SKELLIG

The Tales Of Conor Archer, vol. 2

E.R. BARR

Illustrated by Howard David Johnson

This book is a work of fiction. Names, characters, places and incidents are either the product of the author's imagination or are used fictitiously. Any resemblance to actual persons, living or dead, or to actual events or locales is entirely coincidental.

The publisher does not have any control over and does not assume any responsibility for author or third-party websites or their content.

Cover and interior illustrations by Howard David Johnson

Published by Telemachus Press, LLC
7652 Sawmill Road
Suite 304
Dublin, Ohio 43016
http://www.telemachuspress.com

Visit the author website:
www.talesofconorarcher.com

Categories: FICTION / Fantasy / Urban

ISBN: 978-1-948046-85-5 (eBook)
ISBN: 978-1-948046-86-2 (Paperback)

Version 2020.03.27

ACKNOWLEDGEMENTS

I owe a profound debt of gratitude to Rev. Albert Giaquinto, Rector of Theological College, Washington D.C., (1982–1986).

One day before I was ordained, he told me that, as a priest, I was to be a storyteller of God. I was to gather the people lost in the darkness around the fire of God's love and warm them with tales of his love and mercy. I'll never forget what he said to me, and I have worked hard all my life to fulfill his expectations. This book is dedicated to him. Thanks to you, Fr. Al, for making me what I am today—A Storyteller of God.

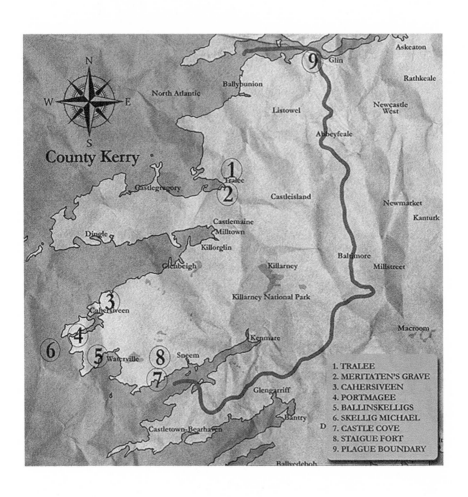

Skellig Michael

0   1/8 mile

1. MAIN LANDING SKELLIG
2. UNDERGROUND PASSAGE
   TO MICHAEL'S HALL
3. PORTAL TO MICHAEL'S CHAPEL
4. SECRET ENTRANCE TO COVE
   BEACH AND ANCIENT SHIP
5. MICHAEL'S HALL

Isle of Skye
(Otherworld)

1. DUN SCAITHA (SCATHA'S FORTRESS)
2. CAVE OF TREE OF THE WORLD
3. PORTAL TO OTHERWORLD SKYE
4. ENTRY PORTAL TO OTHERWORLD SKYE

SKELLIG

THE TALES OF CONOR ARCHER
Volume 2

WHAT CAME BEFORE

CONOR ARCHER IS a seventeen-year-old musician who plays the tin whistle in a pick-up band at the *DerryAir* Pub in downtown Chicago. He's very talented, even with his syndactyly—slightly webbed hands he's had since birth. The only relative he has is his mother who is dying of cancer.

One night, Conor shows up to play and meets a biker, named Rory, who claims Conor is one of the ancient shapeshifting species called the *Roan*. They are the People of the Sea who supposedly fell from heaven with the rebel angels. They are selkies—seals in the ocean who can change to people on land. In disbelief, Conor allows Rory to lead him down to the Chicago River where the biker bites Conor in his hand, telling him that Conor will now begin to transform. Rory changes into something like a seal and disappears into the river.

Conor wraps his bleeding hand and takes off towards home. Cutting through Millennium Park, he heads to Buckingham Fountain to wash his wounded hand. There, a beautiful woman accosts him and looks at the bite. She seems to know who did this to him and what it means. She wraps the wound in a piece of her dress and tells him he must return to his home town and lay his body down where the willows weep by the Wisconsin River if he hopes to survive. The woman begins to change into an old crone as she weirdly washes her hair in the fountain. Unbeknownst to Conor, she is the Morrigan, an ancient Celtic sorceress. Her last words to him are that he should hurry to his mother before she dies.

Conor barely makes it home in time. His dying mother notices the wound, knows who made it and tells him that he must go to his home town of Tinker's Grove, Wisconsin and see his Aunt Emily, whom he has never heard of before. Bereft in sorrow, he holds his mother, Finola, as she passes away.

Feverish from his wound, Conor travels to his home town. Collapsing on the street after leaving the bus, he is helped by a dog named 'Troubles'

i

and twins Conor's age who come up to help him. They are Jace and Beth Michaels who soon become his closest friends.

Conor has come to a strange place. Tinker's Grove was founded by Irish Tinkers after the Irish famine of the 1840's. Benedictine monks led them to this country and built a monastery on the hills above the town. The monks provide education and medical facilities to the people who are descended from the Tinkers, a version of the gypsy people.

In the midst of the gathering crowd, Abbot Malachy from the monastery and Aunt Emily show up at the same time, pushing through the people. With Jace, Beth and the dog, they whisk the unconscious Conor away to the monastery infirmary.

The Abbot knows exactly what's happening and takes Conor down to the Wisconsin River and lays him under a willow tree on top of an old Native American burial mound. It's evening and the Abbot knows that the inhabitant of the mound will come to help.

But there is an ancient Native American river demon named Piasa lurking in the waters. It has been expecting Conor's arrival. It has watched the town for some time, for the Tinker's have a secret. Long ago, some of the Tinker males had relations with the *Roan* who gave birth to their children. That meant that some of their progeny were different from humans. Their genetic make-up has been passed down through the years.

Those who inherited the *Roan* genes are called the 'dark ones'. They have dark eyes and webbed hands and are shapeshifters from birth. It is a talent they grow out of around puberty and seem to have no memory of, but they are protected by the denizens of the village and the monastery. Piasa knows they are there for a reason and he has long awaited the coming of the one who will set their powers alive again. Conor has the same shapeshifting powers as the 'dark ones'. Piasa also knows that Conor possesses the secret of merging both this reality and the Otherworld, sundered for millennia. Once that re-union happens, Piasa and the creatures of the Otherworld can walk freely in our world. The crucial problem is how this takes place. If Conor is allowed to become who he is called to be, the merger could bring a reign of peace. If Piasa corrupts him and the other 'dark ones', the coming together of the worlds will bring destruction and death.

Conor is healed by Madoc, an ancient Celtic chieftain who is one of the *Roan* and has lived in the Indian mound for many centuries. He is the implacable enemy of Piasa. Piasa has made an alliance with the chief landowner of the area, Caithness McNabb and her evil trinity of sons. They seek to discover the secret of the 'dark ones' and use it for power and profit.

The McNabbs have brought in a bio geneticist, named Dr. Nicholas Drake, to build DIOGENE, a research facility dedicated to discovering the secret of the genetic mutations present in the village. He knows of Piasa and, with the help of the McNabbs, tries to turn Conor to their side.

Conor resists and eventually discovers how to use his powers, though he is a very reluctant savior. He discovers that Madoc is his father and that Rory, the biker, is his uncle and feels they could have done much more to save his mother. Rory and the reappearing Morrigan are ambiguous players in this saga, sometimes helping, sometimes hindering Conor's progress at self-discovery.

Eventually, Dr. Drake, the McNabbs, and DIOGENE make their move to capture the 'dark ones', experiment upon them, and discover their secret in the hopes of finding a way to control the coming together of the two realities.

Conor falls in love with Beth and in a youthful indiscretion makes love to her. She becomes pregnant and immediately a target of the McNabbs and Drake's nefarious plans. In their attempt to capture her, she is killed. Conor fights against the McNabbs and his turn to the good side makes Drake crucify him on the Crossroad's Oak which is really the Tree of the World, the source of life and death for both this reality and the Otherworld. The Morrigan and Aunt Emily rescue Conor and save his life, while Troubles loses his trying to help Conor.

Conor and his friends fight Drake, the McNabbs, and Piasa, and, in a climactic battle, many in the town are killed. Forced by the battle, Conor learns to shapeshift into the Thunderbird, the mortal enemy of Piasa. Conor and Jace kill Piasa, but in the process, many townspeople die. Dr. Drake, however, is a casualty as are two of Caithness McNabb's sons.

The story ends with the *Roan* coming from across the sea through a portal to rescue the 'dark ones' and take Madoc and his hidden people back home. They go with the *Roan*, but Madoc chooses to stay. Aunt Emily and the Abbot, fearing that Conor may still be in danger, send him away to Ireland.

THE SELKIE SONG

White as a swan on the lake she was,
Singing of the sea, of the sea.
White as a swan on the lake she was,
Singing of the sea, of the sea.

"Who will take me home
        to the sea, to the sea?
"Who will take me home
        to the surging sea?
"For once, I swam in the heart of my love;
But that was long ago in the sea."

"I will help you lass to be free," said he;
"I will help you lass to be free.
"One kiss I ask, then go from me;
"Go to the surging of the sea."

He held out to her, the roan skin warm;
He held out to her, the seal-skin bright.
His tears flowing from a heart 'twas torn.
Ah, the sadness in his eyes made her face beam with light.

Then a wondrous thing came aborning that night,
Whilst embracing the lovely lad.
        Kissing his warm sweet lips, she did,
        Her selkie skin warm in her hand.
        She touched the skin gently,
        "Follow me, follow me,
        "Follow me beloved beneath the sea,
        "To my lovely home beneath the sea."

In silence, he brought her to where waves ran wild,
There they parted on the sand, on the sand by the sea,
For he was a man and home was the land,
But she was a selkie free.

She was of the Roan; she was of the People;
She was of the People of the sea, of the sea.
Gone she is now, to the depths, to the depths,
To the depths of the deep blue sea.

A tear rolled down his face;
His breath so deep and slow;
He could not leave her now;
He could not let her go.

They say, he walked the shallows,
Then dove deep beneath the waves.
"Drowned!" said many.
"Saved!" said the brave.

But this I know and this I say,
On the first full moon,
Of the spring, of the spring,
Two seals can be seen on the waves.

And if you watch a while, for a while,
Two shall walk the sands
By the sea, by the sea;
Together in their love,
They are free, they are free,
By the waters of the ocean they are free.

My verse, but the story is a common one in Celtic lands. The basic gist is that a young man falls in love with a woman he meets on a beach. He realizes she is a selkie—one of the People of the Sea who is a seal in the ocean but a person on land. He takes her seal skin, hides it, and for years she lives happily with him and bears his children. One day she discovers the skin and happily goes back to the sea. My part of the story adds the fact that she comes back for him and together they enter the sea never to be parted.

PROLOGUE

JACE WAS LYING on the Indian burial mound Sunday morning after All Hallows Eve when he felt the earth shake. Ah, he thought, stepping sideways again. That's what the Abbot called it when one went from this world to the Otherworld. Though for Jace, there wasn't any real movement, cradled as he was in the lap of the Morrigan, her lustrous red hair flowing around his body. Briefly, he lifted his head and saw the world grow larger as the Otherworld merged again with his reality.

"The worlds are bumping together more often, now," said the Morrigan. "They wish to blend permanently. It remains to be seen how that will happen."

It truly was happening more often now, and Jace couldn't say he minded it. A glorious All Saint's Day, a beautiful autumnal morning after such a night of horror. Red, gold and green grass surrounded him and a warm early sun touched his brow. He didn't really mind the Morrigan stroking his head of short blond hair.

None the less, a wet sob stuck in his throat, darkening the dawning of the day. If only his sister, Beth, could see this sunrise. She loved the misty morning. But she was dead, killed by a sadistic warlock doctor—a geneticist steeped in science and magic.

A snuffling in the woods caused a laugh of joy breaking into the midst of his grief. Not everyone had passed away in the dark of night.

"Come here you beast!" he said, lifting his head and turning around. "I know you're there." Troubles, the chocolate Labrador retriever, stepped into the clearing, coming up to nuzzle Jace's neck. He thought the dog might have survived the past night, when deadly magic was alive, but he wasn't prepared for what he saw. The Labrador was much larger, and there was an intelligence in his eyes not there before. Given renewed life in the Otherworld, Troubles was what a dog was supposed to be in all reality. And, thought Jace, he was awesome.

The dog walked up to face the boy and looked at him with sad brown eyes. Placing his forehead on Jace's chest, he moaned a long slow cry. And in Jace's mind he clearly heard Troubles say, "Loss, pain, sorrow."

"I miss her too" said Jace, sobbing into the dog's furry neck.

But then the dog lifted his head and licked Jace's face, and the boy heard him again, "Must go to Conor."

"I know, I know. I have to go too. But not yet. Mom and Dad—I can't leave them yet, but I will be with Conor soon. Tell him that will you?"

The dog yipped agreement.

Jace smiled, "Now go on!" waving Troubles out toward the river. "You'll know how to find him. Take the secret way!"

As Jace stood, the dog leapt into the river, beating a swift stroke to the middle of the channel and dove for the portal to the Otherworld, the ripple of his otter tail melting away in the current.

Jace hitched his breath again in the early light. Even with the Morrigan by his side, he felt so alone, there in the November dawn. In the morning beauty, he thought he could still scent the smell of death hanging down here in the river bottoms. He turned to climb up the path back to the abbey when he saw them above, on the hill, looking down at him in silence.

They were the 'dark ones'—at least those that lived through the night. Not as many as might be, but still quite a number, thought Jace. Whatever am I going to do with them? He knew they were like fish out of water, these 'dark ones.' They were half breed somethings, bearing genes passed down through generations from the coupling of Tinkers, the Irish gypsies, and *Roan*, seal-like shapeshifters from the waters surrounding Ireland.

To no surprise of Jace, it was Oz who stepped forward and spoke as if he had gone to Oxford, no trace of blankness on his brow now: "Where is Madoc; where has he gone; what of Conor the *Roan*, he who shall be king?"

Oz stood so formal above Jace, he and the other 'dark ones.' Jace found himself saying, "Madoc, the Prince of this land who came from over sea and shelters under stone has taken himself and his remaining kin to the hollow hills, the barrows where they dwell. Conor, prince in his own right, son of Madoc, has gone over the sea to the land of his forebears from whence he one day shall return."

Jace's mind was racing, Geez, he thought, I talk like someone from Arthur's Day whatever kind of day that was. I sound like Madoc and don't even look like him. When the Welsh exile wore his medieval garb, his speech fit the part, but here Jace was in jeans and kicks talking like a bard. He laughed at the absurdity. Definitely not a Madoc.

"You should kill him," whispered the Morrigan, standing behind Jace. "He is an abomination."

"Is that your answer to everything?" he whispered back.

"It has always worked for me," she said sweetly, and then merged back into the brush, silently going away.

Death walks away; death stands above, thought Jace.

The 'dark ones' looked at him somberly. "What?" he said. "What do you want from me?"

They said nothing, but neither did they leave. A chill wind suddenly blew down from the bluff, rattling the branches of the trees and sending gold floating to the ground. Now he was sure of it. He did indeed catch the smell and the stink of fire and char, and the smell of other things that met their end the night before.

In silence, he walked up the hill towards them. Oz blocked his way, looking directly at Jace. A feral intelligence shone in those eyes. Jace wished he knew whether he was dealing with Oz or the other things that seemed to occupy that strange man's body now and then.

"Move aside," said Jace, "and let me talk to the others." Oz moved to the left and Jace stood before several dozen silent 'dark ones', their gold-flecked eyes waiting expectantly

"Of Madoc, I cannot say any more. He comes from a world strange to me and I do not know his ways. But Conor—this I know, and this I promise. He will come back to us again. He will come back to take us with him. I don't know where, I don't know what it means, I don't even understand the half of this but you and I—he bound us together and changed our fate. You will never be alone again. Because I will guard you, and I will keep you safe, and I will watch over you when the terror comes again, and we know it will, don't we? We all felt it with the terrible things that happened last night. But I promised him, and I will keep my promise. You and I, always and forever."

The littlest of the 'dark ones', that would be Noah Riley, came up to him and took his hand. "And we will walk with you, Jace, always and forever."

THE HAND OF GOD

Sunday Morning, After Midnight, 11/1, Ballinskelligs, Ireland

IT HAPPENED THE night the Hand of God appeared in the heavens. Late as it was, only a few saw the heavenly event. Storms over the continent blocked the view, but much of the British Isles would have seen it had they been looking. America still hadn't gone to bed, for the sun still shone over much of the continent. As it was, only the late pub patrons on the lonely west coast of Ireland experienced it firsthand.

Lettie Sporn, whose rump had worn a fine finish to the seat of her "special" *Skellig* Pub's heavy oak chair over the many years, sucked in the last of her Guinness. As she raised her head, her ancient eyes caught the sky.

"Mary's milk! Would you look at that!" The words didn't quite come out that clearly since she spoke as she spat the last dregs of her Guinness into the air.

Moira Sheehy, the pub's owner, heard her clearly enough, and she sighed. The *Skellig* was a fine establishment perched on the east end of the village of Ballinskelligs, just above the beautiful beach that led down to the edge of the shallow, tranquil bay. After midnight, she would usually expect a few patrons, but not tonight. They'd all gone home early, and she was left with Lettie, long a widow woman, slightly teched in the head. Moira sighed. Didn't have the heart to kick her out; the lonely hovel down the road wasn't much to go home to.

"Look at what?" Moira said with a bit of exasperation in her voice. "Look at what?"

Now, whether Lettie was the first to christen it, no one knows, but she stood up, pointed out the window towards the sea, and said, "Look at that! The Hand of God!" Even Moira was impressed, for just to the left of the harvest moon, was a phenomenon she had never seen before. It was a nebula—though she couldn't have put the name to it—and it wasn't where it was supposed to be. Hours before, it had been invisible to earth, 17,000 light years away according to the Hubble telescope that discovered the gaseous cloud years before. But here it was, bigger and brighter than a full moon—and it sure looked like a right hand stretching out toward earth, white fire in its palm.

Choking a little on the last of the Guinness foam, Lettie said, "Moira, dear, out from the palm of his hand comes our doom." In her cups, Lettie always got a little apocalyptic, but she wasn't exaggerating the magnificence of what they saw. The two women, Moira having tossed a shawl around her shoulders, and Lettie with her several layers of men's long sleeve shirts, got themselves out onto the balcony looking over the dark bay and raised their eyes where sure enough, what was once white fire in the palm of the hand was now shooting out from it, towards earth, a fiery comet with a will of its own.

"He threw it, Moira," squealed Lettie, "just like a kid playing ball."

"Shush," said Moira, "that's a bit more info than we really know."

But they both knew the fireball was coming fast. A long tail, a large nucleus, and the comet was easily tracked as rapidly moving.

"Coming to us, I think," muttered Lettie.

"To Ballinskelligs?" snorted Moira. "Nothing important comes here anymore." She took a moment to cast her eyes off to the abandoned development—the hope of the area when the economy boomed. Houses were built; finances then fell throughout the world. Bankruptcy loomed, buyers fled, and now just unborn memories flitted through the newly built ruins.

At Lettie's gasp, she turned again to the bay. The ball of fire now was truly bigger than the moon and steadily increasing in size.

"It's going to hit the bay," said Lettie.

"Doubt it," said Moira. "Most likely it'll land near the *Skelligs*." Those were the small but mountainous islands eight miles off the bay.

In fact, they were able to watch it for five minutes, coursing the sky and seemingly taking dead aim at Ballinskelligs. Moira felt a hollowness in her gut. Like billions of humans before her, she instinctively felt the coming of a comet was the coming of some doom, some fate that would radically change the world. The past two centuries had not brought many visible comets, and none this big. Long dead voices of Irish druids were sure to whisper to the people of Erin Isle, reminding them that comets seldom brought good news.

"Well, will you look at that?" said Lettie. "You were right after all." The comet arced from the sky and both women saw it splash down miles out in the ocean. Chunks of molten rock skipped over the sea, and one of them headed toward the bay where it crashed to rest just in the waters by the abandoned Ballinskelligs abbey.

"Oops," slurred Lettie.

"Tsunami," Moira croaked out.

"What's that you say?" said Lettie

"There should be a tsunami from this, and yet the ocean is as calm as it ever was."

"Ah, pish-posh," said Lettie, "you always were a worry wart."

"It's not the physical damage I worry about." Nodding knowingly, Lettie tapped her pipe on Moira's shawl. "It's what the comet portends that should concern us. But no matter right now. Let's take a stroll on the beach down to the abbey and see where that piece of rock might have struck. It might still be glowing!"

The long beach was deserted, it being after midnight on a cold All Saints morning. The unlikely pair hurried along under starlight, kicking sand up from their shoes. They passed the long-ruined castle tower that once served as protection from raiding pirates and soon came to the abandoned abbey. Long ago, the monks who inhabited the largest of the *Skellig* Isles—*Skellig* Michael that would be—left the inhospitable place and built a large abbey by what came to be known as Ballinskelligs Bay. But the dear Lord Protector—Cromwell the despicable—and the anti-Catholic laws of the reprehensible British conquerors—emptied the abbey. Now only ghosts and echoes remained.

Moira was mindful of the ghosts. With just she and Lettie walking in amongst the ruins, it seemed that the shadows had living wraiths within, and even the rotting cloister pillars looked like the ribcage of some long dead dragon. Lettie must have shared her thoughts. "Let's get out of the abbey; that piece of flaming rock landed in the water, not here." Moira couldn't have agreed more.

Pushing their way through the marsh grass they came to the edge of the bay, the water softly lapping, no sign of any fallen star. They both sought the darkness, but it was Lettie who chirped a swallowed scream. "Look at that now, will you!" She pointed to something white floating just under the water.

"Jesus, Mary and Joseph!" said Moira. "It's a man!" Indeed, it was. And when they both huffed and puffed, hauling the body out of the water they could see he was young with blond hair, well-built and very dead.

"Dead!" said Lettie. "Drowned, I say." But she had just said as much when the man coughed, startling them even more. Unconscious he might be, but, clearly, he was breathing. "And look at his sweater! How could it be Ballinskelligs' weave? We don't even know this man."

Truth to tell, Moira couldn't tell a Ballinskellig's weave from a Portmagee product. Once, the thick white wool sweaters beloved throughout Ireland made it easy to identify where a person came from. Each community had a particular weave, and should a man die out in the sea, when he finally washed ashore, he just might be identified by the sweater he wore. The sea and its denizens could destroy the flesh, but the tough wool of Ireland endured. But those were old times. And Lettie was pretty old. No wonder she knew.

The silence of the night was broken again by the town fire brigade, also checking out the renegade comet fragment. "Thank the saints," muttered Moira, "he's far too big for Lettie and me to carry."

Moira took charge, asking the firemen to carry their unconscious guest to one of the rooms above the pub. She also sent one of the boys to the doctor. "Wake him, even if he is in his cups," she said. "This poor soul might not survive the night. God knows how he didn't drown."

And so it happened. The stranger was ensconced in a large room—often used for tourists during the warm months—above the pub. The doctor—Gillespie it was—did his best to make sure the drowned man still breathed.

"He's very strong," said Dr. Gillespie, "but I'd expect that, him being a Ballinskelligs' boy and all."

"You know him?" asked Moira. She had lived in town for forty years, Lettie many more, and she was sure they would have known him if he was local.

"He's got the weave," said the doctor pointing at the sodden sweater.

"Don't mean anything," said Lettie, puffing on her pipe despite Moira's—and the government's—no smoking policy. "He's as strange as strange is. Look at his hair—gold as the sun. Look at his skin; it's almost alabaster in color. It's as if one of Michelangelo's statues came alive. He's no more Irish than the dim and doughty King of England. He fell from the sky." They looked at her as if she was daft. "Tell 'em, Moira, we saw him fall from the sky."

"Oh, we did not you silly old woman," tsked Moira. "We saw a piece of meteor, or comet or whatever it was hit the bay by the abbey—that's all."

Lettie chuckled. "You think what you want. But we looked for the fireball from the sky, and it's him we found."

THE STONE CIRCLE

Sunday Morning, After Midnight, 11/1, Ballinskelligs Headland

AMERGIN, THE BARD of the West, saw the Hand of God as well. Sort of. Drunk as he was, it was just a trifle blurry. Most people knew him as the leader of the Tinkers, the Irish Travelers. His kin knew who he really was. They respected him mightily and forgave his occasional drinking binge. That thing in the sky—he knew it was something odd. "How odd the Hand of God!" he laughed at his own tipsy humor.

His solitary party was at the top of the headland overlooking Ballinskelligs. Land never claimed by anyone. There was a reason for that. To his left, he overlooked the town; to his right, the *Skellig* Islands only eight miles off the shore. Just this moment, he was close to the edge of the cliff in the midst of a stone circle, a pagan monument at least five thousand years old, so said the archeologists. There was an altar of sorts there in the middle and he was splayed out on it, a bottle in his hand, a drunken sacrifice just waking out of his stupor. The locals stayed clear of the place. Had done so for eons. They were still scared of what and who gathered there in times past.

But Amergin was alone. No druid priest or priestess after his beating heart. The scientists said the druids never did human sacrifices, but Amergin knew better. He'd seen the ceremonial knives in the museums, and the dreams—he seen what they'd done in his dreams.

That wasn't most on his mind just now. The Hand of God was. He wasn't stupid. In fact, he had several degrees behind the Amergin name. Such a well-educated bard. Drunk as he was, he knew the nebula shouldn't be in the sky, shining above him. At 17,000 light years away, it should be invisible to the eye. Irish as he was, he, too, searched for portents.

Amergin looked old, not 'old' old, but nowhere near as spry as he once was. He just didn't feel like getting up at the moment. That's why he was in a perfect position to see the Hand of God toss that fastball. He sat up mighty fast as the comet plummeted to earth. He saw it splash out near the *Skelligs* and saw the errant piece of it skip across the dead, flat, calm ocean into the bay, only to sink out of sight off the ruined abbey.

Putting his black Greek Fisherman's cap on his head of grey, curly hair, he sat up, reached for the whiskey, but the flask was empty.

"Damn it all to hell! I swear they make these silver flasks smaller and smaller to carry less and less."

A warm wind from the ocean blew up and tussled Amergin's hair. He stood up, knowing that the invisible wind, weaving itself through the stark, standing stones was walling him in as efficiently as a stonemason could brick up the space between each of the upright monoliths.

"All right, all right," he whispered. "I know you're here. Haven't seen you in an age. Maybe you're here to take me in my dotage."

A faint haunting laughter whispered through the stones, carried softly on the wind. The crisp call of a crow drowned that out.

"Where are you, you old whore?" said the bard. "Back to cause me mischief? Back to bother me here at the end of my days? Back to see me suffer and scream as you force me to say your damnable name, you feckless bitch?"

By now, his voice cried louder than the crow, and he was standing on top of the altar, spinning around in a circle, shouting at the heavens—but his eyes were studying the stones. Thirteen of them there were. The first, but a foot high, the fifth five feet tall, the tenth ten feet standing, five feet wide. And then the thirteenth standing stone, fifteen feet overshadowing the others and ten feet wide. One of the few stone circles that clearly showed one was to progress *deisil*, sun wise when you did the druid thing. At one time, each of the pillars had had a flat stone top—big enough to stand on. But now, all capstones had fallen except the last.

"Where are you?" he said, turning circles on the altar. That's when he saw the crow on the thirteenth pillar. And that's when darkness seemed to ooze from the bird's mouth, feet and wings, a darkness that rose higher, taking shape in a woman's form. As wisps of ether whisked away in the wind, her face was revealed, wild lustrous red hair blown high, pale marble white arms, and hands with piercing, shredding nails reaching for him. A ruby red mouth opened and she screamed at him:

Mine is the life that is yours,
Mine is the time you have left,
Mine is the blood and the bones,
That hold the soul of Amergin.

It was impressive as rants go, but Amergin took some of the mystery out of it when he broke into hysterical laughing, clapping his hands at her performance. Instead, of ripping out his entrails, which the bard had seen her do often to others in times past, she took a little bow and jumped down to join him.

Leaping off the stone column, her blood red nails touched not his face, but smoothed his hair and caressed his neck. Amergin laughed. "I missed you too, girl. I missed you too."

She whispered in his ear, but the wind took her voice and self skyward. Only he heard what she said, and before the sound of a crow cawing echoed away, he slumped onto the altar and wept at the passing of the years and his failure as a bard. Thinking on what she said, he fell fast asleep on the altar of stone—alone again in the dark of the night.

SPEED BONNIE PLANE
LIKE A BIRD ON THE WING

Sunday Morning, 11/1, Chicago O'Hare Airport

AUNT EMILY HAD thought of everything. First class plane tickets—she must have bought two because no one was sitting next to him on the *Aer Lingus* flight. Security had passed him through with no problems at Chicago's O'Hare airport and even let him keep his walking stick—staff really because it was pretty tall. No one knew that it was really the Spear of Destiny, used by the Irish gods for thousands of years and then disappearing only to appear in the hand of a centurion, thrusting it into the side of the Galilean. But it was Conor's now. At least for a while.

He touched the envelope in the front pocket of his shirt. The past hours were a blur to him. The river flight, the journey to the airport, the rush to get on the plane—it left him breathing heavily, not from exertion, but anxiety. The words of Abbot Malachy echoed in his mind, "We send you away for your safety. You're going to your godmother and hopefully things will calm down. Yet, if they do not, you will find friends along the way. Trust them, for the road you walk now, you should not walk alone."

Yet, the Abbot had also given him an envelope, a message from Aunt Emily. Conor ripped off the end and shook a small, folded letter onto his hand.

My dear Conor,

> *How I miss you already. Though the Abbot will tell you that you are traveling for your safety—no doubt he is right, for things will be busy here with police, funerals and the always inquisitive press—there is another reason we send you away.*
> *Our very reality is changing. Two worlds wish to merge and become one as they once were, the world you have known and this strange reality you have experienced for the past few months known as the Otherworld. How they merge,*

whether by good or ill, is crucial. I believe you are the Light's best chance to affect this union. The Dark will oppose you every step of the way.

Chaos inevitably will come with the joining of the worlds. We send you to Ireland, because the land is one of mystery and magic. The walls there between the worlds have always been thin, more so than any other place on earth. Whatever is about to happen will happen there first.

I have heard that dark things from the Otherworld have already been seen in the quiet and secret places there. Few remember these demons of the Dark; fewer still can stop them. Ireland is not what it once was. The people have lost their souls as well as their ability to sense all things fae—that which comes from the Otherworld. You need to see this for yourself. You need to act, if you can.

The servants of the Dark wish to merge the worlds by evil means. They must be stopped. Stopped by you. So young, yet so powerful. I trust you and your abilities, Conor. Do not be afraid. You have defeated evil once; you shall do it again. When the time comes you will know what to do. Nor shall you be alone. Aid will come when you are most in need.

You will know when to return, but I pray you will hurry back to us, for our need is real as well, here in Tinker's Grove, where your home and your family are and where you are loved.

Walk in the Light my precious nephew.

Love,
Aunt Emily

Conor brushed a tear away as he folded the letter and stuck it back in his pocket. The flight attendants hovered over him. "Can we get you this, Mr. Archer … Can we get you that, Mr. Archer?" Like he was royalty or something, which he guessed he was, kind of. Though how they would know was beyond him. Besides, he was just too tired to ponder the problem. And he was so awfully sad. Only seventeen, yet he had loved that girl, and now Beth was gone. He would not even see her buried. In his anguish and sorrow, he lowered his head. He was asleep before the plane took off.

Conor dreamed. Not of the violence, or of the changes that had wracked his body. Nor of his future or what awaited him across the seas. He dreamt of sadness. Of Beth, whom he lost because of his selfishness. Of Jace, whom he betrayed by his thoughtlessness. Of Troubles his dog, lost in death, who fought the Dark so that he might live. Of the Abbot, to whom he should have listened more closely, wise one that he was. And of Aunt Emily, whom he never appreciated, though she was the only family he really had. Finally of the princes, one who was his father, the other who was, well what was he really? Rory was an enigma who changed him, challenged him, persecuted him, yet helped save his life. Madoc was his father and absentee parent, who, when reunited with his son did absolutely nothing to help him. What a son of a bitch.

Conor jerked awake. Sadness had turned again to anger, and hot streams of resentment and loss flowed down his face as pity overwhelmed him. Wiping his face with his sleeve, he looked up to see the flight attendant offering him a meal. He was hungry. "Thanks so much," he said, with a weak smile. And he wolfed the food down.

He dozed again for hours. When he woke, he looked out the window to see cotton ball clouds floating by, and beneath him, an even thinner mist. Shadowy shapes dimmed the light on the ocean. Then the sun broke from the clouds, shedding a golden light, illuminating the sea and the Aran islands in ethereal glory. These were the outer edges of Ireland, and were they ever green.

To Conor, this looked like the Otherworld, inhabiting the same reality as the world he lived in. It was beautiful. Instinctively, he knew why the Abbot had sent him here. All of Ireland was a thin place. The light was different; how he did not know. But it seemed like it came from a magical, more intense reality. He glanced around the plane. Everyone was looking out the windows, gasping at the beauty.

"Ireland does that to most, even to those of us who have lived here always." A stunning flight attendant with lustrous red hair smiled at him. "I never grow tired of the view. However, it will not take away sadness." She sat on the empty seat next to him and whispered, "I see the hurt in your heart, but believe me, Conor Archer, this island has a way of healing, if you let it into your soul. Dark times surround all of us now, and the night might deepen more, but look to the core of your heart, and you will see the Light, for it has never abandoned you."

He blinked his eyes, and she was gone. He looked for her on the plane, but she was nowhere to be seen. The captain broke in on the intercom, telling everyone to fasten seatbelts; they were arriving at Shannon. In the bustle that followed, he prepared for landing, staring out the window at the fast approaching island of Ireland, with its emerald glory gleaming in the Monday morning sun.

CONOR MEETS SOME FRIENDS

Monday Morning, 11/2, On The Way To Ballinskelligs, Ireland

"MAN," THOUGHT CONOR. "I look like Frodo on top of Gandalf's fireworks cart." Yawning again, he looked to the sky where the sun shone brightest behind the grey cloud cover that seemed to have come from nowhere. He was sitting in the back of a Traveler's wagon. The caravan added the only color to the landscape this November morning, its red body and green roofed shell shining bright against the wintry grey-green grass on either side of the tiny lane.

His pack over one shoulder, walking stick in his other hand, he had been trudging the road south from the Shannon airport, gently refusing people's offers to carry him on his way. He didn't want to think of all that had happened. Wanting just to get a sense of the land, he took off down a side road, still heading County Kerry way. Then the Tinkers showed up. Travelers they called themselves now. The wagon they drove and let him ride in was called a caravan, and it was no engine that moved it. An old brown horse seemed to have no trouble pulling it down the lane. How could he resist a lift in that anachronistic vehicle? It looked like something from an old postcard, its rounded, green roof covering the red wagon that had beautiful blue double doors in the back with ancient scrollwork around the lintel. No wooden wheels, rather, sturdy tires which must have made the ride much smoother than it used to be in days gone by.

It was indeed a real-life Traveler family who took kindness on him. Just a young man, his quiet wife, and their little daughter whose bright blue eyes were shining on this stranger they picked up. And of course, the horse.

"Malby," said the man whose name was Kevin Bard.

"A good beast," spoke Mary, his wife.

Conor smiled at them and then said to the little girl, "What's your name, lass?"

Kevin burst out laughing, "You hear that, Mary? Been off the plane a couple of hours and he's got a brogue already."

The little girl piped up above the joshing, "My name's Laura, and I'm four." This time everybody laughed and stayed smiling.

"Sure do appreciate your kindness in picking me up," said Conor.

"No problem," said Kevin, "but if you are going all the way to … where did you say you were going then?"

"I didn't," said Conor, "but I do want to get to Ballinskelligs. Think I could ride that far with you? I'm supposed to look up the lady who runs the local pub. She's my godmother though I've never met her, at least that I remember."

"That'd be Moira" said Mary in a quiet voice. "We know a fair amount of people down there. Most are good, but we've had a little trouble with her."

"A little trouble?" said Kevin, a cloud coming over his face. "She cheated me out of the last bit of work I did for her—repairing a stone patio out the back of the pub."

Conor paled before Kevin's anger. "Whoa now," said Conor, "just be easy and I'll ask her to make it up to you. Promise I will." He flashed a brilliant smile at Kevin, bright enough to make the Tinker forget his anger and just sullenly huff till an embarrassed smile began to tickle his lips.

"Not your fault lad. Alright then, I'll take you there. Believe me, I want to see Miss Moira too, and not just for a Guinness."

They said little as the wagon slowly made its way toward the Kerry peninsula. In the evening, they stopped off the road under an old stunted oak, and Mary made a great beef stew. Where she hid all the ingredients in the caravan, Conor didn't know, but by the time she added this and that, the stew tasted delicious and rekindled conversation between them all.

Laura was laughing at one of Conor's stories about Chicago, when he took out his tin whistle and began playing. Laura turned to her mother and said, "Mummy, what's wrong with his hands?" She had seen the webbed skin between the fingers.

"Hush, child, that is not the thing to say," said Mary, blushing in embarrassment for her comment.

"No worries, Laura," said Conor with a smile. "I was born this way and it doesn't keep me from playing a mean tin whistle."

Looking thoughtful but saying nothing, Kevin leaned back and listened to Conor play his tune.

"I know that song," said Kevin. "Mary, I used to sing it to you long ago—remember?"

Mary laughed, and tossed her red hair over her shoulder and hit him on his arm. "You're hardly twenty-five!" she said. "We don't even have a 'long ago' to talk about yet."

Kevin laughed wryly and said, "Still, it's a good song."

"Well, sing it to her then," said Conor smiling. "I'll play, you go on."

"You won't be mindin' that?" he said.

Conor answered by starting again at the beginning, but before he blew on the whistle, he solemnly intoned, "Red-haired Mary." And then off he was with the bouncy tune with Kevin singing and laughing at the same time, singing the story of the wooing of Red-haired Mary by a lad who found her at a fair in the spring of the year.

While going to the fair of Dingle
One fine morning last July,
While going up the road before me,
A red haired girl I chanced to spy.

I went up to her, says I, "Young lady,
My donkey he will carry two,
But seeing as how you have a donkey,
To the Dingle fair I'll ride with you"

Now, when we reached the town of Dingle,
I took her hand to say goodbye,
When a Tinker man stepped up beside me
And he belted me in my left eye.

Kevin pantomimed his verses with little Laura laughing and clapping her hands. Conor stopped playing and all three clapped, singing the refrain:

"Keep your hands-off red-haired Mary,
Her and I will soon be wed.
We'll see the priest this very morning
And tonight we'll lie in a marriage bed."

"Now, you know it wasn't quite like that," said Kevin, laughing at the memory. "First, I was the one who belted another Tinker in his eye—stupid Loras would never let you alone. But it was at the Dingle fair we met."

"And we never quite ran across the priest," said Mary, "and we should be taking care of that soon." She looked with love at her young daughter. "The little one isn't even baptized yet."

Sitting there, outside, around the campfire, they watched the stars come out. Laura laughed and pointed at the new nebula in the sky. Old Malby, the horse, contentedly chomped a bag of oats. Conor was peaceful, relaxed for the first time since that awful Halloween night just forty-eight hours ago when Beth, the first girl he had ever loved, and so many other townspeople died.

That was a horrific memory. What he saw now muted the tragedy, at least a little bit. Nice land, nice people, he thought, as he saw the stone-white fences glow in the twilight above the green fields. He put down his tin whistle, and in the comfortable silence, he relaxed and smiled at his newfound friends.

"Your hands are webbed, lad," said Kevin, returning unexpectedly to little Laura's question. "Where would you be getting that unfortunate mark?"

"Born with it, like I said," said Conor calmly, though a chill crept up his spine. "It's nothing really; doesn't bother me in the least."

Kevin looked Conor in the eye. "Around here it means something, especially something to the Tinkers—we Travelers. It means your 'teched' … now don't get turning red on me and getting mad—it's just a saying. It means the Otherworld has tapped you for a task. 'Course, it also means you can do things, and …"

"Kevin!" said Mary sharply, "leave our guest be."

Without turning his head, Kevin kept staring at Conor. "Like I was saying, it means you can do things, and it means you are something, something old, something we have long tried to forget."

Conor stood up, anger seething in his night black eyes. "If I'm such a bother, I'll take my leave. I'll not stay where I'm not wanted."

"Stop it, stop it, both of you!" Mary's voice was loud enough to bring a whimper of uncertainty to Laura's lips. "He's our guest, Kevin, and our guest he'll stay. Remember the lark on the hedgerows? What does the lark say about our guest, Laura?"

With the practiced look of one who had been memorizing prayers half of her short life, Laura screwed up her face, looked to the darkling sky and said,

"The lark sat on the fencepost singing,
'Often, often, often,
  Walks the Christ in the stranger's clothes;
  Often, often, often,
  Walks the Christ in the stranger's clothes.'"

"Beautiful, child," smiled Mary at Laura and then fixed a severe gaze at her husband.

"What?" said Kevin. "He's no Christ, that's for sure!"

"He is our guest though," said Mary.

"That he is, that he is," muttered Kevin, offering his hand to Conor.

They finished their dinner in peace. The silence that had just made itself at home around the Traveler's wagon was bumped away by a grinding noise up on the road. The peace was broken with an old Ford Focus rumbling by.

It squealed to a stop and two fairly big men peeled themselves out of the rusting car.

"Oh, oh," said Kevin.

"What's the problem?" asked Conor.

"Trouble," was all Kevin said. Mary grabbed Laura's tiny hand and shrunk towards the wagon.

Kevin walked forward as the men neared. "Can I help you, sirs?" he said.

"Bloody, blond-haired Tinker," muttered one of the strangers. He was tall with a paunch, but his hands were big, clenching and unclenching like they were waiting to do some violence.

"What do you think, Eddie?" said the other, shorter, but heavier man. "Think, they're up to trouble?"

"Of course," said tall Eddie. "They're Tinkers, aren't they? And they're on the Chief's land."

"Hey," said Conor, standing up and joining Kevin. "We're just camping out, hurting nobody. And who is this 'Chief' you're talking about?"

"You American, kid?" said Eddie.

"Yeah, over here visiting my godmother."

"You shouldn't be hanging around with Tinker trash like this," said the thug next to Eddie. "Especially on the Chief's land—Sir Hugh Rappaport is his name—chief land owner around here." Pushing his finger into Kevin's chest, he said, "You can't spend the night on his land. You'll get to bein' greedy, takin' things that don't belong." He flashed a look at Conor. "You that way—American?"

"I'm hanging around them because I guess I'm 'Tinker trash' too." Kevin shot a look at Conor in surprise. Conor smiled, "I may be American, but I recently figured out where I come from."

"If you're taking up with this kind of garbage, too bad for you," said Eddie. And the two moved closer to them.

Kevin stepped in front of Conor. "Leave us alone, please."

"You thieven' shite," said Eddie as he swung his fist. It connected solidly with Kevin's gut, knocking the air out of him. Doubled over in pain, he was gasping when Eddie's companion went for Conor.

Having had a moment to see disaster coming for his face, Conor backed away, tripping over some stones. The unnamed thug's foot connected with Conor's ribs. Momentarily out of the fray, neither Kevin or Conor could do much when the two strangers went for Mary. Laura screamed, but it was Malby, the horse, who stepped up and blocked their path.

"Out of the way you damned Tinker nag!" shouted Eddie. It looked like he would strike the horse, but at that moment, he felt a hand on his shoulder.

Kevin shoved him aside and stood gasping in anger, blocking the way toward his family.

The other stranger turned his attention to Kevin, and both Eddie and he lunged toward the young man, knives appearing suddenly in their hands.

It was hard to explain what happened next. As Kevin and Mary told it later, a mist rose up behind the toughs, blacking out the fire behind them, so no one could see well in the dusky gloom. But they heard the noise, a guttural growl, and they saw a hand or a claw reach through the murky fog, grabbing the throat of Eddie and snapping it like a twig and tossing the limp body aside. Out of the swirling mist swung another hand with nails like knives that simply punched a hole through the other thug's back. His surprised eyes didn't even register pain as the life dimmed in them. The bodies fell, and the mist dispersed, leaving an unconscious Conor Archer on the ground near the two dead men. Mary ran to him.

"Don't touch him, Mary!" cried Kevin.

"He saved us, husband; have a care."

While they argued, little Laura walked up to Conor and kissed his unconscious brow, picked up a wet rag and wiped the blood from his face and hands, paying special attention to the webbing on his fingers.

"Mummy," she said, "there's something black running up his wrist." Kevin rushed over and ripped open the unconscious boy's shirt—tore it off him in a rage and brought his wife over.

"Look at him! He has the sign." And indeed, the black line raced from the palm of his right hand, up his arm, around his neck and spread sharp shards over his heart and continued, presumably, down his left leg. "And it's glowing there, faintly in the dark—do you see it, Mary?"

"Aye, I do," she said, with a voice not carrying the fear that Kevin's did.

"We've let one of them into our lives—something out of myth and story, and no good will come of it."

"What do you mean?" she said. "He saved us. Do you think these men would have left our family unharmed? No! I agree that Conor Archer is something out of time and legend, but he is real, and he is of us. You know the tales."

"Not human, not human, not human!" cried Kevin as he tore at his hair.

"On one side," said Mary. "But human on the other. He's from them, don't you see, those who sailed away, to the West. We thought them lost, but perhaps not. Are you going to kill him now and leave his body with the rest of this scum?"

For a long moment, Kevin was quiet. Then, he said softly, "No. Of course not. And you know, I wouldn't. But I fear for us if this is found out."

"Then we make it so it can't be found out. It's a long time till the dawn, and the ocean isn't far. We can dispose of the toughs in the sea caves. If they are discovered, no one will know what happened—that's for sure."

"All right," he said. "As usual you are right. We wrap the dead and put them in the back, tuck Conor in the front of the wagon, and head for the sea—hoping Malby knows the best place to put 'em." A nicker in response gave them their answer.

It wasn't difficult at all—they reached the sea caves the horse chose by 3 am, and, under a nearly full moon, secreted the bodies into one of the many crevices on the coast. The coming tide would erase footsteps and hoofprints. No one would be the wiser.

Except Kevin and Mary, who had never seen anyone kill a man before. And they looked in on Conor, still fast asleep, bruises on his ribs already fading. "See, he heals," said Kevin, as if it was an accusation.

"Oh," said Mary, "I think he can do a mite more than that, if he has the will to it."

CONOR AND THE TINKERS

Tuesday Morning, 11/3, On the Way to Ballinskelligs

HE WAS BLESSING the lifeless face of Beth and then reaching out for some strange blue spark floating above the forest path when the dream faded into consciousness. He felt his body rocking gently and opened his eyes. Cuddled like a baby with a warm blanket around him, Conor saw the back end of Malby pulling the wagon forward. Little Laura was scrunched up next to him fast asleep.

A voice from the back of the wagon said, "Are you awake up there?" It was Kevin sounding a lot more at ease than he had been when the lights went out on Conor.

"I am," said Conor. "What happened?"

Kevin came forward and lifted his daughter onto his lap and sat next to Conor. "You took out two men, is what you did. Can't say they didn't deserve it. Had you not, we all would have been," here he ruffled his daughter's hair, "somewhat indisposed."

"I killed them?" said Conor, a vague memory in his mind and a tremor of incredulousness in his voice.

"Shush now," he said putting his big hands over the little girl's ears. "That you did, my friend. Killed them good and gone. You weren't yourself, you know. Just bits of mist and claw and bone."

"Tell me how."

Kevin did, handing the child up to his wife and then leaving out none of the gory details. For a long time after, Conor was silent. They were traveling over the *machair*—the grassy plain leading up from the sandy beach that sprawled for a couple hundred yards before vanishing into the normal landscape.

Ahead of them the sky was beginning to brighten as the dawn approached. Then Conor said, "It's never happened that way before."

"Well thank the Lord for that piece of good news," said Kevin. "Even in this country, which knows a thing or two about the supernatural, what you did wouldn't settle well if it happened too often. Are you catching my drift? Couldn't you at least have told us what you are?"

"And what am I, Kevin? Some monster from one of your Irish myths?"

"You know what you are. You're one of the People of the Sea. You're *Roan*. We've known your kind forever. We've just been down to those rocks by the sea properly disposing of your night's work. And now, we're going to see my kin."

Conor didn't say a word again, thinking of the two dead men, bodies placed forever in one of the sea caves.

As they traveled the *machair* towards a thin pillar of smoke down by the beach, Conor felt his chest tighten, making breathing difficult. What have I become? he thought. What rage takes me and turns me into such an animal? They think me a legend out of myth, but my emotions still are human. Is that how I can tell that I'm still part of the human race? That anger, bitterness, and rage can still crap up my soul? Just like anyone else? Hope I kept the good parts of being human too, but I haven't seen very much of that lately.

His thoughts were as jumbled as the rocking caravan. Then, they were there, in front of a clutch of Traveler wagons, at the caravan park just outside Cahersiveen, with the men smoking pipes or cigarettes in front of a fire, and the women taking care of squalling babies and yelling kids. Conor could smell oatmeal and bacon, figuring it must be breakfast soon.

"What are you bringing to us this fine morning, Kevin?" said the oldest man present. With a red vest and once white shirt, and pants that had seen too many washes, the old Traveler came forward.

Kevin just looked at the man, a bleak stare into the old man's heart.

"Ah lad, what have you gotten yourself into now?" whispered the old one. "Come sit by the fire and tell me all about it, and bring our guest too."

Never having been with a group of Travelers before, Conor remembered Aunt Emily talking about them, of how they were Ireland's and now America's versions of gypsies. Their clans were very old, their ways secret, and they were not to be trusted. Obviously, they were the descendants of the ones who had founded Tinker's Grove. Conor's hand touched his back pocket to make sure his wallet was in place. Without even looking back, the old man chuckled, "Don't worry visitor from afar; we've offered you hospitality. For the time you are with us, be it ten minutes or ten years, you are one of us and our protection lies over you."

"Thank you, sir," said an embarrassed Conor, sitting down with the other two on his own wobbly metal chair. He leaned a bit on his staff for balance.

"I'm Amergin," said the old man.

"Just like the ancient bard," said Conor.

"Just," said Amergin with a small smile. "And these are my people and though we don't make a very presentable rabble, you'll find us true friends. Not like what they say in the stories." He winked. "Now tell us what happened. You first, Kevin."

In the early morning dawn, Kevin told about the attack, its viciousness, and how Conor saved them. "It was self-defense that he killed them. Without him, I doubt Mary and Laura and me would have survived. But Sir Hugh won't tolerate this. He'll take vengeance."

Amergin looked at Conor. "And what's your story? What can you add that might help get us out of the impossible situation you have put us into?"

Conor grimaced at the accusation. "I'm Conor Archer from Tinker's Grove, Wisconsin, on the banks of the Wisconsin River. Your kin founded that little town in the 1800's fleeing from the Famine ... and from other things. I'm just traveling here to find out about my people, my roots I guess."

Amergin stared at Conor long and hard. "A darker tale lies around you like the black mist swirls the sea's breakers in the dying light of the day. You didn't just kill those men out of hatred, did you?" He raised an eyebrow. "No, don't answer. I know what you did. I see your heart and it's nothin' like the murdering kind, is it now? I know what you are. Who you are remains to be seen."

"It was like he was something else," said Kevin. "Something like in the stories you tell. I know it. I smelled it. He is from the sea."

What little privacy there was for the three evaporated with Kevin's words. All around the fire were now listening, faces impassive, waiting to hear what came next. The only sound besides the crackling of the fire was the echo of the sea breakers crashing on the shore.

"You are one of them," said Amergin, not unkindly. "One of the *Roan*, the People of the Sea, and you haven't known what you are for very long. Just a child ..."

Conor felt his anger grow again but cooled himself. He was a guest. Let them say what they will; he could always leave.

But the opposite happened. Amergin stiffly rose and then bent down on one knee. All the others followed, even tiny Laura and the rest of the children. "You honor us with your presence, little one, though you don't know much and can't see two meters in front of your face who and what you really are. Your mothers and fathers who fell to the sea were much like you, at first. Unsure of themselves and their place in the world. The Travelers have always known the People of the Sea. We have few friends, but we do have you and those like you. Stay with us and rest for a while."

"I can't," said a sorrowful Conor. "I'll stay the morning, but then I must get to the pub in Ballinskelligs. The lady who runs it is my godmother. How do you know about me?"

Amergin smiled a bitter smile. "The Morrigan told me."

"The Morrigan? You know her?"

"Yes, I do, and you, apparently do as well. I talk to her now and then. She is … a presence here. I saw her this morning on that far rock over there by the waves. She came as a crow," and Amergin's eyes grew wistful and his voice took on a yearning air.

She of the lustrous red hair,
Beguiling child and beauty fair,
Comes to touch you but beware.

She is the voice that tolls the dead,
In battle, mid wrath, her beauty blood-red.
A withered crone she also can be,
Stone-white her claws, on bones she's fed.

Her scream cries death I fear today,
A crow she appeared on my way, on my way,
To the sea, to the sea, where a people play,
Who fell from the sky on a morn such as this.

With fire and sadness they chose the waves,
Condemned to dwell there till end of days.
Seal folk, selkies, shapeshifters tales say
Call gently of loss over waters grey.

People of power, lauded in poems,
Such are the sea-folk, called the Roan.
Tinkers are we, exiled like they,
To the sea to the sea,
Tinkers we are, near to the sea.

She knew this, the Morrigan, while speaking to me,
To me did she speak of the coming of he,
Who shall be King of his kind, o'er land and 'neath sea.
So say I, Bard of the West, who have been and will be.

The camp was utterly still, even the flames of the warming fire grew silent. Conor saw everything move in slow motion, and Amergin, with piercing blue eyes, said, "Son, you have made a dangerous ally with this Banshee of the *machair*. She is neither human nor *Roan*, and in her attempt to protect you, may hurt you and perhaps kill you. Rest here for a while and eat what we have. Your godmother, the widow Moira, whom I know, is not far from here. Kevin will take you, won't you my son, and keep you safe and hidden for now. It must be done.

So says the crow who spoke in my ear,
So says the death crone who banishes fear,
So says she with the lustrous red hair,
"Safe must he be; 'ere the Eye comes near."

"What eye?" said Kevin. And Mary punched him on the shoulder and began to take Conor to the wagon where he could get some sleep. Suddenly Amergin moved forward to embrace the boy and sign a cross on his forehead. So did all present, solemnly and without a word. They put their blessing on Conor, and a peace he had seldom known, settled in his heart, and his eyes closed as the Tinker couple put him to bed in the back of the wagon and, next to him, his plain walking stick.

THE CHIEF

Tuesday, 11/2, North of Tralee

"WHO FOUND THE bodies?" said the portly man behind the desk.

"Osbourne, Sir Hugh," said the manservant. "He said that there was a gathering of Tinkers nearby the sea caves. Perhaps a connection?"

The man didn't answer. He simply pursed his pouty lips in thought. As one of the last of the ancient gentry families with ties to Great Britain, Hugh Rappaport had been knighted by the Queen herself for his leadership, many charities, and vast wealth. Ireland was a rather laid-back land and 'Sir Hugh' was just too uppity of an appellation for the common folk who generally despised the British. They nicknamed him, 'Chief', and, truth to tell, Hugh rather liked it. It appealed to the baser instincts in him and harked back to a time when the head man of the tribe or village or area held the power of the land by cunning, largesse, and force.

He cut quite a figure amongst the celebrities of Ireland, Britain and the Continent. Making his money from North Sea Oil, so they said, he knew everyone there was to know and could name the sheiks and even many of the tribal leaders of the Middle East, calling some of them his 'good friends'.

But the locals knew him differently. There was a darker side to him. He could be arrogant, cruel one moment, but bold and kind the next. Mercurial some would say, nigh near crazy said others.

Not all of his money was made from oil. Much of it, in fact, came from the drug trade.

"Louis," said the Chief to his manservant, "did the shipment come in last night as scheduled?"

"That it did, Sir Hugh. Seventy kilos, all prepackaged in small bags. I must say, Sir Hugh, RAGE seems to be all the rage these days."

The Chief stood up behind his desk and smiled at the thought of what that many kilos of the drug would bring him.

RAGE stood for *Random Anger Graphic Encounter*. Good thing there was a cool acronym for a boring, pedantic, scientific description of a drug.

Random: the anger of the user was seemingly unfocussed. *Anger:* the proven high of the drug was overshadowed by the intense rage that erupted and closed the end of the drug cycle. *Graphic:* the rage was expressed both verbally and physically in an escalating series of violent attacks. *Encounter:* never simply a solitary experience, the rage that brought the drug's cycle to an end was always an encounter, a violent meeting with another person.

The Chief was the first one with the ability to market the drug who immediately sensed its importance. First of all, it was an opiate-amphetamine compound designer drug, time-released to function in a particular way. It was a capsule and since the shell of the capsule contained some of the ingredients of the drug, it could not be crushed, insufflated, or taken any other way than orally. What made it absolutely the best drug on the market was its cost. Not cheap, but not expensive either. Most anyone could afford it. Best of all, he thought, it was terribly addicting.

What caused its popularity was the way the body processed it. Ten minutes after taking the capsule, an intense opioid high was reached that lasted fifty minutes. Then, sixty minutes after ingesting, the drug produced a bizarre amphetamine high where the frenetic activity was violent anger directed outward toward any living thing. It just felt good to hit and hurt another. The rage lasted only ten minutes, but those who had experienced it loved it because they felt so alive and invincible. Collateral damage was expected and almost always occurred. There was a chaos factor at play here, and for the disaffected youth of the day, the drug produced an irresistible, anarchic high.

Kids, and to Sir Hugh that meant anyone under thirty, took to it immediately and used it to play the Game. The young, detached from society's institutions and full of sloth, despair and entitlement, named it their drug of choice. A group would gather together and have one or two of its members take a capsule of RAGE. Then they would bet on when the anger high would commence. Pharmaceuticals interacted with people differently because of unique body chemistries, but the time-released drug was amazingly predictable. There was never more than five minutes difference between the onset of the last manifestation of the drug. That made the betting precise and within the attention span of the young.

These youth, so Sir Hugh had been told, played the RAGE Game with enthusiasm. When one's bet had expired that person left the group. The one who came closest to predicting the exact time of the onset of anger won the bet but had to stay with the 'RAGER' until it was clear the anger was upon him or her. It sounded dangerous but the randomness in the violent explosion made the person swing and move like a frenetic zombie. Unless you were close to that 'RAGER', you would not be caught or hurt. Usually. Lately, the net, the papers and the vid news were full of stories. There was the college student who ate the face off his friend who had won the bet. Good thing the victim won. He needed the money for the plastic surgeries that were sure to follow. The thrill was there—it was like temporary zombiehood—and was irresistible to a young population that had few dreams, few jobs, and less motivation to truly live in the world.

Sir Hugh knew a sucker when he saw one, and this was a great chance to make money. He cornered the market, made a new fortune, even bigger than his oil wealth. Yes, he should have felt a little dirty, but the money and the power it bought were just too good. Sir Hugh was necessary for the public image, but only the Chief could amass the wealth needed to rule over an entire generation. And besides, this was a means to a darker end. Such possibilities he thought.

Departing, his manservant almost ran into Sir Hugh's business manager and fixer. To most people, Shiro Ishii was young for the responsibility he carried. Keeping the books for the Chief and being the 'fixer', the one who had to make all the big man's dealings look legitimate, was a complicated affair. Yet Shiro came to it naturally. Brushing past the manservant, Shiro crooked his mouth up in a smirk saying to the Chief, "It looks like you already know."

"I do," said Sir Hugh. "Happy though I am with the shipment, I am concerned about my murdered men. Who did it? Rumor suggests Tinkers."

"Don't know yet, but it's no loss. They were no more than thugs. You should never have hired them."

"But they were my thugs, and someone has to do the dirty work. Whoever killed them had to know they worked for me. They had to know and because they did know, they deliberately insulted me. I can take that condescension from the airheaded royals and the privileged continental hacks, but not from someone who comes onto my own turf and murders my men." Sir Hugh paused in his rant. "Any news from America? The first part of our plan is working admirably. RAGE has taken hold and I fully expect Irish society to be disrupted very soon. Continental Europe will be next. Has Dr. Drake succeeded with Phase Two?"

"I've heard nothing," said Ishii. "I expect a call from him later today."

"While we wait," said the Chief, "take care of the Tinker rabble that presumably caused all this. It's Amergin's clan, and they are down at Cahersiveen less than an hour's drive from here. Take care of them all. He and his people have caused trouble wherever they have gone and, since they've been around my land, they've been an inconvenience at best and a bleedin' cancer at their worst. Murder is murder and the whole clan is to be punished. Do I make myself clear?"

Ishii smiled a predatory smile. "Perfectly sir. I'll take care of the matter immediately."

"Take as many men as you need. I'll keep the *Gardai* away—I'll send the law enforcement authorities somewhere else, a wild goose chase that will free you to do what you do best."

CONTAGION AT CAHERSIVEEN

Tuesday, 11/3, Cahersiveen

ISHII DECIDED TO go alone. Easier that way. All he needed was his spray bottle. Usually, it was filled with antiseptic cleanser. Used it all the time in this filthy country of mud and wet, mold and marsh. Ishii knew that people saw this was out and away obsessive-compulsive behavior, but gee, a guy had to have his affectations. He threw it into his Mercedes and roared down the driveway, taking the road to Cahersiveen.

Less than an hour later he spotted the caravan park just to the south of the town boundaries. This late in the year, it was desolate except for the wagons of the Tinkers, broods of children running among them like chicks fled from the nest.

Ishii stepped out of the car and was surrounded by a bevy of brats, squalling and pushing amongst themselves to get closer to the stranger. He literally could not move amongst the hoard, until a strong looking old gent smiled his way past the bairns, held out his hands in welcome.

"I'm Amergin, the head of this clan. And who do I have the pleasure of welcoming with our hospitality?"

Ishii didn't even look at him whilst he spritzed his hands with what seemed like cleanser. Vacantly smiling at the closest children, he patted their heads and then looked at the old man. "I'm Shiro Ishii, business manager for Sir Hugh. He wanted me to pay a visit to you and see if you knew anything about a couple of his men falling into some foul play last evening."

Amergin lifted his eyes to the heavens and said, "Ishii ... Ishii. Do I know your family from somewhere? Let me think." And in that moment, Amergin's eyes turned hard as he stared at Ishii. "True, not many Japanese natives settled round these parts in ages past, but with immigration being what it is now, you can find all kinds of races and tribes here in dear old Erin, and all are welcome even if some do not appreciate what this land truly is. But I'm not thinking I know you or your kin from here but rather from across the seas to your native land. In fact, I believe I knew what must have been your great-grandfather of the same name, Shiro Ishii."

The Japanese man blanched and stepped back. "Doubtful sir. I ... he would have remembered such a remarkable event."

"I'm sure he did and does remember, Ishii," said Amergin. "I was walking not far outside of Kyoto, before the war, and had fallen, twisting my ankle and breaking my arm. He kindly stopped his automobile and offered me a ride to his hospital to treat me. I was just visiting, but in such pain, that I took him up on the opportunity. I stayed at his hospital for three days ... before I escaped."

"Escaped?" snorted Ishii. "What in the world do you mean? You're old alright, but not that old. It would be impossible for anyone alive then to be alive now."

"Impossible?" said Amergin. "Improbable, yes. I know well why I am alive, but you ... you are a freak of 'gentech', an abomination of a science run mad, a monster walking among the human race. You laughed when I said I escaped, but I remember you well. You set my arm, much appreciated by the way, but you had more in mind. At night, I heard the screams from the other hospital wards, so haunting I could not sleep. I walked the halls of your hospital and no one saw me. It is a talent I have. And I saw. I saw what you did in your surgical theaters. Vivisection, obscene organ removal just to see how long a patient might live minus a lung, a stomach, or a pancreas, injections of plague bacillus given to pregnant women to see what happened to their unborn children."

"You were not there," snarled Ishii. "No one knows what really happened there or why."

"You do," said Amergin. "And so do I. I am a Walker, a Walker of Worlds, and after three days as your patient, I decided to walk by your side, unseen, unnoticed, but there, there to witness everything you did in that hospital from hell. I saw what you did to prolong your life, gene manipulation at the highest level and far beyond any science that exists today. You were brilliant, brilliant and madly psychotic. But I could care less that you lengthened your lifespan. I too have lived very long. But when you opened Unit 731 in Manchuria, you opened humanity's soul to the darkest evils imaginable. The things you did in Kyoto were but child's play to what you did in that house of horrors."

"You could have stopped me," said Ishii.

"I could not. I am a Walker of Worlds. I observe, I persuade, and most importantly, I find the heroes of the Light to stop the evils of the Dark. But there were no heroes in that land, neither in the day nor in the night."

"So you say. But you knew my work was blessed by my government and later by the Americans. They saw the good in it."

"No, they saw the profit. You are an incarnation of he that fell to this earth so long ago. Men are capable of great evil. Few have actually made themselves into evil. But you are one who has done so. All you do is bring sickness, suffering and death."

A cough sounded behind Amergin. "As I have here it appears," said Ishii and walked away.

"Amergin," said a small voice. He turned and saw one of the children, one of his own nephews, whose head had been benignly touched by Ishii just a few moments before.

"What is it child?" said Amergin.

"I don't feel so good." Amergin saw the boy cough again only this time spitting up blood as well. He moved to touch the child, but others around him began coughing. Blood spilt from their mouths as their lungs quickly clogged.

Mothers came running, screaming. Amergin turned round and round searching for Ishii. A drizzle began to fall from the skies, but he spotted him on a little hillock above the caravan park, black duster whipping in the misty wind. Dark shadows capered around him in silent glee and Ishii, himself, had a feral grin on his face. He stretched out his hands over the Tinker gathering.

"I thought I had brought my hand cleanser. Looks like I picked the wrong bottle. All this, Amergin, is for your meddling in the affairs of Sir Hugh. He has no mercy for those who have no respect for him or his men."

"They had nothing to do with the death of his men. Neither did I. Spare these children."

Ishii shook his head in mock sorrow. "I cannot. The master said an example must be made."

Ishii's hands did not fall. Instead, he now clenched them into fists, and suddenly the tiny campfires exploded more brightly into flame and embers settled on the roofs of the wagons. In seconds, despite the soft rain, there was a conflagration with wood spitting flame, children and now their mothers collapsing from whatever sickness was on the hands of Ishii. The men rushed forward to try to take Ishii captive, but he simply laughed and watched them crumble to the ground as well, frothing blood as they tried to climb the hill he stood upon.

It was a mighty burning. It was a terrible dying. It was a rending of the peace of the very earth, and Amergin could do nothing. He held his wife as she died and cradled the head of his dead nephew. It was over in minutes. As Amergin held his beloved, Ishii looked down upon him and said, "A Walker of Worlds cannot be killed by me. But look around. This world you walk is doomed and you can do nothing to stop what is coming."

Amergin screamed wordless invective at Ishii, but Ishii only shouted the louder, "Go ahead, do like your poet said, 'Rage! Rage against the dying of the Light!' It'll do you no good. There's more to come and all you will be able to do is witness it, you impotent, useless, powerless old man."

A HORRIFYING DETOUR

Tuesday, 11/3, Cahersiveen

THEY WERE ONLY a few miles out of Cahersiveen when Kevin happened to turn around and saw the smoke. "Something terrible is going on. That smoke is coming from the caravan park."

"It is luv," said Mary gripping her husband's arm. "Don't wake the boy but turn around and let's see if we can help."

It must have been Malby's increased speed and the force of the bumps on the road that wakened Conor. Opening his eyes, the first thing he saw as he looked to the front of the wagon, past the figures of Kevin and Mary, was a thick cloud of black smoke smearing the horizon.

"What is it?" he asked.

Kevin didn't turn his eyes from the road. "Nothing good, Conor, nothing good. It's a fire I think and it's coming from the caravan park."

"The Tinkers," whispered Conor. "Someone's burning them out." On the flight over, Conor had done a little reading about the prejudice and violence often done to the Tinkers. It was the first thing he thought.

"Aye, lad," said Mary. "Though I'm surprised you know how we are treated here. But I have to tell you this is different. A bad word, a tossed tomato, a bruised eye—that's usually the most to it, but this is bad, bad as I've ever seen."

Nothing else was spoken till Kevin turned the wagon down the path to the caravan park. The fire brigade was already there but nothing was happening. There was nothing to save. Ambulances were present but only figures covered in sheets were being put into the vans. A chill wind blew in from the sea.

Kevin saw his father wandering aimlessly among the smoke and flames. "Da," he cried. "Amergin!"

The tragic eyes of the old man turned his way, and as Amergin saw his son, he fell to his knees. Kevin rushed over. "Where's Ma? Da, where is she?" Kevin enveloped his kneeling father in his arms.

"Gone," he said. "Gone to the hospital. But not alive, mind you. She died as did everyone else except me. Gasping out every last bloody breath."

"Dead?" said Kevin. "She's dead?"

Conor came up and touched his shoulder. Angrily, Kevin shook it off. "What do you mean, she's dead? I just saw her."

"Shiro Ishii was here," said Amergin. "Sir Hugh Rappaport's top henchman. Blamed us for the deaths of the Chief's two men. Said Sir Hugh had to make an example of us all. Ishii killed them with a pox he brought with him. Fast acting. No chance for any of them."

"A pox?" Kevin turned pale. "What about Laura?" He turned to run to the wagon.

"It's not contagious anymore," said Amergin. "It was so viral it burnt itself out within minutes. The authorities will never figure it out."

Conor backed away. I'm responsible for this, he thought. I did this. For a moment, he thought his heart was going to stop and then he smelled it. The foulness, like the putrescence of the swamp. He stepped toward the middle of the circle of Tinker wagons and, for a moment, he felt his stomach lurch, and he almost lost his balance. The smell was stronger here, and things were walking amid the still burning fires. Black shadows darted furtively amongst the ruin. Conor saw they were Changelings, but they were not alone. No. Someone else. Then he saw her. Bent like an old crone, claws like a crow. That bitch, thought Conor to himself, that fucking bitch. The Morrigan was in the shape she used when she walked the fields of finished battles. She swayed in her grey ripped rags and swirled in a circle around the places where bodies had just been removed. The Morrigan hummed her little keening death song, seemingly oblivious to all surrounding her until her eyes lit upon Conor.

"Is that who I think it is?" she whistled through her rotten teeth. "Is that the Seal King Who Shall Be who comes to save? You are too late boyling. The witch doctor is gone, and that is good for you, for you are no match for him yet. True, you fought the wizard who wanted to be a famous genetic physician, fought him well and killed him dead, but this one ... He is a doctor who wishes for more than science, who has an alchemist's heart but not for gold, no, for power, not to mutate elements but to change living things. He is far worse than the one before. An even older and ancient magic runs through his veins. But why worry about that now? Dance with me lad, the dance of the dead, for who will honor them if not you and me?"

The Morrigan's foul breath touched Conor's face and he saw her rotten teeth and stringy white hair. He was mesmerized as she twirled around him. She took his hands and was about to lead him in the dance of death, when a thunderous voice threw her to the ground.

"Get thee gone, battle whore!" Amergin spoke with fighting fury, present sorrow turned to rage. "We may have been friends once, we may even speak now and then, but when you are like this, you are death's doorway and not fit company for the boy who shall be King."

Turning to Conor, Amergin said, "Listen to me carefully lad. My son has already told me about your willingness to take blame that is not yours. You did not cause this, not a bit of it. But neither are you innocent. You are the catalyst."

"Aye," giggled the crone. "He changes things ..."

"Shut up!" they yelled in unison. Conor ran his hand through his mop of black hair discreetly wiping the tears off his face. Amergin seemed not to notice.

Amergin said, "What happened would have happened anyway but has occurred now because of you. You do change things, and though you are not the cause, you damn well are part of the solution. I for sure am going to help you succeed in whatever it is you are supposed to do. Look at my son over there. A good, decent lad with a heart of gold. And he loves his Mary and that sweet little Laura. Beautiful aren't they. At least they are still alive."

Amergin choked back a sob and continued, "Kevin cannot even see us here. I just made us step sideways into the bigger world, the Otherworld, where evil can be sensed more clearly, and great deeds can be done more grandly. Here, I am both the Walker of Worlds and the Bard of the West, the singer of tales, and my songs have power. I can be a help to you, and I will do what I can. For I look at your round black eyes, seal eyes, and only hurt and pain lie there. That cannot be permitted. Look around, evil is everywhere here, but it is not the only thing present. Even now, I hear my wife's song from beyond and know she is not dead forever. I wish Kevin could hear, but he is not the heir of this power. You are."

"Me?" said Conor. "How could I possibly be your heir?"

"Not mine really. The Land's actually. I have held it a long time, but I held it for the coming of you." He looked at the Morrigan. "A little bird told me recently."

Conor looked incredulous. "You've held it for me? All those years? Why, and why me?"

Amergin smiled bleakly. "The ripening of future events and those who partake in them take time. Your coming and your quickening are of those things. Why is it so hard for you to accept?" He reached out with both strong hands and, like his son had done the night before, ripped the shirt off Conor's chest. The black loop of skin flowed up his right arm, around his neck and cut contours across his chest till it crossed his heart. Amergin, however, was gazing directly at the scar just beneath Conor's heart. "Look at you, the living breathing proof of prophecy." Touching Conor's forehead, thrice he intoned,

Three times pierced,
Three times wounded,
Thrice to bring the king to birth,

Tracing the bite marks on Conor's right hand and following the dark line of *fae* skin till it rested over his heart, Amergin said even more solemnly,

Once, comes the Otherworld,
Twice, the pains of Change,
Thrice pierced, a Kingdom gained.

When he uttered the word 'twice', Amergin stayed his index finger above the scar where Drake's dagger had been driven close to Conor's heart in a killing strike only healed by the White Stag of the Forest. The rest of the words he simply sighed:

So says the crow that flies above,
So says the barrow prince hidden in the mound,
So says he who walks the twilight bound.

"How about a little song, Bard of the West, you who 'walk the twilight bound'?" smirked the Morrigan, who like the carrion crow she was had yet to leave this field of slaughter. "How about the song you should have sung to have stopped this massacre of your clan?"

For a moment, he said nothing. But then, in a soft sing song voice he sang,

You walk amid the tortured dead,
You sing their song of praise,
You listen to their last words said,
But never new life raise.

"Go now and mourn those who passed," Amergin said to the Morrigan. "Your presence here offends me. Give us some peace."

"How about eternal peace?" she coyly said. Looking at them expectantly, she added, "Well, I could go and mourn them somewhere more privately." And in a huff-filled explosion of feathers, she launched herself into the heavens, the cawing, carrion crow silhouetted against the leaden sky.

RAGE

Tuesday noon, 11/3, Cahersiveen

WHEN THE MORRIGAN had left, Conor looked to talk to Amergin once more, but the bard had turned away, walking back through the drizzle towards Kevin. To lose wife, mother, and clan. How would they recover? The pain of loss descended heavily upon the boy again.

Then, he chanced to look south, down the beach. O my God, thought Conor, it's him—that Japanese guy, Ishii—the one that Kevin mentioned. He noticed the long black coat whipping behind the man. Looked pretty tall for a Japanese person. But Conor wanted answers, and he wasn't going to let the man's austere appearance chase him away. He walked slowly toward the figure, who never once looked at him.

When Conor was about ten feet away, the man lifted up his face and spoke. "I am Ishii," he said, "and you must be the young pup that has brought the problems of America across the sea to lovely Ireland. I take it Drake did not succeed in finding the source of your strangeness."

Conor swallowed hard. "How do you know about Drake?"

Ishii turned his head, "We work together. You, or rather the village that you descended upon was his project. Yet, apparently, he failed."

"Drake is dead."

"I thought as much."

"He died a couple of days ago," said Conor. "Shot because he was trying to kill me and the villagers. He was evil. Glad he's gone." Conor's eyes grew hard as he stared at the man.

Ishii hissed and moved like lightning. Before Conor could even react, the man had him in a headlock and was thrusting a capsule into Conor's mouth. Taken by surprise, Conor gagged and tried to push away, but Ishii was strong and relentless. A long finger poked the capsule deep into the boy's throat and instinctively Conor swallowed.

"What did you give me?" Conor gasped finally pulling away from the man.

"Just a little something to calm you down so we might talk a bit. It's all the 'rage' with the young folk around here. You might as well get used to it since you'll be offered it sooner or later." Ishii smiled a false smile once again as he motioned for Conor to take a seat on the sand.

Conor actually wanted to leave. He couldn't know it yet, but the exterior of the capsule had already melted in his throat and the powerful opioid had already begun to relax him. He found his legs collapsing as a warm peace began to flow through him. He looked at Ishii as the Japanese doctor sat by him on the sand.

"Can you hear me, Conor?" said Ishii. "Do you understand me?"

"Of course," said Conor, feeling more at ease with the man.

"Do you want to know why I did what I did with the Tinkers?"

Conor thought it might be quite nice to know, even though the event was terrible. Perhaps Ishii had a motive that would explain why the deed was done.

Ishii told the lad his story. About how he was a research scientist both before and during World War II. About the terrible experiments he had done in order to help the war effort. About how much he gave up in order for the Emperor to succeed.

"You see, Conor, my family was of the royal bloodline. My father could speak to the Emperor as easily as I speak to you. The Emperor was a tiny man, somewhat strange—but he hated America, and he promised me ... things if I could help him succeed. I'm a good swordsman, and our father made my brothers and me into fine samurai, but I knew my path did not lie in physical combat. It was my mind that was supreme."

Conor thought the man was a little full of himself, but as he spoke, the doctor convinced Conor of his greatness. Look at all the man had done: developed a water purification system to protect Japanese soldiers from cholera, made huge advances on discovering bioweapons, and even advanced genetic research from its infancy stages back in the day. But he was not appreciated. Even the Emperor refused to notice him. But that all changed.

Momentarily distracted, Conor picked up again on Ishii's narrative ... "It was the plague that saved my work. Finally, success. And the Chinese heathen demonstrated to all the morbidity of the disease. I had it sprayed from the air, put in their water, sown in their fields, and they died by the tens of thousands. I was hailed a hero by Prime Minister Tojo, himself. And when the Americans came to punish us for Pearl Harbor, I took every American prisoner I could find and turned them into either specimens or monsters. Want to know how long a man can live without kidneys? Ask Corporal Luke Sparrow from Coeur de Lane, Idaho. Want to know how long a man can live if I freeze his right leg and left arm solid? Ask Sergeant Harry Boyd from Boston. Can a man survive a head transplant? Major Emory Marx from

Denver could tell us that … or not. That experiment didn't go as well as I had hoped."

Conor had never felt this good. Every muscle was relaxed; his mind was floating, and he just loved listening to Ishii's voice. Part of him rebelled against the content, but then the soothing sound of the Japanese doctor lulled him into supreme comfortability again. Conor thought Ishii just fine, even though he seemed to speak forever.

Then the doctor asked him a question. "Have you ever heard of 'The Night of Cherry Blossoms?' No? You truly don't know your history. I planned it. It was set to bring down the United States of America. And it would have worked if not for the nuclear bomb explosions your leaders set off in my beloved country. The Emperor was preoccupied with surrendering. Many thought him a weak fool, but he must have known the time was not right. The 'blossoms' would have worked though. I haven't had the chance until now to replicate and strengthen those … 'blossoms'. But I will make it happen here, and not long from now. Not that you have to worry about it."

Suddenly, Conor felt annoyed. Ishii was talking down to him, condescending to him, the man who would be Seal King. If only Ishii knew that.

Ishii smiled at the discontent rippling across Conor's face. "I forgot to tell you, lad, the last fifty minutes were the last fifty you would ever feel this good. The capsule I gave you has certain effects, and you are about to experience the most important of them all—true, inspired rage. And that's good. You'll need it to fight me."

"You?" said Conor derisively. "You're just a pissant with your books and your bottles of plague. Killing in secret. Killing in the dark. What a coward!"

The doctor laughed. "That's the spirit; let that rage flow through you. If I was as weak as you say, then how could I do what I did to the Tinkers back there?"

Scrunching up his face, Conor tried to understand, but he was feeling the blood pounding through his body, and as good as he felt before, now he just felt angry. "You're right," he snarled. "Those could have been my friends back there, but you snuffed them out before I even got a chance to know them." With a howl he launched himself at Ishii.

Suddenly there was a katana, a Japanese curved short Sword, in the doctor's hand. But Conor didn't care. Indeed, Ishii could have impaled him right then and there, but, instead, simply stepped back and lightly sliced open the skin on Conor's chest. A thin trickle of blood dripped down his torso.

"Just a scratch," dismissed Conor. Faster than Ishii could see, Conor swept his legs under the taller man and the doctor fell, letting the katana drop. Conor didn't want it. He wanted the man. Jumping atop Ishii, he began swinging at his face. But Shiro Ishii had decades of experience and the blows never hit him. He was up in a moment kicking Conor in the ribs. It seemed like eternity that they wrestled though it was only minutes. Conor increasingly devolved. His eyes lost contact with his soul. Animal grunts and gRoans came from him. Deep within himself, he tried to hold the madness at bay, but it was not to be. Consciousness receded and primitive instincts took hold. Conor screamed like a beast and kept attacking, but Ishii easily pushed him aside. No rational mind guided the boy's actions now.

Glancing at his watch, Ishii said, "Enough. It is time."

"What?" said a momentarily confused Conor. From the depths of his heart his psyche began to reassert itself. Groggily, he said, "I still have time to kill you." Though to tell the truth, he didn't feel much like doing that anymore. He was dizzy and suddenly felt weak. "What's happening to me?"

Ishii didn't answer, but only bent down and grabbed the katana. Self-preservation kicked in and Conor turned and ran, lurching and stumbling towards the sea.

Ishii chased him along the beach, laughing, exhilarating in the chase. Then, Conor found himself caught before a huge sea rock. He turned to face his pursuer, his mind still cloudy, but the visceral rage in his gut was vanishing enough for him to groan out loud, trying to reach the elemental energy within him. He had to shapeshift. "Now that I need it, it's all gone, gone." Conor fell to his knees in the sand.

He watched the moral monster approach, a smile on his merciless lips, katana swinging. "Slice and dice, Conor. No need for you to be a part of this drama anymore. Whatever happened across the sea, hasn't followed you here. The Tinker and his dam and that by-blow waif aren't in any position to help you. And the RAGE, well that's taken you and you are spent. My master's financial backers thought they were getting a drug that would hype the soldier in the wars that are coming. Not a chance. He and I know this is only a plague, a manufactured one, a powerful one that will simply bring destruction."

He laughed as he walked up to Conor. "You are in exactly the position a man takes when he is about to perform *seppuku*—disemboweling himself in shame and guilt. You don't know about that, so let me help you."

Ishii slashed and neatly ripped open an even larger cut on Conor's torso. Again, a jet of blood fell down his heaving chest.

"I should have you do it," said Ishii. "Then you could watch your guts spill out on the sand and die the slow death you deserve. But I see you are in no position to do such. So," he bowed, "allow me."

As the madman bent low, katana touching the ground, Conor flicked a handful of sand into his face. "Take that, asshat," he said, flinging himself up and running towards the ocean. He'd give anything to change right now, but he realized an effect of the drug was to paralyze his ability to meld mind to bone and shapeshift. He stumbled as fast as he could toward the sea and dove into the first breaker that touched him. He did not surface.

Ishii didn't even scream. The sand was painful. Kept him from doing the deed, but he bet on the ocean's waves and rocks doing it for him. Conor was weak and disoriented. Whatever gifts Conor had just weren't working very well for him. Brushing himself off, Ishii looked to the empty sea, and turned to walk back to the camping ground.

It was a good bet on Ishii's part. Conor was in deep trouble. Diving into the breaker was easy, but what was left of his clothing and those damn heavy shoes, were dragging him down. The rip current helped, sucking him out and down, right into a big rock that bashed his head and made him see stars, until blackness grabbed him, and he knew no more.

IN THE ARMS OF A SELKIE

Tuesday Night to Wednesday Morning, 11/4, Cahersiveen

COUGHING AND SPLUTTERING, he woke wondering why water wasn't pouring into his lungs. He could feel his burning chest, and he was so damn cold. It was dark out, and the gristly sand rubbed his legs. Very uncomfortable. But someone was holding him. He got a look at an arm, a strong, but feminine arm. And he was in her lap. He glanced up to see a dark-haired woman looking down at him, lips curved in a curious expression. It was her eyes that caught him. Deep, liquid, round, dark eyes that seemed to look into his soul.

"You must have saved me," he coughed, trying to sit up.

"I must have," she said smiling now, eyes staring intently as she gently pushed him back down. She had a strange foreign accent and spoke as if even the forming of words was new to her. "Do not try to get up. You are sorely hurt."

"I'm sorely sore," said Conor, coughing again, feeling liquid in his mouth. It tasted coppery. Blood, he thought. He must have bitten his lip.

"No," she said answering his unspoken question, "you have bitten nothing, but your ribs have punctured your lungs, and you are bleeding inside. Internally, as you say. Your skull is fractured as well, but there is no brain damage."

"Thanks, doctor" he said sarcastically. "But I feel like crap, and ..." Conor started coughing again, and a sharp pain lanced through his core. He began wheezing. "I was just wondering," he gasped, "if we are going to sit here all night or if we ought to go to a hospital."

"Help is on the way," said the woman. "I have called them."

"Them who?" asked Conor.

"My sisters. The one who flies above told us to be on watch for something to happen to you. So, we have watched, and been ready."

"That insufferable witch," gasped the boy. "She flits here and there, knowing everything, but never stopping anything. You'd think she might intervene now and then before bad things happen."

The woman smirked, "You are right; she can be difficult. But look, you are in luck. My sisters come."

She pointed out into the water. The moon and the stars, the Hand of God nebula and the luminous waves gave plenty of light. At first, he couldn't see anything, but then, he saw an almost human head break the waves, then another and another. They did not move, but simply popped up and down like bobbers on a fishing line. More appeared, and then Conor recognized what they were. "Seals!" he wheezed in wonder.

"My sisters," she said proudly. "We are the *Roan*. We come to help you, Conor Archer."

"You're a selkie!"

"One of the things men call me. But you can call me Scatha. These," she pointed again, "are my sisters."

The seals moved sleekly through the water, hauling their bodies up on the beach. They lay there in a straight line, the water barely touching them. Then they morphed. Their eyes did not change, but it was as if their seal skin sloughed off in one piece. Conor could not believe his eyes. As they stood, they wrapped their skins around themselves, not as cumbersome furs, but as a sleek, skin covering. Long black hair, round, dark eyes, each of them a woman beautiful but somewhat alien. Conor no more thought he was looking at a human being than at a Martian.

My God, he thought, I can't be one of them.

"But you are," said the woman who continued to cradle him in her arms. "You are of our people."

"But I'm human," he wheezed again. "At least kind of."

The woman laughed. "Partly maybe, but more like us than you think."

Conor groaned. The sharp pain lanced through him again. This time, blood gushed from his mouth. And the blackness returned.

He awoke again to find himself still cradled, but now a dozen additional pair of eyes stared down at him.

"You are dying my King Who Shall Be," said Scatha softly, "but we can heal you if you let us. Only one thing is necessary. You must allow us into your mind. When our people are injured, it is not just the body that is wounded. The soul suffers too, and must be healed if the body is to get well. Will you let us touch you? Will you let us walk the pathways of your thoughts?"

Even in his pain, Conor rebelled. "Everything? You get to see everything in my mind?"

"We can see everything, relive your entire life if we choose. But these things are not necessary to heal you. As we heal the scars on your body and soul, we will be close to your recent memories, but I promise you, we shall not pry more deeply."

"Then do it. I feel like cow flops."

Scatha arched an eyebrow in question.

"Um … cow waste … crap … shit … you got to know what I mean."

Scatha looked solemnly at him. "You do feel badly. Silence. Let us work."

They touched him. Nearly everywhere. That was a bit embarrassing since it was then he discovered the few rags he was wearing covered virtually nothing. He only thought that for a second, because he felt something even more strange. He felt their minds seeping into his thoughts, and his consciousness grew grey again, and he neither felt nor remembered anything.

He awoke wrapped in a seal skin. It was hours before dawn on Wednesday. A small fire burned in front of him and Scatha was alone with him.

"My sisters have gone," she said.

"I … I feel better," said Conor.

"You are healed, but it was not easy. Several of your hours it took. The wounds the substance caused and the bashing your body sustained on the rocks would have ended your life surely. The Sword cuts that the evil man inflicted upon you were minor. But something else was a more immediate threat. In fact, it was killing you."

"You said you wouldn't go deep into my memories," said Conor, anger flashing in his gold-flecked eyes.

"We did not have to. The pain was there for anyone to see. Even those humans who cannot soul-see would be able to read the story on your face. Loss, death, betrayal, loneliness, fear—all these things poisoned your soul and would have led to death. We could not take those emotions away, but we could delay their poison, at least for a while. And we understand you better now King Who Shall Be. You have done wrong, but not with malice in your heart. Your guilt and shame are far greater than any sin you committed, yet in the depths of your soul you believe you deserve to die— you want to die. We could lessen that, but you will have to decide whether you really deserve such hate from others. You are not alone. So many love you who have not even met you, yet they already know of your existence. And that friend who thinks you betrayed him—you know him well and measured his character perfectly. He will not leave you, nor will his anger come permanently against you. I, Scatha, have said it. It shall be so."

Conor sat up and wrapped the seal skin around his body. He felt much better. He looked at Scatha in the dim firelight. An electric charge rippled through his body. She wore nothing but her long hair draped down her front modestly and some sort of sea kelp thing that left little to guess at but still chastely covered her. She smiled at him.

I found something in the ruin of whatever you call those things that covered your legs. She tossed it to him.

"My whistle," exclaimed Conor. "You saved it."

"Of course, and glad am I that I did. Your thoughts betray the heart of a bard and a musician of great repute."

Conor blushed. "Not really, but I do like to play that whistle."

"Play something for me," said Scatha.

"All I play here on this island are Celtic things and you probably heard enough of that. There is a song I know that I learned back home. It's got a Celtic feel to it, but it is as American as anything I have ever heard. It's famous back home. In fact, it is called 'Homeward Bound'."

He poured himself into the song, and the whistle echoed over the waves and sent his loneliness and the independence that always fought each other out in that haunting melody. He put the whistle down and sang the refrain of the song, and he wept while he sang.

When the summer's ceased its gleaming,
When the corn is past its prime,
When adventure's lost its meaning,
I'll be homeward bound in time.
Bind me not to the pasture. Chain me not to the plow.
Set me free to find my calling and I'll return to you somehow.

"You miss your home," said Scatha, brushing the lock of hair over his forehead. Mist in his eyes, he thought he would be embarrassed again, but then he heard voices echoing back to him from the sea.

"My sisters return," smiled Scatha. "They hear and answer your song."

Leaping through the waves they came, diving a last time and rising to walk as women, carrying their seal skins through the breakers and onto the sand, singing themselves ashore.

So hauntingly beautiful were their voices that Conor picked up his whistle and played counter point.

Scatha stood and Conor did the same, and as her sisters sang, she spoke, and as she spoke it was as if her sisters also communicated through her as they sang. Conor knew it was magical because Scatha's dark eyes flecked gold and grew more golden as she looked at Conor. His pain lessened as she chanted:

Born, born, born to be King,
Here in the sea where the Roan do sing.
But home is not here for the boy King to flee.
Home is where rivers meet far from the sea,
By the walker, by the prince, by the crow who frees
There he is loved, there shall he be,
Till the crow who flies above the ground,
Till the prince who seeks a kingdom found,
Till the walker who walks the twilight bound,
 Names him singer of song,
 Calls him son righting wrong,
 Frees him to meet a destiny strong.
Then home shall he be,
Home shall he be,
Far, far, far from the sea.
Far, far, far from the sea.

SCATHA

Wednesday, Dawn, 11/4, Cahersiveen

WHILE SHE WAS chanting, the pre-dawn mist gathered behind Conor, shutting him off from the grotesque death field of the caravan park. Ahead, a golden moon began to shine more brightly through the patchy fog, and Conor could hear the seal women calling to him where the sand met the sea. Their forms were shadows by the waves, and he could understand how, in the past, they had been mistaken for mermaids and sirens.

Then they began to sing again. Almost human in sound with melodic voices, and if Conor couldn't catch the words, this time he certainly caught the meaning.

Loss and woe floated over water and sand. Something had brought them sadness long ago, and the haunting memory tugged at Conor's heart. He found himself drawn forward, wanting to comfort them, but their song changed, stopping him in his tracks. They wanted only a recognition of what had happened, and a promise not to surrender to the Dark. Then, Conor caught the undercurrent of the melody, and to him, it sounded like a hint of hope. Always, an undercurrent of hope.

Then Scatha took his hand and sat him down on the beach. He closed his eyes, listening to the singing, and when he opened them, he found himself looking up at the face of the selkie woman, clad only in seaweed and the tasteful draping of her long, silky raven hair. Conor knew she wore next to nothing, but he didn't think a bride could look more chaste than she. Good thing, too, because he discovered his head resting in her lap again—he could get used to this—and her long fingers stroking his hair. Fine webbing connected the fingers of her hands, and he was speechless before her beauty. Her full mouth came close to his forehead and her lips brushed his skin. He blushed remembering the tattered rags he wore.

"Dawn is only hours away," said Scatha. "Our people have a saying that when the shark hunts, one must flee or else fight with cunning and stealth. Which will you choose, for the shark hunts you?"

"Don't I know it," said Conor. "You saw what happened up there in the car park. You know who did this."

"We do," said Scatha. "That is what my sisters sing about. We have known of the wanderings of Shiro Ishii for many decades. Wherever he walks, pain and darkness follow. He knows of us; indeed, has tried to study us and discover our secrets. He plans to change this land and its people and all living things within it. This Isle of Erin is as much our mother as is the sea, and when the time comes, and it approaches soon, we shall defend her. And you must lead us."

"Hey," said Conor, standing up, "not so fast. I'm not leading anyone. I told you I don't like this Messiah stuff, and I'm not even quite sure what I am yet."

"You know very well what and who you are," snapped Scatha, leaping to her feet. "It is time you start recognizing the details." She bent down and picked up the seal skin she was sitting on.

"Learn the lesson of the seal skin," she said, unfolding it in front of him. "Our home is the sea, but we walk the land as well. Shapeshifters are we, fallen from grace, fallen from the stars. We are not human, but our power is vast and real. We have one weakness—our skins. We must shed them in order to become human on land, and if we do not hide them well, and someone takes a seal's skin, that selkie will be in thrall to whoever possesses such a relic. Until he or she gets it back, the selkie is no longer *Roan* and forgets much and serves his or her master until that master returns the skin voluntarily, or the selkie discovers its hiding place. Shiro Ishii had many skins, and he held many of our people in thrall, performing unspeakable things upon them."

"What happened to them?" whispered Conor, hoping she wouldn't answer.

"They died, crying out into the night, and no matter how far away they were, each of the *Roan* heard their death song."

Tears ran down Scatha's eyes, but they were not tears of sorrow or weakness. They were tears of rage. "We should have been held in wonder. We should have been looked upon with awe. For we are beautiful, and our fall long ago never harmed us as it did the elders. But men can be cruel, not just Shiro Ishii. Few honored us, more feared us, and many hunted us. Over the long years, the voices of so many of my brothers and sisters have been silenced. And it shall not be like that anymore. You will see to it!"

So strong did she say these words, that the protest on his lips died and became an honest admission, "I do not know if I am strong enough to help you."

She smiled, "You are. I know what you did across the seas. More so, I know the prophecy, a prophecy you find yourself in the middle of, not at the end. It has been laid upon me by the *Roan* that I am to teach you what you need to know and train you to have the strength to act."

Now, he was going to protest, but she placed a finger on her lips. Bending down, she took her seal skin, wrapped it around herself and held out her hand. He took it. "First lesson," she said. And she walked him into the sea, her sisters following them into the waves.

GODMOTHER MOIRA

Wednesday Morning, 11/4, Cahersiveen to Ballinskelligs

HE WOKE UP to bouncing and muttering. Bouncing on someone's shoulder. Muttering going right into his left ear. What the hell?

"Awake now, are we?" said Kevin, huffing a little. "Found you on the beach, barely dressed, shoes gone. What the hell has been happening? And can I put you down now?"

"Yeah," groaned Conor. And found himself deposited by the side of the Tinker's caravan.

"Where have you been? Been looking for you all over. Between Ma's dying and Da's grieving, I lost track of you. It's already Wednesday morning."

"I've been to sea," said Conor, and coughed. A gout of sea water shot from his stomach.

"Oh, geez, did you almost drown?" said an unsympathetic Kevin.

Conor said nothing, just climbed into the caravan.

"Mary and Laura stayed at the hospital to take care of things. Da told me to look after you. Said it was most important. Even more important than taking care of my own mother's body."

"I'm sorry about your mom. It was terrible what happened."

"Aye, and don't I know it." Kevin shook the reins, and Malby began to trot out of the caravan park and onto the road south out of Cahersiveen. "We'll be going to your Godmother's place now." With that, Kevin closed his mouth and didn't say another word.

Which was okay with Conor, because he was remembering. Under the sea with Scatha. Like seals they were, or maybe they were seals. Conor could hardly think for the wonder of it. He could swim fast, see far, and he had never been able to hold his breath long enough to see much underwater, but now he could and his sight was crystal clear. Scatha and her sister *Roan* cavorted under the waves and shot straight up out of the water in a dance of sea spray, moonlight and seals. Somehow Conor had no trouble following them and it was amazing.

His memory faded as he looked out onto the road towards Ballinskelligs. It was wilder, less civilized here in this part of Ireland. Though the road cut across country, he knew he was still close to the sea where the ocean was tumultuous, crashing outside tranquil bays or against tall headlands.

It was coming up to noon when Kevin suddenly spoke again. "You see that tall headland out there about a mile away? The top of it is no man's land. If you look sharp you'll see the *Skellig* Circle—old standing stones they are— up there as well. That's why no one has ever claimed the property. Not ever. The headland's beautiful. You can see the small copse of beech trees close to the standing stones. But the circle—spooky as can be. I never go near it."

"Why not?" asked Conor.

"Because it works." Kevin would say no more.

At the base of the headland, a man who looked to be in his later 50's came out of a two-story thatched house as Kevin drove up.

"Malby, how are you?" said the man who plucked a carrot from his pocket and gave it to the horse. "Kevin," said the man in a neutral tone of greeting, nodding toward the younger man as he stepped off the caravan.

"The Shandyman," said Kevin. "I guess it's good to see you, but I hope you have nothing for me to do. I don't have time to dicker price with you, you miserly bastard."

Tom Shandy smirked but paid no mind, setting his eyes on Conor. "This must be the visitor Moira said we should look for."

"Conor," smiled the boy. "Conor Archer. It's good to meet you."

The Shandyman smiled back, but said, "Where's Mary and little Laura, Kevin? Drove them away too?"

Kevin scowled and said, "You don't know what's been happening."

"That I don't," he said, "so come on in, let's have a glass of holy water and you can tell me all about it."

Conor thought the Irishman awfully religious as he sat down at table in the quaint kitchen where a peat fire was merrily burning. A portrait of Christ and his mother looked down from its place on the wall.

All religious suppositions vanished in Conor's mind when the holy water turned out to be three glasses of generously poured Bushmill's whiskey. As Conor sipped and coughed his way through the drink, Kevin talked softly about what happened.

"I can't believe it," said the Shandyman. "A contagion you say? And it acted that swiftly? Caused by Sir Hugh's fixer? I always thought him a shady sort. For Amergin to lose his wife and you, your own mother—what a terrible thing." For the first time in talking to Kevin, the man sounded sincere.

"Not just me," said Kevin, "all those kids; all those Travelers. Gone, except for my Da, me, and my family. It will be a sore loss to us all."

They were all quiet for a time, slowly sipping the whisky in memory of those gone.

The Shandyman raised his head, looking at Conor. "So, what's your story, lad? Moira said you were coming but didn't say why. How's your mother? She was a bonnie lass, a ray of sunshine wherever she went."

"She's dead, too, Mr. Shandy. Seems like everyone's dying."

The Shandyman coughed in surprise. "Tell me it's not so. Seriously, Conor, tell me now. And don't call me 'Mr.' My friends call me, 'the Shandyman' so's I suppose you should too." Conor told him why he came, keeping the account as brief as possible. He felt there was enough sadness going around today.

"Your mother was a fine woman," said the Shandyman, discreetly wiping a tear off his cheek. "I remember the first time she came to see Moira years ago. She was carrying you; about six months pregnant she was. She came all that way to ask Moira to be your godmother. Could have called, but she came from America just to see her." He waved his glass and said, "You, Conor lad, are important. If you don't mind my asking, why might that be?"

"Enough," growled Kevin. "Just come along and introduce him to Moira."

Conor's stomach took that moment to let out a loud groan.

"Where's my hospitality?" tsked the Shandyman. "You fellows are probably starved. Let's head down to *Skellig* Pub for a pint or two and something to tide us along till supper. Moira will have something on the stove for us."

The three made their way into the village of Ballinskelligs and headed to the pub. Quite the crowd there this time of day, and Conor saw a woman outside, tying up her hair in a scarf.

"Who did you bring along with you Shandyman? Besides Kevin, that is—and you are welcome here Traveler." She looked him straight in the eye. "I haven't forgotten what I owe you. Tom Shandy, introduce me proper, to our other guest," said the woman with a smile.

"Moira, it's who you've been looking for. It's your godchild, Conor Archer, from America."

Moira dropped her hands and let out a little gasp. "Finola, Finola, you've sent me your very own." She came up to Conor and took his face in both her hands. "I've seen pictures, but none lately. How you have grown! You are much more handsome in person. Lad, I'm so glad to have you here. I'm your godmother. Malachy called and said you were coming but I didn't think to see you so soon. Ah, poor boy," she said as she smothered him in a hug, "the news about your mother broke my heart. But here you are, bringing us all joy instead of sadness."

Conor found himself without words and blushed at her obvious happiness to see him.

Kevin coughed and Moira smiled, "Like I said, I haven't forgotten what I owe you, Traveler. I think I can make it right today. Here now, you all must be hungry. Let me scrounge up a bit of something for each of you."

More than something. Moira soon had a veritable feast of sandwiches and crisps, burgers and soup, sausages and potatoes hot out of the pub's kitchen. Conor had smelled the food as they pulled up, but Kevin was marveling at the crowd. Never got this crowded unless there was a funeral, a race, or a town meeting. There was quite a murmur going on as they stepped into the establishment.

All eyes gazed on them as they entered, and conversation ceased. Just like at home, thought Conor. Then introductions were made and Conor heard a dizzying list of names as he nodded and greeted everyone. The Shandyman told those gathered Kevin's terrible news. After the stunned silence, murmurs of sympathy toward the Traveler went all around the pub. Then a shrill little voice spoke up.

"Ah now, you're the long-lost godchild," piped Lettie Sporn from her usual spot. "If you take after your mother, she must have been a handsome lass. Such a strong young man. Welcome to you Conor!" she said raising a shot of whiskey to him.

He took the attention well, but asked Moira, "There's so many people here. Kevin said the town was small, but you must have half of it in this pub. What did we miss?"

"Ma's gone and got herself an alien." The voice belonged to a young woman behind the bar. Her mousy hair was short and blond, and her nose pierced. Rather plain faced, the girl turned to Moira. "Tell them, Ma, tell them what happened."

Moira did and spared nothing of the details of four nights ago. She talked about the strange sight in the sky—a nebula, the radio was calling it—and she mentioned the mysterious visitor that had washed up on shore. As she spoke, her daughter, named Philomena—Phil for short—topped off everyone's drinks and kept bringing munchies for all.

When Moira was silent, Phil urged her on. "Tell them that he hasn't woken up. Tell them what Dr. Gillespie says."

Moira frowned at her daughter but said to the crowd, "He still sleeps, and the doctor thinks it's a coma he's in and wants to take him to hospital. I won't permit it."

"Why not?" asked the Shandyman.

"Because he fell from a comet," said Lettie with a glare that shut him up right grand.

"Told you he was an alien," said Philomena with a wink at Conor.

"Enough mocking of me, you little sprout," said Lettie.

"Don't know about him being an alien, Phil," said Moira. "I was there. Parts of the fireball skipped up the Bay and when we looked for the one that fell next to the abbey, well, like Lettie said, it was him we found."

"And the crowd?" asked Kevin looking over all the pub crawlers.

"They're here to see him," said Philomena. "We've been doing a great business since he landed. Not every day or night one gets to see a man from the stars." She said it with a mocking twist to her lips.

"They're not going to see him," said Moira, arms crossed as she stood by the kitchen surveying the curious crowd. "But I am going to feed the lot of you. Maybe that will quell the curious and get you all talking about other things."

The Irish never forsook a chance to have a bit of *craic* and something to eat. They moved from the bar stools to the tables as Moira and Philomena bussed more food out to them.

Phil sat a plate of ham sandwiches and crisps in front of Kevin, Conor and Tom, saying, "I'll get you some of Ma's carrot soup—it will take the damp out of you. You must be tired from traveling the road."

As the customers busied themselves with lunch, Moira and Phil sat down with Conor. For a change, he didn't mind telling most of what happened to him. He talked of Shiro Ishii but got rather cloudy when it came to relating the encounter with Scatha and her sisters. In fact, he kept it as himself just rushing into the ocean and rather miraculously being cast up on shore.

"I've heard of this drug that monster made Conor take." Lettie downed another shot of whiskey and stood up beginning to pace the room. "Kids around here talk about it. Some have tried it. Hasn't turned out well."

"Sit yourself down, old woman. I won't be letting that evil into Ballinskelligs anytime soon," said Moira. "Kevin, I'm so sorry about what happened to your family. You and Mary must be grieving terribly and little Laura without her grandmother. Amergin and I go way back and the loss of his wife must devastate him." Looking at her godson she quietly said, "God has blessed us with your life, Conor. How you escaped both plague and assassin, I just don't know."

Conor nodded gratefully for her comment, and everyone continued eating in sadly sobering silence. He was surprised when Phil bent down and whispered in his ear, "Eat fast, excuse yourself for the water closet and find me in the hallway—I'll show him to you."

Intrigued, Conor didn't say much to his companions, just wolfed down the food—the carrot soup was the best; they just didn't make it like that in America. Excusing himself to go to the bathroom, Conor got up and followed Phil's instructions to the letter and found her waiting for him at the bottom of the stairs in the hallway.

A STRANGER ON THE PREMISES

Wednesday Early Afternoon, 11/5, Ballinskelligs

"DON'T STEP ON the third step; it creaks" she said, "or my mother will hear and that will be the end of this adventure."

Saying nothing, Conor followed her up the steps. They wound around the corner and when they reached the top, Conor saw a long hallway before him.

"Ma lets rooms. She remodeled the place not long ago and usually fills up this second floor all through tourist season. He's down the hall to the big room on the right."

They walked quietly the length of the hallway, past old pictures and drawings of the Ballinskelligs area, finally stopping at the last room on the right. Putting her hand to the latch, Phil bent it down slightly, till she heard it click and quietly pushed the door open.

The first thing Conor noticed, was the huge window overlooking the bay. The ruins of the abbey stood out in relief from the grey skies behind.

"Going to rain soon," said Phil.

"Aye," said Conor, noticing that he was starting to talk like the locals. And then he saw the bed, a crucifix on the wall above, and a figure lying there on the mattress. Walking into the room and approaching, he saw it was a young man and a big one at that—certainly no alien. He was flat on his back and his longish curly blond hair framed his pale face. Eyes closed, he looked to be dead.

"He is alive," said Phil, "though barely breathing. That's what has the doctor so worried."

"He's a big guy," said Conor. "How did your mom and that old lady, get him up on shore?"

Phil laughed quietly. "Never mess with an Irish woman. The hand that stirs the pot and serves the kettle, could bench press 100 kilos if motivated." Phil looked at him and cocked a Spock eyebrow. "New Irish saying. Just made it up."

"Amazing," said Conor drawing closer to the stranger. "I heard from one of the tavern patrons that he was wearing a sweater with some kind of an identification that said he was from here."

"Ballinskelligs weave. I'll find you a sweater that has it. It's a way of identifying drowned lads who went to sea and returning them to their native town. But this man was never here. Nobody has ever seen him."

Conor was entranced with the stranger. He could see only his face, but he felt he knew him, or had seen him before, or at least had heard of him. Crazy, he knew, but there was something about the man.

A groan rumbled through the room and Conor and Philomena jumped back. The stranger moved restlessly and two bare arms appeared wrestling with the covers.

"He's waking up," said Conor. "Go get your mom."

"Wait, wait," said Phil, "he's settling down again."

Indeed, he was. That made them draw even closer. As they bent over the bed, the stranger's eyes flashed open, and, gasping, they threw themselves back so fast they both landed on the floor looking up at a man who braced himself on one elbow, gazing down at them.

"You," he said, pointing with his free hand at Conor. "What in the cosmos are you doing here?"

"Umm..," said Conor, momentarily at a loss for words.

"Speak up, little brother," said the man, not unkindly.

"How do you know me?" said Conor.

"Exactly," said Philomena. "How do you know him? And what's your name, and where are you from?"

"Lots of questions, little princess," said the stranger with a smile on his face. "My name is Michael, and I came from Ballinskelligs ... a long time ago."

Conor hauled himself upright, helping Phil to do the same. "No, you didn't." Conor's eyes hardened. "There's a lady downstairs that says you rode a comet into Ballinskelligs' Bay the other night."

Michael matched his piercing glare. "Did she now? Don't be too sure how I came to be here. Your world is but a speck in the universe, important as it may be. Many things are moving in this space and time, and most not for the better. I come back to what was once my home, because the nexus is here for what is happening. The Dark is rising."

"I read that book," said Phil. "Back when I was a kid."

"And I heard that phrase many times in the past months," said Conor. "So, what makes it unique with you, Michael of Ballinskelligs?"

"So young, so important ...," mused Michael, "and so stupid." He made to rise up from his bed and fell back with a groan.

Philomena rushed over to him. "Are you okay? Do you need anything?"

Michael opened his eyes again, gazing at her. "How can someone with such a beautiful face mar it with tattoos," he touched the dove on her cheek, "and disfigure that same face with spikes in tongue and nose?"

"Tattoos are in," snapped Phil, "and what I do with my piercings is none of your business."

"Sorry to offend, princess. I should not always speak my thoughts."

"And stop calling me 'princess'."

"As you wish … princess," said Michael as a grin started to sneak across his face.

"Leave her be," said Conor. "She's only trying to help you."

"That she is, and glad I am of it," smiled the man. "Now help me get up."

Pushing himself up, he began to throw off the covers. "Stop!" said Conor, quickly realizing the man had nothing on. "Phil, do you have something for him to wear?"

She was gazing frankly at Michael. "I'm sure Ma does. Why don't you go ask her."

"Phil!" said Conor.

"Oh, right," she muttered, and scuttled off to find some clothes. She returned in just a moment. "These were outside on the bureau dresser. Ma must have set them out earlier. Hope they fit." She shyly handed them to Michael.

"We'll get out of your way, now," said Conor, pushing Phil out the door. "Join us downstairs. There are a few people who want to meet you."

They had just reappeared at the bar when all eyes turned to them. Damn the Irish, thought Conor as he scowled at them. They sure had a nose for gossip.

"And where have you two been?" demanded Moira, one hand on hip, towel in the other.

"Shush now," said Lettie Sporn. "They're two young'uns and perhaps they were just getting to know each other."

"Ah, no," said the two together.

"Actually …," said Conor.

"We were just visiting the stranger whose name is Michael and who is coming down promptly," said Phil catching her breath in a bit of nervousness.

And there he was. Right behind them. The patrons gasped. Michael was big, toweringly big, even over Conor's height. But what the folks in the bar were really looking at were his eyes. Conor turned to follow their sight and he hissed in a breath as well. Yeah, he thought, they were blue but there was a special word for that kind of blue. Having always a facility for words—must come from singing all those different songs—he quickly picked the word he wanted. Cerulean. Yeah, that was it. Michael's eyes were like blue jewels, and it sort of made it look like lightning was flashing across his face. Harsh, noble and almost alien.

Michael must have noticed the way the people reacted to him, because it seemed that his eyes dimmed and a pleasant softness suffused his face.

"Who," he said, "do I thank for taking care of me?"

"That would be me," said Lettie, "and, oh, of course, Moira, the proprietress of this establishment."

"I knew your mother and father, Moira," said Michael, "but that was long ago."

"Indeed, it must have been," said Moira, her voice tinged with suspicion. "They passed away years ago. You must have been a child when you met."

Michael smiled, as if reliving a memory. "Yet, I met them. Good people. Is the pub still called *Skellig?*"

"Yes," said Moira.

"Good," said Michael. "It is a rock, a mountain of human life that we will need in days to come."

"Why would that be?" said someone in the crowd, a man with longish grey hair.

"Old Paidric," said Michael, "always the questioning one but in this case a necessary question I think."

A heavy hand laid itself upon Conor's right shoulder. "Have you met this lad?" said Michael.

"Just," said a few voices.

"Well his name is Conor Archer. From America. And he's come to visit us," said Michael. "And all of you will not tell another soul who is not from this village that he is here. He is under our protection. Guardians we are, of a most precious treasure."

Conor blushed in embarrassment as the hand of Michael ruffled his hair. "How do you know ..."

"What do you mean, 'guardian'?" said the Shandyman. "He's got his godmother here and she's no stranger to his kin."

"Ah, yes, the renowned Aunt Emily, from Tinker's Grove," said Michael, "a guardian of sorts herself."

"What exactly are we to be guarding the boy against?" said the Shandyman.

"Tell 'em, Moira," said Kevin. "Tell 'em what happened and see if this is what the stranger is talking about."

The pub grew quiet again as everyone wanted to listen. And Moira spoke of what had happened among the Travelers. She asked Kevin to give the details about what occurred at the caravan park, but both glossed over any role Conor might have had.

The crowd murmured as they always did when news was fresh and understanding but not yet so clear.

Michael said, "There is more to this tale. What about the one who brought the plague? Why no explanation of him? And what about the boy? It's as if he wasn't even there. Come now. Out with it."

The Shandyman and Kevin just stared open-mouthed at Michael, and Moira pursed her lips, but Conor stepped forward and spoke, "There was someone else, someone really bad and I think he's coming ..."

Conor never got to finish that phrase. Suddenly, there was a loud whistling all around, and all eyes looked out the huge windows of the pub towards the bay. Even in the overcast daylight, the balls of fire streaking across the sky looked brilliant, plunging into the ocean far and then all the way up to the bay. People instinctively ducked. The whistles were drowned out by the hissing of the cooling meteorites. Latecomers they were, from the comet the night before. Scaring the bejesus out of the pub's patrons. But they had no time to even talk about it, because around the south end of the bay crept the prow of a huge black freighter.

THE *DULLAHAN*

Wednesday Afternoon, 11/4, Ballinskelligs

"COME," SAID MICHAEL, "we must see this ship down by the bay." The crowd kept pace with him out of the pub as they walked together down to the beach.

"What is it?" said Conor matching Michael stride for stride. "Why the big problem with the ship?"

"Watch and learn," said Michael. "It is a portentous omen."

Conor thought he would have to open a fresh section of his brain for the new vocabulary Michael was bringing into his life. But there was no denying the ominous ship. Completely black, except for its white printed name, *Baleros*. Conor asked what the name meant. Michael told him it was Celtic for "The Deadly One." Conor was going to ask what in the world that meant, but everyone's attention fixated on the vessel.

As it drifted around the point, they all noticed someone standing at the stern. A portly fellow. He didn't wave. Still as a statue, he seemed to watch the crowd. Michael walked forward, his tall stature and white sweater standing out. He didn't wave either. Instead, he raised his fist, and the moment he did that, a flash came from the stout man on the ship, and a whoosh of air flew across the bay and knocked Michael backwards several feet onto the sand. Then, the portly man cheerfully waved and bent down, seeming to release some sort of lever. Immediately, a black viscous liquid like oil came gushing out of the stern of the ship at water level. As the ship turned and pointed itself toward the *Skellig* Islands, the liquid pooled behind and then began to extend itself into the bay.

Rumbles from the crowd raised the apprehension of all as the black substance killed the waves and approached the shoreline. As it widened and progressed, the pollutant seemed to taint the air with a putrid, sulfurous smell. Even the overcast sky began to darken, portending an approaching storm from the west. The ship decreased in size as it pulled away from the bay, its black superstructure silhouetted by blue black clouds over the horizon.

Lettie and others brushed their hands through their hair and Moira wiped her eyes as a noxious oily breeze struck their faces. With that came a sound like a train roaring in the distance. Conor looked out over the ocean and saw something that appeared to be a funnel cloud far in the west, only it was twisting and turning in ways not possible for a tornado.

"Look," he pointed. "It comes closer!"

Apprehension turned to fear in the crowd, and people began to push and shove so they could get away.

"Stop!" cried Michael above the fray. "Do not run! The evil that approaches can find you anywhere. Stand together and we shall prevail."

What looked like a waterspout or tornado twisted swiftly toward the bay, growing larger and larger. The closer it came, the less it looked like a grotesque work of nature. People began to discern things in that cloud, flying things.

"Ravens!" shouted Phil. "Thousands of ravens!"

So many, thought Conor. In fact, the ravens were the cloud. Flying in a circular tight formation, they wound their way toward the crowd on the shore.

"Steady," said Michael. "No one break."

Wonder upon wonders, no one did. The swirling murmuration of birds paused, as it towered over the beach, and then, one by one, ravens dropped from the sky. Wherever they landed, a puff of mist rose up from the ground enveloping each, and the birds within changed and grew tall. They stood upright, their black plumage becoming long ghastly robes, their beaks retreating towards beady eyes already shrouding as the feathered heads became hoods out of which bony corpse like faces, wreathed in shadows, stared. As they moved toward the crowd, hopping like the birds they seemed to be, they lined up two columns parallel from the edge of the beach towards the *Skellig* Pub. Then they each raised what should have been a wing, but now appeared as a twisted, robed arm and pointed a corpse-like finger toward the mass of humanity cowering in fear.

Conor thought he heard the people shushing one another to be quiet, but it was not them. It was those things speaking. He heard a word in all that sibilance: *sluagh, sluagh, sluagh.* Turning to Phil, he whispered, "What's a *sluagh?*"

Phil took his hand. She was shivering in fear. "*Sluagh* are the restless dead, damned and evil souls that even hell doesn't want. Doomed they are to haunt the world seeking more souls to join their ranks. They come from the west, always from the west. Usually, they take the souls of people who are sick, about to die. That's why at night, if there is a sick person in the house, we shut all windows and doors that face the west. We did the past nights for Michael, when we closed the pub. The *sluagh* are like birds, ravening ravens seeking food, only the food they want is us—the living. Usually, they haunt the shadows of night. Something must have brought them here, in the daylight. They normally prey on people in the dark. Easier that way, but sometimes they will take healthy, unsuspecting souls going about the business of the day. Like now. I think they've come for us."

But nothing happened. As the whispering of the crowd died down, the mist grew thicker, darkening the day. It was as if the columns of the restless dead were waiting for someone or something.

"Beware!" cried Michael. "Stay close to one another and do not leave. To leave is to be lost."

A scream shouted in the fog a little ways away from the pub patrons. Another sounded.

"Disobedient fools!" said Michael. "I can do nothing to save them. Stand still the rest of you!"

His rant was cut short as the oily water of the bay began to roil. Bubbling and shifting, as if some great beast was shambling up the shallows. Something was. They should have seen a head surface, but only shoulders and arms appeared. It looked like the corpse of a man but it was stiff and upright, riding something else that soon appeared. A *kelpie*. Conor was sure of it. He had been studying Aunt Emily's books and he knew that Caithness McNabb was riding a *pooka* just a few nights ago, but this was not that. This was a *kelpie*, a water horse, that looked scarcely like a horse and more like some bad biogenetic experiment gone wrong. No skin, just black flesh leaking green fluid. A horse face, but one with fangs and flashing red eyes. A tail, yes, but serpentine, like something some prehistoric sea monster would have.

Conor looked at the headless horseman. He did not know what it truly was. Half-naked, it was wreathed in a black cloak and on the pommel of the *kelpie's* saddle, sat the corpse's head which should have been between the specter's shoulders. Conor almost vomited. Some in the crowd did.

The head was smooth with no hair except for a shock of white near the back of the skull. A smile split the moldering face from ear to ear, its eyes open and red, flicking back and forth, looking, gazing, seeking. But it was the smell, like spoilt cheese that gagged the onlookers. In its left hand, the specter snapped a whip. Bony and crackling, it seemed to be made out of vertebrae wrenched from human spine.

Moira cried out. "It's the *Dullahan*! It rides to kill us all!"

Shouts of "The Dark Man", "The Dark Man is here!" could be heard among the wailing crowd. All felt death clutch at their hearts.

Michael put his arms around Phil and Conor and whispered between them. "The *Dullahan* is one of the fiercest of the *fae*, the *faerie* host of this land.

It rides the countryside spreading pestilence and death, woe and despair. Watch closely; watch what it now will do."

The *Dullahan* had the *kelpie* it rode prance through the shallows and come up upon the beach. The *kelpie* pranced through the open path between the *sluagh* and came to rest halfway. The specter took one corpse hand and reached for its head, grabbing the shock of hair. It held the head high and some sort of preternatural glow illuminated the head with a sickly pallor, casting a *fae* light upon the people. The eyes of the corpse head continued to flick across the crowd, and Conor understood that this was how the demon saw what was before him. The silence of both the *kelpie* and the headless horseman was more unnerving than if the head began to screech or call out names.

"Why are you here?" cried Michael. "Whom do you seek?"

The monster lifted its arm, raising its head again and looked over the crowd. The flickering eyes went still and Conor felt the cold brush of death settle upon him. He had felt it before and knew well what it meant.

"Can't have him," said Kevin, striding out from the crowd.

"Won't let you," echoed the Shandyman joining him.

They stood without shaking before the *Dullahan*, and the Dark Man rode forward, through the *sluagh* sentries, and stopped not three meters from the men. Again, it said nothing, just lifted up its head to look more closely.

"Leave now," said Michael to the Dark Man. "While you still can."

He made to join the other men, but suddenly the Dark Man spoke.

"Tom Shandy. Kevin Bard," it hissed.

"Oh, no," said Moira. "No, no, no!"

"It speaks their names," said old Paidric. "It seeks their doom. And now they die!"

At that the *sluagh* began to wail a high keen, and the *Dullahan's* hand that held the whip of spine flicked its wrist and lashed out at the Shandyman and Kevin. The whip wrapped round the two, and the Dark Man drew the men toward them. This happened so swiftly that they found themselves before the fanged head of the *kelpie*, staring up at the headless being. The *Dullahan* let its whip fall to the ground and with the free hand lifted a small bucket that had been hanging from the pommel of the saddle on the other side of the *kelpie*. With the other hand, the Dark Man pushed its head down towards the two men. The head glowed its supernatural sickly light, and it opened its mouth and screamed. Just at that moment, the *Dullahan* threw the bucket at the Shandyman and Kevin.

Blood—red, red blood splashed over their faces, covering their bodies. They tried to cry out but could only gurgle the agony they felt. Falling to the ground, they writhed and contorted as if their very bones were being torn from their flesh. From the bodies of the men came an ethereal vapor which drifted toward the open mouth of the *Dullahan's* head as its arm ripped the whip from their torsos.

Padraic spoke up again. "The Dark Man sucks their souls from their bodies. Doomed they are! Doomed and now dead!"

"Enough!" cried a voice. Lettie Sporn walked forward towards the Dark Man, and as she did, she pried off her pierced earrings. "I've had enough of you, you black demon from the depths of hell! What's the matter, the slums of the netherworld not have enough for you to do? You come to bother these precious guests? Well back to hell with you!"

She threw her tiny earrings at the *Dullahan*. One hit the headless horseman in the chest and the other struck the corpse's head, sticking in its pulpy brow. Smoke and fire burst from the Dark Man, and the head screamed its pain. Flames suffused the demon and then began to sizzle the flesh off the *kelpie,* which wailed its suffering. In an explosion of fire, the Dullahan and its mount disappeared.

That's all it took for the crowd to get moving. Screaming, they ran back to the pub, except for Moira who rushed to Lettie's side and Michael who held on tightly to Conor and Phil. The *sluagh* looked at one another and then lifted their heads to the blackened sky and screeched in unison. They launched, and the raven whirlwind formed again, fleeing to the west. That danger passed, Michael let go of Conor and Phil, who ran to the blood drenched bodies of Tom Shandy and Kevin. To their amazement, the two were not dead, at least not yet.

"Drag them to the ocean," shouted Michael. "Wash that blood off."

Conor and Phil took Kevin, while Michael dragged the Shandyman and rolled him in the water. The oily black of the water was gone as if it had never been there, and the waves quickly washed the blood away. Yet the two men still were unconscious, and their bodies were twitching as if they were touched with electrical wires.

"How did you do it?" said Moira to Lettie. "What a brave thing that was, but how did you know it would work?"

Lettie was gasping a bit from the exertion and fright, but said, "I threw my earrings at the Dark Man. It was the only thing I had of gold. When I was young, they read us stories of the evil *fae*, the bad ones of the *faerie* host. Scared us to death. But I remembered the *Dullahan* and its weakness. It cannot abide gold. Like other *fae*, iron makes it uncomfortable, but only the *Dullahan* is poisoned by gold. I don't think I killed it, but it is feeling mighty poorly somewhere in hell tonight."

"Brave lass," said Michael. "You saved many this evening." Looking at his little group remaining on the beach, he said, "Come, we must move swiftly. The *Dullahan* has infected the bodies of these men with pestilence. What's worse—you saw the vapor that leeched from their bodies? Their souls were drawn out, but before the *Dullahan* could consume them the monster vanished. Now, their souls linger unseen near their forms and, dissevered as they are, the Shandyman and Kevin will die unless we take them to the healing holy well."

"There's many in the area," said Moira. "Which one?"

"None here. We must travel far," said Michael. "We go to the Well of the Wethers."

THE WELL OF THE WETHERS

Wednesday Evening, 11/4, The Well of the Wethers

"WE CAN TAKE them in my car," said Moira. "The Well is near Ardfert, up near Tralee, and I think we can make it in an hour and a half or so."

"Not the auto," said Michael. "It will go faster if we take Kevin's caravan."

"Michael, it's a wagon," said Conor. "It's not going to get us there at all before tomorrow afternoon."

A smile crossed Michael's face. "We're taking a back road, a *faerie* track, if you will, that winds across the land. Stay on that road, and you're in the Otherworld, and distances and time don't really matter." More somber now, he said looking at the two unconscious men, "It's the only way, and even that might not be enough."

They put the Shandyman and Kevin in the back of the caravan; Moira and Lettie climbed into the rear as well. Philomena went to join Conor up in front, but Michael waved her to the back. She started to complain but stopped when she saw the firmness in his eyes. He checked the horse's rigging and then came around to the animal's face, looking up into Malby's eyes.

"Do you remember me, faithful friend? It has been a long time. Malby's not your real name you know." Touching the forehead of Michael, the horse lightly neighed. Michael held their heads together and chanted:

Malby, Malby horse so fair,
Humbly pulling Tinkers' ware,
Day by day, in plain sight,
Never revealing the blinding Light,
Shining your heart, shining your eyes.

Shine, shine and show your soul,
White as the foam on the waves that roll,
Snow of the peaks and ice of the sea,
Near white as the angel of victory,
Bright is your heart, bright are your eyes.

Brian, Brian, with true name rise,
Take to the seas, wing to the skies,
Hooves pound the land, angel-mane flowing,
Outrace the wind, courage be growing,
Strong is your heart, strong are your eyes.

Change, change, become who you are,
Little one, little one, Brian my star,
Let me ride, let me ride; I lead you free;
Together we conquer; the Dark shall flee,
Brave is your heart, brave are your eyes.

Michael lifted his head and looked at Conor, who saw the stranger's face shine with an unearthly glow. His strong arms encompassed the neck of the horse which itself began to transform from a kindly brown-maned beast into something magical. Ripples of white-like muscles of lightning flashed back and forth across the horse as it grew larger. And from its shoulders sprouted flesh and sinew covered with feathers as white wings lifted high. The horse let out a cry of challenge but did not break the bridle or rein, though they too seemed to grow thicker and larger. All the while, Michael held the head of the horse and whispered to it gently like a friend welcoming a loved one home.

"Come here," ordered Michael to Conor.

Reluctantly and with a little fear, he climbed off the caravan and approached Michael, marveling at the size and beauty of the horse which shone in the dying light like the evening star rising.

"What did you do?" said Conor.

Michael said nothing but beckoned him forward, making Conor stand in front of the horse.

"Touch his mouth, let him breathe in your scent. He knew you when he was draped with the form of Malby, but now he must know you as he truly is, Brian, the steed of Michael Victorious, the Ranger of the Heavens."

Conor was almost in a trance as the stallion bent down to breathe in the scent of the boy. He couldn't believe such a being let him touch his face and mane. And then he shook his head, remembering the words that Michael said.

"You!" said Conor. "You aren't human, are you?"

"No," said Michael with a smile. "But you aren't completely human either. And it's the 'either' that gives you the right to see me briefly as I appear in this realm."

The one named Michael transformed, although the revealing nearly blinded Conor. He knew he was seeing an angel, but it was an unearthly experience. Hints of wings, a taller being, a glimpse of a trident in his hand, but the same cerulean blue eyes, and the same smile. Conor knew he should be afraid, but he wasn't. It was as if he was seeing a more famous member of the family.

"*A dhearthairín*—little brother," said a deepened voice. "I call you that, for that is what you are. We are kin, you and I. Different destinies, but made of the same star stuff. I am here to guide and protect you and my valiant steed Brian, the same."

"Brian?" said Conor.

"Not in Celtic," said Michael. "His name is pronounced, Bree-ahn, and he is magnificent, don't you think?"

"Aye," breathed Conor. "Never have I seen such."

"Look behind you," said Michael. "Do you see those in the wagon gawking?"

Conor nodded.

"They are not seeing exactly the same as you and I. We know how to see the bright mountain behind the mountain—the Otherworld, the Real World as it were. They do not. And yet, they are attuned to it. They do not see a horse with wings, though they see he is now white as snow. They do not see me in my angelic form, though I am luminous to them. They think magic is near, but it is just reality seen, as your friend the Abbot says, stepping sideways. We travel this way till we get to the well. Now climb up on the wagon and let's be off."

Conor thought they would fly, but no such luck. Michael simply took the reins and Brian took off across the countryside following a shining path ahead of him.

"The special way," said Michael. "We travel in the Otherworld now, and it won't be long until we arrive."

The journey was so beautiful that Conor couldn't speak. Whether changing climate had given Ireland a warmer autumn, he did not know, but autumn leaves were still on the trees here in the Otherworld, and they even reflected gold in the starlight. Brian kept his wings folded, but trotted confidently on the path, looking right and left to make sure that nothing would surprise them on the way.

"He is a warrior horse, Conor. Without him, I could never have driven the Usurper from the heights." Michael, looking normal again, smiled gently at Conor sitting next to him. "I know I can be intimidating when seen as I truly am, but do not be afraid. Think of me as the guardian of this world and your guardian as well, for that is what I do."

"My mom used to tell me that I had my own guardian angel."

"Ah, such a wise woman. Did she tell you the angel's name?"

"No."

"Well, that would be me."

Conor gasped, "Why?"

"Because, little brother, I am the guardian of this world, and it is facing its greatest danger since the Savior walked this earth. And it is not time for him to come again. So, I have you, and you must succeed in what you are destined to do."

"How come I've never seen or felt you before?"

"Not my problem. Once you became more attuned to how the two worlds are merging together, you became able to sense and see the higher realities. Not perfect yet, but you are such a quick study. What you did several days ago amazed even one such as me. And I have seen much in my existence."

Conor couldn't help himself. As amazing as this knowledge was, he was just so tired. His eyes began to drift shut.

"*A dhearthairín*, let your eyes close now. Sleep amidst this beautiful land, for I do not know what we shall meet at the well."

Conor jerked awake as Brian came to a halt. He could hear the three women in the back moving around as they awoke. Before he even looked ahead, he turned and said, "Phil, how are Tom and Kevin?"

A moment later, "The same I think. Hardly breathing but still warm."

"They are dying," said Michael. "We need to get them into the enclosure."

As Conor looked ahead, he saw in the brilliant starlight, an enclosed copse of wood. Pasture-land surrounded it on four sides. Holly bushes formed a living fence ten feet tall and huge beech trees soared like the high towers of a castle. A green, daisy strewn path led up to it.

"Fantastic!" whispered Conor.

"Come, it is dangerous out in the open," said Michael.

Wordlessly, the women and Conor lifted the unconscious men and walked behind Michael. He held his hand palm forward and the holly broke open to let them pass.

As they walked by him, he said, "In the world you live in, this is but a simple metal gate. But the power of this place is revealed here in the true reality. Behold, *Tobar na Molt*—The Well of the Wethers."

They laid the men down just inside the opening. Conor looked up at Michael and said, "Why do they call it that?"

Phil broke in, "Wethers are neutered sheep."

"That's right," said Lettie, "and this place got its present name over three hundred years ago when the British were persecuting the Catholics. Priests used to say Mass here, right by this huge rock. It's called the Mass Rock, and one day, the priest and the congregation were discovered by soldiers. The people ran and the priest high-tailed it out across the fields. It was then that the miracle happened. Three sheep burst up from the well, surprising the redcoats surely, distracted them and led them on a wild goose chase across field and vale. Priest and people got away."

Conor looked further into the enclosure. He saw the Mass rock where the priest and people had met for prayer so long ago. He looked to his left and saw a little stone building and to its right a small pond surrounded by cut stone—the well he assumed.

Moira continued the commentary, "St. Brendan the Navigator, the one who discovered America, was baptized here. A mighty saint. He grew up here and was schooled by St. Ita, a tough little Celtic nun who taught him to love God and the land. Her grave is just beyond the rag tree."

Conor started. "There's pieces of cloth on that tree."

"Indeed, there are," said Moira. "That's why they call it the rag tree. People have come to the well for centuries and said their prayers. The pieces of cloth represent their intentions and they hang them on this tree. The belief is that by the time the rags rot away, their prayers will be granted."

"They still do that now?"

"Yes," said Michael, speaking for the first time inside the holy place. "Things are not well in Ireland. Even the faith is dying, and those coming into this land know nothing of its mystery. It literally shouts with the energy of the Otherworld but they cannot hear it. Conversely, because they cannot hear and answer, the Otherworld begins to die, just like in your land, Conor Archer. There is an interconnectedness between the realities. When people and all rational beings begin to forget that truth, the worlds begin to die. And yet. There still are faithful ones here who come to holy places such as this. They know the power this holy well holds. They pray for the land and for their own needs. Is that not right you three?"

Moira and Lettie nodded, but Phil scratched her foot on the ground saying, "I'm not much of a religious person."

"And still," said Michael, "you feel the power."

"Enough chattering," scolded Lettie. "Are we just going to let these men die?"

AN UNEXPECTED REUNION

Wednesday Evening, 11/4, The Well of the Wethers

"BRING THEM OVER to the water," said Michael.

When Kevin and the Shandyman had been laid by the side of the well, Michael continued, "They had to come here. In this part of Ireland, the Well of the Wethers is known for its strong healing properties, but also for being an exceptionally thin, 'thin place'. Their souls are still close to them and they hover nearby but are vulnerable to dissipation in your world and even in this realm by the slightest touch of magic. The holy well will help tether their souls to their bodies till we can complete the healing."

"And just how to you plan to do that?" asked Moira, skepticism ringing in her voice.

"By linking the well with the healer who is buried here, that 'tough little nun' as you say—St. Ita, a powerful abbess and foster mother of many Irish saints," instructed Michael.

"Like, I said," replied Moira, "her grave lies inside the mound beyond the rag tree."

"Her grave is not what I need," said Michael. "Her presence is. But see. Already, she is here."

A breeze kicked up, and the branches of the beech trees swayed, casting starlight shadows across the faces of the gathered. Conor, however, heard something else. The swishing of cloth and the small sound of footsteps from the far end of the enclosure near the grave of the saint.

"Guests in the middle of the night—blessed am I," said an ancient voice. An aged woman dressed in a gray robe with a gray veil framing her face, walked around the rag tree and addressed them as she leaned on a simple wooden shepherd's staff.

"Christ be with all here," she said kindly. "This is my well. Peaceful it is, don't you think? Do not mistake me. The Summer Country, what you call Paradise, is a wonderful place, but on nights such as these, I still love to walk in this lovely garden and be by the well where so many holy ones were baptized.

I sent them forth into the land, living lights of goodness, hope and healing. Now, who are these who lay sick and injured?"

"A good man who I just met, Tom Shandy, and my new friend Kevin Bard," said Conor.

"Ah," said the old woman. "And who may you be?"

"Conor Archer from America," he said.

She laughed and slapped her free hand against her thigh. "America! I should have known. Here I thought your accent sounded like a barbarian's. I sent Brendan there you know. Brave man, one of the best. Now a visitor from there comes to me. We shall talk later. First tell me how these men fell ill."

Before anyone could speak, there came a wailing on the wind, like a horse screaming in defiance.

Ita cocked an eyebrow at Michael, "The *Dullahan*? You did not tell me you were tracked by the Dark Man himself."

"Apologies, noble lady," said Michael with a bow of his head. "We have been besieged by darkness half the day and now this evening."

"The *Dullahan*. It is many ages since I have seen it. Come quickly by my side," she said to Michael. They stood back to back in the middle of the enclosure, slowly circling, gazing at the enclosure walls of holly.

Conor looked to the gate and remembered what he left in the caravan. He darted towards it before anyone could say anything, and the holly branches parted for him. The caravan was just outside, and he reached under the driver's bench and grasped his walking staff. He looked down the path and there, at the end, a shadow rose with a luminescent corpse head in its hand. Hurriedly, Conor dashed back into the enclosure screaming to the bushes, "Close, close, close now!" The bushes slapped shut.

"Can it get in here?" asked Philomena. Her voice quavered with fear.

No one said anything but simply stared toward the entrance.

As if in answer to Phil's question, the holly wall gate smashed inward and the headless horseman came through. Its black *kelpie* steed snorted wisps of flame and pranced completely around the enclosure, pausing finally over the dying men. Conor stepped forward to confront it, but the *Dullahan* held up its corpse head and surveyed its audience. When its eyes struck him, Conor stilled in fear and did not move. Above the unconscious men, two ethereal clouds hovered, their souls close to them at last.

"I see what you want," said Ita to the *Dullahan*. "You wish to take the souls of these unfortunate men. You have called their names, and you think by right to claim them as your own. But you have no rights here. This is the Well of the Wethers, my well, and you have been around long enough to know that here there is no darkness that can extinguish the Light."

The corpse head's mouth split into a maniacal grin.

"Why doesn't it speak?" whispered Conor.

"Because," said Lettie, "it may only speak once an evening and it has already done so. But make no mistake. Even now it is plotting, even now it is readying its hand to snatch the souls, even now …"

The corpse head screeched as it looked at Lettie. Its other hand picked up the bucket of blood again but did not throw it at any of the assembled. Instead, it leaned the opposite way and dumped the contents into the well itself.

Enraged, Ita snapped at the monster, "You dare poison the waters of my well? You think you can block the emergence of aid from those waters with your foul pestilence?"

Michael held her back from approaching the *Dullahan*, as a small cackle came out of the mouth of the head. The Dark Man cast the bucket aside and reached for his scourge of severed spine.

"Whip an old woman tonight?" said Ita. "Powerful *fae* you are. Tell me, that whip of human backbone—how many good people did you flay to make it? No, no, don't try to speak, corpse head. You've used that power up for tonight. Now you look like just a bloated carp guppying your mouth to catch some air."

The *kelpie* began to stamp and snort again while the Dullahan's face sneered at the woman.

Conor said, "Ah, ma'am, ah, sister—to hell with it—Ita! You're pissing them off. Don't think it's a good idea."

Ita stamped over to Conor and looked up at his face. "Don't think, *a dhearthairin*. Just don't think right now. I know your name, Conor Archer. Every bird that flies under the sun has whispered it the past few days here at the well. But just because you are someone special doesn't mean you know everything."

She took her finger and poked it into his chest. "I knew your mother and aunt, so I know what it is you must do and why you are here. But the Dark Man has that knowledge also. That's why Michael guards you, and I must get to know you better. You have to live beyond tonight, and we are not doing so well right now."

The whip cracked and wrapped around Ita's neck. Dropping his staff to grab the foul thing, Conor raked the flesh off his hands as they slipped along each vertebrae of the whip. Ita began choking, and Conor thought her doomed to be dead for sure, but then she was dead, wasn't she? But this was the Otherworld and maybe things didn't work the same here. He bent down and grasped his staff with his blood drenched hands and a wonder happened.

He gasped as his eyes flared gold and the dark skin winding around his body luminesced. The staff crackled liked lightning, the wood expanded and became a marvelous Spear, the Spear of Destiny. Conor suddenly remembered what is was like to hold that magnificent weapon when he was the Thunderbird facing *Piasa*. But this was no time to reminisce. He brought the wood of the Spear down upon the whip and the malevolent weapon shattered with the blow. Cartilage and vertebrae spilled onto the ground and Ita staggered back, gasping and able to breathe again.

Michael leaped at the *kelpie* and punched the *Dullahan's* mount in the head. Like a stone, it fell with a thud to the ground, momentarily stunned, The *Dullahan* jumped while the *kelpie* fell, managing to hold on to its head. Conor couldn't figure out why he did it, but he threw himself at the *Dullahan* hoping to pierce its body with the Spear. The monster simply backhanded the Spear away, and Conor crashed into its torso and was immediately assailed by the stench of death and decay. Bouncing off the Dullahan's body, he found himself gasping for oxygen next to the fallen Spear. As he staggered up, everyone froze in place as hundreds of keening screams filled the air. From the darkness dropped the *sluagh* from the sky, many, many of them, coming to rest inside the enclosure.

Michael sprang into action, a flaming trident suddenly at his side. Screaming at Conor to protect the fallen, he slashed through the ranks of the *sluagh*, severing each one he sliced with its connection to the Otherworld. Just a touch from the seraph's trident was enough to snap the linkage the *sluagh* had to physical reality. He laid waste to them and each one touched by the three-bladed Sword dissolved into mist.

Moira grasped the hands of Lettie and Phil and pulled them down into the shade of the rag tree where for the moment they were unmolested.

"Stay there," said Ita, "and say a prayer to the Christ that I get this right." Moving swiftly to the well, she bent over the stone wall and plunged her hand three times into the water, letting the liquid splash back into the well.

> *To the One who made the waters of earth,*
> *To the Son whose heart-water gave man new birth,*
> *To the Spirit who gives water blessed power and worth,*
> > *Here me now I pray,*
> > *I, Ita of thirst,*
> > *Release this water*
> > *Destroy the fae.*

The water answered. The blood-red color vanished, and the water began to bubble and roil. Then, once, twice, thrice, it shot high into the air like a geyser pushed skyward by the warming fires of earth. Any *sluagh* touched with but a drop of this water hissed into non-existence, making Michael's passage of carnage that much easier. However, it seemed not to have an effect on the

Dullahan which had now remounted and moved toward the well, toward the bodies of the Shandyman and Kevin Bard.

Conor again moved forward to block the monster and its mount. But just as he was about to charge the *Dullahan* again, the well fountained once more and then erupted in an explosion of water. Up from the waters dark, up from the chaos below, into the night, into the maelstrom of battle burst a shadow with gold flecked eyes and bright, sharp teeth. It howled a challenge to the *Dullahan* as it flew through the air, crashing into the headless horseman's body and catapulting it off the *kelpie* mount. Conor ran the *kelpie* through the heart with the Spear and its deafening cries cut off in a wail. The dark shadow from the depths of the well loomed over the *Dullahan* ripping hunks of whatever passed for its flesh out of its body.

"The head," cried Ita. "Find the head and destroy it. It is the only way."

Conor found the head near the Mass rock, its luminous face blinking and leering up at him. He stared at it for a moment, then flipped the Spear over and plunged it into the corpse head's left eye. A terrible scream rent the air, and the head burst into flames, while the body of the *Dullahan*, hands around the shadow's throat, suddenly went limp. At the same time, the keening of the *sluagh* stopped when Michael sent the last one out of the Otherworld.

Conor breathed hard, turning as swiftly as he could toward the *Dullahan* and shadow fighting it, wondering if he'd next have to fight this new strange being. But the shadow turned towards him and set its gold-flecked eyes upon Conor. And as it looked upon him, it began to whine and bark.

"Troubles?" said Conor. "Troubles? Is it you?"

The shadow leapt toward the boy solidifying into the largest chocolate Labrador retriever either of the worlds had ever seen. Troubles crashed into Conor and both went rolling on the ground, Conor laughing and crying at the same time.

"You were dead, and now you're alive!"

"The second reason why we had to come here," said Michael as he approached.

"You knew?"

"Only that we would meet someone who would help us. Hear what I said, Conor, someone, not something. He is not what he once was. He has been changed by the One. Hear his voice."

And Conor did. Into his mind came a breathy sigh with words, "Conor, I have come. Conor, my friend, my very life. I am here."

And a huge tongue licked the boy and Conor thought to himself that this was way better than Timmy and Lassie any day. Then he laughed out loud.

The others came around as well, marveling at the size and the gentleness of Troubles.

"He's yours?" asked Phil.

"Well, he was. He died last week saving me. I thought he was gone forever."

Ita spoke, "I have some little way with animals. Let me look at this dog." She came over. He was so large and she so small that she stood on her toes so they could look each other in the eye. She gently touched his muzzle and put her head on his cheek. He stood stock still for her and they communed in silence.

"Glad he's back?" said Michael, a gentle hand on the boy's shoulder.

"I thought he was gone forever," said Conor through a new rush of tears.

The nun turned toward him and said, "I have spoken with your companion and you are indeed blessed. He came at a time to save us all and intends to stay till the task is finished. His heart and soul belong to you, Conor. Treasure him always." She gently kissed the dog on its face and endured a sloppy lick in exchange.

"But now," said Ita, "we must do what you came to do."

She led the group back over to the dying men. She prayed a prayer of healing over them. Michael came forward and raised his hands as if he was lifting them up. And lift them he did. As they floated in the air above the well, he gently lowered them into the water.

"Take the Spear of Destiny, Conor, and thrust it into the water. Long has it been a holy Spear, first for Lugh, the light bringer to this land, and then to Longinus, the centurion who stabbed HE WHO LIVES in the side and let loose the holy heart water. In sorrow for his deed, the soldier reforged the Spear, melting into it one of the nails used to crucify our Lord. It was a fierce weapon before, but since that time, it possesses the power to heal. Out of suffering comes life. Submerge it into the well. Cleanse the pestilence poured in by the *Dullahan*. Let the Spear release the power of the water so that its strength may be a boon to our companions."

Conor did as he was told. For a moment, nothing happened, but then a pure white ethereal mist coalesced above the two submerged men as their souls gathered to them once more. They descended into the water and suddenly the bodies made great movement as they struggled to emerge.

"Women," said Michael, "get them up and revive them."

Quickly they moved, tending to them. Conor saw Ita walk over to the body of the *Dullahan*. She raised her arms in prayer and said words he could not understand, but the body of the *Dullahan* did. The headless horsemen dissolved into dust and blew away on the wind.

"Ach," tsked Ita as she turned towards Conor with a smile. "I cannot have such refuse taint my little garden now, can I? Remember that lad— always clean up your mess when you are finished." With a wink she passed by Conor and went to help the others treat the now conscious men.

As the Shandyman and Kevin revived, an anxious Conor quizzed them. Were they okay, where had they been, did they know what had happened to them? They could not answer him, for healed they may have been, but exhaustion had hit them. Moira and Lettie led them to the caravan to lay down.

Phil said, "I've never seen anything like this."

"Well," said Conor, "until last summer neither had I. But something's happening. A restlessness in both worlds and a building of violence. I don't think anyone is going to be in the dark for long about what is occurring. I doubt the *Dullahan* has ridden this openly in thousands of years. And those wretched *sluagh*, surely they were heard through this night."

"People have a way of ignoring what's right in front of their faces," said Phil.

"Maybe, but I didn't tell you much about the man I met early last morning, the man named Shiro Ishii."

"Who is he?"

"I'm not sure, but evil reeks off him. He says he's some Japanese wartime scientist, but he looks less than thirty years old. He forced me to take some drug—RAGE he called it. It was awful."

"RAGE?" said Phil. "But that's the designer drug that's flooding into Ireland kilo after kilo. Terrible things come from it."

"Don't I know," said a rueful Conor. "You get a nice high for a while and then turn into a raging lunatic. Enough people get on that and things are going to go swiftly downward."

Phil frowned in worry. "There have been isolated problems, bad stuff I hear. But in just a few days, Tralee is going to have their winter music festival. Thousands will come."

"O there will be problems, I think," said Conor. "Shiro Ishii wants to spank this country bad. He and his boss, Sir Henry, may have their chance."

Troubles had been laying quietly by Conor, but sensing the inner turmoil in his beloved companion, he placed his huge head on Conor's lap and gazed up into the boy's eyes.

Conor stopped talking and the tears flowed again. Never had he been so happy to see someone again. As the dog looked upon him in silence, a new sense of peace stilled the anxiety in his heart. He wished he could tell Aunt Emily where he was and that he would be okay.

JACE AND THE SAINT

Thursday, 11/5, The Well of the Wethers

DAWN, WITH ITS rose tipped clouds, was breaking as Ita puttered about *Tobar na Molt*—such a better name in Celtic than the English 'Well of the Wethers'—cleaning up residuals from the night's encounter with the *Dullahan* and the *sluagh*. As the sun touched the grass, she saw the stains of whatever passed for blood in those Otherworld creatures.

"Can't have that," she said aloud. Leaning on her staff, she bent down over the well and collected some of the holy water. Twisting a branch off the rag tree, she used its still green leaves to sprinkle the entire grounds, and as she did a perfume rose up and the stains disappeared. She wove the holly gate back together with a weaving of her hands. Wherever she walked, the tiny daisies so prevalent in the land sprang into full bloom and within an hour the sun was shining over a perfectly beautified well enclosure.

"There," she said, pushing back a wisp of white hair into her veil, then wiping her hands on her hips. "As if nothing dark had ever touched this place."

For a moment, she listened to the birds that always managed to sing every morning in the beech trees surrounding the well. Suddenly she started, as the well began to bubble and fountain once again.

"Oh, of all that is precious and holy," she said aloud, "I don't think I can abide any more excitement." But the well never heard her as it continued to geyser into the air.

"Oh my," she said as the well vaulted a body through the water and mist. The huge lump thumped upon the ground groaning, and Ita took herself toward it as fast as she could move.

"Oh … my … God!" said the person, for even Ita could see that it was human. "That hurt!" Jason Michaels tried to push himself up but began coughing.

"There, now," said Ita, wanting to pound him on the back but seeing a Sword in the way. "You have got some water in your lungs; cough it up now." Jason hacked a fair amount up and gasped some welcome air.

"Where am I?" he asked.

"Well, before I answer that," said Ita, "I will be asking who you are and whether you come for good or ill. It has been a bitter night and I will not be having any more shenanigans from the *faerie* folk or anyone else for that matter."

"Ah, sorry ma'am," he said trying to plaster on a smile. "Jason Michaels is my name. Jace for short, and I'm just myself. You don't have to be afraid of me. I don't plan on doing any evil. Saw too much of that lately."

"Humph!" said Ita, helping him up. "Good thing, because though you are a big lad, I have taken down many like you who sought to do me harm."

He just couldn't help himself. As he looked at the tiny woman holding her staff, he began to laugh, streams of well water still rushing down from his blond hair. Ita started laughing as well and for a minute they were caught up in a joy that just wouldn't stop.

"I am thinking you are a right fine lad," said Ita getting control of herself. "I can tell from your laughter you are as happy as me to be rid of whatever has befallen ourselves."

Jace stopped his laughing. "It's been terrible. The things I've seen. And my twin sister ... we buried her just a few hours ago."

"Ah, now," clucked the saint. "Such sorrow on a morning like this. You will have to tell me all about it. Not that you look starving, but a full stomach will loosen your tongue and you can tell me what has happened over in America." She looked at him slyly. "For that is where you come from, am I not right?"

"Right you are, ma'am," said Jace. "I come from Wisconsin and I have to tell you, your place here is almost as beautiful."

"Almost?" she said. "No matter. Come sit on my little hill over here while I get you something to eat."

He couldn't believe it. He walked past this tree festooned with little strips of cloth, and saw the daisies under his bare feet, and found himself not even chilled in the November dawn.

"Why is it so beautiful in here? I mean, don't get me wrong, but it's November and things ought to be a little dead and dormant."

"It is November lad, but it is November in the Otherworld, so a little cooler maybe and as you can see some golden leaved beech trees, but still green grass and flowers in this little Paradise."

They had arrived at a small hill and she bid him sit down on the soft grass. A tiny fire was already burning off to the side and she puttered there for a while whisking things and browning bacon. Jace's mouth was watering with the great smells and he found himself powerfully hungry. He had no trouble digging in when she handed him a hollowed-out loaf of bread full of freshly scrambled eggs and thick pieces of bacon. As he ate, she went near the fire and poured out a cup of what appeared to be milk and gave it to him as well. For a few minutes, there was absolute silence between the two as Jace wolfed down the food.

"Absolutely spectacular!" he said as he tucked in to the bread bowl as well.

Another small smile graced Ita's face as she said, "Well, you are certainly a special lad. My Brendan ate like you. But that is not what makes you special. You see, a bite of this food should have set you sleeping here on my grave."

Jace choked on a piece of bread and leapt to his feet. "Your grave? Holy crap! I mean, I'm sorry you're dead and all. I mean, what do you mean your grave? You're here."

"Yes, I certainly am," she laughed. "But I died about fifteen hundred years ago your time."

"How? ..."

"You know how, young man. The very fact that you aren't sleeping the sleep of ages tells me you know the Otherworld well."

Jace nodded.

"No one from your world can spend time here and eat in this place or anywhere in this realm without basically dying. Reality is too powerful here. I know things are changing. I can feel it. The worlds are drawing closer, perhaps even have begun to merge, but only someone with a destiny, only a Champion could come here and do what you have just done."

"Yeah, okay," said Jace, "But exactly how are you here if you are dead?"

She opened her hand to him and he saw a perfectly white round stone. She tossed it into the air and it split into three stones, swirling above the saint and the boy like protons circling one another in an atom—at least that's the best Jace could describe it later.

"The Three-In-One Stone was given to me when I was very young. Our beliefs were young then too, and the Stone was here to help me remember the One who as Father created all, and the Chief of chiefs his Son who redeemed us, and his Spirit which enlivens and makes holy all things."

"I don't understand," said Jace, brow furrowing.

"Neither do I, very well," said Ita, "but I've seen the One and walked the deathless pathways in the Kingdom of the Summer. But every once in a while, he gives me leave to come back to my little well, and I sit here a while. Lucky for you."

Jace smiled, liking this lady very much. She might even give Aunt Emily a run for her money. "Lucky how?"

"It was whispered you were coming. A nagging crow told me. And told me about your friend, Conor Archer."

"Conor!" said Jace. "He was here? Where is he now?"

"He was and is fine. Sit yourself back down." She paddled on his posterior with a spoon that suddenly appeared in her hand. "I am not done with you yet."

Sheepishly, Jace sat back down, but whispered, "Conor."

"Yes, your friend I think, though I can see you are troubled by him."

"My sister died because of him."

"Really now. Is that what truly happened?"

"Yes, and no. I mean he is responsible, but he didn't really cause it."

"Ah," said Ita. "But there is a terrible hurt in your heart."

"Yes, and I just can't forgive him. Sometimes," he said with fists clenching, "I want to pound him into the ground. Sometimes," he said jumping up again and drawing the Sword, "I want to kill him for what did."

"For what he is responsible for," said Ita.

"Yeah," he said, embarrassed. They both were quiet for a moment.

"You carry the Sword of Light," said Ita. "Aren't you just the surprising one?"

"Abbot Malachy gave it to me just a couple of days ago."

Ita laughed a clear rich laugh. "Malachy? There's a name and a person I have not seen nor heard from for many a year. If he gave it to you then he meant you to be the Champion."

"That's what the Morrigan said, though she thinks I'm to be her Champion. Malachy says I am to protect Conor."

"Perhaps both. A watcher over the carrion crow and the King Who Shall Be."

"What?" said Jace.

"Nothing," said Ita, brushing her wispy hair into her veil again. "Malachy sent you through a gateway, a portal."

"Yes, ma'am. Said I had to go. I was needed. Didn't even have time to pack anything. It was just after my sister's funeral. I went down by the river, kicked my shoes off and dove for the portal in the middle of the channel. I sent a dog this way, I think. Seen him?"

"Well," said Ita, "you just missed Conor and that massive dog of his."

"Maybe I can catch up to him and Troubles," said Jace looking for a way out of the enclosure.

"That is not meant to be yet, lad, though be comforted. It will happen."

She took his hand and drew him back to the green soft grass. Reverently, she ran her fingers along the blade strapped to his back. "The Sword of Light is a wondrous thing. So many who have gone before you and possessed it have done such great deeds. Let me tell you a little tale, not about them, but about me so you know why you and I have met.

"Long ago, when I was young, I didn't just stay by this well. I walked these hills among my people, and I got a certain reputation."

"What kind of reputation?" said Jace suspiciously.

"Why that of a prophetess and miracle worker. What did you think? That I was a *fae* witch of some kind? I assure you little Champion, that I earned my repute. Anyway, I was here one day, when word was brought to me that the local chieftain's son, strapping lad that he was, had gone to war with his father, and gotten himself decapitated. Obviously, the battle had not gone well and his father's sworn enemy took the son's head. The father was left grieving over the body. The clan came to me and begged me to do something. Sweet Virgin Mother of the Son of Stars! I did not know which way I should turn. And then I remembered my Three-In-One Stone." She pointed at them still swirling above Jace and her. "I took them out and looked at them and quieted my mind and the One spoke to me, and I knew what to do and where to look."

"What did you do?" asked Jace, spellbound. "What did you find?"

"I took off over the hills and skedaddled miles till I found the chieftain's enemy and took back his son's head. I brought it back to the grieving father and said to him, 'This is not death's day. Your son will live.' Young and inexperienced as I was, they had a mite difficult time believing me but not after I affixed that lad's head back upon his shoulders. I called down the blessing of heaven upon him and he was whole again, barely a mark where the Sword had cleaved. I gave him back to his father and told them all he would live another seventy plus seven years. And so, it happened. He took his father's place in time and became a great warrior. And died in battle again." She sniffed, "At least that's what the legends say."

She laughed to Jace's surprise. Smiling at him, she said, "We were such barbarians then, almost as bad as the dreaded northern raiders of later days. But we got better over time."

She patted his hand. "I tell you that not to boast, but to say I never lost that art of healing or the gift of prophecy. I also tell you this because though your thick blond head is securely on your shoulders, your heart is cleaved from your body. So much suffering in such little time. And you cannot be a Champion if you are filled with anger, sorrow and guilt. Now tell me how your sister passed." He did, and he didn't mind the fact that his tears flowed freely. When he was done, she reached out her hand and placed her palm over his heart. "Be healed you good and decent man, so that you can be at peace and change the world with your friend Conor Archer whose Champion you are."

And Jace fell backward, and lay upon the grass staring at the deep blue sky. To him, he felt like he breathed for the first time. The ache in his heart receded, and as the pain fled, a peace filled him. He thought he might be able to forgive Conor. And as he breathed in peace, he sat up and gasped in wonder. Before him on the little hill, stood a great throne, and on it sat the saint, still garbed in grey but with her robes flowing down the hillock and a silver circlet around her veil. Taller and more regal, she held the Sword of Light in her hands. He got up on his knees and bowed his head as she touched each shoulder with the blade. "I prophesy the future to you, Jason Michaels:

A Champion shall you be,
To she who walks battlefields free,
To the Seal King Who Shall Be,
To the past that is lost,
To the future that comes,
Upon you turns their destiny.
You shall not fear,
You shall not flee,
You shall not run,
You shall not see
 Final Defeat,
 Never ending Despair,
 A Coward's Death,
Unless you betray.
One weakness you have,
One weakness must you slay,
Do not betray, lose not your way
Do not betray, else lose the day
Giving night its sway.
Giving night its sway.

"I, Ita, prophesy this," she said as she gave him back his Sword. And with her free hand she opened her palm, and there rested the Three-In-One Stone. "A gift to you, to remind you of who I am, and the One that you serve. It will guide your way in the dark to find the Light. May it be comfort in times of strife."

"I don't know what to say," said Jace, as she placed the Stone in a little leather bag and gave it to him. He put the pouch in the pocket of his jeans.

"Say nothing but get up off your knees. The strange clothes you wear are dry, but you can't leave here as barefoot as some *fae* cavorting through the forest. Here, a pair of boots freshly made. A deer gifted them to me.

Wear them and be fleet of foot. Take this scabbard made from the same, and this Sword you bear—it shall be invisible until you need it, and until you use it, it will simply mold itself to your form so no one will suspect what it is you carry. It will be an easier burden to bear."

"Where am I to go?"

"Ach, I am just an old lady after all, forgetting what you truly need. A destination for a destiny. It is not time for you to find Conor. Instead, seek out the man who strives to destroy *Skellig* Michael, the hermItage out in the sea. He is not what he seems. He is old, older than I, cunning and strong, and evil his eye. He is called Sir Hugh Rappaport, but that is not his real name. You are the Champion. You will see what he truly is, the bane of all that is good, and holy and true.

"He has a familiar, a depraved man who dares to do even more evil. Find them both and wait for Conor. He readies himself even now, though he does not know it. Your paths will intersect when it is time. Go now, for the daylight is hastening, and you must do much before the night."

She kissed him on the cheek, led him to the holly bushes which parted before her, and sent him on his way, upon a path strewn with star flowers. He turned to bid her goodbye, but she was already gone. Surprisingly, he felt no loss in his heart, but instead, his mood lifted as he set upon his way.

A VALE OF TEARS

Thursday Morning, 11/5, Back to Ballinskelligs along the Faerie Track

THE TRAVELER CARAVAN moved slowly this time down the same Otherworld path Michael had used before. It was dawn, and the rose-colored sky illuminated the mist rising through the verge. The soft drops of condensation could be heard all around them. Brian's wings were folded tight and Michael did not ride him. Instead, he held the halter, whispering to the mount.

Conor couldn't hear what Michael was saying, but he didn't care. The others fell fast asleep again in the rear of the caravan, but Conor and Troubles were up front, silently together.

Beauty after horror, thought Conor. As bad as the *Dullahan* and the *sluagh* had been, they were just more grotesque monstrosities visited upon Conor and his companions. He couldn't help feeling guilt, that, somehow, he brought all this upon them. Then there was Beth, dead just these few days. He couldn't get her out of his mind—how she died when he was dying. How he couldn't save her. How he had really paved the way for her brutal death. Conor couldn't feel his tears, but they were flowing like the rain, down his cheeks and onto the huge head of Troubles who flipped his eyes upward to eye the boy.

"Such sorrow," spoke a voice into Conor's heart. Conor jerked a moment not sure where that came from but then looked down to see the dog's huge dark golden eyes looking at him.

"Sorry, boy," said Conor. "Just being selfish with my thoughts. I haven't even told you enough about how glad I am to see you. You saved our asses out there."

"Little Master," said the dog, verbally this time, pausing to sit up and bend down his head to lick the tears off the boy's face. "You need not apologize. So much has happened; so much has changed. The Battle at the Crossroads and River that took so many lives have transformed you and me. I am different now and my role with you is not the same."

"You're not leaving again are you?" said Conor, fear gripping his heart.

Troubles snorted, "Nay. But something happened to me at the moment of my death. I shall tell you the story shortly. But first, place your head against my chest. Until you weep, until all the sorrow in you has flowed through your tears, you will not be able to move forward, and joy will forever escape from your grasp. Look at the mist in the morning dawn, see the morning dew on the grass, hear the droplets of water splash upon tree and ground, and know that the earth and its life weeps with you now—for you in your pain and for Beth who travels another road. Join your tears with the land and rest your head against my chest and so fade sorrow."

Conor did. He sighed a deep moan from the depths of his heart and put his face in the soft fur of the dog. Troubles placed his head on top of Conor's black hair and looked out the caravan towards Michael. The guardian turned and gave a sad smile to Troubles. Only the soft sounds of snoring in the back of the caravan, and the quiet sobbing of the boy disturbed the peace of the vale. The boy slipped into sleep and Troubles used the moment to place his story into the mind of his human.

WHAT HAPPENED TO TROUBLES

Thursday Morning, 11/5, Back to Ballinskelligs along the Faerie Track

IT HAD HAPPENED before, when Conor and Beth were fleeing town, trying to get away from Dr. Drake and the McNabb boys. Troubles had stopped them and somehow had put thoughts, pictures, really, into Conor's mind in an attempt to communicate. They were chaotic, primitive, emotion laden, but Conor was able to figure out what the dog was trying to say.

This was a different experience, just like Troubles was now quite a different dog. The images flowed smoothly, as if the eyes of the dog were camcorders sucking up the surrounding landscape.

At first, all was dark, but then a blurry image began to form in Conor's resting mind. The dog was on an ancient, wooden table, and bent over him was the face of Madoc, the prince of Gwynedd. The Morrigan had brought the fallen hound down to the Indian mound by the side of the Wisconsin River, where Madoc and the remnant of his people lived. She had given Troubles to him saying, "Do what you can with this noble creature."

Conor couldn't believe it. When he was crucified on the Crossroads Oak, he witnessed the death of Troubles at the hands, claws really, of Rafe McNabb. He had seen the monster snap the dog's neck as Troubles rushed to protect Conor. The dog had been deathly still on the ground. But now, the pup was in the realm of Madoc, and the prince was talking to Troubles.

"Faithful beast, well done!" exclaimed Madoc. "To sacrifice your life for my son, to try and protect that poor girl—'tis a gallant act and no fault of yours that a monster which should never have existed took your life. But the spark of existence is not easily extinguished in some. You are one of those. She who walks the battlefields found you on the ground, after the fight at the river, and to anyone else you would have appeared dead. But your spirit still adhered, though barely, to your body. The *neart*, the life force, the grace in all things living, still resided in you. And so, she brought you here, where once

I restored you to life long ago. Now I have done it again, for we need you—my son needs you."

Troubles lifted up his head, broken neck knit back together, and feebly licked the hand of Madoc.

"You are welcome," said the prince. "But having brought you here, you are already changing. Your first time as a pup was so brief as to be almost insignificant, but you have been here awhile. In the Otherworld, where we now dwell, things revert back to the original intent of the One, the Creator of all. I know you understand me clearly. That is the first of the gifts, but only the first."

Conor felt it also, a power in Troubles that had even the dog wondering what was happening. It seemed like the Labrador retriever was expanding, both physically and mentally. The image was from the dog's point of view, so Conor could not see Troubles growing, but he knew it was happening. The changes in the dog's awareness, however, were much clearer to Conor. It wasn't as if the dog's mental processes were becoming more human. They were still strange, emotional and possessing deep feeling. But Conor could sense the dog was able to reason and think in ways that the boy could understand.

"You may come down from the table now," said Madoc. The dog tried to stand, wobbled for a moment and then leapt off the wooden table. There was a mirror in the rock-walled, stone-floored hall, and Troubles had landed on one of the many thick colored carpets that covered the floor. As the dog's head swung towards the mirror, Conor gasped as he heard the dog yip. The image he saw was of a beast considerably larger than the Labrador that had wandered with him through the river bottoms and hills of southwest Wisconsin. He was even more beautiful. His chocolate colored fur was thick and rich, but what was truly striking were the intelligent eyes gazing from the huge, blocky face. The dog was hardly stupid before, but the dark golden eyes held depths of knowledge that Conor had not seen previously.

"While you were unconscious," spoke Madoc to Troubles, "this world transformed you into what you are truly meant to be. All that was real in your world was but a shadow of what actually exists in its fulness in this world—the bright mountain behind the mountain. You now know with a knowledge you should always have had. You now understand with a comprehension of why you are tied to my son. You now are wiser than any other beast in your reality, with a wisdom instilled by me for the coming trials. You are what you should be."

Troubles opened his mouth and tried to say thank you and made a reasonable attempt, but Madoc simply laughed. "Human speech will not come easy though your attempts will not entirely be in vain. Changed though you are, your anatomy remains the same. Yet you will easily communicate with your own version of language. Through the vocalizations given to your kind, you will attach thoughts and emotions so that you may speak in a way able to be understood by humankind. 'Tis a great gift, only seen or heard in Conor's world, if then, at Christmas, when animals have a vague memory of the time before the worlds were sundered, when darkness had not yet come, and all were united in peace and each could understand one another."

Conor experienced the dog taking in his surroundings and even experienced a bit of déjà vu himself. He had been in this room long ago as a baby, after *Piasa* had attacked him and his mother and Madoc had finally revealed himself protecting them. Gleaming candles cast warm light everywhere. Now it was strangely empty, Madoc's people mostly gone back over the sea.

Just then a blue light, like a will 'o the wisp, flashed by the side of the dog's head. Out of instinct, Troubles snapped to the left trying to catch it in his mouth. He missed; the light instead hovering by the side of Madoc.

"That would not be tasty," said Madoc with a laugh. The ball of light began to dance around the dog, and though Troubles did not snap again, it still floated just outside the reach of those jaws.

A low throated growl of confusion rumbled in the dog's throat, and it was obvious to Madoc, and the watching Conor, that the beast had just asked what this strange sight might be.

Madoc's eyes grew sad with memory. "It had to be done. He would have died without my intervention. The girl had been hurt too badly. Her destiny was the Summer Country, and it was not yet his time. I preserved him like this for now, till Conor can come back and claim him as his own."

Troubles yipped in frustration, clearly not understanding who or what this was.

Madoc cupped the blue light in his hand and gazed at the dog. "You must get to know him, Troubles, and protect him always. His name is Lugh, and he is Conor's son."

A CHANGE IN REALITY

Thursday Morning, 11/5, Back to Ballinskelligs along the Faerie Track

CONOR SNAPPED OUT of the dog's mind and smacked the back of his head against the caravan's side. He was breathing heavily, wondering in fear at what just happened.

Troubles looked down at him in concern and Conor heard the dog chuff at him, "Little Master, did you not know?"

"No," said Conor, "I did not know. I thought the child died when Beth passed. And what was with the blue light? Is my son even human? I've got to go back."

"You cannot," said the dog. "The child is fine in the form he is in, and the prince of Gwynedd is guarding him, keeping him safe, and keeping him secret. But what happened this morning at the well convinced me that once again, the two worlds swirl around you. Something momentous is occurring, and you are at the crux of all events to come."

"That is true," said a voice. Michael had walked back to speak to Conor and the dog. "Yes, Conor, I can hear him too." He ruffled the fur on Troubles' head. "Amazing! Long has it been since I have seen another beast like Brian in this world, fully developed, his potential realized. Clearly, the Creator is moving more directly here than he has in many years."

Conor could barely hear them. The shock of finding that his son was alive and that he really wasn't in any form to drink from a bottle, learn to walk, or speak his first words had rather fried his brain. He felt Michael's hand on his shoulder.

"Come out of the wagon for a moment. Bring the dog and follow me. I want to show you both something."

Conor had not really been paying much attention to where the *faerie* track was leading them, but as he climbed out, he looked around and found the forest had faded and they were parked in front of a cliff. He could hear the ocean surf pounding out of sight, far below the edge of the precipice.

Michael stopped to unhitch the horse, and the four rapidly climbed to the crest. There, Conor gasped in awe. Before him lay the north Atlantic with the view to the west. Clouds and mist were rosy red with the dawn's early light, but that is not what grasped Conor's attention.

Before him, eight miles out, rose the *Skellig* Islands, glowing in the dawn in the unearthly light that surrounded Ireland.

Michael pointed out to sea. "You glimpse them as they truly appear in the Otherworld, massive spikes of rock, as if two fists were rising out of the ocean. *Skellig* Michael to the left, my namesake, is the larger. In your world, Conor, it soars 700 feet above the waves. Here in the Otherworld, it is much larger, and if possible, even more dramatic. I have several homes in your reality, but this was the first, the place where I watched the falling of the Light Bearer. He fell like lightning crashing from the sky—and those who formed alliance with him fell as well." Michael turned a piercing gaze to Conor. "Indeed, I saw your ancestors fall, though their guilt is less and they were not forever condemned."

"I know that place," said Conor. "I have been on the island—me and Jace, when we fought *Piasa*. The demon came in the guise of my mother on that rock, and I almost fell for the ruse."

Michael nodded, "*Skellig* Michael is a place of power. Often, evil has tried to conquer good on those rocky peaks. Never has it succeeded, and it cannot conquer now. An attempt still will be made, however, a push by evil not seen since the stars fell from the sky. Like comets in the night, they plummeted to the sea and on the land. The truly evil were cast even from your world. But there is one who has passed through that gate again, and the darkness he spreads is rising. You, Conor Archer, have not yet fought your last battle. You have not even reached your potential. Thrice pierced said the prophecy, I believe, and only twice has your body been touched like that, once by Rory, your father's brother, and once when Drake nailed you to the Tree of the World. I am sorry. The burden you bear is a heavy one. But you will not bear it alone. Behold, out upon the waters, already the Shadow comes."

A darkness roiled out from the back of the island, far below the summit of *Skellig* Michael, casting a far too large shadow upon the island and the sea crashing around it.

Conor's arm tightened around the neck of Troubles, and suddenly, as the dog whined, he heard the beast speak again. Conor turned to look into the face of one who had willingly died for him, saw the deep golden eyes pierce his own. Wondrously, a single tear from one eye spilled onto the dog's face, and Conor heard Troubles say:

Amid your fellow travelers
On these rocks piercing skyward
From surging sea,
You stand alone,
Here at the edge of the world,
   At the end of all things.

On that fateful day to come,
The mountain will crumble into the sea,
As the rider of the waves,
Rises beautiful in visage,
Powerful in form,
Strong in purpose,
That Ranger of the Heavens.
He shall come to your aid,
Mounted on his steed,
And with him,
I who cheated death twice,
And the Champion who hates but loves.
Alone for only a moment are you,
For we will be by your side,
Here at the edge of the world.
   At the end of all things.

No one spoke and silence reigned. Only the ocean far below, pounded the rocks and sand. Conor knew who the Champion was, and he wished Jace was here, with him now, to take away the fear that gnawed his soul.

AT THE *FOAM AND FINN*

Thursday Morning, 11 / 5, Portmagee

HIS RIDE DROPPED him off in what passed for downtown in Portmagee. Jace waved goodbye and stared to his left at the bank of houses and shops that bordered the wharf. Down a piece, was a hotel and bar named *The Foam and Finn*, and the guy who gave him a ride said it was nice, renovated and affordable, so Jace thought he'd give it a try.

The bell rang as he opened the door and a matronly voice wafted through the downstairs, "I'm coming!" said Niamh Finn, and sure enough, she bustled right in to the foyer, wiping her hands on a dish towel. "And who might you be?" she said, a tight smile on her face. "Just so you know, check-out's at ten so if you're going to be visiting anyone, it will have to be short, and if you want to stay, check-in's at two, a bit of a while from now."

She was blustery that was for sure, thought Jace. A bit of Dort Martin in a buxomy body. "I was just dropped off—way early it seems. Name's Jason Michaels."

For the first time a warm smile appeared on the woman's face. "Jason Michaels. Ah now, there's the name. He said you'd come. My name is Niamh Finn, the proprietress of this place, and I've been waiting for you. The cell call I got the other day didn't really say when you'd show up, but I'm glad you're here. I was to make you welcome and tell you this: You might be here a while, but you are not to worry about the room cost or the food—'tis all been taken care of by your friend Malachy."

"Malachy? Really?" said Jace, honestly surprised that the Abbot would even know that he was going to be here in this town.

"Really, dear. Now let me show you to your room. Check-in is now for you. It looks as though you need a morning nap."

Jace grinned as they headed up the stairs, silently gaping as she opened the door to his room. One huge room, studio divided, with a bay window looking out at the wharf and two islands far in the distance.

"It's beautiful," he said. "What are those two islands way out there?"

"That'd be the *Skelligs*, and the main reason Portmagee is even here. Oh, we're a fishing town, but I'd doubt we'd make a living without the tourism those islands bring. The big one out there is *Skellig* Michael, named for the archangel. Of course, most young ones like you never remember the name. Instead, it's 'that place Luke Skywalker hid out when he was hunted as the Last Jedi.'"

"But that's just a movie," said Jace.

"From your ears to God's lips," she said. "You'd never know it by the way people talk. They filmed the movie there, that's all. But its real importance is much more ancient. It's Michael's Mount. There was a monastery there once for eight hundred years because it's the place where the archangel watched the rebel angels fall from the heavens and saw their kin, the *Tuatha de Danaan* and those that became the selkies fall with them. Most nobody now believes that."

"I do," said Jace quietly.

Niamh turned sharply from the window and stared at the boy for a long moment. "I believe you do," she said quietly. "Maybe you're as special as Malachy said you were. But enough of that. He said you would come with nothing but told me what size of clothes you wear. I put some in the dresser drawers for you. Bar's closed for another hour, so I'll make you some breakfast and bring it up to you."

"Thanks, but please don't fuss over me," said Jace.

Niamh smiled and touched her short brown hair. "'Fuss' is what I do, Mr. Jason Michaels. Now take a shower and I'll be back up in a few minutes with something to eat."

The hot water splashing his face took him back nearly a day when he had been tossing and turning in his bed in Tinker's Grove, Wisconsin. Trying to get a nap after Beth's funeral in his own bed back home. He couldn't sleep. He closed his eyes again, but something suddenly thumped his back.

"Get up! Get up now," said a voice. Big as he was, Jace was fast. Turning swiftly, he grasped a wooden stick and followed it forward into the hands of Abbot Malachy. He didn't look right, thought Jace. Almost a shadow rather than a real body.

Those musings were cut short when the Abbot spoke again, "No time to waste. Danger is coming to this town and it will head straight for you if you remain."

"But, we just buried her! What will my parents say?" protested the boy.

"You can't stay. Too dangerous. I will make it so they shall not miss you."

"I don't want go. Besides, where would you send me where I'd be safe?" said Jace.

"You'll go now if you care for your life and the lives of your loved ones."

"Where? Where am I going?"

"Just get dressed. Someone will find you and point your way. When you get to where you're going, others will find you and take you where you may not wish to go. But no matter, go you must. Now!" With that the Abbot wrenched the crozier away from Jace's hands, using it to knock him to the floor.

Stunned just a little, Jace looked around but found his visitor gone. He was beside himself. His sense of duty and the love he had for both his parents and sister tugged at him, almost dissuading him from going.

The empty room down the hall which once was Beth's haunted his soul. He pulled on his jeans and shirt and padded down the hallway. Sitting on the edge of his sister's bed, he felt the emptiness all around him.

Beth and he were twins, and when she died, a hole ripped open in his heart. He couldn't even weep so hollow did he feel. Now that she was gone, he realized that a part of his very self had left him. He knew she walked the Summer Country. He liked that name for heaven and was grateful Conor had taught him the words. But the very thought of Conor caused anger to flare up in him again. Unfair, he knew, but he didn't care. Maybe he wasn't really responsible for her death, but he was the catalyst. Had he never come to Tinker's Grove, she'd still be alive.

Jace was thinking that very thought when the blue light popped in through the window. He had seen it once before, just when Beth had passed away. The life that had been born from her and Conor's union. A baby he supposed but something more—otherwise, it wouldn't be a blue light floating right in front of him.

"You're Conor's little one. What do you want?" he asked gently. No answer but a flitting movement towards the door. Jace followed the light out into the hallway, stopping only to grab his Sword. Out the door and through the streets of the town he walked as dusk settled in, led by the silent light. Past the quiet abbey and down the hills to the river it led him.

"I can't walk on water," said Jace, smiling a little as the light tried to coax him. It hovered for a moment at the edge of the beach and then floated out to the middle of the channel.

"Really," said Jace, "I can't."

Like sprinkles of stardust, the revolving sphere cast motes of light back towards him that fell on the water like a path. Thankful that he could at least swim, Jace kicked off his shoes and tentatively tried out the path. He found it bore his weight, and so he gently put one foot in front of the other towards the light on the water. Pretty cool, he thought. Just like Peter coaxed out onto the Sea of Galilee by Jesus, he could walk on water. Jace laughed out loud when he reached the light but gasped when he sank like a stone into the black depths. Just like Peter.

Back in the shower at Portmagee, Jace gasped again, sucking in some water as he remembered the strange feeling of traveling through the gateway. Same one that Troubles had traveled, he reckoned. He wasn't drowning but he was moving fast, and then upward into the waters of *Tobar na Molt*, the Holy Well, and then flat on his face in front of that ancient nun.

Now he was here in the tiny town of Portmagee, and he didn't know why, except that Abbot Malachy was obviously involved and had planned the whole thing. Monks and nuns and little blue lights, thought Jace, coughing out water and shaking his wet hair. Stepping out of the shower, he wondered what waited for him next.

Cleaned up and fed, Jace felt a lot better and decided to walk down to the wharf before he napped. Portmagee was rather a charming place on this beautiful but bleak peninsula. He loved the bright colors of the houses, and the boats on the water looked like fishing was indeed a major activity here. Still, it was a small place and as Jace walked the quay he spied a little shop called *Roddy's Skellig Tours*.

A young man, only a little older than Jace, was mopping out a twenty-foot boat. There was a glassed-in cabin, but most of the vessel was open to the sky with padded benches all around.

"*Failte!*" said the lad cheerily. He was quite dark skinned but with blond streaked brown hair and brown eyes. Looking up at the overcast sky and feeling the damp, Jace wondered how anyone could get a tan in this country.

Jace had picked up enough Celtic to know that the older boy's greeting meant 'Welcome!' "Same to you," he said. "Name's Jace Michaels."

"And I'm Hercules Columba Roddy. My Grandpa Joe started this business and my Da continues it."

"You're Irish?" said Jace. "Pardon me for saying that you look like you hail from somewhere else."

The young man smiled, "They all say that, but I'm as Irish as they come. Born and bred here, except my Ma emigrated from India. What she was doing this side of Ireland I just don't know, but she wandered into one of Portmagee's bars on a wet and dreary night, and my father dropped his pint on the floor—and even though it was my mother that caught his eye, it was a waste of a good Guinness. Anyway, he fell for her on the spot and married her not much later. I'm the result of all that."

Jace laughed and said, "So what's with the name? Hercules isn't exactly Irish."

"You got a point," he said. "It was my Ma's idea. She'd grown up watching Bollywood versions of Hercules the hero and just liked the name. Da didn't really care, but Fr. Greavy sure did. Said Hercules was no saint's name and so slipped another name in all by himself. 'I baptize you Hercules Columba Roddy'. It's such a mouthful, everyone just calls me Colly."

"Well, Colly," said Jace, "it's great to meet you. Looks like you give some tours out to the *Skelligs*."

"Truth to tell," said Colly, "it's our main business. Six months a year we sail; the rest we fish. Fishing's okay, but the *Skellig* Tour makes our daily bread. Government has limited the number of boats that can go to the islands. Only seven sail daily now, and each carry twenty people. It's exotic and we are never short on customers. 'Course the season is over now, so I'm just fixing the boat up."

Jace looked out over the water at the *Skelligs*. "I saw the islands driving in. They look as wild as I remember," he murmured. "Like the poet says, 'No sun shines peacefully on those splintered rocks'. They're all angles and edges. What a place."

"You've been before?" said Colly, puzzlement washing over his face.

Jace spluttered a bit, knowing he had said too much. "Just in a dream. Maybe, I can see it for real someday."

"Well, that would be in about an hour if you want. I don't usually go over there in November, but we got word that the seas were unusually calm today, especially at *Skellig* Landing, known to us locals as Blind Man's Cove."

"Hey thanks," said Jace. "I appreciate the hospitality."

"Don't mention it. Bring a warm jacket and, of course, eighty euro's in cash. I don't drive strangers around for free." Colly laughed, happy at being able to make a bit today.

Jace wasn't sure where he was going to get any money, but when he returned to the hotel, Mrs. Finn had put an envelope on his bed. "Expenses" was all it said, but when Jace opened it, a wad of Euros met his gaze along with a note from her saying that Malachy wanted his needs taken care of.

"I've got to start doing more things for that Abbot—if I ever get back there," whispered Jace to himself.

An hour later, he was back at the quay and found Colly standing by an empty boat.

"Look," he said, "I was yanking your chain a bit. No tourists today, but I need to go out and get some supplies to the student archs out there and I could use a hand."

"Archs?" asked Jace.

"Yeah, archeologists, student ones repairing the monastery and excavating for any ancient buildings undiscovered as yet."

Jace smiled, "Sure I'll, help—for eighty euros."

Colly laughed. "I was only joshing you. I would have taken you for free anyway. You seem okay."

Jace hopped in the boat and saw a bunch of supplies scattered around.

"This here's the *Scatha Sloop*, named after a great Celtic warrior woman. She's never let me down. She'll be good for the voyage today."

But Jace was barely listening. He looked across the waters at the islands and saw that something was wrong with *Skellig* Michael. "What's that?" he asked

"Don't know," said Colly. "Saw it starting just a bit ago. It's pitch black on the leeward side of the island."

"Let's find out," said Jace. "Got a feeling we need to see this up close."

It didn't take long to come near the islands, particularly with a powerful engine on the *Scatha*. It quickly became apparent that the dark splotch they saw was an add-on, not part of the island at all, but instead a huge black cargo ship wending its way from the westward side of the island and casting a strangely sharp shadow for the overcast day.

"What the hell is that doing there?" snarled Colly.

"You know that ship?"

"Sure as I do," said Colly. "It belongs to a man by the name of Sir Hugh Rappaport who fancies himself a modern noble over near Tralee. He's a sonofabitch of the worst sort—at least we fishermen think so. Oh, he's so beloved by the *Taoiseach*—that's our prime minister—and the elites love him as well, but I can't stand him. You know what he calls that ship? He calls it *Baleros,* named after one of the worst Irish demons ever to walk this green land."

Colly took a breath and then shook his fist at the ship, "Looks like a cargo ship and I guess it is but it's also a research vessel. Looking for gold he is. Just a few years ago, he parked that hulk in Clew Bay north of here and declared he was going to mine the gold in *Croagh* Patrick, St. Patrick's holy mountain, right there on the shores of the bay. He lost that fight, though just barely. Now I've heard he's setting his sights on the islands, and there'll be gold there. The archs got the geologists to check this past summer, and it's there all right. He wants it, no matter what it does to the *Skelligs*. Officious prick!"

Jace was taken aback by his new friend's outburst. "He sounds like a gem."

"Murderous asshole actually," said Colly. "One of my best friends disappeared last year. He was driving over near Cahersiveen and was run off the road by some goons of Rappaport's. The *Gardai* wouldn't even write them a traffic summons. Just let them go. Bastards. Found the car, never the body."

Jace found himself placing a hand on Colly's shoulder. "Hey, man, I'm sorry."

Colly grimaced. "Not your fight. But let's have some fun with that ship."

With that, Colly changed course, and sent the *Scatha* plunging through the gentle waves toward the vessel. It took about five minutes but the cargo ship soon loomed above them. Colly let loose the throttle and the boat went merrily circling the *Baleros*. A few sailors appeared far above them hanging over the rails shaking their fists at them, but Colly just laughed and soon Jace joined in. When one is small and faces a bully, sometimes just laughing at them is enough.

Except that wasn't the end of it. Another man appeared on the cargo ship's deck. Tall and Asian, he carried a rifle. Aiming, he fired towards them, plunking dozens of bullets five feet from *Scatha's* hull.

Jace shouted in fear as Colly wrenched the wheel and sent the tiny craft plunging away with Jace losing his footing and smashing into the side of the cabin.

"Jesus, Mary and Joseph!" cried Colly, and Jace thought it was more of a prayer than anything else. "You know who that was?"

"Ah, no," said Jace getting up and rubbing his shoulder.

"That was Shiro Ishii, Rappaport's right-hand man. He's the one that always does his master's dirty work."

As their boat plowed toward the island landing, the cargo ship sailed the opposite way, no more bullets sent their direction.

They were silent for a while, but then Jace said, "He could have killed us you know."

"Yeah, but he didn't."

"I know," said Jace, "but before you twisted the wheel, I got a good look at him. He was shooting rounds into the sea. Only his eyes were aiming at us. He was looking straight at you and me. I have a feeling he was memorizing our faces, like he planned to see us again."

STAR WARS SUCKS

Thursday Afternoon, 11/5, Skellig Michael

THEY LANDED WITHOUT incident and found the student archeologists waiting to help them unload the supplies.

"Saw your cat and mouse game with the cargo ship," said one of the archs, whose name was Tommy.

"Yeah," said Colly, "stupid of me, I know."

Tommy grinned ruefully. "They were anchored on the other side of the island, sending some divers down with equipment. Gold prospecting, I think. Thank God they didn't land here. They don't seem the friendly sort."

Jace and Colly agreed but left the archs to sort out the supplies. Colly wanted to show Jace the island.

"Seven hundred steps carved into the rock by some monk as penance for his sins. That's what we got to climb," muttered Colly and started off on the path towards the monastery. Jace was entranced. Even though it wasn't that warm out, he was soon sweating as he climbed, completely in awe of what he saw. The peaks were jagged and stark, but in clefts and hollows, green moss still shown bright. They finally reached a small level meadow about five hundred feet above the ocean, and Colly excitedly beckoned Jace to follow.

"And here's the place where Luke Skywalker stood, the Last Jedi, while he was hiding out and trying to figure out how to stop the resurgent empire." Colly waved his hand to where the meadow ended in a sharp cliff over the western side of the island.

Jace raised an eyebrow as the wind caught his blond hair. "*Star Wars* sucks, Colly."

Colly gaped at him. "I thought ... I thought you'd be like the others. Tourists I mean. They always want to know about the movie."

"Really, Colly? I'm not an idiot sightseer. Thanks for trying to entertain, but 'Star Wars' doesn't have a thing to do with what this island is all about."

"Sorry, man." Colly looked sheepish. "Just trying to have some fun. But since you've gone all serious on me, you might as well know where you really are standing. This is 'Christ's Saddle', the *machair* or meadow that connects the two parts of the island. All this to your left, leads up to the 'Needle's Eye' and the 'Stone of Pain', places where monks and pilgrims for fifteen hundred years went to do penance. I can't take you there. It's just too dangerous."

Jace looked around, feeling very small and insignificant. It was as if he was resting in the palm of a half-closed monstrous fist thrust up from the waters of the sea with gannets and other seabirds wheeling around the cliffs and spires of rock. "Definitely been here before," said Jace under his breath.

"What?" said Colly. "Well anyway, everything to the right and up that hideous last hundred feet of steps leads to the monastery, and it is cool as cool can be. Come on."

And like some mountain goat, Colly took off, climbing the steps swiftly, Jace right behind.

"It's amazing," said Jace at the top of the steps, looking at the small collection of beehive huts that made up the ancient monastery. Still watertight and sturdy, they had stood for well over a millennium. Not a bit of mortar or planking held them together—each stone fit precisely.

"The monks lived here," said Colly, "carting soil from the mainland to fill this garden and grow what they needed. It must have been grand back then in a way. Did you know the climate was warmer back in the day? There was a Little Ice Age in the 1200's that drove them to Ballinskelligs on the mainland to set up a new monastery and then only visit here occasionally."

"Kind of beats *Star Wars*, huh?" said Jace.

"Yeah," said Colly with a smile. "Just a bit. Hey, maybe I can show you something I found close to the Needle's Eye when I was out here yesterday."

Jace followed him down the steps, across the saddle and then up an almost invisible path that led into the spires on the southern side of the island.

"There's the Needle's Eye—too dangerous to go up there," said Colly. "But that's not what I wanted to show you. It's over here, at the base of the final climb to the needle."

Colly led him over to what looked like a small set of standing stones one or two feet in height, and right in the middle, shining green in the noonday sun, was an emerald scale, like something shed from an ancient dragon.

"Now how brilliant is that?" said Colly. "I've been up and down these rocks all my life, but only yesterday did I find this. These miniature standing stones have been here forever, but nothing was ever inside the circle, until I discovered this."

Jace bent down to look. Colly said to him, "You won't be able to pick it up. I tried; it's stuck fast."

None the less, Jace put his fingers underneath the two by three foot dragon scale and lifted it easily. "*Piasa*," he said.

"What did you say—how did you do that?" said Colly. "I tried for an hour to pry that up yesterday."

"Remember when I said I had been here before in a dream? Guess it really wasn't a dream. I was here a couple of days ago, with a friend of mine. And, I know you aren't going to believe me, but we were battling a dragon here—or something like it—and this is part of the beast. Its name was *Piasa*, and it died in my own country, by the banks of the Wisconsin River, but for a while, we fought it here, Conor Archer and me. And I think that Sir Hugh Rappaport may not simply be looking for gold."

Hercules Columba Roddy just stared at Jace. He had already told his new friend that he had always wanted to leave this barren, bleak and boring area of Ireland and, like most young folks, wanted to see the world. But he wasn't stupid. He knew his land was rich in history and mystery. And this kid who dropped in on him today was a mystery indeed. "Jason Michaels, I don't know who or what you are, but you are about the most exciting thing that's happened to me in quite a while. Let's go home. I want you to meet somebody, somebody that might shed some light on all this stuff."

"Can we throw this thing into the ocean?" asked Jace. "It's from an evil you can only imagine."

"We can't throw it from here. We could drag it down to the landing, but the archs won't let us leave with it. Maybe we should just leave it here and get rid of it later."

Jace reluctantly agreed, but a nagging feeling in the pit of his stomach told him he would regret this decision.

FATHER GREAVY

Thursday Afternoon, 11/5, Portmagee

AN HOUR AND a half later, Colly and Jace stood outside a thatched cottage. The house was surrounded by a stone fence with holly trees fronting the entrance and hyacinth bushes all around the fence line.

Colly pounded on the door but no one answered. "He's out back, tending his garden, I suspect."

"Who?" asked Jace.

"Father Nathan Greavy, the curate of the Portmagee Parish. Come on." And Colly jumped the fence and headed round back, Jace following.

Sure enough, someone was in the backyard. A pudgy man dressed in black, straw hat on head, was bending over some of the most brilliant roses, Jace had ever seen. He couldn't believe they were still blooming in November. The priest, however, didn't even turn around.

"I can tell that it's you, Hercules Columba Roddy. You walk like a cart horse. And whoever you brought with you doesn't walk much more softly."

"Father Greavy," said Colly. "I want you to meet a friend of mine."

With that, the man turned, and Jace saw that underneath the hat was a round, full face with wire rim glasses and a shy smile.

"I'm Fr. Greavy, lad," he said, taking off a glove to shake Jace's hand. "And who might you be?"

"Jason Michaels, but most just call me Jace."

"Ah, American," nodded the priest knowingly. "I'm very pleased to meet you, Jace, though I already question your judgment because of your choice of friends." He scowled playfully at Colly. "Do you like my roses, now?"

"They're grand," said Jace.

"See," said Fr. Greavy to Colly, "picking up our way of talking already. So, what are you boys here for; certainly not scoping out some roses for Philomena—the girl who doesn't know how much you care?"

"A girl I like," said Colly sheepishly to Jace. But then his gaze hardened. "Can we talk to you, Father? Something happened out on the *Skelligs*."

"You look serious, lads. Let's walk to the pub for a pint and you can tell me everything."

Mrs. Finn ensconced the trio into one of the back snugs of the pub. The high back booth was very private, and Fr. Greavy told the boys they could talk freely which they did between grateful slurps of frothy Guinness.

"There's something evil about that ship," said Colly. "I mean, I've seen it before, but today when it rounded the island it looked like a dark shadow— a black hole bleeding upon land and sky."

"Aye," said Fr. Greavy, "you're not far off. The name of the ship is *Baleros*. It's ancient Celtic for—"

"'The Deadly One'," finished Jace.

"And how did you know that, lad?" said the priest. "Been dusting up on your Irish back there in America?"

Jace blushed dark red. "Just knew, that's all. Sometimes I know things."

"No need to be embarrassed," said Fr. Greavy. "Knowledge and wisdom are great gifts. And you are right. The name of the ship means 'The Deadly One', and Colly's right too that it is an evil thing. You've read the newspaper, Colly. You know it's both a cargo container ship and a research vessel. Rather a cumbersome thing I suppose and impractical but not if what you are researching is big and dangerous, or expensive and rare."

"You're talking about the gold," said Jace.

"Suppose I am at that," said the priest. "He wanted to pillage the holy mountain, *Croagh* Patrick, but the outcry was so great from the people that he had to slink back from that idea. His plan to rape the *Skelligs* of that ore has gotten much less publicity. He's learned that fame and fortune aren't always an ally. But I'm less worried about that than what Colly says about the man who shot at you—Shiro Ishii. Do either of you know much about him?"

"Just that he's chief thug of the Chief himself," snarled Colly. "Can you believe that? Trying to scare us off with a rifle? He could have killed us!"

Fr. Greavy gingerly sipped his Guinness. "If he wanted you dead, you'd be dead. He's had great experience in that area."

Jace's mind was swirling. Since he had tasted of the Great Catfish that he and Walter had caught a week ago, his idle thoughts had been racing. It seemed he had tapped into a vast fund of knowledge with the added benefit of understanding what it meant and how to use it. The gift came and went, like a darting dragonfly over the swamps of the back sloughs of the Wisconsin River. Right now, knowledge, wisdom and understanding were overloading his brain.

"Shiro Ishii—Japanese name," said Jace. "And not a nice one. That name belongs to the worst war criminal of all time. But surely this can't be him. The guy on the ship was young. The real Shiro Ishii should be long dead."

"All I know," said Colly, "is that he's a bastard to the nth degree." Colly soaked up some lentil soup in a hot roll and stuffed it in his mouth. Just then, there was a scream and a crashing sound from the other room. Before they could rise, a shadow drifted over their table and all three looked up into the sneering face of Shiro Ishii.

"Just talking about you, Shiro," said the priest. "You are welcome to sit and speak with us a while if you wish."

"Don't need your hospitality, priest. Back in Nagasaki, a long time ago, some Jesuit missionaries had myself and my family over for lunch one day. A nod to our royal connection to the Emperor. It was a stiff, uncomfortable situation for a child. Never liked priests, particularly ones that should not have been in our land."

"And yet," pointed the priest, "here you are in a land of priests and Catholics."

"I didn't stop by to do wordplay with the likes of you, Fr. Greavy. I simply came to tell the lads here that if they ever pull that stunt again out on the water, it will be the last thing they ever do."

Fr. Greavy's round face grew red. "I'll not be having my guests insulted and threatened like that, Shiro. You've said your piece now let me say mine. Touch these boys, harm one hair on their head and I'll emigrate you to the dark side of the Underworld where there will be wailing and gnashing of teeth for one such as the likes of you."

Shiro placed both hands on the table as he leaned over almost appearing ready to rip a piece of the priest's face with his mouth. But Fr. Greavy smiled at him and immediately Shiro uttered a loud scream. The steak knife the priest had been using thunked soundly down into the wooden table, Shiro's hand in between. Blackish red blood spurted from the wound, but rather than extricating himself, Shiro reached his free hand to his side and drew his katana.

Jace had only seen one of those in pictures but he knew what it was and what it could do. Shiro was already swinging it at the priest's neck. Time slowed down for Jace, just as it had when he fought *Piasa*, and he felt himself standing and pushing the thug away from the table. The knife popped out, causing Shiro to scream again and crash to the floor. But before Shiro hit the ground, Jace had already drawn his Sword.

Ishii gasped in surprise, cradling his hand, and Jace could hear Fr. Greavy and Colly suck in their breath. Just as the nun had promised, the Sword had been invisible in its sheath on Jace's back.

"Where did you get that?" snarled Shiro clutching his bleeding hand. "That Sword was lost long ago. My employer has described it to me in detail over the years. Even he has not set eyes on it for millennia. It has a mate, young man. Not a Sword, but a Spear, the Spear of Destiny, lost only recently, around the time of the Second World War. You have one; where is the other?"

"Quiet, Jason Michaels. That Sword and Spear must be very important to him to want them so badly." Fr. Greavy casually wiped the dagger free of Shiro Ishii's black blood on a nearby cloth napkin.

"Fools, you don't even know what you are talking about." He tried to rise but Jace gently touched the tip of the Sword to the henchman's neck. As his skin made contact with the blade, there was a flash of light and Ishii screamed again.

"It's the Sword of Light, asshat," said Jace, "and I know very well what it is and what it does. And the Spear is safe, with a friend of mine."

Ishii grew silent in his pain, his eyes suddenly taking a crafty look. "An American too? Perhaps so. Perhaps he even preceded you here. You should have listened to the priest. You talk too much. I have seen your friend, though he carried no Spear."

"Conor?" said Jace without thinking. "You've seen Conor?"

"Conor Archer," said Ishii, with a smile. "I knew of him before I ever met him just the other day. Precocious lad, smart boy, talented with the smell of destiny around him. Then, not now, I'm afraid. He's gone, alas."

"What have you done with him?" screamed Jace, pressing the Sword point into Ishii's neck so blood flowed freely.

Ishii howled again. "Press any harder and you'll never know."

Fr. Greavy pulled Jace's arm back. "Easy lad. He's not going anywhere for a moment at least. Let him speak."

Shiro Ishii glared at the three. "He should be dead and drowned in America. But something went wrong didn't it? Something Drake failed to do—am I right? No matter. I found your precious Conor up in Cahersiveen, in a trailer park with the Tinkers. He managed to upset my employer. His special talents gave him away."

"How do you know all this?" asked Jace. "How could you possibly figure out who he is?"

"The world cries out in agony, Jason Michaels. Haven't you heard it weeping? Even the Otherworld is in tumult, as it seeks to merge with this one to ease the pains of what will be a new creation. I have known many things in my life, but the rise of one who seeks to bring the worlds together is no real secret to me.

"When Sir Hugh noticed the disruption, he knew it was the birth pangs of something never seen before, and that there was some doubt as to what the new creation would be when the worlds merged. Sir Hugh loves the chaos, the night, and the abyss. He will have his way, and that will be the new world order. But he also knows there will be those who resist."

"New world order," said Jace. "What a drama queen."

Ishii ignored the insult and went on. "He sensed the greatest pocket of resistance in the tiny town of Tinker's Grove, Wisconsin where you come from, Jason Michaels. Amazing, isn't it? Known for nothing but giving birth to something and somehow resisting the darkness that is my master's domain. Though we didn't know exactly how that resistance would manifest itself, we sent one of our best scientists and most talented mages—don't look so surprised Hercules Columba Roddy. You live here in the midst of myth and story and you think the days of magic are over? Far from it. The man we sent from here was skilled in both arts."

"Drake," whispered Jace. "You sent Dr. Drake, you piece of vicious scum. Sorry to tell you, he's dead now."

"I thought as much," said Ishii. "Otherwise, Conor would not be here. How he and you and your allies managed to defeat such a talented man as Professor Drake eluded me for a while. Until I met Conor. He's not your ordinary boy, is he? In fact, he's hardly human at all. Or was hardly human."

"What are you saying? What have you done with him?" Jace rose up again and pointed the Sword.

"I'm saying he's dead. I wished it by my hand, and by the katana I wear at my side, but such was not to be. He ran into the sea and sank beneath the waves. I did not see him again. He's gone—forever, Jace." Shiro's face twisted into a sneer.

Jace cried out in grief and pulled back the Sword to begin a stabbing blow, but Colly grasped him around the chest.

"No, Jace. Not here, not like this. He wants your rage. He's got something he's holding back. I don't know what's going on, but I know if you strike him, something terrible will happen."

"Colly's right, lad," said Fr. Greavy. "Let it go for now. We can sort it later."

Jace was gasping and tears were running down his face. "You're a monster!" he raged at the man lying on the floor.

And Shiro Ishii began to laugh. "That I am, and all of you are so blind to what is happening. The Dark is rising, and I am its herald. You would find me hard to kill, but I must admit, I cannot defeat you here, not with that Sword in your hand." He wobbled a little as he staggered to his feet, saying. "But there will be another time."

Ishii turned to leave, but swift as the winter wind, his unharmed hand grasped his katana and his arm whipped it around aiming for Jace's neck.

Jace barely moved, but his Sword arm lifted and the Sword of Light blocked and shattered the katana, its broken pieces falling to the bar room floor.

Laughing again, Ishii said, "Brilliant! But I had to try. And it was my second-best katana. You'll pay for that insolence, boy. But for now," he said backing away both hands held forward, his left one bleeding freely, "I will leave you, until we meet again. And we will, Jason Michaels, we definitely will." With that, he turned and strode out of the bar and hotel.

Mrs. Finn rushed in crying out, "Fr. Greavy are any of you hurt?"

"No, none," said the priest, "but what about you? We heard you scream and then came an awful crash."

"Ach," she said blushing, "he startled me so. I tripped backward over my own feet and smashed that brilliant tea set that's been in our family for years. Clumsy of me, but I'm no worse for wear. 'Tis nothing. Now get yourselves to another booth while I clean up this mess. I'll bring you all something stronger than a Guinness to get over this fright."

Just her bustling brought a smile to Jace's face and he looked at his two new friends and sighed. The Dark is rising, thought Jace. That's what that snake said, but if it was rising, Jace was very glad to have the priest and Colly on his side.

THE HOLLOW MAN

Thursday Afternoon, 11/5, Around Portmagee

SHIRO ISHII WAS in powerful pain. Fr. Greavy's dagger should not have even pierced his skin, but it had sliced into him like butter. He hated it when someone other than he and Sir Hugh had access to magic or science the two of them did not possess.

When he got back to his Mercedes, he found a cloth in the glove box and wrapped his bleeding hand. He could already feel it healing. Tissue regeneration was one of the benefits of the gift of longevity he had discovered. He rammed the gear shift into drive and sped out of town musing on what he learned. The Conor kid had allies but how powerful? The Sword of Light was a new twist and already he lusted after it. Must he tell Sir Hugh about its presence?

Sir Hugh. Shiro Ishii owed him much. In 1959, Ishii's small yacht ran into engine trouble just off the coast of Kerry. He had fled Japan and prepared to disappear completely. Not that it would be that terribly difficult. The United States had simply not prosecuted him for his war crimes and he was clearly the worst of the war criminals in either the Nazi or Japanese armies. America had needed him despite the obscenities he committed at Unit 731. As Korea had descended into chaos after the war, and the Union of Soviet Socialist Republics, the U.S.S.R., rose to prominence, the United States needed to keep ahead of the communists in both nuclear and biological/chemical weaponry. Nuclear research was for someone else to worry about but Shiro Ishii had everything America needed to remain number one in the bio/chem weapons area. Prosecuting him was out of the question. Democracy needed his knowledge. And he gave it to them. Almost everything he had. Amazed at his brilliance, they never questioned whether he knew anything else, but he did.

He knew the secret to eternal life. Or the next best thing to it. During the war, he constantly experimented. Before the war, he had noble goals. Discovering a water purification system meant the Japanese army could fight in the field without the cholera and dysentery so easily caught throughout central and southeast Asia. That meant the empire could expand with fewer losses. But he quickly lost interest in what would have been a great life-saving technological achievement. He soon became mesmerized by his ability to tweak biology and invent chemical compounds that changed humanity or brought quick death. The Japanese High Command didn't mind. Whatever he set his sights on, he succeeded and helped bring victory to the Emperor.

Experimenting on humans brought him great joy. At first that embarrassed him. His father, a member of the royal family, had little mercy but was definitely not into torturing the peasant class. He would beat Shiro frequently when he caught him brutalizing the family pets or abusing the servants. But Shiro grew up, and his father died. And the Emperor liked the progress Shiro made with science.

One day in the lab, he found it. He managed to develop a compound that seemed to retard the corruption and degeneration that accompanied the body's exposure to infectious bacteria and viruses. His discovery was even more fortuitous since genetic research was in its infancy. Had he known then what he knew now, he could have perfected the compound without the hundreds of deaths he had to cause to make it perfect during the war.

He told no one. He justified it because, to validate its efficacy, it had to be tested on humans. He took his results and a sample of the compound directly to the Emperor. He met with Hirohito on August 25, 1945, hours before the atomic bomb exploded over Hiroshima.

It was just the Emperor and himself in the throne room. The small, scholarly ruler exerted a presence far beyond his size. Ishii was humbled to be honored with a private meeting.

"The war is lost, Shiro." The Emperor looked at him unblinking through his pince-nez glasses.

"That cannot be, Majesty," said Shiro, truly shocked that the god-king would say such a thing.

"But it is true. We shall fight to the death, but the Americans will win."

"No! Never! Majesty, I have brought you something that will save us, all of us."

"Shiro," said the Emperor with a sad smile. "you have done so much throughout the war. Whatever you have, it is too late."

"It is eternal life."

"What do you mean?" asked the Emperor sharply. And Shiro told him.

The Emperor was an amateur scientist himself, a good one. But he had a hard time believing the doctor had actually invented anything like he was describing. Shiro offered to test it on himself and injected the substance into his body right in front of the Emperor. There was no immediate change, except for one thing. Hirohito had noticed that Ishii was going grey. By the time the meeting ended, Ishii's hair was completely black. Impressed but unsure, the Emperor ordered Shiro to Nagasaki. He was to stay there a few days at one of the royal palaces and then return to Tokyo for another audience with the god-king.

Ishii was already headed for Nagasaki when the bomb obliterated Hiroshima. He had no idea that the Americans had come so far in nuclear research. He knew the Emperor would not surrender, so he instructed his bodyguard to continue to the city. He was there when days later, hell descended upon him.

He should have been burned to death. Burned he was, but miraculously, his wounds healed before his eyes. His clothes were vaporized, but his heart and lungs worked normally. He walked past the shadowed dead—bodies destroyed but their images imprinted on buildings. He refused the outstretched arms of corpses shattered in the explosion. He recoiled from those already suffering radiation poisoning. All he wanted was a mirror, and he found a broken one in the rubble. Cleaning it off, he looked carefully at himself and found a young, vibrant, healthy young man looking back at him.

Within a day he appeared before the war-weary Emperor once again. Whispers of rebellion were everywhere; people wondering whether the god-king would surrender.

Seldom did the Emperor show any emotion. But when he saw Ishii with flawless visage and skin before him, he gasped. "It worked! You have achieved the impossible!"

"Yes, Majesty," said Ishii. "And now we can defeat the Americans."

"There is no time," said the Emperor sadly. "They have threatened more bombs. We cannot survive. I have told my advisors that we must surrender."

Ishii did not say a word. At that time, he had absolute faith in his Emperor and divined that surrender or fight on, the Emperor would ultimately be victorious.

"I do not know what to say, Majesty, except to express profound sadness."

The Emperor smiled. "You have done well. So well in fact that I have a gift for you. You have granted yourself long life, but there is still something I can grant you."

He walked over to a little gold Shinto shrine in the corner of the room and picked up a small casket of silver. Opening it, he took out a bottle and gave it to Ishii.

"It is the strength of the samurai," said Hirohito, "an ancient potion created by the Shinto priests. I haven't a clue what is in it. My family has had this casket with the vial in it for centuries. It was to be used when the Heavenly Kingdom was threatened with its very survival. That time is now.

Drink it for there is little time. I must help you through this, and my retainers will soon be here to take me to my generals. Drink."

Ishii took the vial and drank, never worrying for even an instant that the Emperor might be trying to kill him. His trust did not wane when he was seized with violent convulsions and thrown on the ground. The Emperor cradled him until the spasms passed.

When Ishii had recovered, the Emperor helped him stand. "How do you feel?" he asked.

"Fine, the same as before. I feel no stronger."

Hirohito said, "You will, in time. The strength of the samurai is both spiritual and physical. There will have to be a catalyst to empower each. You will know when this happens. Go now. We shall not meet again. Years will mean nothing to you, but when you sense your destiny approaching, act for the good of the Emperor. I expect nothing less of you." Hirohito walked away.

Shiro Ishii said, "Yes, Your Majesty," to the retreating figure and then made his way out of the palace.

In the chaotic days to come the physical strength of the samurai was enacted within Shiro's body. Many times, he had to fight in order to escape the madness that was post-war Tokyo. He physically fought soldiers and peasants with a strength he never had experienced and found it was impossible for anyone to inflict a mortal wound upon him. But he never experienced any spiritual awakening. And he wondered.

That enlightenment waited until 1959, when his yacht lost power and ran aground on Bull Rock off the coast of the Beara peninsula just south of County Kerry. It quickly sank, and though exhausted, Shiro Ishii did not drown. Not knowing where he was, he simply held on to that piece of godforsaken rock in the North Atlantic, until Sir Hugh Rappaport sailed by to save him.

It seemed odd though to Shiro, in his half-drowned stupor. Bull Rock had a hollow tunnel straight through it, and the voice that spoke to him spoke on the other side of the tunnel. Shiro could see the man leaning over a boat looking though the passageway.

"Well, will you look at that?" said the Chief. "The estimable Dr. Shiro Ishii clinging to Bull Rock." Sir Hugh Rappaport was alone in that small outboard, but a sleek yacht was only a hundred yards away.

"How do you know my name?" gasped Ishii.

"We immortals have to stand together. I've known you long and followed you for many decades. The stench of evil is strong about you and even here in the Emerald Isle, I sensed you. Far away it is true, but not so far that I couldn't bide my time and wait for the right moment. Seems to be that time now."

"I would thank you for rescuing me."

"Indeed, you should," said Sir Hugh, "and I can rescue you if you will only swim through the passage. Did you know this islet used to be known as *Tech Duinn*, the Rock of Donn, the House of the Lord of Death. Souls would be taken by the Dark Lord through the passageway to hell. Do you want to go to hell, Shiro Ishii?"

"Who are you?"

"Shhhh. There will be time for introductions. But let me say how proud I am of you!"

"Proud?" said Ishii, not comprehending.

"Yes, proud. No human has ever achieved through science what you have managed to accomplish. It even rivals any magic I have seen. In fact, I have a proposition for you. Would you like to meld your science with my magic? I can offer you power unimaginable, and you can help me change the world."

"There is no magic."

"But there is, good doctor. Your Emperor gave you a taste of it long ago, and it has made you vigorous and strong."

"What must I do to gain this power? What will I owe you? My allegiance is and always has been to His Imperial Highness."

Sir Hugh's eyes narrowed, and his smile grew cold. "I will forget you said that because you do not yet know me very well. And I am sure I will eventually change your mind. All you have to do to is swear loyalty to me as well. Just swim through the passageway here at *Tech Duinn,* while you look into my Eye."

Shiro Ishii had thought the man had merely misspoke, but he saw no harm looking into Rappaport's eyes. The man could not conceive what loyalty to the Emperor truly meant.

The Japanese doctor swam the passage while he gazed into the Irish chieftain's eyes. But only for a moment. The face of Sir Hugh Rappaport blurred before Ishii's vision and something strange happened to his savior's forehead. The skin began to move and twist as if some living thing moved deep within.

"Think nothing of it," whispered Rappaport. "Just look. Just see."

And as he swam, Ishii did look, and he saw. The skin began to break apart and leak blood, and Sir Hugh reached up and tore the skin away, again and again. To Ishii's horror and amazement there was a living thing beneath. It was an Eye, but like no eye he had ever seen. It moved with malice and darkness and pierced deep within the doctor's brain. The more Ishii looked the more fascinated he became. He felt Sir Hugh's hands on him, dragging him into the boat, but he could not stop looking at the Eye.

The Eye drew him in and began to impart knowledge. What it revealed was indeed familiar to him. Emotions sparked his nerves. Feelings he hadn't experienced since he stood before the Emperor and since he performed the experiments at Unit 731 churned in his stomach. A kinship grew between the orb and himself, but then in black fire, the eye enveloped the totality of Ishii's sight and the doctor knew this was not kinship at all.

There was a depth to the depravity before him that he could not duplicate, but it did not make him shrink away. He saw possibilities he never conceived before and felt the invitation to be a part of something new, a changing of the world into a reality decadent and grotesque. Black fire again, consuming his mind, and as he stared at the Eye he knew beyond a doubt that an endless night drew close. He fell to his knees in that boat and worshipped the fear and shadow that loomed before him. Sir Hugh held his new friend close, there on the other side of Bull Rock at the end of the passageway that sinners entered on their way to hell.

BACK AT THE *SKELLIG*

CONOR AND MICHAEL said little the rest of the way to Ballinskelligs. When the pub was in sight, Michael whispered into the ear of Brian and the horse, with each step he took, began to transform. The wings retracted, and the body shrunk. The luminous white coat once again became dusty brown.

Michael broke the silence, "It won't do any good for folk to be wondering why Malby looked all grand and wonderful. The disguise is necessary."

"What about Troubles?" asked Conor. "He's so big, he's bound to cause wonderment."

"Perhaps, but with him it's a little easier." Turning to the dog, Michael said, "Brave one, you must remain in possession of your powers at all times. I can cast a glamour over you that will somewhat bewitch those who see you. But, Conor, make no mistake, people will still see Troubles as a large and noble beast. You better have a story to tell about him. But hear me well. He never leaves your side unless absolutely necessary."

Conor nodded and put his arm around the dog's neck. "By my side, forever."

Rustling in the back of the caravan told the three that the rest were waking. Sure enough, Phil poked her head out the front and said, "Home yet? I can't tell you how starved I am."

Conor laughed and said, "Better talk to your Mom about that. I'm a piss-poor cook."

"I heard that," snapped Moira, "and as soon as I get my hair pinned up, I'll be out and about. But I'm shooing three vagrants out to you now."

From the back of the wagon descended Lettie, Kevin Bard and Tom Shandy, looking remarkably well after their ordeal.

The Shandyman stretched and said to no one in particular, "Doubt much whether we're going to be able to tell the pub crawlers about what we've been doing this past night."

"You think?" said Lettie, pulling out her pipe and packing it with a bit of tobacco, lighting up for a smoke.

"Got to call Mary and Laura and check on Da," said Kevin, reaching for his cell phone. "They must be powerfully worried."

Each were busy with their concerns but Conor saw Michael drift back and walk into the bracken. Before he disappeared, he gave Conor a slight smile. The boy nearly spoke to ask where he was going, but then he realized that his guardian would be back when there was need.

Breakfast at the pub was as good as Moira had ever made and they talked little about what had happened. Then Moira spoke up. "Don't want any of you, especially you Phil, to get all talky and spill what happened at the holy well. We've walked both worlds and you know what that means."

"We're teched," said Lettie.

Phil laughed and said, "You've been teched in the head for quite a while, everybody says so."

Lettie harrumphed and blew smoke at the girl and the tension lessened as Moira's point was made.

Kevin shoveled breakfast in faster than the others, stood up and said, "I've got to take the caravan back to Cahersiveen and pick up my family. Mary says Laura's ok but Da is still pretty broken up over Ma's death. I'll bring them all back here as soon as they're able. Got a feeling we aren't done with all of this yet."

Everyone silently nodded in agreement as Kevin left. Moira took charge of those left telling Phil and Tom to do the dishes and Lettie to clean the tables. "And Conor," she said, "get that beast out of my pub and meet me out back. I need a few words with you."

Conor and Troubles waited for Moira by a broken down shed a few yards from the back of the pub. When she appeared, she was drying her hands on a fresh apron. Conor was afraid she was angry, but a smile appeared on her face as she brushed away a loose strand of black hair.

"I have to admit," she said, "you have been the most exciting guest I have ever hosted, even when compared with Michael. Can't say I mind the hurly-burly and all. Sometimes Ballinskelligs is so quiet even the dead stop haunting we who remain. It wasn't always like this. Ten years ago, developers were everywhere. Ireland was booming with the tech revolution and we were supposed to be part of the great expansion. That's what they called it. Then the bottom fell out of the economy. You saw those beautiful homes scattered all over the outskirts of town. All empty, none sold. What the speculators expected never happened. Our greed was our own death. And now we hang on, as the Irish have ever done. And then you come along, with all your mystery. A drowned man comes to life. Legends appear to persecute us all. The richest and most powerful man in the country suddenly finds this area interesting, and everyone with an Irish soul who was about here last night or at the well knew, whether they could explain it or not, that this world and another were merging together and change was coming, change like we've never seen before." A sadness crossed her face. "I'm not sure it's going to be a good change, Conor. And I fear for my daughter."

"I know," Conor said quietly. "Wherever I have been these past few months, I seem to have brought sorrow, hurt and even death. I'm so sorry I ever got you, your family and your friends into this."

"No, no, no!" said Moira reaching out a tentative hand to brush his shoulder. "Don't misunderstand me. I've got a good sense of people. I run the pub you know. And you ... well you are not the problem. In fact, I welcome you here. At times I look at you and you are just a boy, but last night, you were something else. There is something powerfully noble about you, Conor Archer, and I'm just glad to have you around."

Troubles woofed a low agreement. Moira laughed. "And though he's all full of hair and slobber, I'm glad he's here too." Troubles held his head high and looked away pretending to be offended, but then trotted over and slopped a kiss on Moira's face.

She laughed again, "Don't take liberties with me you rascal. Just take care of the boy so I can get a little peace here and there these next few days."

"What's happening?" asked Conor.

"Well, we have a *celidh* on Saturday night—that's a night of music and *craic*—you know, fun—down at the village hall. Everyone will be there playing instruments, singing and dancing, and I've got to organize it. You and the others in the pub can help. And then, Tralee is having their Winter Festival this weekend. I know, it isn't even winter yet, but it's just like us Irish to have it now and talk about the memories when it gets colder and darker. Keeps us going till spring."

"But," said Conor, "the things that happened here last night—won't the people be freaked, scared out of their ever-lovin' minds? I mean, how can they celebrate at all?"

"Don't know us very well, do you?" said Moira. "You won't hear a public peep about what happened. Maybe some whispering in the pub, lots of talking in houses with doors and windows closed. But publicly? It'll be as if it never happened. We Irish are a chattering bunch, but the world doesn't believe in the *faerie* realm, and most folks outside the island think we are all a bit daft. Besides, so many new folk in the land don't know our traditions. We don't talk much in front of others about what we know to be true: that there are things that go bump in the night and can reach out a claw from the darkness and grab the unwary one or the unbeliever. The folk of this land may not even talk to you, Conor, not because you are an outsider but because you have the smell of *faerie* upon you. The Otherworld lies deep in you, and everyone here can sense it. Don't be offended; they will be grateful for the good you did and will do, those who know of it. One thing will happen— they'll be real friendly to you and you will probably never have to buy another Guinness here again."

"Ma!" yelled Phil from the door. "The ladies are here to go down to the hall. They want you there."

Moira winked at Conor, "We've got two days yet and you think the *celidh* was just in a few hours."

"Can I help?" he asked.

"Absolutely," she said. "You and the Shandyman and Phil can move tables and clean up the place. They always leave it in a mess, and I won't have the party of the year taking place in a pigsty. So says Moira, proprietress of The *Skellig*." With that she bussed a kiss on Conor's cheek and went back inside.

A CONVERSATION IN THE BRACKEN

Thursday Morning, 11/5, Ballinskelligs

MICHAEL SAW HER up ahead perched in the empty hollow of an old shrine ensconced in a tumbledown stone wall.

"How in the world did you get here so fast?" said Michael with a smile.

Fluttering her eyes, Lettie said, "I have my secret ways Ranger of the Heavens."

"Few have called me that in centuries," said Michael.

"Yet, that is what you are, and I'll have a word with you if you don't mind."

Michael lifted himself up on the old stone wall and said, "When has my permission ever been needed with you?"

"What happened last night made it real for me. This world is ending isn't it?"

"So it seems," said Michael.

"Pretty complacent about it all, don't you think?" said Lettie.

"All things pass, little one."

"I'm not so little and I'm certainly not young."

"Ah," said Michael, "the *fae* are so touchy."

"Thousands of years, Michael. That's how long I've walked this land. Maybe I didn't see your compatriots fall from the sky, driven by your steed and Sword, but I'm almost that old."

"Haven't aged a day since," laughed Michael.

She blew smoke in his face. "We met on the *machair* just there above the beach. Remember?"

"Yes, Lettie, you were torturing a hobgoblin."

"I was teaching him respect," she said. Michael lifted an eyebrow. "Well, perhaps I was a bit rough, but they were all over the place then, after your folk came around."

"But we sorted it, didn't we?"

"Aye," said Lettie, "that we did. But this merging that's happening—the Archer boy is responsible?"

"Not responsible, but indispensable. It can't happen without him." Michael shrugged his shoulders. "The Otherworld has been separated too long from this reality. Now both are dying. They were meant to be together. The Great Divide that happened so long ago didn't benefit either world. Now they must come together or both realities cease. But it matters how it is done. Conor represents all that is good in both worlds. And his talents are many. As a shapeshifter, he adjusts to either reality, and is at home in both. As human, he can reign and rule. As *Roan*, he can gather all creatures and even the elements into harmony. But he is not strong enough yet. And you know humans; they bend like reeds in the wind. I am not sure he will stand true. He has many enemies, including the oldest foe in this land."

"Balor of the Evil Eye," whispered Lettie.

"Aye," said Michael looking out towards the ocean. "And Balor is just as vicious as he always was."

"Then take him out," said the *fae*, "just like you struck the Ancient One so long ago."

"It is forbidden. This world and its perfect complement, the Otherworld, belong to humans and those creatures like yourself who were made to live here or there. The battle with Balor is yours, not mine. But I need not be absent. There is room for wisdom, and a guiding hand."

"Humph!" blustered Lettie. "So, you have a front row seat for the action, but can't do much but laugh or cry at the performance."

"Cynical, even for you, Lettie."

"I care about these people, about this land," she said. "Most everything lives but a breath of time here, but what they live is precious to them. We can't simply let them fend for themselves."

Michael smiled a sad smile, "You will have your part to play since you are so anxious for the fray. And I won't let any of you be alone. But the outcome, at least in the short term, is yet to be determined."

She puffed on her pipe and held a silence for some moments. Then she looked at him and said, "Amergin suffered a grievous blow yesterday. Will he recover?"

"I think not," said Michael. "Amergin and his wife loved each other deeply, and the Travelers held them in honor for centuries. The Bard of the West must fade as many good things will in the change that is to come."

"But who will sing for us, Michael? Who will sing for the people and for the land?"

"Amergin will decide, before he leaves us. Don't fret so. We are not simply surrendering to the inevitable."

With that, Michael stepped back as he rose up in the air hovering ten feet above the ancient Lettie. "Show off," she said, and then, she shrunk into a little ball that began to whirl, a blue sphere with motes of light circling around her.

"A finer wisp I have never seen," said Michael, and he raised his head as wings unfurled, and he shot heavenward over the Ballinskelligs headland. The will-o-the-wisp followed him swiftly in the sky.

Anyone on the ship named *Baleros* would not have been able to see them, for a dark mist covered the ship again as it anchored on the west side of Skellig Michael.

"What do you suppose they are doing?" said Michael hovering high above the ship. The wisp, cupped in Michael's hand, glowed more brightly.

"Aye," said Michael, "it's a filthy mist alright. Even I cannot see through it. But I cannot have Balor dropping anchor and digging for gold on the ocean floor right in front of my own outpost. You up for a look see?"

The wisp didn't even respond but simply floated above Michael's hand and then dropped like a stone towards the ship. The wisp had seen much in her time, but the black fog that enveloped the vessel and surrounding ocean was something new and dangerous. She had always been fearless and so was more curious than afraid. Yet the moment she plunged into darkness she halted her descent. She heard not a sound, and so she let herself drift slowly downward hoping anything in the mist was as blind as she. Compressing herself and dimming her light as much as she could, she drifted for a minute and then suddenly the mist was gone and a ship full of lights glimmered below her. There were hundreds of men working on the deck. Some huge project was going on, and now she could hear a thrumming coming from beneath the center of the deck. Darting down a hatchway, she made her way through the depths of the ship, hiding behind the myriad of pipes and tubes towards the noise and found what she was seeking.

There, in front of her was a mining drill, busily punching a hole into the sea floor and taking samples. She saw the test plugs and began bobbing up and down in excitement. In the dim light, their golden glow was unmistakable. The Chief had been right. There was gold in *Skellig* Michael.

Down by the drill, Sir Hugh Rappaport was checking with one of the engineers on the progress of the drilling. Suddenly, his nostrils twitched and he lifted his head, letting his eyes rove over the room. He felt that he was being spied upon but no unauthorized person was down by the drill with him. And then he saw her. Not quite sure what she was yet, but he smiled a toothy grin, cocked his finger like a gun and pointed it at her, pressing his thumb like it was a trigger.

"Got you babe," he said, and pushed his thumb forward. But no invisible gun fired, no sound came forth, no shadowy bullet flew. Instead, a third eye opened on his forehead, bloodshot crimson, pupil pulsing, and from that hideous orb spewed out a black, inky nothingness that flew forth from his head toward the little wisp, high in the corner of the room.

She didn't wait. Fast as she could move, the wisp zipped out the hatch she had used to slip in. At first, she thought she had escaped, but the inky blackness followed her, like an ocular torpedo, and it rushed through the hatchway, up the stairs following her to the deck.

Never had the wisp moved so swiftly. She had caught a whiff of the snake-like shadow and was reintroduced to the smell of corruption and all things foul and dead.

Reaching the deck, she did not pause but shot up through the mist toward where she thought Michael might be waiting. Almost free, she thought, but then she looked back. Out of the blackness following her, dark as the night, there exploded hundreds of black and white gannets, snapping their yellow bills in the air as if they were diving for fish. Their blue eyes flashed not toward the sea but to the wisp above them, now only slightly in front of the pursuing flock.

She did not think she'd make it. Through the mist enveloping the ship, she flew, higher and higher. Suddenly, she burst into the sunshine, gannets right behind, and she issued a mental scream to Michael—and he was there. Eclipsing the sun, shining with his own light, brandishing a trident, he was there and he enfolded her with his other arm. The trident pointed down at the gannets now swirling below.

"Get you gone, birds of the Eye. You have no power here. Back to your master who waits below you." The trident flashed bright, and the gannets screamed as one and fell senseless back into the mist. But the whirling shadow which had brought them swirled more fiercely and in its darkness an Eye appeared.

"So," said Michael, "you are back to harry humanity. You were defeated before. It can happen again. Come abroad this openly again, and I will smite you myself. Bring terror upon the ones I guard, and you shall feel the might of the heavens once more. Now, out of my sight, and away from my island. This is no place for you. Begone!"

It seemed to the wisp that a bright light flew down into the whirling blackness and though no shout of pain was heard, the wisp felt the atmosphere shudder as the shadow withdrew, back into the ship.

Michael looked down at the wisp in his cupped hand and smiled. "Enough for today, Lettie?" The wisp pulsed in gratitude. "Then let's go home," he said, "and you can tell me all about your visit to *Baleros*. I want to know everything that's going on upon that vessel."

ON *BALEROS*

Thursday Morning, 11 / 5, Anchored off Skellig Michael

THE DARK SHADOW snapped back upon Sir Hugh's face like an iron hammer. Giving a shriek, he fell like a stone. The sailors around the drill rushed to his side, but the man was unconscious. The first mate shouted for one of the underlings to get Shiro Ishii from his cabin.

It took several minutes, but when Ishii arrived, Sir Hugh was just regaining consciousness.

"What happened?" said Ishii. "Who did this to you?"

"We had a visitor," said Sir Hugh. "Just a wisp of a one, but she saw what she shouldn't see, and I almost had her. I chased her as far as I could and reached out to clutch her in my grasp, and then ... and then ..." He coughed and spat as he tried to stand up. "And then, someone else was there, someone I haven't seen for a long time. I was ... unready for him. He snatched the spy and dared raise his hand against me."

"Are you injured?" said Ishii.

"Just my pride," smirked Sir Hugh, "but I have enough of that to go around."

"What are we going to do?"

"First we move away from here. My adversary is powerful and I do not want to fight him so close to his place of strength."

"Who is he?" asked Ishii. "Why have I not heard of him before?"

"He is not your concern. I have a different task for you rather than fight a being I should have destroyed myself long, long ago. I want you to mount an assault on Ballinskelligs."

Ishii laughed. "Sir Hugh, it's just a tiny village. What harm can it cause us? Besides, I'm busy with our Tralee strike."

"My enemies and yours are there or will be soon. You've already met two of them, that boy with the Sword and Conor Archer. More are gathering. In two day's time, a *celidh* will be held and they will all be together. You can act where I cannot. Use your science and the magic given to you by your

Emperor and me and bring pestilence among them. I will send you a helper, the *Dearg Due*, "The Red Thirst", and you can have your way with all of them so they cannot interfere."

He reached into his pocket, pulled out what looked to be an ancient map on parchment, all the writing in Celtic script. "Take this, use it and find her. Bring her to Ballinskelligs. Take her to Tralee, and together destroy them all."

Shiro Ishii glanced at the parchment, bowed to Sir Hugh and rushed up to the deck, shouting to be carried to shore.

I am not myself, thought Sir Hugh. Then he laughed. Hadn't been for quite some time. The Other that lived in him had never manifested itself so blatantly before. But he felt its power and its promise to him. Lately, he had thought himself losing touch with his own personality. Dreams and even daytime musings seemed to belong to the Other. The bargain was clear. He would have to surrender himself, but he would keep his personality and share in the power. The Other had not walked the earth for millennia, and Sir Hugh had both the public position and wealth that made him irresistible to that entity. Sharing personal space was disconcerting, but both sensed the twinning was worth the effort, because their power was growing and soon the Other could be revealed.

A LITTLE NIGHT MUSIC

Thursday Evening, 11/5, Portmagee

JACE HAD SPENT part of Thursday afternoon catching up on sleep after the violent meeting with Shiro Ishii. He, along with Colly, had been invited up to Fr. Greavy's rectory after dinner for a further explanation from the priest as to what was going on.

Colly appeared in the reception room of the hotel just as Jace was finishing dinner. There was mist rising and the fog made their footsteps echo as they walked through the lane towards the cleric's house. Far away, came the howl of a wolf, and both stopped at the haunting cry.

"I didn't know Ireland had any wolves," said Jace.

Colly shivered in the damp, "Not for hundreds of years. Maybe we heard wrong. The mist does weird things with sound."

Just then, there were several answering howls from different directions.

"They sound like they're getting closer," said Jace.

"Can't be," said Colly. "There just aren't any in the land."

"Don't know about that," said Jace. "After the few things I've seen in the day I've been here, I wouldn't be so quick to doubt. I didn't tell you what happened to me on the way to your town just before I met you this morning." With that, Jason talked about the Holy Well and the mysterious St. Ita.

"You're kidding, right?" said Colly. "I mean, my dad always told me to respect those old holy places, but I sort of do it out of tradition not real belief."

"Better change that hands-off policy toward legend," said Jace. "I have a feeling; things are happening above our pay grade."

A snuffling in the bracken to their right caused them to stop.

"Hear that?" asked Colly, fear creeping into his voice for the first time.

"Yep," said Jace, as another snuffle to the left caught their ears. The lane was clear of mist and Jace made an instant decision. "Don't run; just walk like we know what we're doing, and we'll see what happens."

Colly's wiry frame fairly bounced on the roadway. "I'll fake it, but I won't feel it."

They were quiet then as they walked, the rustling in the bracken following them but nothing appearing on the road. They soon saw the priest's house ahead, and both sighed with relief until several howls broke close around them.

The doorway opened and Fr. Greavy stuck out his head. "Get yourselves in here, lads, the land's children are singing the music of the night."

Both boys didn't hesitate and breathed a sigh of relief as the door closed behind them.

Jace looked carefully at the priest and said, "You don't seem surprised to hear the howling of wolves."

"No, I'm not," said Fr. Greavy. "If Colly ever picked up a newspaper, he could have told you that there have been reports of a return of wolves to Ireland. Nobody knows where they come from, they've been gone so long. Somebody imported them, they say. But those that have seen them describe animals bigger than regular wolves. Dire wolves perhaps or some wolf-dog hybrid perhaps."

The priest chuckled as he led them into the sitting room, motioning them to take a chair in front of a peat burning fire. He looked at them through his wire-rimmed glasses and his pudgy face broke into a knowing smile. "Nobody knows, say the media. But I know. They come from the Otherworld."

Colly snorted in derision. "Father Greavy stop telling those children's tales. Otherworld stuff and all—you really don't believe that?"

"Of course, I do," said the priest. "Strange things have been happening throughout the country these past few months. Stories out of legend coming true, so the ordinary folk that remember the old stories say. I agree with them as to why. It's the Otherworld. That reality behind the one which we all see. It's been coming closer to this world and touching it every once in a while. When that happens, there is a break between the worlds, particularly at the thin places like Holy Wells, pagan sites, churches and such."

"But why?" asked Colly, slouching in one of the chairs. "Why would such things be happening now?"

"Because both worlds are dying," whispered Jace. Fr. Greavy raised an eyebrow in surprise. "I don't mean to get all 'end of the world' on you," said Jace in apology. "But I know something about this. My friend, Conor Archer—my friend who I have to find—has got something to do with that merger. He's in danger and I promised I'd stand with him. That's why I'm here."

"What do you mean, 'dying?'" said Colly.

"Come on, Colly," snorted the priest. "Surely, you've seen what's been happening throughout our land. The old ways are gone. The sense of 'something else present' that Ireland has always been famous for is just leeching away. Our people, seduced by the newest tech, the latest rave, and now the newest designer drug are so much less than they were. Have you ever seen people in the midst of a RAGE experience?"

"No," said Colly. "Just heard about it. I mean it's just a drug."

"No, it's not," said the priest. "It's something different. Oh, it will test out as a designer drug, but something intangible got added to it. It makes those who take it into demons. There's only one man on the island who could have made it so popular and could corral the business side of it. You met his associate today and saw that man's ship."

Colly gasped, "Sir Hugh? He's behind RAGE?"

"Aye, lad, it's my thought that he is. He brings a rot to this island that sinks into the very stones."

"I'd never heard of him till this morning," said Jace. "But I've got to tell you Colly, what Fr. Greavy says rings true. There's a pall over this land, and I know it's got something to do with me and Conor." Looking at both of them, he said, "Sorry, I didn't tell you what I knew when we met earlier."

The priest smiled again, "But you didn't have to, Jason Michaels. Malachy told me all about you and Conor. He's kept me up to date over the past few months."

Colly looked back and forth at both of them. "I don't get it. How could you possibly know about Jace? And who's this Malachy guy?"

That's how Jace began to relate the story of his and Conor's adventures, and especially what the last week had brought upon them. Fr. Greavy added a few details, but Jace did most of the talking as Colly sat there, mouth agape.

"I can't believe all that's happened," said Jace, "and now we have supernatural wolves on our ass. I don't know what to do."

The fire merrily burned in the hearth, the peat spreading a homey smell of comfort throughout the room. But the lights were dim and the atmosphere became heavy and almost dreamlike. Colly and Jace both yawned.

"No sleep for you yet, lads," whispered the priest. "They're here."

And at the edges of the room, shadows began to appear. Large, inhuman things. Dark they were, but gradually they took shape and as they stepped forward Jace and Colly hissed in fear. Around them stood seven huge wolves, their golden eyes gleaming.

"Ah," said Fr. Greavy, "I wouldn't move if I were you. They don't want us dead or that would have happened already. I thought they might pay us a visit though. When I saw you this morning, Jace, I knew you had been touched by the Otherworld. The Sword you carry—ah yes, I can see it—has not been in this land for millennia. And you know things that no seventeen-year-old should. Malachy told me about that. I just didn't believe him until I saw and heard you for myself."

He stopped for a moment as the wolves panted, saliva falling from their mouths. Then two of the beasts moved forward. The Alpha male and female. They made their way in front of the fire, turned and faced the three. They were as huge as the Dire wolves of old, and there was a feral intelligence in their eyes that Jace had not seen in animals before, except for the newly re-born Troubles.

Fr. Greavy looked solemn as he said, "You are welcome here."

The pair slightly bowed their heads in acknowledgement as the priest continued.

"I am sorry you have been ripped from your world where green things grow and the hunting is good. But you are needed here, and you know that even the Otherworld is not spared the slow death of decay. Yet, when you stepped through the rift—that broken space in the middle of the glade where you love to run—the balance in this deadly game of chance shifted slightly toward the direction of the Light."

The female Alpha whined in question.

"I know," said the priest. "But you've felt it yourself—another world, this one as a matter of fact, drawing close to yours. But your experience is different from ours. We sense beauty, majesty, a richness never divined here. But you—I see the hackles raised—you sense only decay, death and destruction among us. And you are right. The boy named Conor Archer is not here tonight, but his Champion is. Conor set the worlds moving together faster than has ever happened before, and it's fortuitous that he did. Nobody but a few expected this. He is a force of nature that seeks to unify that which was broken long ago. I believe there is another, an old demon who once styled himself a god, who lives within both realms, who has long been moving the worlds back together for his own dark purpose. I assure you it is not for the sake of unity. It is not for the sake of making things whole once again.

"There are good Irishmen that remember the name of Balor Evil Eye and shy from it, but this being did not reckon on the boy or that lad's power. Balor has little fear, but what he does have has begun to tickle the back of his evil mind. Conor is the unknown, and Balor will move swiftly now to head off any possible problem.

"This is where you come in, children of the night. I cannot see the future, but everything portends to a crisis coming to our land very soon, and somewhere near where we are this evening. You can range over miles swift and unseen. I ask you to do so, seeking out that which is unnatural and evil. If any people of this land are involved, stop them and save them if you can. But if not, defend the good against those who would destroy even unto death, yours or theirs. I, Greavy, give you this task. Take and accept your part in redemption."

The Alpha pair moved close to Greavy as he stood before his chair. They were nearly as tall as he and both licked his face. Then one by one, all the wolves came forward and did the same. Jace sat still as a sphinx and Colly couldn't press himself more tightly into his chair, but they were not unnoticed. The Alpha male turned and looked at both of them and spoke. The words were low, almost a growl, and barely understood, "Champion—you and your companion here shall meet us again when we are in desperate need. You fear us now, but when we next see each other, we will need your help. Do not desert us in our fateful hour."

"We won't," said Jace.

"What?" said Colly. "What the hell are you saying?"

"Shut up, Colly," said Jace. "If they need us, we'll be there."

The wolf nodded in acknowledgment as Colly spluttered in outrage. "Don't you be promising for me."

Jace smiled a sad smile at him. "Sorry about that. But if the world needs you, where are you going to hide from it? I'm new around here, but you'd stand with me, right?"

Colly shook his head. "I'm surrounded by wolves, a crazy priest, and someone who thinks he's Sir Lancelot. I'm not in a position to say no."

"Well," said Jace, "that's done then. Welcome to our little company."

Without another sound, the wolves backed toward the walls, blended with the shadows and were gone.

Fr. Greavy cocked an eyebrow at Jace and Colly, "A spot more tea perhaps? Just to take away the evening chill."

Jace and the priest burst out laughing and even Colly joined in smiling a rueful smile.

DOWN BY THE DOCK

Thursday Night, 11/5, Portmagee

JACE AND COLLY walked back to *The Foam and Fin* hotel under a sea of shining stars, the Hand of God nebula burning high in the sky. Stifling a yawn, Jace looked at Colly and said, "I'm bushed. I think I'll turn in. See you tomorrow?"

"You bet," said Colly. "It really was great to meet you, and I'm glad you'll be around for a while. Haven't had this kind of adventure in a long time."

Jace laughed. "That's me. Always fun, never boring. Catch you in the morning."

With a handshake they parted. Colly watched him go into the hotel and a strange look, almost of pity, came over him. He sighed and walked the short journey down to the dock to make sure the boat was secure. Such a quiet night. Usually the waves slapped loudly against the quay, but tonight they were just a muted plash against the old concrete. Except something was in the water. It lifted its head to stare at Colly who managed a little smirk.

"Scatha," he said. "You're out late."

A seal head bobbed up and down, limpid eyes staring at him silently.

"What?" said Colly. "Lobster got your tongue?"

The seal bobbed under the water and what surfaced next was a woman with long raven hair and a mischievous smile.

"Shifter," she said in greeting.

Colly scowled. "I told you before, don't call me that."

"But you are a Changeling. What else should I call you?"

"Not anymore," he said, his voice growing louder.

"Shh," she said *sotto voce*. "You will wake your new friend."

He glanced up toward the hotel and saw Jace's second floor room light blink off.

"Doubtful," he said. "It was a stressful day for us."

"Does he know what you are?"

"Of course. I'm Hercules Columba Roddy, son of Joe Roddy. I've lived here all my life."

"Not all your life."

"Most of it."

"The Roddy's real child was a still birth, and someone replaced it with you, a whelp from the Otherworld."

"That's a cold way of putting it, even for you," sneered Colly. "But whatever was placed in that crib changed the day I was baptized. I wasn't rejected, and they think I'm as human as anything else."

"But I know differently." Scatha leapt gracefully out of the water and stood with her long hair modestly draping around her. "You are a Shifter. Always have been and always will be."

"So are you," he snapped. "Seal spawn."

"Temper, temper," she cooed, caressing his cheek with her long fingers, the webbing on her hand still glistening with seawater. "But I am not a Changeling. I am *Roan*, and I needed to see what you thought of our visitor."

"He's strong," said Colly. "And kind, and single-minded about this Conor Archer fellow. His best friend he says. In some kind of trouble and here on the island."

"Oh, I know all about Conor Archer," said Scatha, and told him what had happened the day before.

"Things are happening then," said Colly. "Everything we've prepared for is moving to its climax. I'm not going to betray Jace, if that's what you're worried about. He's an ally I think, and so's the priest. How that man has never figured out who I really am is beyond me."

"We've got problems, though," he continued. "Big ones. That katana weaving douche bag you saw this morning visited us at noon. He's in league with Sir Hugh, and there's something about Hugh Rappaport that's not quite right. When we hazed his vessel, it seemed like a shadow of a true ship, like it wasn't completely in this reality. He's not what he seems, and Shiro Ishii, powerful as he is, is himself but a weak shadow in Sir Hugh's wake. Didn't like confronting Ishii. I dare say the captain of *Baleros* will be even more trouble."

Scatha looked at him quizzically. "What do you suggest we do?"

Colly said, "The wolves came tonight. Up at the priest's house. Smart creatures they are. Didn't reveal who I was. I was surprised to see them here so soon. I was up at Killorglin the other day and walked out to *Mac Tire* Rock and put the marker out in the cleft of that stone. It's a path to the Otherworld and the wolves check it regularly. They've known I've been here for years. When I was younger, I often ran with them. Not here of course, but in their realm. Yet, they still recognized me tonight. If they are here, our time is short. Great evil is about."

"It is already here," said Scatha. "What Ishii did to the Tinkers—releasing the plague and all—I've never seen anything so contagious and deadly. It was all I could do to save Conor from Ishii's attempt to take his life as well."

"What's he like?" asked Colly. "Is Archer the One?"

"I don't know. I think so. But he's so young. He can shift. He has power, but little knowledge how to use it. Yet there's something in him so deep. It is destiny, I think. It hangs on him like a king's robe. He wears it well."

"Keep an eye on him, Scatha. We'll try to hook up with him tomorrow. Jace has got the scent and I don't think I can keep him on my boat investigating the coves and beaches of Portmagee. He's on a search for his friend, so I best keep him pointed in the right direction."

"Going to tell him who you are?" asked Scatha.

"Not a chance. My people don't have a very good reputation with humans."

"Thought you were claiming a bond with them," teased Scatha.

Colly's face darkened, "I'm more like them than I was. So, get off my back, Seal spawn."

Scatha laughed and leapt high. Before she slipped into the sea, she whispered to him, "Later, Shifter."

Colly spat into the water. "Feckin' witch," he said. Then he turned and saw two wolves in the shadow of the ticket house staring at him with gold flecked eyes. For some reason, he felt embarrassed. "Sorry," he said. "She just gets to me sometimes. But you ..." He walked over to them and ruffled the fur of the Alpha male and female. "It was so good to see you tonight. After all these years. Thanks for not showing the priest and Jace that you knew me. Can you feel it? We're coming into our own. This world has yet to see what we can do." He paused and looked at the slowly rising moon. "You know, the night is still pretty young. Want to go running?" He quirked his left eyebrow high and both wolves yipped softly.

Anyone looking down at the quay would have seen a man talking to shadows. But then that human would seem to mist and shift in the night. By the time anyone had really focused their eyes, he would be gone and a huge wolf would be standing there, and not alone. Two others like him walked by his side. Pausing for a moment, they lifted their heads to the shining stars and howled a cry that coursed through the fields, there by the side of the sea. A cry that was answered.

In the blink of an eye, they were gone, at least to the casual observer. But the land took notice of their presence. The rabbits and the nesting birds saw them too. They did not fear their nearness. So other was that pack, that the animals and the earth itself knew they were hunting for different forms of life, stuff that seldom lived in this reality. Most people only heard them in their dreams, as the wolves of the Otherworld did the rounds of County Kerry, making sure that the dread they feared would not come upon the land that night.

TOWARD A NEW ALLIANCE

Friday Morning, 11/6, Portmagee to Ballinskelligs

"MRS. FINN," SAID Colly, standing in the reception area of the hotel holding his fisherman's cap in his hands, "would you think that Jace is up yet? I told him I would stop early in the morning."

The proprietress of the establishment smiled and stood on her toes to ruffle Colly's brown and blond streaked curls. He couldn't help smiling in affection back at her. She had always been kind to him, when others had not. She and his mother were fast friends.

"He's in the dining room finishing breakfast. Why don't you join him for a moment and I'll bring you a plate."

"Thanks ma'am," said Colly and strode into the dining room to find Jace shoveling the last of an omelet into his mouth.

"Oh my God," said Jace, "she cooks the best food I've ever tasted!"

Colly laughed and sat down saying, "Glad you're almost done. I was wondering if you'd like to go salmon fishing this morning. Whatever we catch we can bring back to Mrs. Finn. They're biting up the river, so I hear."

Jace paused. "I don't know," he said slowly. "I was kind of hoping to tour some of the nearby towns and see if I can find my friend, Conor."

"We can do that, sure," said Colly, "but first, wouldn't you like to see if you could catch dinner for tonight?"

Jace smiled, "Yeah, of course. But only for a little while, okay?"

Colly smiled, jumped up, turned and planted a fast kiss on Mrs. Finn's cheek as she placed a plate of food down. "Got to go," he said, stuffing some toast with marmalade into his mouth. "We're getting dinner for you and your guests tonight." He moved out of the room with Jace close behind as Mrs. Finn shook her head, exasperated with the boys.

Colly had borrowed his dad's car and quickly drove to a place where he promised Jace the salmon were biting. They put out into the water on a small boat, their rain slickers handling the early morning mist and chill. Two hours later, they had a great catch, easily enough for the hotel's chef to make a feast.

Driving back, they had to pass Fr. Greavy's house and found him at the edge of the road as if waiting just for them. In fact, he was. As Colly parked, the priest stepped over to the driver's side after Colly lowered the window.

"See you were fishing," noted the priest. Without waiting for an answer, he said, "I've got a proposition for you. I can see by your faces you've got a successful catch so let's go give Mrs. Finn half the share and take the rest down Ballinskelligs' way to the pub and give it to Moira. I'm telling you this because I have it on good report that Jace's friend Conor might be there. We should check, and I don't doubt there will be friends to meet and adventures to be had." He winked and smiled. "What do you say lads? Up for some fun?"

Colly and Jace looked at each other and laughed, not unkindly, but the idea of the portly little priest offering them adventures was rather funny. But Colly smiled and said, "Get in, Father, and let's see what the day will bring."

After dropping off the fish at Jace's hotel, they sped over the roads towards Ballinskelligs. About three miles from the town, they saw someone walking in the same direction—a little old lady, thought Jace, moving as fast as Aunt Emily always seemed to do.

Colly stopped the car, but it was the priest who stuck his head out the window and said, "Lettie? Lettie Sporn? What in the world are you doing walking the country road this cold morning?"

Lettie smiled at the priest. "Well if it isn't the good Fr. Greavy. And two handsome gentlemen as well." She came closer and looked at Colly. "I know you, you're the Shif—"

"Colly's my name, Miss Sporn. You used to tell us kid's stories at the school when I was younger. Remember?"

Lettie squinted her knowing eyes at him, beginning to slowly nod her head. "Ah yes, that must be where I remember you from. And you, young man," she said, smiling a quick smile at Jace. "Just who might you be?"

"Jason Michaels—Jace for short. From the USA. Over here looking for a friend of mine. Conor Archer's his name. He'd be new here, but I know he's in the area."

"'Course I know Conor," said Lettie. "Just met him yesterday. Good lad as well. You're lucky you nearly ran into me." She scowled at Colly. "I happen to know where he is. Give me a ride and I'll take you right to him."

Jace whooped and Fr. Greavy got out of the car to usher in the old woman. In less than fifteen minutes, they were pulling up to the *Skellig* Pub. "I think," she said to the three travelers, "you'll find him in there."

A FUNERAL AT THE FORT

Friday, 11/6, Ballinskelligs

THAT FRIDAY MORNING, Conor woke to the smell of eggs and rashers of bacon wafting up from the kitchen. Taking a quick shower, he dressed and bounded down the stairs, hungry as if he hadn't eaten in a week. His sleep had been dreamless, and he felt amazingly refreshed. Even Troubles had to rush after him to keep up with the young man's race to the dining room.

Phil was already eating, her mouth full of food and quirky hair stuck out all over. It was blue streaked today. She motioned him to join her and he did, a full plate of food suddenly appearing in front of him. Looking up he smiled at Moira's beaming face. "Eat up, lad, and my daughter here will fill you in on what's happening today."

Conor barely heard anything as he ate. Something about finishing the town hall for the *celidh* and sprucing up the empty homes in the development to welcome paying guests who were coming from all around for the Saturday festivities. But he stopped eating when he heard the word "funeral" come out of Phil's mouth.

"What?" he asked. "What did you say?"

"Amergin's wife's funeral will be tonight. It won't be in any church. The Travelers are just not that way. Instead, it's going to be inside *Staigue* Fort up near Castlecove—a little town not far away." Phil's eyes began to dance. "It's going to be freakin' awesome, Conor. Do you know what the fort is?"

Conor shook his head.

"It's a five-thousand-year-old stone ring fort, and Amergin wants the funeral there at sunset tonight. It will be brilliant!" She paused and reflected on her exuberance and calmed herself down. "I mean sad and all too, but really fabulous!"

"Funerals aren't much fun for me. I mean I'll go, but I watched her die and Amergin was so sad. The life just went out of him, and I'm thinking he's not going to be okay."

"I know, Conor. I didn't mean to sound like I didn't have a care for the dead. But it's an extreme place for the burial fire. That's how they'll do it you know. They'll use a caravan, place her and all her favorite things in it, and then torch it. It will burn like a beacon in the night, giving her a grand farewell."

"Grand," said Conor, putting his head down and thinking that the evening would be a sad one indeed.

Just then, the door opened and Lettie walked in. "I've been out and about this November morn and look who I picked up on the road."

Fr. Greavy walked in and Phil and Conor stood to say hello. Moira appeared at the door of the kitchen. But it was Conor who gasped aloud. A boy about his age, with curly brown and blond streaked hair and a fisherman's cap walked in but Conor didn't even notice. Jace was behind him and Conor had a shocked look on his face as if he was seeing an alien. They looked at each other for a moment. Conor felt guilty, seeing his best friend for the first time since *Piasa* had been destroyed and Beth had died. He didn't know what to do. It was Jace that broke the awkward moment. He quirked a smile, strode toward Conor and hugged him hard.

"It's good to see you, man; I mean really good to see you. I just couldn't let you have all the coming fun by yourself."

Conor laughed, seeing that Jace was, well, not as angry as before.

Jace introduced Colly saying, "This here is Hercules Columba Roddy, my new friend, a fine fisherman, and though he doesn't really know it yet, he's helping us in whatever we have to do here."

Colly shook Conor's hand and walked over to Moira with a bundle wrapped in newspaper. "These are for you, Moira. It was good fishing this morning."

Moira was wiping her hands on a cloth. Quickly giving it to Phil, she ruffled Colly's hair, (making him squeak, "Does everybody have to do that?"). "Well you brought me some salmon now. I'll have that cooked for tonight. Aren't you a generous one, Colly Roddy."

"And a real suck-up," said Phil as she placed a kiss on Colly's cheek. "You could have brought flowers," she whispered in his ear.

Embarrassed, Colly muttered, "Your hair is blue."

"Right you are, observant one. As blue as the skies of Ireland when it isn't raining."

Fortunately, Moira had some strong coffee for everyone as Fr. Greavy asked them all to sit.

"I brought the lads here," he said to Conor, "because of you, dear boy."

Jace interrupted, "He knows Malachy, Conor, and the Abbot sent me to find you. Both he and Fr. Greavy think bad things are happening here that we might be able to do something about. And from what I saw at the holy well ..."

"Well," said Conor, "then you know bad stuff is happening. I don't know what it all means, but it's tied up with the Travelers and there's going to be a funeral tonight for the wife of the Traveler Leader. We're going."

"But not," said Moira, "till we get the town hall ready for the *celidh* tomorrow."

Their morning was a busy one and Conor was kept occupied with the preparations for the *celidh*.

"What's with the Japanese lanterns we're hanging on all the light posts of the streets and doorways of these empty houses?" asked Jace.

"It was Mum's idea," said Phil. "The Tralee 'Cherry Blossom' Festival opens this weekend—that's the Winter Festival she was talking about—so we thought we'd carry over the theme for our own celebration. Been planning it for months."

"Phil," said Conor, "it's November; there aren't going to be any cherry blossoms even if the Japanese gave you guys the hardier version of the trees than we have in the U.S. Just the wrong time of year."

"Oh, you might be surprised," smiled Phil. "We Irish are simply stubborn. Tell us we're going into the depths of winter and we will find ourselves something to hope for. This *celidh* is our best shot for a bit of *craic*— you know, fun and stuff—before the winter comes. And we're going to make the best of it, funeral or not."

It was about noon when fifty caravans rumbled slowly through town followed by men on horses and beat-up old cars. A sad thing really. The bright colors of the Travelers' homes seemed faded and washed out under the graying and lowering sky. Black bunting swirled around the hanging lanterns on the wagons, and some of the men walking behind played mournful reels on their tin whistles. As slow as they were going, it would take much of the afternoon to get to Castlecove and then on to *Staigue* Fort.

Conor paused respectfully and made the Sign of the Cross, just as his mother taught him in Chicago, when the funeral procession went by. He was standing by the road with the priest and Phil. This sad march for death and mourning was a melancholy thing. Then, Conor saw Amergin, almost the last in line. Kevin was clasping his father's hand, and Conor could see tears running down his cheeks, but Amergin's face remained dry, his eyes hard, staring ahead.

"We'll leave later this aft and catch up with them on the way. Don't worry, we won't miss this. It really is important to all of us," said Phil.

"What's happened to everyone else that was killed? There must have been at least a dozen kids and parents in the campsite when we were there," said Conor.

"Mum was talking about it this morning. They buried the rest last night, quiet and private. It's what they do."

Conor looked at her closely, "Thought you folks didn't much like the Travelers."

"We don't," said Phil. "They cause a powerful lot of trouble, but this bunch is special. Amergin is more than just a Traveler, he's a ..." Phil paused for words.

Conor smiled. "He's the Bard of the West."

"How did you know?" said Fr. Greavy.

"Just do," he said. "Kevin told me. Said his Da's music holds the land together."

"Indeed, it does," said a new voice, joining them. It was the Shandyman and the four looked in silence at the sad procession. Jace and Colly walked up and introduced themselves to Tom Shandy.

"The land is falling apart," said the Shandyman, "and few remember the old ways. That's why this country has lost its soul. But no matter. Amergin still holds it together, at least for now. But you felt it a couple of days ago didn't you Conor, and then yesterday—the darkness and all that. Something is coming—is already here, I guess—and it doesn't bode well for us. Once the funeral is over, Amergin has to make a choice and upon that choice we will either live or die." The Shandyman nodded his head at the other four. "Mark my words."

"Sheesh," said Conor to himself. "I'm just out of the frying pan and back into the fire."

***

It was later on towards evening that Moira, Phil, the Shandyman, Conor and Troubles tumbled into the van and set out for *Staigue* Fort. They managed to squeeze in Jace, Colly and the priest as well. Phil held the picnic lunch on her lap, and they had just started out when Lettie rounded the corner in front of them. Moira hauled on the brakes saying out the window, "Lettie, in the name of all that's good, you're going to send my breath out to the far-off hills."

Lettie didn't respond, just waited for Conor to get out and hold the door open for her. There was a last space just for her.

They rode tightly in silence until Lettie said, "I can't believe I'm going to this. Amergin's wife—pity. You should have seen her when she was young. What a beauty! And now we go to send her on."

"Aye," said the Shandyman. "And maybe Amergin, too. He's not doing well, I hear. If he follows his wife in grief, what will become of us?"

No one had an answer. Conor had thought they would get an evening rainfall, but instead, the mist began running down from the hills.

Conor already had a name for it. 'Mystic fog' he called the stuff. Made everything look like it came from another time, another place as it rolled down the hills and drifted over the *machair*.

By the time they got to Castlecove—just a tiny town, really—the mist was beginning to obscure vision. Moira parked the van in a little car park next to a picnic table and told them all to get out and eat while they could.

Just then, a Mercedes rolled past them. Conor's back was to the vehicle but he had time to glance at it as it passed, and he sucked in his breath. He could swear the driver was Shiro Ishii. What in the world could he be doing here? He watched as the car drove through the little town and pulled into a parking place next to a pub called the *Blind Piper*. The driver was too blurred by the mist for Conor to see if it truly was the crazy doctor.

"What's wrong?" said Phil. She had heard a growl from Troubles' throat and saw Conor looking down the road intently.

Conor grabbed a tuna salad sandwich and some crisps and said, "Don't know really. Just thought I knew that guy who just passed us." No need for him to tell them he thought it was Ishii. Everybody had enough problems on their minds.

As soon as they were finished eating, they jumped in the van again, driving the last few kilometers towards the fort. When they passed the pub, Conor strained to look through the windows, but he saw no sign of the man who had beaten the hell out of him on the beach.

Lots of people never saw *Staigue* Fort, famous as it was. It was on a farmer's land, off the main road a piece, just at the bottom of the hills. But it was crowded now. Not with tourists, but with Travelers. Their caravans were parked away from the fort which rose ghostly in the mist. The white limestone walls seemed to glow in the fog and Conor whistled lightly. It was beautiful in a mournful sort of way. For millennia, it had stood watch with the hills behind it, grazing land in front, and the sea a couple of kilometers away to the west. There still were breaks in the mist where Conor could see the waves lapping the shore. Someone had put torches around the top of the ring fort. It looked positively stone age, and he got just a hint of what it must have been like in its heyday. A chill ran down his spine, as if other, unseen mourners had gathered as well.

One caravan had been taken into the ring fort. Wood and brush had been piled underneath and around it. The door was open and Conor supposed Amergin's wife was shrouded inside. As Conor stepped across the threshold of the fort, he stopped as if a great hand pressed against his chest. Thresholds were thin places, and his second sight kicked in. He rested on his staff, his vision blurred, and all the Travelers, Amergin included, faded until they became like shadows in the night. But the caravan stood out boldly in all its brilliant colors. Green roof, red chassis, blue trim, all freshly painted

gleamed grandly. It shone in the deepening twilight, a refuge midst the grim
gloom gathering around.

Conor saw the shadow of Amergin come forward and light the pile of
wood from a flaming branch in his hand. Then Conor realized that his second
sight let him see what no others saw, because there upon the battlements,
next to torches burning brightly in ancient sconces, men stood dressed
strangely as in thousands of years gone by. Celtic warriors looked down upon
the little caravan catching fire, and then their eyes turned as one on Conor.

"She comes," they said. "'The Red Thirst'. She comes."

"Wha ... what do you mean?" asked Conor. The chill running up his
spine was back and made him stutter.

One of the warriors pointed a torch at him. "We are the watchers of the
land. We see. She comes, and you must save the lost souls of this island from
her ravening thirst."

"Again?" said Conor, his eyes hardening, his fear retreating. "That's all
I ever get. Get involved, save this one, save that people, make sure the land
is okay. Make way for the Otherworld. And I'm getting tired of it. I'm just a
guy and admit I can do some strange stuff, but this Messiah gig is a little
much."

"I do not understand," said the warrior. "You are strange, and your
words make little sense. If a messiah is a champion, then a hero you are called
to be. She comes. 'The Red Thirst'. And you have to stop her, or all those
you love shall die. So many things have passed away." He waved his hand
around the land. "The beauty that once was is gone. Only we remain, and
watch. The people of *Eire* fade. When we look, they are now but shadows.
They are unattached to earth, water and sky. But we know what we see. We
see you, clearly. The King Who Shall Be. So, do what you were destined to
do. She comes. 'The Red Thirst'."

Just like that it was over. Whatever was pushing on his chest was gone.
Conor could breathe again and the warriors had disappeared.

"What's wrong?" asked Jace coming up and placing a hand on Conor's
shoulder. "You were talking to yourself."

"Did you see them?" asked Conor. "The soldiers on the battlements?"

Jace quickly looked up and around. "There's nothing there, Conor, but
you know I don't doubt you saw them. This place is ancient, and even I can
feel that we don't walk here alone."

Amergin began to sing a lament for the dead. Quickly the flames
advanced upon the caravan, eager to consume and allow the spirit of she who
had passed to depart.

But whatever might have left, did not, and Conor gasped as he
walked closer. A woman was there, beautiful as the dawn, standing at the
doorway of the caravan as flames licked the frame. It had to be Amergin's

wife as she once was. She smiled at Conor and walked down the pyre, through the flames toward him, and the boy was not afraid. For there was peace in that smile and a love that flowed out from her radiant face.

"Ah, Conor, I see you once more," she said. He nodded speechless. "Do not be afraid." Cupping his face in her hand, she said, "Amergin has talked much about you, and you are as he hoped you would be. I should have been with you on this journey, but so much evil walks the land that it took me before my time. But you can prevail, if you have the will and desire."

"Deirdre," spoke a grief-stricken voice. Conor looked to his left and saw the bard, knowing that Amergin could see what he saw. "Deirdre, come back to me please."

"My love, I cannot. This you know. But unseen, I will walk by your side. You will touch my face in the wind and hold my hand when yours grows cold in the winter snow." She kissed him on his lips. Amergin fell to his knees, hands over his weeping face. She knelt with him and in silence they embraced as the fire flickered high.

"Now Conor," said Deirdre, standing and turning to him. "You know what to do. Send me to the Summer Country."

Conor gaped at her, "I cannot ..." and he paused and swallowed. "But I can. I don't know how or why, but I can." Some long-forgotten memory, not his but in his possession, raised up to his consciousness. He lifted his staff, as if in farewell, and said,

Go home, Deirdre, of the many sorrows.
Go home to your home of autumn, your home of winter, spring and summer.
Go home to the Summer Country,
Where grief is no more and tears are not shed.
Walk forever with the One who created you
And gave you a love stronger than the shadows that remain.
Sleep now and rest, and so fade sorrow.
Sleep now and rest, and so fade sorrow.

She touched his cheek again, and turned from him, walking through the flames, through the other side of the caravan, and into the mist. And she was never seen in the land again. Amergin wept openly on his knees before the flames.

Conor left the bard to his grief and went over to the wall of the fort, sitting down with his back against the ancient stones. Everyone was so intent on watching Amergin, that only Troubles walked up to the boy, and leaned against him.

"I saw something, Troubles," said Conor. The dog woofed in agreement. "And I'm betting you saw it too. Something's coming real soon and it's going to put to shame all the other weird things we've seen since we've come to Ireland."

He couldn't talk anymore because Amergin was now speaking. The bard told the Travelers of the love of his life, the beautiful woman he had married. How they had loved, had a child, walked the land, sang the stories of their people, and tried to stop the slow erosion of the magic that once dwelt so visibly in this island.

"But I cannot go on. My time is done." A gasp rose above the crowd. "So many years have passed since I first stepped on this ground, and my strength ebbs. It is time for another. If you would accept him, there is your new Bard of the West." And his finger pointed straight at Conor, who, if he could, would have melted further into the wall. "The song of the sea within him rings true, but I was only of the land. In him, the mysteries of water and earth commingle, and though he is young, you may trust him as you have trusted me. Take my hand Conor. Come here and let them see you."

Conor hitched himself up on his staff and walked with Troubles toward the old man, standing proud here at the last. Conor saw him reach out and he did the same, taking his hand. They started walking closer to the burning caravan and Conor saw to his horror that Amergin was not going to stop.

"You understand, Conor, don't you lad? I thought I could go on without her, but such strength is no longer within me." He gave a soft, sad smile to him. "Do not be afraid, little one," he said. "It is your time now. The flames cannot touch you. This is how I was born so long ago. As it happened to me, so now to you." And he clasped Conor to his chest. As he was held, Conor felt himself change. His heart raced. And his awareness became like a physical presence, his very person reaching into the land under stone, entwined around hawthorne and heather, and he heard the voice of the land, a voice of pain and sorrow.

"Do you hear it, lad?" said Amergin. "This is what I have heard for so many centuries. Only, there is an urgency now. The land breathes its last. I don't know how to stop this death from happening. People no longer drink of the lifeblood of the land. They no longer see the secret ways and trod the hidden paths. They could still, but they do not care. They await another salvation. And they shall be so disappointed.

"Perhaps you will have more success. I leave to you the power of my song. You will need it to preserve the land. The song has the ability to go beyond the borders of this realm, for it belongs to the world and holds together the structure of all things. It is the voice of *neart*—the grace of the One who blessed all things into being. The song of the sea is already in your heart. For you are *Roan*, and you have always possessed the music of your kind. Join them together now, the voices of land and sea, and meet the darkness that is to come."

Amergin reached out his index finger and touched the tongue of Conor. Again, Conor felt he was losing himself, but, no, that was not it. Instead, he felt the land again. No longer a passive recipient, a benign watcher, an unused instrument, he felt a song in his heart that sang with his whole being as the melody joined with the music of the sea. While no one but Amergin heard what was happening, that voice inside Conor, his own voice empowered, sunk into the land and was recognized. A certainty came into the boy's mind that he was meant to walk both worlds on the lands and waters and sing them into survival, helping both them flourish again as one. He didn't really understand, but it did not matter. The grace of the land, its very self, and the voice of the sea that sounded within him, both from this world and the Otherworld, accepted him. For now that was enough.

Amergin held him close once more, and Conor let out a yelp of terror. Amergin's clothes were on fire, and so were his own. He reached out to help smother the blaze but Amergin pushed him gently away. Conor was amazed to see flames lick up and down his own arms and legs. "There is no pain," he said to himself. "None at all." Nor were his clothes consumed. Amergin backed away from Conor, saying, "My body returns to the earth now, and my spirit will join my wife as we stand before the One and account for our stewardship of this land. Farewell, boy, and never betray your trust."

Tears ran down Conor's face, and as Amergin became a star of burning fire, Conor held out his staff whispering, *"Sleep now and rest, and so fade sorrow. Sleep now and rest and so fade sorrow."*

"What is this?" said Colly who had walked over to Jace. "What is happening to your friend?"

"I don't know," said Jace, "but he's not the same as he was. I can feel that."

"So can I," whispered Colly to himself. "He has the smell of the Otherworld on him. I wonder if it means good or ill for me."

A cry of grief rang throughout the fort. It was Kevin running forward and kneeling close to the flames. "Da!" he cried. "Da! Come back! Come back!" All Conor could do was put his arms around the grieving son. For a moment, all was silent except for the snapping of the flames, and, then, Conor felt something take his wrist. It was Troubles, and the dog led both he and Kevin back from the flames, all untouched by the burning ring of fire. The Travelers within the fort stared at Conor. The Shandyman came forward and led Kevin back to the group as Conor stood with Troubles in front of all of them.

One after another of the Travelers began to stamp their feet and clap their hands in a primitive beat. Their voices held not words but began to hum in an ancient rhythm as they circled Conor and Troubles. It would have been absolutely creepy to Conor, if the faces turned toward him were blank, but they were not. There was joy on them, and as the circle grew wider and more joined them, Conor could see them all, tears still drying on their faces as they welcomed the new Bard of the West.

He looked up and saw the warriors on the wall once again, moving above them in a circle around the fort, thumping their Spears in time with the Travelers. Only the priest stood off to the side, but he was blessing all of them. Conor's heart was lifted, and he knew he was not alone. When the dancing suddenly stopped, the crowd roared, "We accept!" and Conor fell to his knees, hands outstretched. It was his way of saying, "Then I will serve." But as overwhelmed with what this all meant, a foreboding leeched into his mind, and he remembered what the warrior said and wondered what his words foretold. "She comes. 'The Red Thirst'. She comes."

THE RED THIRST

Friday Evening, 11/6, Castlecove and Staigue Fort

SHIRO ISHII HAD eaten a leisurely meal at one of the tables in Castlecove's *Blind Piper* pub, but now he stood and took a seat at the bar next to a scruffy Traveler who had just quaffed the last of a pint.

"Another sir?" said Ishii, "With the promise of a story from you."

"T'anks a million," slurred the man. "Appreciate your kindness and I'd be happy to tell such a tale as you might want. Name's Hurley, and who might my great benefactor be?" He smiled a gap-toothed grin.

"Just a fellow traveler looking for some very old information." Ishii stopped for a moment and they both looked out the large glass window to see Travelers' caravans passing by.

"Ah, that would be the funeral," said Hurley.

"Funeral?" asked Ishii. "At this time of night?"

"Aye, we Travelers have our ways. This was a big one, and I should have been there. Wife of a great bard and *seanachie*, storyteller, I mean. Died of a tragic sickness, most unexpected."

"Why weren't you there?" pressed Ishii.

Hurley looked at his drink and sighed, smiling softly, "I was a bit delayed. No matter, what tale was it you wanted?"

"Ghost story, really. As you can see, I'm not from around here, and in my world travels, I have a habit of picking up odd stories about ghosts and demons and such—vampire tales, mostly. Know any of those that might come from around here? I have an old map of this area, and there's a mark here indicating a spot up in the foothills above the fort and town. The man who gave it to me told me I might find something there that would interest me."

"Well," said Hurley taking a drink, "it's none of my business why you want to know about them things, but Ireland really only has one vampire tale worth telling and the tale has roots right around these parts. I can't say the name loudly here," and his gaze shifted to each of the pub denizens still left.

"But the deadly thing you're talking about goes by the name of the *Dearg Due*. But she wasn't always a vampire. In fact, she was a lovely thing so many centuries ago. She was besotted with a boy of the village. They were sweet on one another. He was handsome and she was beautiful; but she was rich and he was poor. And her father—aye, her bastard father—he wouldn't hear of her marrying low like that.

"Here's how it went, at least as the story was taught to me:

Twenty centuries ago—imagine that—so much time and so much pain—there was a winsome lass so beautiful that anyone who saw her loved her dearly. She was in love with a lad from the village, a good boy, a strong boy, a smart boy—but, unfortunately, a poor one. And her father, a very rich man indeed, but poor in every other virtue, would not hear of such a match. So, he married her off to a man much older, a cruel chieftain who had use only for her dowry. In fact, he hated the very sight of her.

Her father cared nothing for her misfortune. He had grown in standing by the marriage, and the cruel chieftain had given him contracts and cattle, and enough gold to fill a leprechaun's kettle at the end of the rainbow.

The woman's husband only touched her when he beat her. And when he was done, he would take a silver knife and draw her blood. Some say he drank it, if you know what I mean." He tipped his pint towards Ishii. "*Afterwards, he would always say, "Tell me you love me darling dear; tell me you love me darling, darling." Each time, he made her answer back in the midst of her pain and shame. She was forced to say, "I'll love you forever darling dear; I'll love you forever darling, darling." Imagine that, if you will, bleeding her and everything, then saying the words, "Tell me you love me darling dear; tell me you love me darling, darling." Then hearing her choke out the bitter answer, "I'll love you forever darling dear; I'll love you forever darling, darling." Afterwards, he would shut her up in his tower, until the next time.*

She kept hoping that the peasant boy from the village would come to rescue her. Day after day, month after month, and then year after year her confidence never wavered. But he never came.

Hope finally left her. Her husband never did. Always the tortures. Always the blood. Always the words, "Tell me you love me darling dear; tell me you love me darling, darling." Bereft of any salvation from her one true love, she whispered in despair, "I'll love you forever darling dear; I'll love you forever, darling, darling."

Her last day of life, shadows flew around the tower, and a powerful darkness leaked from the small windows there. Village folk whispered these things happened because she renounced the Light and promised vengeance on all who had forsaken her. But I think she was touched by the Morrigan. It weren't shadows flying around the tower. It were crows. Someone else was in that tower with her that night, and though others skip this part, I think it truly was the Morrigan. Something went very wrong up in that tower that final evening. For it was there that the young woman turned into something unnatural.

When her husband came for her later around midnight, he found her dead on the floor, a black feather there on her throat. Dead from neglect, horror and terrible abuse.

They buried her the next day, under a tree down Waterford way. It was tradition then as now to place stones on the grave so that the spirit would never wander. But the people remembered her as so meek and mild that they left the grave bare. Much to their sorrow.

A year passed and she was nigh near forgotten, but on the anniversary of her death, she thrust a pale hand through the sod, and then the other, and hauled herself up like some grub from the ground, an undead corpse with a thirst for blood. Beautiful she still was, but no longer human. A small wailing sound came from her mouth, and she floated over the grass-clad ground like the deathless thing she had become.

First, she went into the village, and searched for her one true love, the peasant boy. She saw him with his wife and children. All she felt was betrayal, and she tore that family apart, and when they were found, not a blood stain was upon them nor a drop of blood in their ravaged bodies.

Her thirst not satisfied, she went for her father who had abandoned and forgotten her. She silenced the shriek that bubbled on his lips when he saw her ghostly form. She drank him dry like a Tinker drinks a gallon of whisky. Almost satiated, she went back to her house, to her tower.

Her husband heard scratching from up there and wondered what it was. Surely, he had latched and closed the tiny windows. Nothing could get in. He slowly went up the stairs and entered the darkened room. Suddenly, looming in front of him in her white funereal dress, she reached out a cold, dead hand and grasped his throat. Then she whispered in a keening voice, "Tell me you love me, darling dear; tell me you love me darling, darling." She tightened her grip, "Say the words!" she screamed. "Say them now!" And she loosened her claw so he could gasp, "I'll love you forever darling dear; I'll love you forever darling, darling." She smiled, and blood dripped from her teeth.

They found him the next day, dead and drained, but they did not find her. In her hate, in her abandonment of the Light, she had changed from the beautiful girl she once was to the Dearg Due—'The Red Thirst'—for that is what they called her now. Her desire for blood is never quenched, and so she wanders the land and calls out to the living. The last words they hear is her sing-song rhyme, "Tell me you love me darling dear; tell me you love me darling, darling."

When Hurley said 'darling' for the last time, he shouted the words in Ishii's face. "Scared you, didn't I?" he giggled.

Hurley took a drink from his pint. Shiro Ishii said, "Good tale but they must have captured her."

"Indeed, they did, many times. Took her screaming back to her grave, or dug her a new one. Only those times, stones were placed above her so she could not escape. But the funny thing is, she always does. Sometimes decades go by, sometimes centuries. But 'The Red Thirst' is never quenched, and she arises to feast again."

"Where is she buried now?"

"Most people don't know anymore," said Hurley with a glint to his eye.

"But you do, don't you Mr. Hurley."

"Yes, I do, and I'll be happy to tell you for a price and a look at that map."

Shiro smiled. People were always the same. He had learned long ago that most could be bought, so he nodded and said, "Name your price and tell me."

Hurley told him what he wanted, and then after Ishii had agreed, said, "According to the map, she's buried not far from here, just a click or two from *Staigue* Fort."

"Take me there now," said Ishii.

Hurley blanched, "Now? In the night? In the dark?"

"Now, if you want to be paid."

The Traveler drank down the last of his pint and grumbled, "Let's get it over with, then."

Hurley stumbled into the passenger seat of Ishii's car, and the two went up the road to *Staigue* Fort. They parked in the tiny parking lot and looked into the fort to stare at the quickly cooling coals from the burned caravan. Not a soul around.

The mist had cleared and the stars were out. The Hand of God still burned brightly in the sky and the moon leant its silver light. Easy to see the path that Hurley led Ishii upon. They were going due east, into the foothills. Hurley was like a human GPS tracker. Ishii was amazed that he knew so clearly where he was going.

"How do you know where she is?" he asked.

"Been at her grave once or twice. It matches the mark on your map. Only a few of us know. Even most Travelers don't know. Most of us don't have commerce with the Dark Ones. But some of us, myself included mind you, think it's a good idea to know about both sides, if you catch my drift, Mr. Ishii."

Shiro just nodded and urged him onward. In a few minutes the rocky ascent leveled out for a small stretch. Little cairns dotted the landscape. The Irish fascination with stones had led hikers and wanderers to fashion tiny dolmens, miniature fake graves here and there in that barren place. Ishii had seen it before. It's what attracted him to these people, who knew in their souls, even if they chose to forget it now, that a more real world was just beyond their sight.

"Aye," said Hurley. "The hikers and folks from around here don't know 'The Red Thirst' rests in this spot, but they sense it. That's what turns their thoughts to death. That's what makes them build these cairns. Here we are."

He led Ishii over to a pile of stones behind some bracken. "Here it is," he announced.

"This?" said Ishii. "There's nothing here but stones. No marker, nothing."

"That is as it should be. The last ones who buried her didn't want nobody knowing where she was. But word gets out … over time. Now give me my price. I've brought you to her."

"Indeed, you have," smiled Shiro. "But before I pay you, remove the stones. I want to see how they buried her."

"Nothing there but rock, sir," said Hurley, nervously shifting foot to foot.

"Humor me and remove the stones." Ishii's voice held just a bit of threat, but Hurley didn't pick up on it. He was too busy slamming down his fear so he could reap the price the stranger had offered him.

It didn't take Hurley long to pull up the stones. To the surprise of both, there was no rock underneath the limestone flags. Rich loam had been carted in. They had no idea how deep it was, but there was a lot of it.

"Looks like they expected her to bloom where she was planted." Hurley's lame attempt at a joke elicited no response from Ishii.

After a moment's silence, Ishii said, "Hurley come here. What was it that I promised you? What was it that you claimed for your price?"

"I wanted a thousand euros, sir. Just a small finder's fee, if you know what I mean."

"That's why I let you come, Hurley. You could have asked for more but didn't. But I sense you also want something else. What is it?"

"Well," said Hurley, "it's just that I've never seen such a creature before, and I'm figuring that you are going to trap her some way. I might be a trifle curious. I'll help you, I will, if you'll let me stay and see."

"I wouldn't have it any other way. But she is dead, and for us to see her, we must call her, and there's only one way to do that. Blood."

"Blood?" whispered Hurley, an octave higher than usual.

"Blood. Yours, I think."

"Mine?" he squeaked.

"Oh, come now, don't be squeamish. I'll double your finder's fee. But I need a vein. Just a sprinkle of your blood on that turf will do the trick, I think."

Greed was always a Traveler's weakness, and a fondness for the strange and unknown. Hurley took a deep breath and held out his arm. In an instant, Ishii had a small knife out and sliced open a vein.

"O my God!" shrieked Hurley, "Did you have to make such a long cut?"

"It'll be fine," said Ishii, patting the man on the back. "Now, just let that blood drip into the dirt." And Hurley did just that.

"Should I wrap my arm now?" he said.

"Not yet. You'll not bleed out that fast you know. Trust me. I do have a little experience with these things."

They were silent about a minute. Only the swift drops of blood striking the dirt making any sound. Then a breeze began to blow. Not from the sea, not from the foothills, but as if it arose from around the rocky plain. It tousled their hair, and as it gained strength, it hit the rocks and began to echo as a moaning cry.

Hurley, never the bravest soul, began to shake. He turned to go, but then he felt a viselike grip on both his shoulders. Ishii had gotten behind him. "Don't mind the wind," he said. "It's not what can hurt you. It's simply telling us that something is coming."

The ground began to shake, not violently but vibrating as if something was moving underneath. Hurley took a glance at the grave and saw the grains of dirt bouncing up and down. How odd he thought, but then he shrieked again as a pale hand jutted from the earth, fingers touching and grasping the ground. Then another hand exploded from below and white shoulders appeared, heaving upward, and a lowered head began to rise. Hurley was sure he would have passed out had Ishii not had hold of him.

"Looks like you were right," said Ishii. "That is her burial plot." The revenant continued to haul itself out of the grave, and Shiro was inwardly amazed that she was not some desiccated corpse. Instead, she was beautiful. Dirt did not cling to her white dress, and her face, though thin, showed no decay. Blond hair cascaded down to her shoulders. But when she looked at Shiro, her eyes and mouth gave her away. They were inhuman. The red slits of her eyelids wept blood, and her mouth, full with crimson lips looked peculiar, as if her jaw could be larger than normal, as if it wasn't hinged right.

"You see, Hurley, she really does exist, and you were so good to lead me to her. Now if you survive her embrace, I'll give you your money, but I fear, she thirsts, and I think she thirsts for you." He pushed Hurley into the arms of the now standing *Dearg Due*. The man didn't even have time to scream, for the Red Thirst simply paralyzed him with one look from her dead red eyes. She paid no attention to the blood dripping from his arm, but instead gently tipped his head back.

Shiro gasped as she disjointed her jaw. Fangs came out, not tiny pointy ones, but long vicious incisors, and in a moment, she ripped out Hurley's throat. It was casual, he thought, like she had done it a thousand times, and he supposed she had. But the almost meticulous way she handled Hurley suddenly disappeared as she buried her head into his throat and ravaged the corpse.

Ishii was amazed at her appetite. He knew what would come next. She threw the corpse aside and advanced on him. But all he did was laugh and pointed his katana in the direction of her bosom.

"Stop where you are or die forever on this spot. I am the master of you, even though you don't believe it. Let me open my mind to you. I'll let you see a little of me, and then you can decide whether I live or die."

He just looked at her and reached out with his mind. The Emperor had truly transformed him, and Sir Hugh had refined his technique. Shiro was grateful for that, and he enjoyed pouring into this alien presence his thoughts, memories and experiences, just enough for her to know who she was dealing with.

She ran her tongue around her lips, and demurely used the hem of her dress to wipe the blood spatter from her face. She smiled sweetly, and as an answer to what he had just showed her, she curtsied and reached for him.

Ishii was not taken in. "You are a monster," he snarled, "but I have need of you for a while. You will rest again in your tomb. No rocks shall be placed over you. But on tomorrow's night, you will rise again and make your way to Ballinskelligs. I expect you to take care of every living human being there, and every other living thing if you wish. But nothing human is to remain alive. After that, you will join me in Tralee for something I wanted to do long ago but have never had the chance. You will be the final act of what I am calling 'The Night of Cherry Blossoms'. It will be the beginning of the end."

They both began to laugh, the Red Thirst because all she really understood is that her ravenous hunger was to be sated, and Shiro Ishii because he would strike a blow to this land that would bring a new darkness to infect the world of humanity and the Otherworld.

CONOR GOES TO THE ROCK

Saturday Morning, 11/7, Ballinskelligs and Skellig Michael

THE MORNING AFTER the funeral, Conor snuck out of the hotel early and went down to the ruined abbey. He felt he needed a little solitude. Amazed at how warm it was for November in Ireland, he found himself an old piece of the abbey wall that faced out toward Ballinskelligs Bay. Sitting himself down to await the dawn, he took out his tin whistle and began to play. He felt the warmth on his face as the sun broke over the land and cast its rosy fingers across the waters of the bay shining like silver glass. Distant sea birds added harmony to his music.

"Beautiful," said a voice. Jace sat down next to him. "Didn't mean to sneak up on you, but I wanted some alone time with you. What are you playing?"

Conor stopped and smiled, "Just a tune from that old movie, *Local Hero*. It's called the 'Wild Thing' but it's so haunting, just like this old abbey."

"I'm glad I found you," said Jace.

Conor looked out to sea. "I glad you're here. When I left you guys last Sunday, I was so scared. Abbot Malachy and Aunt Emily boated me down the Mississippi to Cassville so I could eventually catch a plane to here, but it was crazy. I'd morphed so much the night before, I barely thought I had any human left in me. Couldn't even ask the Abbot about it, I was so confused. Then I get here, and I sort of found an anchor in Amergin and the Travelers. Then all the bad stuff began again. I was lost. Michael was cool—you haven't met him yet, but just wait. He's okay ... and different. But now you're here and I'm glad. I'm so sorry for everything."

"Stop," said Jace. "It's not that I'm totally over everything, but coming here has helped. I met your ancient nun, St. Ita, and she had a few things to say about everything."

"I didn't get to talk to her all that much," said Conor, "but she said she had been waiting for me for a long time. You've got to admit in the last six months our perception of wonders and mysteries has gotten stretched a bit. Every day, something new."

Jace thought about the Travelers and their bowing to Conor. "Yeah, and you're full of constant surprises."

Conor smiled ruefully. "Guess I am at that. But whatever's happening, I've learned I can't do it without you. I mean, I've got some fine friends here—a godmother who seems to care, the Travelers, Phil and even Lettie are good people. But you. I'm just a lot stronger when you're around."

"Then let's see about staying together this time," said Jace.

They heard the motor before they saw the boat rounding the headland.

"That's Colly's boat," said Jace. Unlike himself, who also spent the night at The *Skellig*, Colly had gone home. Looked like he was making early landfall in the bay. They waved to him, and he coasted up to the abbey's ruined dock.

Colly quirked a smile at them. "Up early, I see. I was hoping to find you. Got a proposition for you. I know we promised Moira we'd help put the finishing touches on the hall for the celebration tonight, but I thought if we got an early start, we could make it out to the Rock for a quick visit. I want to show you guys something. Didn't have time to show Jace the other day, but after what's been happening, I thought it might be important. Up for a ride?"

They were, and in forty-five minutes they were pulling into Blind Man's Cove. The trip had been incredibly smooth with only light waves and a blue sky with just a few scudding clouds.

As before, there were no tourists and no archs around either. The school had called them back for the upcoming weekend. Tralee University was a primary sponsor for the city's Winter Festival—the Cherry Blossom Festival—the coming weekend.

The boys had the island to themselves. They were young and easily climbed the steps. At Christ's Saddle, the little meadow between the two peaks on the island, Colly turned left to lead them to the southern part of the island.

"I remember," said Conor in a whisper.

"So did I," said Jace in a low voice. "But it's not as scary as it was the first time. I did find something though."

He and Colly showed Conor the dragon scale they had found on the path toward the Needle's Eye—the spike shaped peak above them jutting to the sky. Conor picked up the scale as if it was plastic, and Colly said, "Am I the only weak one here? What's with you guys?"

"It belonged to *Piasa*," said Conor in a flat voice. "I remember the feel of its skin, and it still smells. Maybe we can take it back with us when we go. Might come in handy in some way."

"That's not what I wanted to show you, Conor," said Colly. "There's something both of you should see—an opening in the rock wall a couple of hundred yards from here. I found it a couple of months ago. I thought it might be a cave, but it looks manmade and seems to go nowhere."

"There can't be anything undiscovered on this island," said Jace. "Too many people have been here over the centuries."

"I don't know," said Colly. "But my Spidey Sense is tingling. I think there's something there."

They reached the place he was speaking about, and Conor immediately saw that indeed there was an opening, about seven feet high, roughly carved out of stone. But it was only three feet deep. No door, no cave here. Conor let his hand trace around the frame.

"Webbed hands," said Colly. "You're going to freak out the people here."

Conor grimaced. Jace said, "Hey, leave him alone. He gets enough grief from folks about it."

Colly's face clouded and said seriously, "I wasn't making fun. Just stating fact. We're a superstitious people, and men and women of legend have walked this land frequently enough that people aren't all that surprised when things are not really what they seem. Sorry."

"No offense taken," said Conor, "but look here, there's more than meets the casual eye."

He pointed out to them some kind of motifs in each corner of the stone wall, and a tiny Celtic Cross in the bottom middle.

Colly said, "Others had to have seen this. If these represent a code for the way in somebody would have figured it out long ago."

"Maybe," said Jace, "or maybe not. The island has been visited a lot, but this area was the dangerous part. The Abbot here would not have liked visitors investigating, and it wouldn't really matter if the other twelve monks or so knew what was here."

"I've got some chalk," said Colly.

"For what?" asked Conor.

"Connect the dots," he said.

"You just carry around chalk?" laughed Jace.

"Hey, we are an island of rocks. Sometimes we have to mark things."

"Well, wait a sec," said Conor. "Let's take a closer look at what these images are. One in the upper left looks like a man. Upper right, the image looks like some kind of a beast. Maybe a lion. Bottom left is a cow. Got the cross in the bottom middle, and an eagle on the bottom right. I wonder why those images."

Jace muttered absent-mindedly. "They're the gospel writers. Matthew, Mark, Luke and John. They're crude, but they are the same style as the ones in the Book of Kells at Trinity College in Dublin. In fact, some say the Book was once kept here for safety."

Colly looked at him with new appreciation. "You could be on a game show, man. Where'd you get all that trivia?"

Conor snickered, "From a river-sucking catfish this past summer. Takes a taste of it and—poof—he's the smartest thing this side of Wikipedia."

Colly looked in awe. "Like Finn McCool with the Salmon of Knowledge?"

"Sort of," said Jace. "Can we get back to the problem at hand? You're probably right, Colly, that we have to connect these images somehow and I do have an idea. Give me the chalk for a moment."

In silence, he gazed at the rock and then took the chalk. He started in the upper left with Matthew's image, drawing a diagonal line to the cross below. Next, he reached up to the right where Mark's image of lion was carved, drawing a diagonal line to the cross below. He drew a line connecting Matthew with the lower image of Luke's Gospel—that of an ox—and then drew a straight line from Mark's sign to the eagle symbolizing John's Gospel at the bottom of the rock.

"Of course," said Jace. "Do you see? This island is Michael's Mount, so that's why it is the letter "M", but we're missing something. A cross doesn't float in the air; it's attached to a base, and all the gospels have to be connected so a straight line from Luke to John has to be there. Likewise, from Matthew to Mark. It's not a door; it's a frame, like a window or picture frame."

"But nothing happened," said Colly. He patted Jace on the cheek. "Maybe your fishy insight is faulty here in the old country."

"Don't think so," said Jace. "It just takes somebody special to open it with a little more spiritual mojo than I have. Like maybe the *Roan* King Who Shall Be. What you think, Conor?"

He didn't say a word but stepped forward and traced his fingers the exact way Jace had. And where he touched, the rock luminesced. A network of lines appeared in the space between the frame and as the lines thickened, the boys could see blackness beyond.

"Would you look at that," said Jace. "I think it's a portal."

"To where?" said Conor.

"Inside the mountain," said Jace and Colly together.

Tentatively, Jace reached his hand toward the space and it passed through. He jerked his hand back swiftly because as it passed the blackened barrier it disappeared.

"Geez, I thought I cut it off."

"Come on," said Colly. "Let's see where it goes."

Each stepped over the frame into the darkness. They looked back and saw the outside where they just were. The grid lines appeared again, and faster than they could move, walled them in.

There were three fast intakes of breath, but no one yelled in the pitch black surrounding them.

"Anyone got a light?" asked Colly.

"Don't think we'll need one," said Conor. "It's getting brighter." As their eyes adjusted, they saw a faint illumination on the walls, not flashlight bright, but enough to see by. They were in some type of a passageway that gradually widened ahead, presumably to a cavern, and they could hear the sea.

"We're down by Seal Cove," said Colly, "but I've never seen this before. C'mon."

Leading them down the passage, Colly hadn't gone more than fifty meters when he stumbled into a larger cavern. Above them, an overhanging rock jutted out over the sea. It was low tide. Colly guessed the opening was barely visible most days. The water extended into the cavern, but there was a sandy beach higher than the highest tide level. The gasps that came from Conor and Jace weren't from the absolute coolness of a cave beach. It was the wreck of a ship that listed there on the sand. Not a big boat, but clearly one meant to sail on the sea. It looked terribly old, but the cave environment had preserved it. Colly wouldn't bet his life on it being seaworthy, but in its day, it must have been a swift sailing vessel.

"How old is this thing?" asked Conor.

"Well," said Colly. "It's an old design and it's not European. More Roman Byzantine, I'd guess."

"Why in the world is it here?" asked Jace.

"There's a legend," said Colly.

"Of course, there is," sighed Jace. "Like you said, this is Ireland."

Colly quirked his little smile and explained, "It's about the Seven Coptic Monks from Alexandria, Egypt. Things were a little dicey politically around 460 A. D. in Egypt, and the legend says the seven sailed west to escape all the turmoil and eventually wound up in Ireland. The people of Kerry said they made contact with St. Patrick. Just a legend, but seeing this, maybe not."

Conor hadn't said much, but he looked into the boat. "There's lots of stuff here. The metals are rusted but there are benches and oars and some rotted cloth like sails or something. Nobody's ever ransacked this ship, and there are no holes in it that I can see, so what happened to the monks?"

"Maybe they ended up staying or going back to the mainland another way," said Colly.

Jace was busy climbing some worn steps that ended at the top of the overhanging rock. "There's another level up here. The cavern goes back a bit more." They followed him when he let out a low whistle. "You guys got to come and see this."

The third level of the cavern was dry as dust, out of the way of the salt sea spray. It was smaller but much deeper and against the far wall was an altar, and, above it, painted frescoes which even in the dim light looked absolutely brilliant.

The center painting showed the seven monks arriving on *Skellig* Michael, but that wasn't what captured the boy's attention. The painting on the right front wall caught more of the light from the entrance to the cave.

"It's a fresco of the War in Heaven. There's Michael throwing out Lucifer and the other angels falling ... and other beings too ..." Jace glanced at Conor who was looking with intense interest. "Conor, they're falling down around Ireland and these islands."

"You know," said Colly, "the Irish say that the fallen angels went to hell, but these other creatures, some of them vaguely human became the *Tuatha de Danaan*. Those that fell on the land became the *faerie* folk and those that fell into the ocean, became the *Roan*, the People of the Sea."

"Yeah," said Jace with voice full of irony. "So we've heard."

Colly tilted his head like he didn't understand, but no question came from his mouth because Conor whooped and said, "Look at this."

Conor was pointing down to the right of the altar where three slabs of stone were laid next to one another, each about two meters long and raised half a meter above the ground. He rushed to the other side and saw four stones laid exactly the same. "Looks like they never left."

"What do you mean?" asked Colly.

"They're grave stones," said Jace. "There are inscriptions here." He picked the first stone far to the left and let his fingers trace the carvings. "This first part is *ogham*—the Celts primitive written language; the second part is in hieroglyphics, and the third is in Greek."

"How do you know that?" said Colly, suspicion dripping from his voice. "You study that stuff in high school or did you get it from your magic fish as well?"

"Maybe," said Jace, looking embarrassed. "Since this past summer, I found I had a knack for languages."

"So, what's it say?" asked Colly.

Jace concentrated as he let his fingers drift. "The first part, the *ogham* inscription is a name—Serapion, I think. Must be the name of the monk. The hieroglyphs are jumbled a bit for me, but the Greek is easy. It says,

> *Eight years after the Council, I sailed with my fellow monks to this farthest point west where we found like-minded brothers who worshipped Christos. We brought them the Spear and the Cup as gifts, and they showed us great things,*

the greatest being the Messenger. Here we stay; here he teaches; here he protects us from the Dark One who seeks our lives. Here we wait for the King Who Shall Be. A mighty battle comes, but we will wait, and we will prepare.'

"That's it, that's all it says. Who's this Messenger?"

"Ah," said Conor. "This is *Skellig* Michael so maybe it's the archangel himself?"

"The angel?" laughed Jace. "I highly doubt it. He's got lots to keep him busy, and I think he would not be tied to this rock."

Jace was still shaking his head when he noticed the change in the light. It was moving and shifting color. As if something was behind him and coming closer. He and the other two turned as one and saw the ocean had been blotted out by a riot of color and flame, moving and spinning. Any other time, and from a bit farther away, the three of them might comment about the light being beautiful, but now it just looked frightening and powerful. No real shape, but the light probed ahead as if it were walking towards them. Two ropes of flame suddenly erupted from its center mass and looped around Conor and Jace. They both yelled, but in surprise not pain. They were lifted high and pinned against the wall of the cave above the altar.

"Who comes to my house?" said a voice. "Who comes to disturb the Seven Sleepers?"

Colly looked up and saw Jace and Conor staring at the thing that held them. Then he watched the consciousness drain from their faces as the ropes of flame slowly set them down on the floor of the cave.

Colly's nostrils flared in anger and a sneer appeared on his lips. "You! Why did you do that to them?"

"Shifter," said the voice in greeting.

"That's not my name. Don't call me that," he yelled.

"Changeling, then, if you want to be so reminded."

"I don't like that much better," muttered Colly.

"Reveal yourself," said the voice.

Colly spat on the ground. "I'm not in awe of you like the others, you know."

"Reveal yourself," said the voice more insistently.

Colly spat again. "As you wish." The clothes Colly was wearing sloughed off him as he grew taller and heavier. His shape was humanoid but his body was totally different—more muscular, with his knees bent the opposite way, and his arms long and gnarled. His face lengthened too, but it was like a mask, few facial muscles moving. And he was a dark green with skin like leather. As he spoke, his voice was low and raspy. "Happy now?" he asked.

"You are as you were made, a Changeling."

"No," he said. "I'm not like them. I've lived my life as a human. I'm not like the others."

"Your form is twisted, but I am told you have a soul and perhaps that is not depraved."

"You know I've been put here for a reason."

"The One has his reasons. This I know. But I must be truthful. You make no sense, and I do not see the purpose of your presence. Nonetheless, here you are, and with two I am sworn to protect. What is your business with them?"

"The bigger one found me. Trouble follows him like gannets to fish. We ran up against Sir Hugh yesterday and his," here Colly spat a third time, "loyal minion, Shiro Ishii."

The presence shimmered in intensity. "Sir Hugh I am familiar with. He also is not what he seems, though he may not know what inhabits him. The other ... malice and power flow through his veins rather than blood."

"If you must know, I'm also watching over these two."

The presence laughed, "I am much relieved now that I know you care for them. Your kind is so reliable."

Colly flared, "Reliable for the past eighteen years. I was sent here to await the time, to prepare when two shall come from across the sea."

"There have been many who have come to you from all places."

"True, just tourists though, not like these two. The wolves saw them last night. They say that Conor and Jace are the ones awaited."

"We shall see," whispered the presence. "Now it is time to wake them and let them see me in a form they will be able to accept. Conor already knows me in that guise. But mark my words, Changeling, betray them and you shall face my wrath. Many of your kind still writhe in the flames I flung them in. So, take care."

Colly nodded nervously as the presence shimmered again and withdrew around the corner of the cave. He heard Jace and Conor groan and shifting to his human form and throwing his clothes back on, ran to help them.

"What happened?" said Conor. "There was this light, and then I blacked out."

"Me too," said Colly helping a wobbly Jace to his feet.

From around the corner of the cave, a small boat appeared in the narrow opening and a man yelled at them, "You lads alright? I saw a light and heard voices."

"Michael!" shouted Conor, running to the end of the rocky ledge.

"Here's where you've gone off to. Moira said you all might skip the finishing work on the ce*lidh*, but you could have found easier places inland to hide."

"Michael, you've got to see this." Conor hopped down the steps and ran to help Michael beach the boat. "These are my friends. Jace, from America, and Colly from Portmagee."

Michael heartily shook Jace's hand and did the same with Colly but gave him a piercing look. "Hercules Columba Roddy? I've heard of you, and met your father. He's good people, so you're likely the same. And Jason Michaels from America. Conor has told me much about you. But what is this you all have found?"

They showed him the frescos and the graves. "The Seven Sleepers," said Michael.

"You really think so?" said Conor.

"Don't know who else they'd be. They were seven Egyptian monks, learned and wise. They sailed west to escape all the scandal and heresies of the day and sought a bright land of learning, new to the knowledge of the Christ, but old in spiritual wisdom. When they found it, they stayed. It is even said they helped St. Patrick, not that he needed it, but it sure didn't hurt. Everyone thought they just up and vanished, but that is not quite true, hmm?" He looked at the boys with a narrow gaze. "The fresco is tended, the graves have not eroded or decayed. Somebody has cared for them over the ages. I wonder why?"

"Oh, me too," said Colly with a sarcasm that only Michael noticed. "Ireland's an island of secrets so there's a story here for sure."

"There's something weird about these graves," said Jace kneeling down before the last two on the right of the altar. "All the tombs have one name except this second to the last one. There are two names inscribed here, John and Constantine. Were they buried together? I wonder why?"

Colly snorted, "Monk midgets, maybe."

Conor burst out laughing and Jace snickered. Michael just glared at Colly.

"What?" said Colly, "I'm just saying maybe they were saving space."

"But that's the thing," said Jace. "If that's true, what's in the last grave? There's no name on here, just a picture. It looks like a big kettle or pot, like a ..."

"Cauldron," said Colly under his breath. Michael flexed his hands as if he were about to strangle Colly.

Jace nor Conor saw. Conor just said, "Well we can't just dig up this tomb. We'll talk about it later, but we should get back. Lots to do yet."

Colly lagged behind, looking at the seventh grave. "It can't be. It just can't be. No wonder ..."

"And not a word of it to anyone," snapped Michael to the fisherman. "It is not your secret to tell. Come along now, in silence if you please."

Bundling them into the boat, Michael ran them around the side of the island and tied it up next to Colly's. "I'll ride with you lads, if you don't mind. My original ride's already gone back and this little *curragh* would not make for a comfortable trip."

It was a silent forty-five-minute journey back to the mainland under a cloudless sky, the beautiful view hiding their restless thoughts that they hadn't yet seen the last of the Seven Sleepers.

THE *CELIDH*

Saturday Afternoon and Evening, 11/7, Ballinskelligs

LETTIE WAS WAITING for them as Colly pulled the boat up to the dock at Ballinskelligs. She hailed Michael first. "I've been wondering where you got to but I see you found a bunch of rapscallions shirking the duties that Moira put on them this morning."

Conor blushed saying, "Not fair, Lettie. She just said we had to get them done, not when they had to be done."

"Humph," said the old woman. "Suppose you are right, but I've got my own agenda here anyway. Michael's got to help the band set up the sound, and I'm looking for an extra tin whistle player." She arched her brow at Conor.

"Sure," he said. "It'd be cool. Jace, here is a maximum bodhran player, if you need him."

"Is he now?" said Lettie coming closer and looking him up and down. "Perhaps he is. Bring him along."

Jace grinned at the old woman and, dutifully, Conor and he followed her up the path.

"I can sing," yelled Colly.

"Don't need an extra singer," said Lettie, nose into the wind. "Got enough without your help."

Colly slouched at the dismissal, his nostrils flaring with repressed anger. Jace glanced at him and Lettie, feeling the tension. Michael made it all worse by pushing past Colly and catching up with Lettie.

Hanging back, Jace said, "What's going on? They seem not to like you very much."

"It's a Portmagee thing," explained Colly. "Most folks resent the tourist dollars we bring in for ourselves, so they make their feelings known. No big deal, really."

By the time they reached the town hall, the disturbance was forgotten. Most of the prep work had been done, but Michael took charge of the sound system, while Conor and Jace met the members of the band who were present. They seemed enthusiastic to add two more musicians, even though they made Conor and Jace play a few songs to make sure they were up to speed.

Colly left the hall and found Phil, the Shandyman and Kevin hanging up more Japanese lanterns on the streetlights in the little abandoned suburbia next to the hall.

"Stupidest thing I've ever done," said Tom Shandy. "Japanese lanterns in November."

"Oh, not the stupidest thing you've done, I bet," said Phil, smirking at him. "I seem to remember one New Year's night not long ago and you singing songs in the snowy road, shirtless and with a pint in your hand."

"Okay," said the Shandyman, "maybe this isn't quite the dumbest, but, really, couldn't we have a better theme?"

"Blame Tralee," said Kevin. "It was the city council's idea to thank the Japanese for the trees. Didn't want to wait for spring."

Colly's hands began to shake as he looked at the colorful lanterns moving softly in the breeze, and he lifted up his head when he thought he heard a faint howling on the wind. He looked up the street at the abandoned houses and noticed a group of men hanging Japanese lanterns on the central traffic island that held the town's five cherry trees, also a gift of the Japanese ambassador.

He muttered to himself, "The world is changing."

"What do you mean, 'changing'?" asked Phil looking at him, her head cocked to one side.

"I don't know," he said. "Something's just not right. Maybe it's these abandoned houses, maybe it's the weird theme, but can't you feel it? Things are unsettled. You know those guys over there, decorating the trees? That tall one looks familiar."

"Nope, never seen them before, but lots of volunteers are here today. Colly, I know this looks like a ghost town now," said Phil, "but by this evening it will be filling up. We've been through all the houses, made them ready for guests whose reservations we booked weeks ago. It'll all look normal again soon."

"Don't think so," said Colly, turning away towards the hall. "There's bad luck in the air. I can smell it."

Phil watched him leave. She went to school with him and he normally was all full of smiles. But there was always something about him, secretive. She found him a little fascinating. They were friendly, but she'd never tried to get to know him better. Still she was happy he was staying for the evening. Everybody said he had a bit of the wild streak in him, so maybe he'd be up for some fun.

The afternoon passed swiftly, mostly because people were already pouring into town. Ballinskelligs was a favorite summer haunt for people, but the advertised promise of the *celidh* was a magnet for folks who didn't want the crush of the crowd in Tralee but were still intrigued what a Cherry Blossom Festival was doing in a November Ireland.

Conor and Jace were in awe of the amount of food and drink being consumed by everyone. Colly took them around and had them sample the various foods. Fifty years before, everything would have been boiled and served with potatoes, but with immigrants coming into the island, great varieties of food were now cooked. Conor and Jace appreciated the cosmopolItan atmosphere. Conor thought it almost looked like one of the Chicago festivals. The Japanese lanterns were lit and cast a warm glow on the evening and the town hall was filling fast.

Moira looked nervous though. Conor caught her eye and went over to her.

"What's wrong?" he asked. "Did we forget something?"

"No, nothing like that," she smiled too quickly. "The *Gardai* just told me there was an altercation in Castlecove. Bunch of RAGERS, just young kids, really, but high on that stuff that's been being thrown around the country. A couple of them got badly injured, went crazy and attacked some of the pub crawlers up there. RAGE or not, they were no match for the toughs. Got beat up pretty badly. Just hoping groups like that don't come down here. The night is off to a good start. Hate to see it spoilt."

"You worry too much, Moira," said Conor. "Come on into the hall and let's listen to the music. I play soon, and I'd love to hear what you think of it."

She ruffled his thick hair. "You are all charm, aren't you? I never met your father but you aren't the rascal your mother was, so all your sweet smiling must come from his side of the family."

"I plead guilty. A charmer I am," he laughed and flicked her a little salute, offering his arm as they walked into the hall.

He met Jace inside the building and they looked in wonder at the gathering. Conor knew what a *celidh* was; he'd just never been to a real one. The *DerryAir* in Chicago threw a pseudo-one every St. Patrick's Day, but it was pretty touristy. This was the real thing. Nobody was fancy dressed. Comfortable casual seemed to be the norm, and boots—lots of boots, not cowboy stuff but things called brogues. And ribbons on girls' hair. And of course, music. The band was lively, but Conor could see it wasn't some professional gig. The musicians were townsfolk, he guessed from the friendly first name calls the crowd gave them. He felt a surge of pride that they had asked he and Jace to play with them. Nice to be welcomed in a foreign land, even if he did feel strangely at home.

The crowd was a mix of out of towners, Travelers, and local denizens. Whatever differences they had melted away in the music that wafted over them and the dances that were called. Conor and Jace listened for a while and when the set ended, they made their way up to the stage to get ready for the next.

THIRST FOR DESTRUCTION

Saturday Evening, 11/7, Castlecove

THE PUB CRAWLERS up near Castlecove were all local toughs, hard men who earned their livelihood from scratching a living from the fields or fishing the seas. When the gangs of RAGERS appeared that evening, the hopped up, drug-addled bunch were not a threat to them. Even when they passed into the destructive phase of the drug experience, they could not really threaten the hardened locals who, knowing what they were, set to them with pipes, stones and chunks of wood—whatever was at hand—and beat the living hell out of them. RAGE had another peculiar effect on those who took it. It enabled them to endure pain and bodily damage that would otherwise seriously incapacitate or kill a person. While the RAGERS were beaten to within an inch of their lives, none of them died. The locals knew about the effect and left them lying in their own blood, confident that time would sort them out and send them back to wherever they came from. The townies went back to the *Blind Piper* pub and celebrated with as many pints as they could quaff.

But the coppery smell so noticeable around spilt blood lifted into the air and drifted north over old *Staigue Fort* and the surrounding hills. Humans wouldn't notice the diluted odor, but something did. And she stirred in her grave.

She pushed the dirt upward as she had done the night before. Easier this time, since it had been turned over by the now dead and consumed Traveler. She pulled herself out of the earth and sniffed like a rat scenting decaying meat. She remembered her task given her by the wizard thing that had commanded her last night, and she had every intention of fulfilling his wishes, but the smell of blood captivated her. She thought she would find its source on the way, but she had far to go this evening. Floating on the bits of wind present would pose no problem, but flight was not a speedy thing for a creature like her.

There was one who might help her, and she called in her strange sing song voice for him, but he never answered. However, something else did. She felt it first before she saw it, galloping from the nearby ocean. In the light of the quarter moon, she saw flashes of sinewy flesh and glistening scales with a mane like seaweed flowing in the wind. It stopped before her and bowed its head. It had no trouble recognizing a greater presence of evil than itself.

"Mistress," it breathed. "I heard you call my Master and I have come."

"Where is he?" she whispered. "He has never refused my summons."

"True. But he has seldom been disembodied before."

"What do you mean?" asked the revenant. "He is dead?"

"His kind cannot really die. But they can be indisposed," said the *kelpie*, swishing a serpentine tail over its flanks. "He must be remade from blood and dirt."

"Then come," she said. "I know where we may … reconstitute him. I have need for him tonight, and for you."

"Yesss, mistress," hissed the *kelpie*, bending its body down so she could mount. Together they galloped off to the southwest, both their noses scented to the smell of blood.

No one was out walking on the streets of Castlecove. Those who were awake were in the pub or tucked in their homes watching the telly. But the bodies of the RAGERS were still in the streets. Some were moving slowly, but most were still unconscious. When the Red Thirst galloped in on the shadowed *kelpie*, she sucked in a useless breath in greedy delight. Leaping off the beast, she took the moving ones and drained each of them of their blood. They had no time even to scream. It was luckier for the unconscious ones. They never knew what she did to them. She opened their necks with her sharp nails and let their blood fall to the ground. She gathered them into a small mound and had the *kelpie* run over them, stamping their bodies with its cloven hooves. Then, she sang in her sing song voice:

Dullahan, Dullahan hear my call.
Awake this night and cast your pall
Upon this land where death shall fall.
Dullahan, Dullahan hear my call.

Dullahan, Dullahan heed my cry.
Form from this midden a body to try,
Ride forth this night under moonlit sky.
Dullahan, Dullahan, heed my cry.

Dullahan, Dullahan, rise to my spell.
Wherever you wait, wherever you dwell
Forgotten, alone, burning in hell,
Dullahan, Dullahan, rise to my spell.

Her elegant, beautiful form, in her white burial shroud, simply tramped around the corpse pile like some primitive witch woman of old, but her words had the effect she wanted. A black, putrid mist rose from the midden and began to swirl until the bodies of the RAGERS disappeared and a form in the shadows took shape—a headless specter with spine-woven whip in hand and on his belt, a grinning corpse head, eyes alight with a hellish glow and a welcoming smile to greet the Red Thirst.

Those in the pub had heard the commotion but they thought it was simply the RAGERS recovering consciousness, gathering themselves and leaving. Then they heard the howl of the *kelpie* greeting its master, and involuntary chills ran up their spines. As one body, they leapt from their chairs and gathered at the doorway to see what was happening.

By the time they pressed outside, the *Dullahan* had mounted his *kelpie* steed and the Red Thirst was walking towards the townies. Smiling coyly, she sweetly said, "Oh tell me you love me darlings dear; tell me you love me darlings, darlings."

She reached out a clawed hand to rip the throat out of the nearest tough, when a larger man pushed through and faced her.

His scarred face twitched in anger, "We hate you forever darling dear, we hate you forever, darling, darling."

The Red Thirst stilled her movement, hissing in frustration.

"My mother taught me what to say as protection," said the man clenching his fists, "when we asked her to scare us with a story about Ireland's greatest vampire. Never thought I'd have to use it."

She backed away till she bumped into the flanks of the *kelpie*. For a moment there was silence, and then the *Dullahan* lifted its head from its belt and held it high. The head looked at the crowd and then began calling names, one by one.

"Liam," it said. A man fell in front of the pub's front window.

"Clancy," it said in its toneless voice. Another collapsed in a heap on the side walk.

"Do not listen to the names!" cried the large man. "Stop your ears with your hands. Get back inside the pub."

Crowds have their own lives, almost a hive mentality. A few smart ones did as they were ordered and ran either down the street or went inside the pub with hands over ears. But most simply panicked. And the voice of the

Dullahan went on, and more bodies collapsed on the ground, until at last the voice said, "Niall."

And the large man turned. So busy had he been hustling people inside the doors that he had not put his hands over his ears either. As he turned, he felt his heart flutter, but he steeled himself and lurched towards the *Dullahan*. He made it all the way to the *kelpie* before the *Dullahan* swung the whip and wrapped him in its embrace. The specter pulled Niall towards the empty space between its shoulders as if it was watching the light die from his eyes. Then the *Dullahan* tossed its old head into the pub and it burst into flame. The demon's hands twisted so swiftly that even the Red Thirst was amazed that Niall's head was neatly pulled from his body. The *Dullahan* threw the body to the vampire who greedily drank, and affixed its new head on its belt, the eyes already glowing with hellish fire as Niall's soul fled from the darkness.

The few left alive did not die, for the *Dullahan* swept up the Red Thirst behind itself and they galloped around the peninsula heading towards Ballinskelligs. The *kelpie* cried out now and then, a herald of death and woe as the night deepened.

LOCAL HERO

Saturday Evening, 11/7, Ballinskelligs

THE BAND HAD tossed the opening song of the second set to Conor. Normally, he would be really embarrassed to take the lead like this but they were so damn nice about it that he couldn't refuse. Besides, Jace was urging him on as well. Trying to think of what to do, he suddenly had an inspiration.

"Ladies and gents," he said. "The band has asked me to open this set." Good natured cheering greeted these words. "I thought I'd do something from my side of the Atlantic, and it's one of those Irish Canadian tunes that I know you know, but it fits this wonderful party so well that I think we ought to do it. It's an ancient reel, maybe over 600 years old, but the lyrics form a modern song. Called St. Anne's Reel for the Virgin Mary's mother's sake, it's great fun. And it's about a sailor stranded in a tiny town. Sort of like me, I guess, because he loves this little place and the people in it. And he hears fiddlin' music on the wind. He gets everyone involved in listening to it, so make it your own. It starts out with the tin whistle."

The song could be played fast or slow, but Conor always liked it fast, so he piped that whistle loud and strong and though the crowd let him do the solo, the minute the fiddle started in, everyone began to clap and head for the dance floor. It was wild and fun, there in the glimmering Japanese lantern lights, and Conor got the band to stall the lyrics while people danced their heart out. He heard a buzz in the crowd from the Travelers who weren't dancing but who were smiling big and strong. "The King Who Shall Be is playing," they said. "He doesn't know it, but he's calling her to come to him."

Conor didn't have a clue to what they were talking about but they were laughing and smiling knowingly at him, and he didn't sense any danger. He noticed Jace watching the Travelers carefully, and though Conor's hearing was heightened to an animal's sensitivity and Jace's was not, his friend seemed to have no problem reading the lips of the watchers. Even Michael seemed to be enjoying the song, clapping with the others while he sat far back on the stage watching over the tech.

Just as the folks on the dance floor couldn't move faster and began laughing and gasping for air at the same time, the doors of the hall blew open. Conor's whistle and the band's music faded away. Everyone stopped and gaped. There in the doorway stood Troubles and he looked every inch the massive dog from the Otherworld. Next to him, hand on his thick neck, stood Scatha, wrapped in a green gown that Conor swore could have been made from seaweed spun like silk. Raven hair shining with a circlet of gold glistening in the light. Troubles led her into the hall and the crowd parted to let her pass. Conor thought her beautiful and, mesmerized, walked down the stage steps to meet her on the dance floor.

Heads nodded in approval, a few people began to clap, several Travelers yelled out, "Scatha—*Failte! Failte!*—Welcome! Welcome!" The music started again only this time Jason sang the lyrics. He knew the song well and figured he might give it a go. He was getting to like this weird stuff that Conor had introduced him to months before.

It was timeless, magical, mystical. That's what Jace thought as he sang and watched the people move as one—strangers, lovers, friends—all caught up in the magic of each other's smiles. Conor had the same thought, only for him, no one existed but the woman before him. He had sensed the depths present in her when he met her days before, currents of deep emotion flowing like the ocean waters. He had never met anyone like her. The breeze that gently floated by him, kicked up by the passing dancers, lifted the front of his thick black hair. He smiled a little secret smile, just a touch on his mouth, like he knew Beth had liked, and Scatha smiled back, lips parted lightly to show a glimpse of artic white teeth.

And then the lyrics ended with:

And sometimes on November nights,
When the air is cold and the wind is right,
There's a melody that dances through the town.

The reel began in earnest again, and Conor danced like he never danced before. Scatha was a natural, and to the beat of boots on the floor and Jace's *bodhran,* Conor raced through steps he didn't know he knew and forgot the crowd and saw only her. Grinning at him now, she matched his vigorous pace and though sweat poured off his face, he was laughing with her as they made the rounds. Gradually, even more couples joined, and only those too old to dance stayed seated, but they pounded the tables with their drinks until the whole hall was as one with the music.

Just as the song reached a crescendo one more time, the doors flew open again, and a howling began that deafened the hall. Seven wolves paced in taking their places around the dance floor. They paid no attention to the people, but all faced the doorway they had just entered. Surprisingly, no one screamed or fled the hall. They were fascinated by the intensity of the wolves staring at the doorway, waiting.

Colly knew why they had come, and he slipped to the back of the stage where only Michael saw him.

"What is this?" said Michael placing a hand on the back of the young man's neck.

Colly didn't even try to dissemble. Looking up at him with dark black eyes, face set cold as an autumn morning, he said simply, "The wolves are mine. I placed them around Ballinskelligs and told them to come if danger was near. I'm sure Conor told you what happened at the funeral last night. Something bad is coming. Best we be prepared."

Michael looked at him for a long moment and then briskly nodded. "I did not know about you until today. Seems like you have a role to play that is not at odds with mine. See that you don't get in my way."

Colly bobbed his head. Stepping behind the curtain, he shifted to his wolf form and padded out to the floor to join the others.

He wasn't the only one on edge. Jace's fighting senses heightened as soon as he noticed that the animals had placed themselves strategically around the hall as if guarding the crowd. Troubles moved to cover Conor and Scatha. A heavy silence weighed amongst those gathered.

Then a stench assaulted all their senses, as if a grave had opened directly over death itself. Tears came to people's eyes, but it was not from the smell but from memories of loved ones lost, of family dying, of sickness taking, of death destroying. But the reek was gone in a moment and a fresh breeze drifted into the hall clearing the place of the fetid odor.

"What was that?" said Conor, turning till he met Jace's gaze.

No one answered him. But one of the wolves, Colly in his shifted form, lifted his muzzle and howled. As one, the pack moved and shot out the door, obviously chasing after something. Troubles whined but did not join them and Michael came down the stairs and stood by Conor.

"Death is in the air," said Michael, "and I smell the *Dullahan* and something else."

"But we killed that thing," said Conor.

"Not really," said Michael. "We just knocked it out of this reality, but it seems to have found form again. I am worried less about it than about the other thing with it. Not the *kelpie*, but a guest the *Dullahan* has brought."

Conor gripped Scatha's hand. "I know what it is," he said. "They told me last night at the funeral."

"Who told you?" asked Phil, as she and their other friends came close.

"The sentries on the battlements. Ancient soldiers. I saw them there and they spoke to me. It's the Red Thirst. That's what they called it."

"No!" said Scatha, eyes darting around the hall. "That can't be. *The Dearg Due*. She's gone. She's buried. She hasn't been seen in centuries."

"None the less," said Lettie overhearing them, "if that's what Conor heard, then she has taken up traffic with the *Dullahan* and these are sore and terrible days indeed."

The crowd inside the building broke down into little groups muttering amongst themselves, but Michael saw flashes of light outside the building and pushed his way through the crowd followed closely by Jace.

The two of them stood looking down the beach, out to sea, and saw on the distant horizon, lightning reflected from an approaching cloud bank. Overhead, the heavens were clear with a quarter moon and the Hand of God nebula brightening the night.

"I must go," said Michael.

"Where?" asked Jace. "You can't just go and check on what's happening out there. Stuff is happening here."

"I can and I will. You, on the other hand, need to do me a favor. Malby is Kevin's old nag that draws his and Mary's caravan. Get that horse and bring it to the beach. Watch it carefully, and if things go badly here, simply whisper in his ear, 'In Michael's name, I have need.'"

"Then what?" said a bewildered Jace.

"Then do what comes naturally to you." Michael laughed and ran down the beach disappearing into the darkness.

Jace could have sworn a tiny blue ball, glowing in the dark, followed after him. But Jace did as he was told and sauntered up towards the car park where the caravans were, found old Malby and brought him down to the beach. Such a calm animal, he didn't even feel the need to tether him. He heard a flapping of wings as a crow settled on Malby's harness.

"Wondered where you were," said Jace.

The crow just clacked a guttural mumble.

"Wherever there's a hint of death, there you are," said Jace.

The crow tilted its head and shot him a beady-eyed glance.

"No need to answer. But you're a little late. Something bad has just passed by, and a bunch of wolves have just taken after it."

The crow seemed to grow and its shadow slipped off the horse's withers. On the other side of the animal, Jace could see a dark shape and hear an old crone's voice.

"That bad thing passed by because I stood up by the crossroads to Castlecove and sent that dark little trinity on its way. Too much to do yet for carnage to hit this town. But your friend Conor was right. He suspected it was the Red Thirst, and indeed it is, but she is with the *Dullahan*—damn his penchant for reconstituting himself—on a particularly nasty *kelpie*. Conor was destined to battle the vampire, but I could not let it happen. He has something greater to do. They've gone north toward Tralee. I sent the wolves after them."

"Well then I guess you have it all sorted out as usual," said Jace, bitterly. "All going according to your plan." He stomped away from her and headed back to the town hall.

"Champion," she whispered, "oh, I will have need of you this evening as well. Prepare yourself." But he never heard her, anger churning in him drowning out her manipulative voice.

THE RACE TO TRALEE

Saturday Evening, 11/7, Ballinskelligs

COLLY YIPPED A quick command to the Alpha male and female wolves who transmitted his orders to the rest of the pack. The fetid stench that assaulted the partiers was still fresh in his nose as he streaked with the pack toward the crossroads on the way to Castlecove. He was in the lead when he spotted a figure all in black standing in the middle of the road. Colly had heard of her of course but had never seen her in person. Slowing the pack, he allowed himself to transform into his Changeling shape, a tall, almost plantlike figure, that looked more than a match for the Morrigan, especially as the bent old woman she appeared to be.

"Threatening me, Shifter?" cackled the ancient crone, stringy white hair falling on her withered face. "I'll take your tortured body and splinter it for kindling if you don't show me some respect."

Colly laughed, "They describe you truly, ancient one. I'm honored to meet you."

"Charmed," snorted the Morrigan, grudgingly accepting the compliment. "I suppose you know, I'm not here for you or your companions. I sent the things you chase away from here. Their thoughts said Tralee, but I could also divine they intended to make a stop at Ballinskelligs. Couldn't have that this early, I'm afraid, so I hastened them on their way to the city."

Colly's eyes hardened, "It's twice they describe you truly, ancient one. For it is said you hold human life lightly and gladly throw it away. I have friends in Ballinskelligs, people I have grown to love. Simply delaying their demise is not a plan."

The Morrigan stepped forward and shrewdly sized up the Changeling. "There's more to you than to the rest of your kin. Almost a conscience, a courage, a destiny even. Perhaps a test just to see what you are truly made of. I am not a heartless bitch, despite what some say. The thing called the Red Thirst is mounted with the *Dullahan* on a *kelpie* and they are keen on bringing death to the people in Tralee. That wretched wizard …"

"Shiro Ishii?" said Colly. "He's involved in this as well?"

"As I was saying before I was interrupted," said the Morrigan raking her nails across the Changeling's cheek, but not even marring his rough visage, "the wizard plans to slaughter the entire town at the festivities this evening. He needs the Red Thirst to accomplish his task. So, why don't you and your friends—come here my lovelies—try to stop them." The wolves wagged their tales and crowded around her laying on their backs with tongues hanging out.

"Thanks for the support, you guys," said Colly ruefully. "Morrigan, what is it you want us to do?"

"Catch her of course. The *Dullahan* and *kelpie* are less important. She's the one crucial to the wizard's plans. Lure her to Meritaten's Glen and take her there. Kill her if you can, though many have tried." Something caught her attention in the weeds on the side of the road. She bent down and snatched it in her claw.

"Look at this," she said. "This is a *droc ula*—a twisted little vampire thing."

Colly grew up watching vids of the original *Star Trek*. One of his favorite episodes featured round shapeless balls of fur called Tribbles. This little *droc* looked like a Tribble on steroids, a fairly shapeless furball with patchy scales. Unlike Tribbles, the *droc* had muscular little arms with grasping claws and feet to match. Though the pesky space aliens on the show were harmless, this guy had a mouth full of sharp teeth. The better to rip your throat out, he thought. He felt a whispering buzz in his head and realized it was the *droc* chattering in his mind.

Mixed with the Morrigan droning on, he was getting a headache. "You know how the worlds are coming together," she continued. "Perhaps you were even sent here to do something about that. But it's a strange occurrence. The Otherworld is dying. Huge swaths of it are barren desert now, though much beauty still remains. The things that are beautiful don't cross over here much—except for me of course." She smiled with her rotten teeth. "But evil things cross willingly. Food for them is becoming scarce in that reality. In the wake of the Red Thirst, the worlds are touching again and the tiny *droc ula* can cross over." She thrust the thing at Colly and he stepped back, especially noticing the fangs on its twisted, dwarven body.

"All they do is feed," said the Morrigan, "and there are many that are following The Red Thirst this evening. She has a plan for them. You must kill them as well, for they will cause great destruction." She held the thing up, and then crushed it in her hand. Dark slime oozed out her palm and onto the ground.

She stood looking at him in silence. "Well? You know what to do. Get you gone and strike that wicked wizard a blow while you're at it. I think he will find her. He needs her to put his plan into motion."

"Why not come with us?"

"Can't," said the Morrigan. "My place is in Ballinskelligs for now. I have a garden growing there this evening, a garden that I must tend. I shall follow as soon as I can."

Absolutely senile, thought Colly, but he changed to his wolf form again and quickly caught the scent of the evil ones. Yipping once, he got the attention of the pack and they raced off into the night.

THE NIGHT OF CHERRY BLOSSOMS

Saturday Evening, 11/7, Tralee

THE LITTLE *DROCS* proved to be more nuisance than danger for the wolves. The more they caught up with the Red Thirst, the more they heard the rabid little creatures. As they sped north, closely following the N70, the pack had little trouble snatching them up and dispatching them with quick crunches of jaws. Yet, for the local wildlife, the *drocs* were like the passing of a wildfire. Whatever they touched died. They were even able to drain the bodies of life without pausing in their race to keep up with the galloping *kelpie* and its riders.

It was a race and a chase of Otherworldly beings, and so the klicks swept by faster than thought. In less than an hour, they were at the Blennerville Windmill, a tourist trap vacant at this hour. It was there that Colly, even in his wolf form began to figure out why Shiro Ishii had needed the Red Thirst. She was corralling not wildlife, but people, stragglers who either had not yet made it to Tralee for the Cherry Blossom festival or just folk unfortunately out and about. The sight of her and the *Dullahan* caused every mortal who saw to flee faster into the city where there were greater numbers of people and hoped for safety. The *drocs* cast a pall of horrific expectation ahead of their passing and served to extend the Red Thirst's terror as she approached the festival.

Colly had noticed lightning in the far west over the sea towards the Skelligs, but as he and the pack approached Tralee, the storm seemed to come closer to land, thunder beginning to sound around him. He knew he would not catch the *kelpie* before it and its riders reached the town, but he and the pack poured on speed in hopes of disrupting whatever destruction Ishii had planned.

Once in Tralee, Colly saw the streets were a horror happening. The *Dullahan* was guiding the *kelpie* toward the town park near the city center, and the Red Thirst was laughing hysterically as they galloped through the panicked crowds. They touched no one, but did not have to. Just the sight of them caused people to trample one another.

For a while that evening, the town park had looked beautiful with Japanese lanterns glowing in the night, brightening the cherry trees gifted by the Japanese ambassador and planted by the town council earlier that spring. The trees were a special cultivar. They were bred to bloom twice, most brilliantly in the spring, but also in the autumn. They were blooming now, not as much as they would in spring, but startling prolific anyway. A freak of 'gentech', the blooms were beautiful amidst the falling leaves. The smell of the blossoms and the glowing lanterns warmed the night. Families enjoyed walking under them as the music played and people danced.

Before the living nightmare of the Red Thirst appeared, the lightning bolts came out of the cloudless sky, smacking into the town. Surprisingly, few hit the crowds of people. Most pounded the cherry trees with their energy. The sap exploded, blossoms were strewn high into the air, and in the midst of the cracking of the trees, smaller sounds could be heard. Tiny explosions from inside the lanterns came from little canisters hidden within the silken fabric of the festive hangings, releasing powder that filtered through the air, falling upon the crowds of people.

The lightning ceased and for a moment all was quiet as people looked up quizzically at the beautiful cherry blossoms gently falling in the night like a silent pink snowfall. They caught something besides the smell of cherry blossoms in the air, a slight acrid odor making their noses twitch and their eyes glaze.

Colly and the pack of wolves saw it all. They weren't affected, but they weren't human either, but every man, woman or child they saw suddenly stopped what they were doing and froze in place. Colly saw the Red Thirst leap off the *kelpie* and mix in with the crowd. He followed her path of destruction through groups of people that couldn't defend themselves. She killed them where they stood, stopping briefly to feast. The *Dullahan* stayed mounted but swept through the crowd swinging his whip. As dreadful as that slaughter was, it was minor compared to what Colly and the pack now noticed. People were popping out of their RAGE-induced state, and with looks of fury on their faces turned on one another. Fights broke out everywhere and nothing inhibited the people's anger. The pestilence spread its invisible hand everywhere and quickly. Ishii had accelerated the drug's metabolic affect.

The mad doctor saw everything as well, but he was above in the park's round tower. When the lightning exploded the trees, the beautiful blossoms did make the park look like a fairytale. He thought of years gone by and of how this scene should have played out in Washington, D.C. It would have been beautiful then, too, but the Emperor was not willing to allow it. Such a god-like being could not make a mistake, but Shiro Ishii always wondered at that decision. The fall of Japan happened swiftly after that. But now, he had a chance to see if the pestilence he was also releasing could really unleash the terror he sought. If so, it could be used again. He had manufactured it by using his old biotoxin from the war and mixing it with the new drug RAGE. The toxin insured lethality and contagion, and the drug gave a visible sign of the plague to those not yet infected by it. As chaos erupted below in the park, Ishii sighed with relief. The Red Thirst had done the job of herding people toward the park and the added horror she and the *Dullahan* provided would spread the news even faster of what had occurred here.

He noticed the wolf pack, slinking through openings of the crowd toward the demons wreaking havoc in the park. Hissing in anger and frustration, he hurried down to confront them. He was too slow, and by the time he pushed through the rioting mob the wolves had attacked.

Colly and the Alpha male and female wolves leapt at the Red Thirst ravaging the crowd while the others harried the *Dullahan* mounted on the *kelpie*. No matter how close they came to the vampire, she always managed to slip through their jaws. The same occurred with the *Dullahan*, steering the *kelpie* with speed through the people, trampling some, but always heading closer to the terror in the white funeral garb. The monster swept his free hand and grabbed the Red Thirst around the waist, hoisting her up behind him, and whipped the *kelpie* towards the park exit.

Colly saw they were escaping. Knowing he could do nothing for the raging crowd, he set the pack to follow the demons. At least he could stop them, depriving Ishii of one of his tools of terror. As the wolves pursued, Ishii reached the end of the park and saw them go. He needed to find them, but he had to turn back and look at what he had wrought. Fires, started by the lightning, were beginning to consume buildings near the park, and thousands were still rioting. What the violence and flames didn't kill, the contagion would and with luck would spread to surrounding communities. Not bad, he thought. Just decades too late.

MERITATEN'S GLEN

Saturday Evening, 11/7, Meritaten's Glen, Southwest of Tralee

THERE WAS A road, a detour west into the area of the Dingle Peninsula, that the *Dullahan* and the Red Thirst took in their flight from Tralee. They paused off that road near the battle field where the *Tuatha de Danaan* were beaten by the Scotians, a band of invaders, followers of the woman who led them. Her name was 'Meritaten Scota', and she was a Pharaoh's daughter exiled from Egypt because she married a Greek prince. Briefly Pharaoh, she had to flee in an uprising. The royal couple and their supporters traveled for years, finally ending up in Scotland, giving the country its name, but then emigrating to Ireland, only to do battle with the sorcerers who inhabited the Emerald Isle. There beneath the brooding mountains, the battle ensued. It was fierce but the Scotians prevailed, though the daughter of the Pharaoh perished in the melee. She was buried, there in what came to be known as Meritaten's Glen, though her tomb was never found. At least not by humans.

But Colly knew, and so did the wolves. The reputation of her people and of her as a fierce warrior penetrated even into the Otherworld. He knew where her grave was. Curious that just earlier in the day, he and his friends had discovered the graves of the Seven Sleepers, the Egyptian monks who centuries later came to Ireland to help gift the Christian faith upon the people. Wondering if there was some connection, he thought it fascinating that the last battle with the Red Thirst, a demon left over from the time of those sorcerers, would occur here, for he meant to kill her where demons had died before.

The *Dullahan* and the Red Thirst stopped the *kelpie* next to the ancient stone proclaiming the glen to be the burial place of the Egyptian princess. Only the *kelpie* screamed at the approaching wolves. The headless horseman stayed silent and the Red Thirst smiled softly, singing a tuneless song as the wolves rushed into the glen and stalked their prey.

Colly's only goal was to kill the Red Thirst, but to do that he had to separate her from the *Dullahan*. Sending the Alpha male and female wolf forward, he had them harry the *kelpie*, nipping at its legs and tail. They did no real damage, but they did make the *kelpie* skittish. Suddenly, the *Dullahan's* attention was riveted on keeping his mount under control. It was then, that Colly paced forward and looked directly at the revenant, who was still dripping blood from the mouth that had feasted on the townsfolk.

"Come here," rasped Colly in the closest approximation to a human voice he could make in wolf form. Saliva dripped from his mouth. His lips, pulled back from his feral teeth, made the Changeling wolf seem to smile.

She came to him, drifting off her seat on the *kelpie* and lightly landing on the soft grass of the glen. She knelt, surrounded by the golden leaves fallen on the ground from the beech trees above. Holding out her arms in a welcoming embrace, her dead lips somehow moved the air in front of her mouth so that the wolf clearly heard, "Tell me you love me darling dear; tell me you love me darling, darling."

Colly knew the legend well. The times he walked in the Otherworld, he had heard of its truth. He howled as the Red Thirst tried to transmit her lust for blood through her beckoning arms. He began to pace back and forth and both barked and growled the answer, "I hate you forever darling dear; I hate you forever darling, darling." As she stood, her hands reaching out to grasp him, he leapt at her throat.

The other wolves, all seven of them jumped at the same time for the neck of the *kelpie* and the arms of the *Dullahan*. A headless horseman looks strange at the best of times, but swatting at jumping wolves made the *Dullahan* look spastic and far from fearsome. The Alpha male and female had always hunted together, and they timed their attack perfectly. As the wolves harried both beasts, the Alpha wolves leapt again for the *Dullahan* from both sides of the *kelpie*, succeeding in dragging him off his mount onto the ground.

Perhaps they were lulled into thinking the headless horseman more powerless when off the *kelpie*, but if so, the wolves were mistaken. The other pack members were having no trouble ripping into the *kelpie*, biting huge chunks out of what passed for its flesh, but the Alpha male and female suddenly found themselves at a disadvantage. The *Dullahan* had managed to snag his head from the pommel as he fell, and was swinging it at them like a club as he tried to rise to his feet.

Colly didn't even notice. He missed the Red Thirst's throat and barreled into her chest knocking her over. She rose hissing and bit him deeply in his shoulder. His paws dislodged her and he went for the soft flesh beneath her chin. But she was a monster. Her jaw stretched and bent, and it seemed to Colly that her fangs grew longer. He had to dodge away lest he impale himself on the ivory blades so sharp in her maw. He yipped in frustration, glancing at the rest of the pack.

He could see them clearly under the star and moonlit night sky. While the *kelpie* was down, the *Dullahan* had arisen and was clubbing two wolves with the corpse head. They weren't defeated, but neither were they weakening the headless horseman.

Suddenly, Colly found himself thrown across the glen. When his body stopped sliding through the dew-covered grass, he looked up and saw the Red Thirst floating over the ground towards him, her arms not beckoning with an embrace, but instead brandishing claws with fingernails that had grown into slashing hooks. No sing song tune from her now, only the screech of the undead seeking its prey.

Colly had enough. When he had run with the pack over the years in the Otherworld, they had taught him one move that this reality's wolves never used. Lurching to his feet, Colly ran directly at the revenant. Putting all his weight on his back legs he jumped. The Red Thirst, thinking he leapt for her throat again, reached out to snag him with her claws, but Colly had no intention to come close to her. He vaulted high over her head, and in a maneuver impossible for a normal wolf, he turned 180 degrees in mid-air, landing behind her and immediately leaping at her again. His jaws closed over her neck and he bit, crushing her spine.

Dropping like a rag doll, the Red Thirst fell on the ground. Colly, morphing into a werewolf, grabbed an arm and flipped her over. Her dead, red eyes flashed at him, but for the moment she was unable to move. The Changeling had no illusions, however. He could already hear the bones knitting themselves back together. Full of the blood of her victims, she was healing swiftly.

With no time to waste, he bit deeply into her chest, ripping to close his jaws over her mummified yet beating heart. Finding it more by sound than sight, he crushed it in his jaws and tore it from her body. An unearthly scream pierced the night as Colly jumped up and tossed the heart onto the golden grass of the glen where it burst into flame. He rose up on hind legs to pounce again when a terrible pain ran through his body. Thinking for a moment that the monster had bit him worse than he thought in his shoulder, he came back down as a wolf, and found himself tumbling onto the ground. Looking, he saw he was missing much of his front right leg. Another shriek off to his side made him glance right, and he saw Shiro Ishii, katana drawn, screaming a samurai cry, preparing to strike again.

But the pack was not going to permit such an attack. The *kelpie* used the distraction to limp away; the *Dullahan* was being chased down the glen by the Alpha male and female, and the rest of the pack set upon this new threat. Ishii was too skilled with the blade to allow them to tackle him and he got in a few deep cuts on some of the wolves. He too, however had to flee. This was not a fight he could hope to finish.

Colly dragged himself over to the Red Thirst to make sure her death was secure, but the pain and blood loss caused him to lose consciousness as his head dropped next to hers. With his last bit of sight, he saw a small group of people entering the glen. It was Fr. Greavy and a posse of rescuers.

"Ah, lad," said the priest, cradling the wolf on his lap, "what have you gone and done to yourself?"

Then he saw an old woman, dressed in gray like a nun, leaning over him. "Well, Fr. Greavy, I'd say he's rid this world of an ancient terror forever." She turned to others in the shadows saying, "Brendan, Fintan, Orin—drag the body of this demon over to its burning heart and toss them together with some of the dead branches around here. I want the Red Thirst turned to ash." She looked up at the sky. "And I want it done under the Hand of God before the moon goes any higher. We will be rid of this menace." Then Colly lost consciousness.

He awoke in his Changeling form with his back against the Neolithic stone in the center of the glen. Fr. Greavy was sitting beside him staring at the snapping branches burning the body of the Red Thirst. The old nun was binding his one good arm and shoulder with a bandage and a sling. The other arm, severed at the elbow had a heavy tourniquet on it. Surprisingly, the pain was gone.

"You look familiar to me," he slurred to the old woman.

"Well, I certainly should," she said, "since I'm the one who brought you to your mother in this world long years ago. I'm Ita, and you've done well, child, so much better than I thought you would."

"Indeed," said the priest, "we knew you would succeed in looking for the coming of Conor Archer and Jason Michaels, but to kill the Red Thirst. That is a happy circumstance, and rids the world of one of evil's most faithful servants."

"You knew what I was, Fr. Greavy?" said Colly.

"Of course. Ita and I planned it, many years ago. I was a younger priest then. She's been around here … well nearly forever." He smiled up at her and she whacked him in the knee with her staff, laughing as she did so. "Your father was fishing in the North Sea when Mrs. Roddy had her child, unexpectedly early. No one was with her and her child died stillborn. She too would likely have died had I not come visiting. Unconscious, she had lost a lot of blood. I made her as comfortable as possible. Nothing much more I could do."

"You could have called an ambulance," said Colly amazed at what he was hearing.

"I could have, but then you and I would not be sitting here today. Instead, I called for St. Ita, the guardian of the Well of the Wethers and all the surrounding land, and she came, bringing you, the little Changeling child, and with her healing touch, saved your adoptive mother's life."

The nun reached down and touched the shoulder wound on Colly's left arm. "This bite would have killed a man, but it's barely scratched the surface on you. We needed someone who was from the Otherworld, someone special who could fit in here, and watch for the coming of the King Who Shall Be and his Champion. That event was, as all great things are, a part of an ancient prophecy that foretold the joining of our worlds once again and the tumult that would ensue. I cast a glamour on you for your first few years. You appeared human in every respect. I was able to make you look like your mother. Knowing the abilities of your kind to shift forms easily, I called in the wolves of the Otherworld to teach you over time how to disguise yourself as a human but learn of your true heritage as well. You needed to know things, but not know too much. Now, it's time for you to come into your own."

"They'll hate me though if they find out what I am," said Colly. "All humans hate Changelings and that Michael thing, whatever he is, he's not human and he is suspicious of me too."

Fr. Greavy laughed. "Michael will come around. In your true form, you remind him of a group of beings he had to war against—you do remember the stories don't you—but you are not like them. Indeed, you are not much like a Changeling either. You've been around humans too long, and it seems to have done you a world of good."

The wolves that had chased away Shiro Ishii were back and lounging on the ground. Colly looked down the glen and saw the Alpha male and female returning. He felt their love and concern but knew immediately that the *Dullahan* had eluded their grasp. "It is all right," he said to them, ruffling their shoulders with his one good hand as they sniffed his wounds. "We'll catch him another time."

Everyone was silent for a few moments and then Colly said, "Ita, what do you know about this glen?"

"Everything, child," she responded.

"Did you know there's a grave of the daughter of an Egyptian Pharaoh on that little hill just over there under a buried stone beneath that huge beech tree?"

"That," said Ita, "would be the sixth beech tree that has grown in that place."

"There's more Egyptians out on *Skellig* Rock—seven of them, I think. And a treasure. Any connection?"

Ita looked at Fr. Greavy and then smiled enigmatically at Colly. "Could be. Long time ago, I was here and the grave was visible. You could enter it then. Stairs going down deep underground could be seen. I went a little way to the bottom. There's a locked door down there and hanging in the middle was an ankh—an Egyptian cross. It was a key, you see, and no one knew what it fit. It wasn't meant for the door, at least not that one. I have it here." She reached into the folds of her grey robes and pulled out a bronze ankh which on closer observation was in fact a key. "Perhaps you might know the lock it might open."

Colly smiled remembering the seventh sarcophagus in the cave on *Skellig* Michael. "I think I do," he said.

"But first," said Fr. Greavy, "you've got to get back to Ballinskelligs. It was terrible in Tralee, and I saw lightning flashing down their way as well. I have a bad feeling they are in trouble too. I'm staying here for a while. No telling what I might find as I putter about."

"The land portals are too dangerous this evening," said Ita. "Evil things manifest around them. We will have to go by sea. That's why I brought my friends along. I have a ship on the River Lee. It will take us by the sea portal swiftly to Ballinskelligs. Come," she said to her companions. "Gently carry the Changeling. We have a boat to catch."

MEANWHILE BACK IN
BALLINSKELLIGS

Saturday Evening, 11/7, Ballinskelligs

JACE HUFFED HIS way back to the hall in anger after leaving the Morrigan. He knew Malby would be okay by himself down on the beach. Conor said he was a badass pony. He was going to say more to the Morrigan, but the new preparations for whatever else would happen on this oh so fun evening cut the conversation short.

He found Conor in the hall trying to gather together his friends. He noticed that this Scatha chick stuck to his friend like glue. He could tell she wasn't just an ordinary girl. For a moment, her sultry glance caught his eye. She acknowledged him with a nod, but then the rest of the crowd demanded his attention. Everyone else was milling about, not sure what was going on. The dance caller instructed the band to play, but it was a half-hearted tune they produced. People were just on edge. Then the booming began. Thunderclaps overhead and the flash of lightning visible even inside the hall. Mostly just a sound and light show since the sky above was virtually cloudless. Conor told as many as could hear him to stay put while he and Scatha checked outside. Jace joined them in watching.

Crowded as the hall was, there were still hundreds of people lining the streets where the Japanese lanterns glowed. Whatever fun they were having stopped. The thunder and lightning spooked them, making them look for a place to shelter.

"The lightning is coming from just beyond the *Skelligs*, out to sea. There's a cloud bank there," said Jace.

"Yeah, I saw," said Conor, "but look closely. The bolts aren't random. They're arcing northeast."

"Towards, Tralee," said Jace. Conor looked at him quizzically. "The Morrigan told me. Just saw her down at the beach. Seems like whoever is playing Zeus with the thunderbolts is in league with Shiro Ishii and that Red Thirst you were talking about." He turned toward Scatha. "Conor, like always, hasn't given a proper introduction. I'm Jace, and you?" He held out his hand to her.

She ignored it and said to him simply, "Champion, it is good you are here with your friend. There is so much more power present when two minds and hearts are united in purpose. Look, something is happening down the street."

Shafts of lightning suddenly struck the center traffic island festooned with lanterns and cherry trees in autumn flower. Like a burst feather pillow, the trees let loose the cherry blossoms while the expanding air from the lightning strike threw the flowers high above the town, already mixing with the powder hidden in the exploding lanterns.

Just as at Tralee, the scene was momentarily beautiful, but Conor saw many people down the streets grow still and stand unmoving.

"That sonofabitch," said Conor. "I know what's happening to them. Ishii has gone and made a biochem weapon. There's at least some of that drug RAGE present and I wouldn't put it past him to mix it with that plague that killed the Travelers. Damn stuff is probably contagious. Go," he said to Jace, "get the doors of the hall closed and then get Malby—I've got an idea."

Jace cocked an eyebrow at Conor who said, "I know I'm in danger, but I have a hunch I've caught at least part of this thing already and I lived. Scatha, well, she's special and I'd doubt she's vulnerable to this stuff, but Jace, you've never been exposed. Doesn't matter if you're my friend or the Champion. This thing will kill you if it touches you."

Jace nodded and said, "I'm going back down to the beach. Michael said if things got bad I was to go to Malby and say, 'Michael has need of you,' and then just believe what I would see. The horse would do the rest. If not, I'm probably shafted." He took off at a run.

"What will you do?" said Scatha to Conor.

"It's what we're going to do," said Conor, gritting his teeth. "I don't know this land like you. I think I know how to make my idea work, but you're going to have to convince the ones I call that I'm the real thing. Amergin named me the Bard of the West and, if that's really true, we can save at least some of these people."

He took her hand and they walked over some rocky scree to the road. Ahead of them, bolts of lightning still struck the trees and lanterns that had not yet exploded. But the people, who were as frozen as zombies before, now began to move and scream and attack one another.

"Oh, my God," said Conor. "I hope we're not too late."

"You're not," said Scatha, planting a kiss on his lips. "You are the King Who Shall Be; you are the Bard of the West. The Land will listen to you." Troubles, who had padded up to his master, woofed in agreement.

Conor took out his tin whistle and piped a luting call, like a lark might sing in the evening. It was clear and pure and carried through the night. Though not one person who heard it knew there was an embedded message in that tune, all untouched by the plague felt their hearts lift with hope and their fear ebb away. In the distance, birds could be heard answering from their nests or the trees or rocks where they slept, and a rush of wings approached the tiny town. Conor put the whistle back in his pocket and instead simply let his lips do the calling of the birds. Like a lark he sang. Truly eerie, it sprang from his heart and surprised him as much as it did Scatha. Suddenly, he was able to weave words around the music and he sang:

> *Often, often, often, walks the Light in the midst of song,*
> *Often, often, often walks the Light in the midst of song.*

The birds came, tens of thousands of them on the wing, high in the air. All kinds joined together in a huge murmuration, diving and sweeping together in the night sky, visible as shadows under the moonlight and the Hand of God nebula. Some bolts of lightning cast many down, some birds inhaled the plague powder and were lost, but other birds appeared to take their place. Conor and Scatha, each holding the other's hand, lifted up their arms and sang to the birds. Conor remembered the gathering of the *sluagh* as they approached the town days before, but this murmuration was a thing of beauty. Swirling in the air, wings whispering, songs soaring, the birds veered upward beating their wings toward the burning neighborhood. One bird, a dozen birds, tens of dozens would have done nothing, but tens of thousands created a wind that pushed back at the spreading contagion and conflagration, keeping both from the hall and the rest of the town. Nothing could be done about those infected, and the wind caused by the birds was certainly not strong enough to keep the plague-touched people from trying to infect the entire village. And then, there were still the lightning bolts which struck many of the winged creatures from the sky and threatened anyone outside without shelter.

For a moment, everything hung in the balance. The pressure caused by the exploding lightning began to press more heavily on Scatha and Conor, and he knew they were losing the battle. For a moment he stopped his part of the song, urged Scatha to continue, and then at the top of his voice yelled,

> *Brian, Brian, with true name rise,*
> *Hear my cries, wing to the skies,*
> *Hooves pound the land, angel-mane flowing,*
> *Outrace the wind, courage be growing,*
> *Strong is your heart, strong are your eyes.*

He heard Jace yell back in shock. He could imagine what his friend had done. Jace knew how to ride, so he probably mounted the old horse and whispered into its ear, "I'm supposed to say that Michael—whoever he really is—has need of you." Conor smiled at what he thought was happening down at the beach, and he picked up his harmony with Scatha again. He didn't need to see what was occurring behind him. He knew Malby had transformed into Michael's steed, Brian, and even now was hovering aloft with a shaken Jace grasping the horse's mane. Conor wasn't worried. Jace was born to be a Champion. He'd know what to do.

The horse rose on its beautiful wings above the beach, and Jace quickly took in what had become a battlefield. Ahead of him and the magnificent steed, a neighborhood was in flames and hundreds of people were attacking each other and seeking to storm the town hall. Around Jace and Brian were a multitude of birds singing in their own languages and the music generated was deafening. But it was the wind that impressed Jace. The many birds created a wind that held the contagion back, that kept the flames from spreading, but as wonderful as that was, the birds and Conor and Scatha's song could not keep the enraged people at bay. If they broke through, the plague would spread. Jace bent over the neck of the horse and yelled, "Sure hope you understand, but please, please, please, get your wings beating and let's drive those crazy zombies out of here."

Brian was able to beat his wings faster and faster all the while bringing himself and Jace above the town hall. The steed screamed a cry of battle as he dived and used his wings as a bellows to drive the infected back into the burning neighborhood. Jace drew his Sword and caught any of those unlucky to be strong enough to resist the wind. He hated to do it, but looking at their faces, he saw all humanity had left them, and a feral hatred stormed out from their gaze. He was killing human bodies, but God only knew if there were souls still in them. Jace saw Conor look over his shoulder and grin at him. It was a smile of victory. The steed of the archangel Michael and every bird in southwest Ireland were driving the contagion away from the town and out instead over the sparsely populated fields. Most of those infected were simply blown back, and Jace, the horse and winged fowl held them at bay until they simply collapsed and died from the plague. It was over in minutes.

Such a temporary victory though. Conor and Scatha let their arms fall and their song cease. Released from their task the birds let the murmuration dissolve and disappeared into the night. The horse landed and the three humans, and Brian surveyed the damage. Troubles was less reticent. He bounded down the road and checked the bodies he passed. He, too, seemed immune to whatever remained of the plague. He delivered a coup de grace to the few bodies still crawling on the ground, and when the dog was done, he trotted back to Conor, shaking his massive head in what Conor thought was an expression of horror.

"Could be worse," said a voice behind them. They looked and there stood the Morrigan. "Well done," she said. "Brilliant use of the birds. I would never have thought of it. And you, Scatha, first time in, well many years, that you've cooperated with anyone on land. Must be this young man's fetching personality." Shining in her red robes as the warrior maiden, the Morrigan flashed a bright smile at Conor who blushed deeply red.

"And my Champion," she purred at Jace. "Another fine effort." She touched his face with her hand and Troubles growled. "Quiet beast," she said shortly, "I like you but I won't tolerate back talk." She ruffled the fur on his head and the dog licked her hand.

"Geez," said Conor to the dog, "no need to be such a brown-noser."

"Well," said the Morrigan, "at least the beast knows who his betters are. But enough of this chit-chat. Ahead of me is my garden for the evening. There are dead to take care of, and I must do my appointed rounds. Do not worry about Shiro Ishii's plague around this town. Nothing will be left to infect any living thing. But I cannot say as much for the rest of County Kerry or Ireland herself. The contagion is moving. None of you are strong enough yet to stop that. It will take another." She gazed out toward the *Skelligs* where the sound and light show still was raging and then looked at Brian. Something passed between the two of them. The horse leapt to the sky with Jace hanging on for dear life, crying out "Holy crap, where are we going?"

Brian flew low over the town hall and above the crowd gathering outside on the beach to survey the destruction of half their village. Conor ignored all the pointing at Jace and the flying horse and yelled to Kevin and the Shandyman to gather the Travelers and the townspeople and make some fires on the beach because no one could go anywhere until the plague was securely under control. He wasn't just going to take the word of the Morrigan at face value. She liked the dead too much. Moira and Phil rushed to the hotel to prepare as much food as they could. With what was left from the *celidh*, plus what they could make now, there'd be enough to last the night. Moira had a feeling things weren't quite over yet.

As soon as she thought it, a tremendous flash of light, followed by an explosion came from the top of Skellig Michael. It was so powerful that in moments a shock wave blasted everyone outside of a building to the ground. No one was seriously hurt, but all looked anxiously out to sea. A furious battle seemed to be taking place as a mushroom cloud of fire and light rose over the peaks.

Jace saw it all. Brian had already flown half the distance to the islands when the explosion happened. It seemed that some beam of energy had come from the stationary cloud bank and smashed into the summit of *Skellig* Michael. Jace could see the shadows of stone thrown high in the air.

Buffeted by the shock wave, he saw something else as well. Something was standing on the summit of the island giving as good as it was getting. Huge blasts of energy radiated out from the top of the highest peak, down into the murky cloud. Far from being stunned by the blast, whatever was at the summit was raining copious amounts of power down towards the ocean. Whatever was in the cloud that hugged the surface of the water had stopped throwing lightning to the northeast and towards Ballinskelligs. It was focused totally on its island enemy.

"It's your master, isn't it?" said Jace through the wind into the flying horse's ear. "Is it Michael up there?" The horse neighed a quick agreement, and Jace reassessed the man he knew as Michael. Because whatever was on the summit did not look like a man. It was some being of light, shifting colors throughout, with several overarching and moving appendages. And there was a trident. That was clearly evident. Three-pronged and beaming out its own energy bolts. Conor hadn't told him who Michael was. Just another thing they didn't get to do in all the bustle for the party. But Jace knew what he was seeing. That giant figure at the top of *Skellig* Michael was an angel, a seraphim to be exact with six wings and nary anything that looked human to Jace. He couldn't even pick out a single face. This being was something totally other. Whatever he was fighting must have been some huge motherfucker as well. They seemed evenly matched.

Brian swerved to the right and approached the island from the north. Slowing down he glided across the northern summit with its abandoned monastery of corbeled stone huts. Just a few meters from the top of the summit where the battle raged, the narrow platform of the Needle's Eye, where hermits used to crawl and lay for hours cruciform in prayer, provided all the space the winged horse needed to land.

Shaken, Jace gingerly stepped down onto the ground, holding onto the neck of the steed. "Most fantastic ride I've ever had. Let's do it again, ok?" The horse shook his head and whinnied what Jace thought was a laughing agreement. "But no more tonight, my friend. No more tonight. You stay here. I'm going upstairs to see if an angel needs my help." The horse nickered again, and Jace now knew that he could recognize a sarcastic and contemptuous scoffing of a horse. At least there was one creature that didn't think he was any kind of a Champion.

It was a difficult few meters to climb, particularly since the rocks were shaking every time a lightning bolt or, he guessed it now as a deliberately aimed energy bolt, struck the island. But he made it up to the top without incident and stood in awe of the scene before him.

He had no doubt now that he was seeing an angel, but no painting ever did this being justice. Actually, it looked like a ninja angel, darting its huge form here and there avoiding energy blasts. Once in a while, it stood still and from the very visible trident that Michael pointed at the sea, a huge blast of fire streaked into something there on the ocean.

"Welcome, Jason Michaels," said a placid voice. "Few humans have ever seen what you are witnessing now. The never-ending battle with Leviathan."

"You're fighting a whale?" shouted Jace. "Like some supernatural Captain Ahab?"

Something like laughter hummed through the air. "I'm a better shot," said the being. Then in the same languid voice it said, "Below is the ship you harried a few days ago—the *Baleros*. It belongs, as you know, to Sir Hugh Rappaport who once was a man like you, but long ago sold his soul to the Dark. Watch out!" the voice said, barely changing its tone. From somewhere beneath flashed an energy beam, and without thinking Jace already had his Sword out and swatted it away. Without that instinctive action, he would have been immolated then and there and this conversation would have been ended.

He felt no fear though and instead was intrigued. "You are Michael, right? The one I met today? I mean now you look like what I always thought God looked like."

The same 'Otherworldly' laughter hummed through the air again. "Who is like God? I am certainly not, though it is not wrong for a creature such as yourself to feel awe in my presence."

"Great," said Jace, "a narcissistic angel."

Again, the laugh, this time louder. "I like you human. I sense you are a good friend to Conor. He will need you, but first we must dispatch this ship. It has caused much damage tonight."

"Why not just kill Sir Hugh if he's responsible?"

"That will be very hard to do. There's not much of Sir Hugh left inside the husk of his body. A change is occurring down there. Every living thing on that vessel is being sucked dry of spirit and energy to feed the being coming into this world now. His name is Balor. Worshipped once in this land, indeed all over Europe, as a god, he is a demon bent on the destruction of life. He can't kill me, but he can harm me, for we are made of the same star stuff. It will be a standoff of sorts once I destroy his ship. I will need both you and Conor to help me defeat him, again."

"You've fought this guy?"

"Once before, actually, and at great cost to beings like me and to the two realities that make up what you call Earth—this physical place and the Otherworld which seeks to merge with it."

"Balor is a cancer upon all reality, and though you did not fear me when you saw me in my true form, you will fear him, for by nature you are attracted to goodness and cannot really understand or fathom the darkness and the depravity of evil."

As if Balor knew he was being discussed, several bolts of energy smashed into the summit and the shock wave threw Jace against the cliff face, momentarily stunning him. The crash of thunder was deafening and even Michael knew such a blast would be felt on shore.

"I must act now. Stay here on the summit while I stop this nonsense." Some unseen communication between horse and angel must have happened, for Jace heard Brian scream in welcome and fly up to the summit. He seemed to have grown larger, which was a good thing in Jace's mind, since the seraph was several times larger than himself. He didn't know quite how the angel sat on the steed, but Michael looked appropriately magnificent as the horse jumped to the sky, circled the summit and with a single word from the angel, "Attack!", said in that same placid voice, horse and rider dropped like a stone.

There were a few stray energy beams that Jace almost absent-mindedly batted away with his Sword, but he was mesmerized at the amount of power that poured out of Michael. So bright was the lightning the angel created that Jace could see the ship below, sustaining many blasts and not without massive damage. Great gouts of fire erupted from the deck and huge chunks of steel were torn from the ship. Return fire was noticeably lessening, and still the seraph did not let up. Over and over, Brian dived and Michael pointed his trident and unleashed the heavenly version of hell upon the ship.

Then, Michael gently lifted off the horse and floated down to the deck of the vessel, now listing to port. Jace heard the inhuman voice say, "Balor, you have lost. Show yourself." For a moment, there was nothing, and then the ship exploded. Incredibly, Jace saw Michael thrown backwards into the air. Shrapnel passed through the angel, and for a moment Michael lay in the air cruciform looking up at the sky with, as Jace would explain it later, what passed for six of his faces slightly out of shape. Jace could swear he was unconscious.

But only for a moment. Michael's wings pushed him higher in the air and another explosion sounded from the huge research and cargo ship. Then all was quiet as the ship broke in two, and like the TItanic sunk silently into the North Sea.

Brian gently flew beneath the angel and lifted him up, carrying him back to the summit. Jace could see the angel seemed hurt. Particles of some kind were drifting out of his side rather rapidly.

"Can I help?" he whispered, not sure if he should approach closer.

The inhuman voice softly said, "Yes. Take your Sword, the Sword of Light, and press it against my wound. Do not worry, I will feel no pain."

Jace did as he was told. The closer he got to the angel, the brighter the Sword glowed and when he touched it to the middle of the angel's body, a flash erupted and the seraph let out a groan.

Jace couldn't help smiling just a little. "You won't feel a thing, huh? They tell us in football, no pain no gain, so suck it up buttercup."

Six pairs of orbs that were his eyes lifted in incomprehension. "Suck it up buttercup?" said the voice.

Jace laughed, "Are you going to be okay?"

"Surely. Not many days ago, I washed up on shore after a battle with another evil thing and his minions and I was more damaged then than now."

"You should be happy," said Jace. "Looks like you killed Balor."

"His kind cannot be killed, only sidelined. But I see no body, and I would feel his passing. While the ship was exploding, he escaped and there is only one place he would go."

"Ballinskelligs," said Jace. "I've got to get back there. He'll try to take out Conor and the whole town."

"That he will, but you will not make it in time. He is already there."

"But I'm supposed to protect Conor. He's my friend."

"And you are his Champion, but you can't be everywhere. What you just did here helped me destroy his power base. Had he gone to Ballinskelligs without that happening, Conor would not stand a chance. He might yet prevail."

"Please let me go," begged Jace. "Just let me take Brian and see if I can make it."

"As you wish, my young friend. But hurry. I fear you are already too late."

BALOR

Saturday Evening, 11/7, Ballinskelligs

CONOR LIFTED HIMSELF off the ground after the explosion, quickly checking if everyone was okay. No one seemed harmed, and he was gratified to see Moira and Phil, the Shandyman, Kevin and his family all unhurt. Troubles got his attention though, by barking excitedly and running down the beach.

Conor yelled at him, but the dog didn't stop. Wondering what had gotten into him, Conor took off after the dog and then he saw. Just around the headland, a sparkling path on the sea appeared.

"What the hell?" said the Shandyman.

"It's a *faerie* track," said Mary, arm entwined with Kevin's.

"Sometimes, beings from the Otherworld can travel more swiftly using paths that connect the two realities together. This must be one of those tracks," said Kevin.

All conversation stilled as they saw what travelled that path. Coming into their sight was a small dragon-prowed long ship being rowed by several men. Standing in front, holding onto the prow was the grey-habited nun, St. Ita, looking every inch the medieval abbess, holding her wooden crozier. She raised her hand in greeting and leapt lightly off the ship as it crunched softly into the sandy beach.

"Don't just stand there, my friends," she said. "We have a wounded warrior to tend."

Conor rushed forward and cried out as he saw a blood-soaked figure wrapped in a blanket. The figure of a man lay in front of him.

"Geez, it's Colly!" he said. Everyone, except Scatha, gasped as Conor reached into the boat and effortlessly lifted the wounded man out and laid him on the beach. "Ita, what happened? He's bleeding out!"

"Colly," she said, "had a run in with the Red Thirst and though it looks like he got the worst of it, she is dead and he is still among the living."

Phil knelt down beside Conor and lifted Colly's arm, or what was left of it. "My God, that vampire bitch did this?"

"Not the vampire," said Ita, "but that wretched wizard with his curved Sword. After they spread the plague in Tralee, the *Dullahan* and the Red Thirst made for Meritaten's Glen. Shiro Ishii brought up the rear and was late to the battle. He arrived in time to see the revenant torn apart by Colly and his pack of wolves. He severed Colly's arm up to the elbow. Then we arrived, and he, along with the *Dullahan* and *kelpie* fled."

"Colly has done a great service to us all," she continued, "ridding the land of the Red Thirst and halting this evil trinity from spreading the plague faster, though I fear the contagion will not be contained."

"Something's happening to him!" asked Phil, stepping back in fear.

"He cannot control his form," said Ita. "He has changed several times in the past hour."

"Changed?" said Conor. He looked more closely and he saw the human form of his new friend shift and this time he even stood and backed up in shock. "What is this, Ita? What's going on here?"

It was Scatha who answered. "Conor, he's a Changeling and you're about to see what he truly looks like."

Uttering a cry of disgust, Conor turned away. "Changeling? They're evil. You should have seen what they did back in my hometown."

Ita took his arm and led him back to Colly. "Not all are like that, though I admit it is in their nature to have a dark side. But not this one. He was put here long ago by myself and Fr. Greavy to wait for you and Jason Michaels. We knew when you appeared, we would have need for heroes from either world. Colly is one of the good ones."

Conor wasn't so sure. The figure taking shape before him had an elongated head and a large body with skin like supple wood. Colly opened his eyes and spoke, "Oh no. I can see from your faces that I must have shifted. So sorry, so very, very sorry."

"Nonsense," said Ita. "You are a gifted creature and a hero tonight. Once these people get over their shock, they will accept you."

"Speak for yourself," said Conor bitterly. "I know what they can do— they killed friends of mine. They let the Dark in to Tinker's Grove."

The alien eyes of the Changeling looked at Conor as Colly tried to sit up. He held up his wounded arm almost beseeching Conor to understand, but it only caused everyone to gasp again. A gout of greenish blood spurted from the stump of the arm when he unwrapped it, and Colly slumped, caught only by the hands of the boatmen. He didn't lose consciousness, and he managed a slight grin across his woody face. "Don't suppose this is going to help me win you guys over?"

He held up his arm and concentrated on the wound. Like sticks snapping in fire, a sound of bending and breaking came from Colly's body and he gasped in pain. But his arm was lengthening, and as it did, the blood or whatever fluid passed for that in the Changeling's body stopped and the rudiments of a hand began to form. Phil was speechless as she approached again and gently touched Colly's elbow. He tried to smile at her, and whispered, "One of the perks of being a Changeling. We can regrow an appendage if we are hurt."

In a moment, his arm was whole and Phil clasped his hand. Conor walked up to the Changeling and said in wonder, "I know I can be a horse's ass, but that was amazing, and you did kill that vampire. I spoke too quickly. I do that often. It's just that the Changelings I met weren't quite like you. They were so terrible. I shouldn't have put that on you. My apologies."

"Accepted," said Colly in his strange voice. "But I think it will be better if you see me as you expected me to look." He shifted again and a bare-chested young man stained with blood sat before them.

"Show-off," said Scatha, smiling lightly.

"Oh, for heaven's sakes," said Moira. "Phil, run up to the hotel and get him some clothes."

"I'm going to take a look at the people," said Ita. "I suppose the Morrigan has taken care of those who have died, but I want to see the living. I can cure any who have been exposed to the contagion as long as they haven't fully manifested the disease. Even if they didn't get fully exposed, they could be carriers, and we have to stop the pestilence this very night or the land will be lost."

"But it is spreading," said Conor. "If it raged through Tralee then the spores are drifting north and east. Everyone will be infected before long."

"We deserve this you know," said the Shandyman. "I've traveled the world over. Even made it through Tinker's Grove once, though that's another story. I came back to a land that was losing its soul. I know I whine about this all the time. But to have seen what we were and to see us now— well, you'd tipple a little of the holy water yourself to wash the sadness away. No one has time for the old ways, if they even remember them."

"Old ways weren't always good," said Kevin.

"No," said Mary, holding Laura's hand. "But they were better than now. We had our heads screwed on straight. We knew right from wrong."

"Humph," said Moira. "Funny words coming from a folk who tried every way they could to pull one over on us regular Irish."

"I know," smiled Mary. "But we knew right from wrong even if we didn't always practice it."

Ita looked out over the sea to the *Skelligs*. "Doesn't matter now. Without major assistance from all of you, our island is lost. The plague is just a symptom.

Had the people been truly healthy, body and soul, it would have been a minor sickness. Now, I'm not sure we can stop it. I'm hoping for a little help from a friend. But it looks very quiet out there on *Skellig* Michael. The battle was fierce. No one can kill the seraph, but he could be hurt or sidelined from further action."

Conor was about to speak, but a wailing cry from the ocean caught everyone's attention. It was like an animal's cry, wounded and angry.

"Jesus, Mary and Joseph," said Conor, instinctively crossing himself like his mother taught him. "What the hell is that?"

No one answered him. The cry came again, and Troubles howled to the skies.

A new voice spoke. Lettie Sporn joined them saying, "I'm afraid something has happened to Michael. Whatever he was fighting has come to our shore."

"Jace is out there!" said Conor. "He may be hurt too."

Lettie turned to him and said, "We cannot help them now. Evil has come to us, and we must fight."

The cry sounded again and Conor saw something huge and dark crawling out of the ocean. Tentacled and bloated, it slapped the beach with its corpulent body. Conor had read the great horror stories before, and there was almost something Lovecraftian about whatever this thing was.

"Like Cthulhu," he said.

Scatha entwined her arm around his. "I know that name, but this thing goes by another title. This is Balor, an ancient demon who once ravaged this land. Michael defeated him long ago, but I'm sure this is the same. He is a thing of mud and water, a bloated facsimile of life, loathed by those of us who dwell in the sea and feared by those who walk on land. He comes to destroy us all."

"Moira," said Conor. "Take Mary and Laura. Go with Troubles and send him back with my staff from the hall. The rest of you get the people off the beach as quietly and swiftly as you can. Already, they start to panic. I'll try and keep this thing close to the water."

"Not alone," said Scatha. In her hand appeared a long knife and Conor for the life of him couldn't figure out where it came from. He smiled in thanks for her courage.

"Together with me included," said Colly.

"Ah," said Conor haltingly, "you don't have a stich of clothing on you, man."

Colly looked down at himself. "That I don't," he laughed. "So, I think I'll stand by you in another form." He morphed into a wolf and howled a cry of defiance.

Lettie laughed saying, "Nicely played, Shifter. Might as well join you."

In a moment there was a popping sound in the atmosphere and a bright blue ball hovered where once Lettie stood.

"Is no one here what they seem?" said an exasperated Conor.

Scatha burst out laughing. "She is a wisp. I never would have known. But seriously madam, you can't be in this fight. It is ... not your style."

Conor knew what Scatha was saying, and before the wisp could take offence he said, "I know you want to stay Lettie, but are you able to travel swiftly?"

The blue globe bobbed in affirmation.

"Then do us all a favor and check on Michael. Bring him if he is able, for I'm not at all sure we can defeat Balor."

The wisp shot forward over the ocean toward the *Skelligs*, and Conor breathed a sigh of relief. Death was in the air and he had grown fond of the old woman and didn't want her hurt.

"C'mon." he said to Scatha and Colly, "let's go see what the tide brought in."

They walked slowly to the quivering lump laying on the edge of the sand like a beached whale. It looked like it had the tentacles of an octopus, but its body was bulbous and leathery. They were staring at it when they were struck to the ground by a voice pounding in their minds.

"Welcome, children," said the voice. "I am Balor. You catch me at a slight disadvantage. I've wrestled with an angel tonight and am tired and famished. I need a meal."

A tentacle lashed out and grabbed Scatha lifting her easily in the air.

"No!" cried Conor, but just then Troubles leapt past him dropping the staff into Conor's hand as he hurtled by him toward Balor. Colly, in his wolf shape, was fast in pursuit and together they latched onto the tentacle that held Scatha and bit down.

Balor screamed and dropped Scatha, whipping his tentacle at the wolf and dog and flinging them up the beach.

It gave Conor just the time he needed to transform the staff into the Spear of Destiny and charge the demon, stabbing into the fleshy body.

Balor screamed again, but as Conor wrestled the Spear free, he saw the thing open its eye and stare at him.

"No, Conor, don't look!" cried Scatha as she rushed to Conor and tackled him to the beach. A bright beam of energy flashed from the eye to where they had just been. A huge explosion dug out a massive crater in the sand.

For a moment, Conor was stunned, his vision filled with inky blackness and a shapeless horror that grasped his soul.

"Come back to me, my King Who Shall Be, come back to me," he heard a voice say, and then he felt her lips on his, his vision cleared and he stared at the face of Scatha.

Balor let his gaze drift over the beach. It touched the abandoned abbey and a large chunk of the ancient ruin exploded in molten rock. People still on the beach screamed in fear, trampling one another as they fled. The gaze of Balor caught several and they crisped into ash in the cold night air.

"You cannot look at the Eye," whispered Scatha into his ear. "First he tries to entrap your soul, and then he destroys your body."

"We'll see about that," said Conor getting to his feet and charging Balor again. Off to his left he saw Colly and Troubles grabbing for tentacles and pulling Balor's body in opposite directions. They distracted the demon enough so that Conor could drive the Spear of Destiny close to where he thought Balor's eye was. He knew the Spear had great power and he could feel the charge bursting into Balor each time he thrust. A woeful cry came from the beast and Conor saw the eye opening again. He tried not to look, but it was impossible. Caught like a fish on a hook, he leaned forward to stare.

High in the sky, a voice shouted at him. "Conor, to me, to me!"

Tearing his gaze away from Balor, Conor looked up and saw Jace upon Brian bearing down on them. Jace's Sword flashed in the night sky, and even though shivers of horror still ran down Conor's spine from the short glimpse he had of the eye, he turned his face from Jace toward Balor once more and sent the Spear ramming into the roiling flesh of the monster.

He saw the Eye open again and he knew he was doomed. No hypnotism this time. Hard for just the Eye to convey emotion, but Conor saw hatred there. In desperation, he thrust for the Eye yet again and felt the Spear prick just below the orb as Balor let loose another blast of energy. To Conor, it looked like a flaming version of his own Spear, and, for a moment time slowed. The energy bolt approached him as he threw himself backward.

Conor would have died on the spot, but Jace leapt from Brian swinging his Sword and partially blocked the beam, deflecting most of it into the beach. Yet Jace saw a shaft of energy still strike Conor in the center of his body. Jace thought he could feel his friend's chest explode. Scatha screamed in hatred at the demon as Conor fell still on the beach. She sent her knife flying into Balor's Eye. It was not enough to destroy the orb, but it was enough to allow Jace to ram the Sword into where he thought Balor's heart might be. He struck something vital for Balor's body jerked high off the beach sending dog and wolf spinning into the sand again and flinging Jace back almost to Conor's side. He yelled at Brian, "Get yourself back to Michael! Bring him if he's able!"

Balor just wouldn't stop screaming. As if all the demons of hell were focusing the cries of the damned though Balor, the sound was deafening and despairing. Those still conscious had tears running down their faces so sad and lost were the cries of the beast. It turned itself on the beach and flopped back into the shallows pushing itself back into the sea. Jace was too stunned to move, Scatha too exhausted except to watch the leviathan's escape.

"Conor," said Jace. "Conor!" he screamed. Crawling over the sand he reached his friend. Smoke rose from his body. Jace smelled burning flesh and witnessed the burnt marks on Conor's clothes. Ripping Conor's shirt open, he saw where the beam's shaft had stabbed Conor, just above where Drake's blade had sliced the week before. Only this time, it was worse. Jace could see into the wound, ribs broken, flesh flayed. He was sure he saw a stilled heart, and Conor wasn't breathing.

Jace started CPR. He didn't want to bang on Conor's chest, so ravaged it was, but he did breathe for him. As he did, he heard Scatha behind him utter in her unworldly voice:

Three times pierced,
Three times wounded,
Thrice to bring the king to birth,
Once, comes the Otherworld,
Twice, the pains of Change,
Thrice pierced, a Kingdom gained.

Jace raised his head for a moment and growled, "I'm getting pretty goddamned sick of prophecies. Every time somebody says one, someone I care about gets hurt or dies. Make yourself useful and get help."

He started breathing for Conor again, and as he did so, Ita came swiftly down the beach. "Jace, let me help him. You can do no more."

He tried to push her aside. "No, I can do this. If I stop, he dies."

"Not so," she said gently pushing him away. She laid her hands directly on his wound and Conor gasped in air. "See," she said, "he breathes; his heart beats."

Troubles padded up and whined, licking Conor's face. Surprising everyone, they heard the dog speak inside their minds, "Will he live? I will give my life for him. Woman," he said to Ita, "take my life spirit. Use it to make him live."

"No, you valiant beast." Ita touched the dog's cheek, a tear rolling down her own. "You have much to do before you rest." She looked at the group around her and waited till Moira and Phil joined them. "Where are the Shandyman, Kevin and his family?" asked Ita.

"Up by the caravan," said Moira. "They've been helping people evacuate. They are unharmed."

"Where's Colly?" said Phil. "I don't see him anywhere."

"Here," said voice behind a rock. "I'm fine, but I sure hope you brought me some clothes." He reached up a hand and Phil tossed him the set of clothes, dutifully turning her head to give him some privacy.

Jace looked at him strangely, since he had been helping Michael when Colly first returned to the beach. "Though I'm glad you're here now, where the hell have you been this evening, and why are you naked?"

"Long story," said Colly. "Tell you later."

Ita distracted Jace, clucking softly as she checked Conor.

Jace leaned over his friend. "Why isn't he waking?"

"Because he is near death. I've only prolonged the act of dying."

"Can't you do something?" said Jace.

"Indeed, but I'll need your help to get him into the boat. Philomena, run and get my boatmen. We have need of them. Since Michael has yet to come to us, we must go to him."

COLLY

"COMING WITH?" ASKED Jace of Colly. "We've got to get Conor to Michael."

Colly grimaced, "Don't think Conor likes me much." Jace tilted his head in puzzlement. "Because of what I am."

"What do you mean?" said Jace, confused. "What are you?"

Colly laughed. "You saw the wolf with Troubles? Hope you have a mind that welcomes possibilities. Got a feeling you'll find out about me real soon." A far-off howling caught the ears of both boys. "Maybe sooner than I thought," said Colly.

"Why are the wolves here?" said Jace.

"Well," said Colly, "it's kind of a long story. We ran into Shiro Ishii up near Tralee, and I killed the Red Thirst and set the wolves after the *Dullahan*, who's back by the way. The wolves wouldn't be howling like this unless they were giving chase, and, as they don't chase anyone from this reality, my guess is that they have the *Dullahan* and his *kelpie* steed on the run and he's heading here."

"Wait," said Jace, "you killed … how did you kill the Red Thirst?"

"I bit her in the chest and ripped her heart out. Then I scattered her body over Meritaten's Glen. She won't be coming back."

"How did you do that?" said Jace backing away. "What are you?"

Colly looked at Jace sadly, "Conor said the same thing. It's complicated and I didn't mean to deceive you. Apparently, you've met my kind before, and it didn't go well. I'm a Changeling and a shapeshifter, Jace, always have been and always will be. And my brothers and sisters need me now, because the *Dullahan* is coming, and Ballinskelligs has gone through enough tonight."

He morphed right in front of Jace. For a moment he was Colly, and then in a swirling twist of sand, he let Jace see his true form, that tall almost plantlike figure with the wrongly bent knees and the enigmatic entish face.

He saw Jace gasp and raise his Sword. Colly changed again into a werewolf, running off to find his pack who were yipping and howling more closely now.

Jace would never have struck Colly with his Sword, but he had raised it anyway. Instinct he thought. Nothing much surprised him anymore, except that Colly didn't match his experience of Changelings. No time to ponder that problem. A caw came to his left and he saw a crow standing on the beach. It cocked its head to him and cawed again.

"What?" said Jace, "Are you going to go drama queen on me too?"

The bird seemed to laugh and then obliged, repeating the same little tornado of sand. When it was done, the Morrigan stood there in her warrior maiden form, red robes and golden gauntlets, spitting sand out of her mouth, and shaking her lustrous red hair.

"Look what you've made me do, Champion," she pouted. "I will never get all the sand out now."

"What are you doing here?"

"I have finished with the dead. The boatmen took their bodies away, and I have sent their souls onward. Plague dead are the worst. They never asked for such a sickness, and their innocence deserved a better demise."

"No," said Jace. "I mean, what are you doing here now?"

"Why, waiting for the *Dullahan*, just like you. I think we have had enough of that thing."

"Can't you just take care of him?" asked Jace. "You're the Morrigan after all."

"No, I cannot," she pouted even more and ran a red nail through his close-cropped blond hair. "Besides, we are kin. I am just much nicer than he is. Get ready, Champion, for here he comes."

The *Dullahan* broke out on the beach, chased by the pack of wolves.

Jace recognized Colly immediately. He was the biggest of the wolves, even bigger than the Alpha male and female, and he was leading the pursuit.

The *kelpie* pounded the surf and halfway across the strand, turned and faced the wolves. The *Dullahan* raised its whip threatening the pack as the wolves fanned out to block its way inland. In its other hand, it lifted up its severed head.

That's when Jace started laughing. The head was screaming and Jace knew it was shouting the names of those it planned to kill, but no one heard the words. The surf had become too loud. No longer was the sea glassy and still, but a tide was swiftly coming in and the waves drowned the Dullahan's voice into silence.

Even the Morrigan laughed at the irony. Jace knew what he had to do. He began running toward the *Dullahan*, Sword swinging, and as the *Dullahan* turned to meet him with its whip, it held the corpse head high. Flashing red eyes smote Jason, but he didn't stop. The head's mouth opened and Jace was close enough to hear it yell "Jace ..." but by then his Sword was moving and he cut the Dullahan's gloved hand off at the wrist and sent the head spinning into the sea. "And it's Jason!" he yelled after the head, just before something dark leapt from the ocean and caught the head, swallowing it before it disappeared beneath the waves. With his return swing, he sliced the descending whip in half and fell back breathing hard.

The Morrigan stalked through the pack of wolves and grabbed the bridle of the *kelpie*, pounding her gauntleted hand into the steed's head stunning it for a moment. She looked at the silent *Dullahan* sitting ramrod straight on the kelpie and then gazed into the kelpie's stunned eyes and said, "This world has had enough of you two for now. Get you gone to wherever you ride in the Otherworld."

From a pocket in her robes, she drew out what she later told Jace was bone dust, gathered from her 'garden', and threw it on the *Dullahan* and the kelpie. Jace could swear there were flecks of gold mixed with the human remains as the dust settled on the monsters. For a moment, nothing happened but then, they began to fade into the darkness and in a moment, disappeared on that shore by the side of the sea.

The Alpha male and female stepped forward and pawed the ground whining slightly, and Colly transformed back into his human shape. "I hope he's gone for good," he said to no one in particular. Turning to Jace, he gave him a lopsided smile, "I hope you'll forgive me for not telling you about what I was. By the way, that was a mighty thwack you gave that head. We'll have to play golf soon."

Jace laughed, "No hard feelings. Like I've said before, this has been a year when I've seen a lot of strange stuff. I'll get used to it."

Colly looked at the battle queen and said, "Morrigan, you're looking beautiful as always."

The Morrigan curtsied slightly and with a lascivious grin said to Colly, "And you are looking very fetching yourself this fine evening—for a Shifter."

Jace turned away snorting with laughter and said, "Colly, get some clothes on. We don't need a randy goddess on the beach falling for the biggest badass werewolf around."

THE GRAIL

Saturday Evening, 11/7, Skellig Michael

WITH THE *DULLAHAN* gone, Jace could assist the boatmen as they lifted Conor and set him in the ship up near the prow. Troubles climbed in and stood by his master's side. Ita crossed Conor's arms and set the Spear of Destiny upon his chest, the gaping wound still bleeding as Conor took shallow breaths. Scatha approached and unwound her shawl, made of knitted seaweed and covered Conor's body for warmth. She kissed him on his cheek, and Jace laid his hand on his friend's head. "Don't you give up, Conor Archer. We've too much to do, and little time to do it. Balor is still alive. You know he'll never leave you alone. He'll chase you through death and purgatory for your soul. I saw him look at you. He wants to obliterate you. Come back to us. Please."

Gently lifting up Jace's chin, Ita looked into his eyes. "We will get him to Michael in time. He will help heal him."

"We have something else that might help," said Colly. He reached around his neck and unclasped a leather necklace around which hung the bronze key from Meritaten's tomb. "We have a key. A key to a coffin. I think we should take the return trip to Michael's island with you. We have some monks to visit." He tossed the ankh-shaped key into the air and snatched it back with his hand.

"Where did you get that?" asked the Morrigan, biting her words and glaring at the Changeling.

Colly smirked at her saying, "Found it where it was supposed to be—in Meritaten's Glen. Someone thought I should have it as a gift." He nodded at Ita. "Got a feeling it might be of some help."

Ita bobbed her head, saying to Jace, "You and Colly sit in the stern behind the boatmen." Like the Morrigan, she too had a little bag of dust but of a different kind. Tossing some on the water, it sparkled with golden light leading out through the ocean toward the *Skelligs*. She told her boatmen to row, and like Arthur on the way to Avalon, the body of Conor Archer and

St. Ita's ship floated away on the waves along the *faerie* track. As they sailed, the Morrigan, now a crow, landed on the dragon prow with a soft caw and cast her beady-eyed stare on the islands.

Not long before this, just as the battle with Balor had begun, the wisp had taken off towards the islands. She had made good time shooting swiftly towards *Skellig* Michael. Hearing the sounds of fighting and screams behind her on the beach worried her, but all her focus was on what she would find on the now darkened summit. The tiny blue globe was fast—it was one of the wisp's finest powers—and in minutes she was at the island ascending swiftly to the highest crag. There she found the supine angel lying among the rocks slowly leaking out whatever passed for lifeforce in whatever took the place of veins and arteries in angels.

"Michael," she said. "I've never seen you like this!" If a wisp could splutter and fret, then that is what she sounded like, but to any other witness they would have only heard a series of pops and clicks.

But the angel understood and silvery laughter greeted her care and concern. "You found me like this just days ago."

"But that was in your human form. It's easier to take when you look like a mortal."

"I cannot die—you know this—but I am weakened and glad you are here. Help me, if you would."

She hovered over his wound, somewhere in the area where his abdomen would be. Little sparks of energy flowed out of her and completed the healing Jace's Sword had started, sealing the rent Balor had torn into Michael.

"Ah!" he said in angelic wonder. "It is as the ancient proverb says, 'The touch of a wisp is a healer's blessing'."

"What ancient proverb?" popped the wisp sarcastically.

"Nephilim, actually," said Michael. "Their short and violent sojourn on earth required your kind's ministrations often."

"There," she said, "good as new."

The light shimmered and Michael rose. In silence, he turned his gaze towards Ballinskelligs.

"What have you seen?" asked the wisp.

"Nothing good," said Michael. "Many are dead or dying from the plague and a swift battle has raged there. Balor crawled out of the sea and our young visitors have requited themselves well. Even the Shifter surprises. I did not think we could trust him."

"Are you saying you were wrong?" sparkled the wisp.

A whisper in the wind revealed his irrItation. "I am saying it is possible I slightly miscalculated his value. But I made no mistake on the hound. He protects Conor almost as well as I could. I must go and help. This is not yet over."

"Wait," said the wisp. "Something has happened on the beach." Both could see clearly the end of the battle with Balor.

"May the One help him," said Michael. "Conor has been struck down."

"But not killed, I think," said the wisp. "Look, Ita attends him, and Brian is flying back here."

In minutes, the steed was circling the island. Brian landed and the angel mounted. "Wisp, with me. Down to Blind Man's Cove. It seems that Balor was not enough sorrow for the evening; the bane of the *Dullahan* has had to be endured once more. Jace and the Morrigan have dispatched the *kelpie* and that headless horseman. I also see Ita placing Conor in a boat and it speeds on the *faerie* road here. We have little time. She is a powerful healer, but if Conor was struck by Balor, death is near. She can only delay it."

With a graceful leap, Brian descended the summit, flew over Christ's Saddle, and winged down to the landing at Blind Man's Cove. Michael allowed his form to become more human, though he kept a pair of wings and his trident visible as he dismounted. Lettie resumed her human form as well, as the boatmen rowed the tiny long ship to harbor. Scatha stood upright at the prow over the fallen Conor. Like some Celtic princess of old, she stood tall and proud, looking up without fear into Michael's visage. Troubles seated at Conor's feet barked once in greeting. Jace, Colly and the crow remained silent.

"Scatha," said Michael, "it has been too long since we have met. And now ... in this time of sadness. Hound of God, welcome. You did what I could not. Well done, Champion, and though it will take me some getting used to, well done Shifter. Yet so much woe and sorrow."

The crow cawed in agreement.

"No sadness yet," clipped Scatha. "Conor is grievously injured and still he breathes. Balor struck him with his Eye, but Jace deflected the blow. Still, a shaft of the demon's glance slipped by and has pierced him."

"The prophecy," said Lettie, looking sharply at Michael.

Three times pierced.

"I care not for any prophecy," said Michael. "He is my charge and I failed. If he dies, those are empty words."

"Don't let your self-pity keep you from your task. Your watch is not ended. He yet lives." Though Scatha's words were sharp, her eyes beseeched the angel.

He walked down the landing steps and leaning over the boat, looked over the body of Conor Archer, the gaping wound still bleeding every time the boy took a breath.

Michael lifted him up and placed him on the boat landing. Troubles leapt out of the boat and lay at the boy's side. "It is like Balor to infuse his weapons and the very glance of his Eye with corruption and pestilence. This wound is a terrible one." He plunged his hand into the gap in Conor's chest and even Lettie gasped. But it was an angel hand, not corporeal and filled with light and healing energy. When he withdrew it, the wound looked less inflamed. Then he took the same hand and pressed it directly on the torn flesh. The bleeding decreased to a small trickle. Conor took a deep breath and sighed.

"There," said Michael. "I've done what I can. He will not die yet, but as is common with wounds of darkness, Conor's life energy is depleted. I know not if he will recover. He needs more than I can give."

"I have a key," said Colly. Michael just looked at him. "A key to the seventh tomb in the cave at Seal Cove. I found it at Meritaten's Glen earlier this evening." He showed Michael the ankh shaped key. Michael reached for it, but Colly snatched it back. "You and I don't quite trust each other yet. Best let me keep this for a while. But I think there is something in that seventh sarcophagus that can help Conor. Remember the Cauldron pictured on it and the figures of people dancing around it?"

"What would you know of anything that deals with the Seven Sleepers?" said the angel in a clipped voice.

"I know what my kin say. I know what all the Celts say. The fact that I have this key reveals the truth of ancient stories about what this thing in the tomb is and what it does. I'm not sure we'll find a Cauldron, but the tales say there is a Sword of Light. Jace carries that and wields it well. There is a Spear of Destiny, and it lies clasped in Conor's arm. And legends tell of a third thing represented by the Cauldron. We saw the image of it carved on the lid of the tomb. And around it danced figures of people. If you looked closely others were on the ground, still others sitting up. Some were climbing out of it. It appeared a source of life. Our legends say it could make the dead live. Know anything about that, Ranger of the Heavens?"

Michael fairly radiated hostility. shimmering in what star and moonlight there was. "You know not of what you speak. It is beyond you."

"Maybe, but it might just help Conor."

Jace stepped forward. "Please. If it could help save him, shouldn't we use it?"

The crow flew up from the prow and onto the landing. In a moment of shifting shadows, the Morrigan stood no more in her battle array, but as the old, shrouded crone.

"Too long has it been, Morrigan," said Michael evenly. "Why are you here?"

"Because I am the one who first found Conor and knew who and what he was. And I am not about to let your fascination with secrets keep a boon from the boy that will help him recover."

"I do not seek his illness. I do not wish him to fade from this time. I know what he means and what he must do."

"Then," said the Morrigan, "let us be in league, the Old Ones, the Heavenly Ones, the Otherworldly Ones and the Human Ones. For the lad needs our help. Balor was unexpected tonight and came close to victory. The *Dullahan's* appearance was also unfortunate. The Red Thirst I knew about and helped plan her demise, but what they did with the plague was so much more than anticipated. Mark my words, that wizard from the east is the unknown factor here. His meddling may destroy us all. He wields a power I do not know."

"I know what he wields," said Michael, "but I must admit, I did not consider his presence. The priest warned me, but in my pride, I discounted his advice."

"Seems like all you guys with wings always make the same mistake with pride. Rather than throwing a pity party," said Colly, "don't you think we ought to pay the dead monks a visit?"

Jace snorted and Michael nodded. The angel turned toward the cliff face and traced the shape of a door, similar to the one on the other side of the island that the boys had used earlier in the day. Picking up Conor, he led the group, except for the boatmen who chose to stay, through the entrance and into the heart of the mountain.

The passageway was large and luminesced brightly enough so they could see. Jace noticed other passageways and rooms branching off the center way. He saw hints of golden light shining from them.

Scatha caught his interest and said, "This is Michael's realm here in this reality. Many wonders are hidden in this place. My people—Conor's people—often keep him company here. Perhaps some other time you can see the banqueting halls, the treasures, the throne room."

"Throne room?" said Jace.

"He is a prince of the heavens," said Ita, "though you will seldom see him take that title or show his true form. He was placed here as guardian of humanity and all other living things. He is ancient, but true. This is a holy place and holds back the Dark, even in these waning days and the threat of the end of all things."

"Champion," said the withered Morrigan, "take an old woman's hand and give her someone to lean on."

Jace held out his arm, but stiffly said, "You need no help from me, not here, not ever."

"Indulge my fantasy," cackled the crone. "It has been so long since I have had a man in my life—Cuchulainn was the last I think—and you are so like him my Champion. Perhaps ..."

"Perhaps nothing," said Ita. "You are tolerated here because of your ancient wisdom, but make no mistake. We see you as an ally of necessity not because you or we really wish it."

"Oh, you pious wretch," snapped the Morrigan, "you have been a killjoy since the day I first met you when you took that decapitated prince and restored his life by fetching his head and reattaching it. Always spoiling my fun."

"Silence," said Michael. "We are almost there."

Colly had not been paying much attention to the bickering, though he, like Jace, was truly curious about the other rooms and halls in this vast mountain fortress. However, as they turned the corner, he caught sight of the burial chapel again.

Colly and the others halted in awe as Michael gently lay Conor down before the altar.

Granted, the chapel had looked impressive earlier that morning, but Jace and Colly hadn't noticed everything. Candles now filled the space and the flickering light picked up the gold tiles in the mosaic behind the altar.

"Don't know why I didn't catch this before," said Jace looking at the mosaic. "It's the voyage of the seven Egyptian monks to Ireland."

"And they're carrying a gift," said Colly, pointing to a wooden box carried by two of the monks on the boat. The box was shaped like the Ark of the Covenant.

"Oh, oh," said Jace, "I'm having an Indiana Jones rush here."

"You telling me I should choose wisely?" grinned Colly at Jace.

"You have carried your responsibility well these many years," said Michael to Colly with a tiny smile, "so I'm willing to forget and ignore the insolence that always drips off your tongue."

"It's called smart-assery—being a smartass," said Jace with a laugh. "I gotta admit, I've found it kind of helpful these past few days."

Colly couldn't wait any longer and stepped forward with the key.

"Give it to me," said Michael reaching out a hand to Colly.

"No ... respectfully sir, no. This is something I have to do. Apparently, I'm the only other person that knows about this key besides you, Ita, and Fr. Greavy, so there's a reason I'm supposed to do this. Just point me to the lock and let me do my job."

Michael tilted his head saying softly, "As you wish. Here it is," said Michael, pointing to a tiny keyhole at the base of the sarcophagus. "Just put the key in and turn. What happens will happen." He stepped aside.

Colly, never reverent about much of anything, slowly went up to the last sarcophagus and knelt before it. Gently, he reached down towards the right side of the base. Taking the key, he carefully placed it into the lock.

"Michael, have you ever done this before?" asked Colly.

"I have no need for keys and no locks would prevent me, but though I know the gift the monks brought, I have not looked because I did not think myself worthy."

"You do now?" smiled Colly without his usual sarcastic quirk of his mouth.

"There is need now," said Michael, bowing slightly and backing away.

Colly said, "Here we go. It's been nice knowing you guys." Then he turned the lock.

They heard a series of clicks as some mechanism within the tomb activated. With a tiny puff of accumulated dust, the stone top moved slightly to the right.

"We're in!" said Jace, moving to Colly's side. Carefully they lifted the stone off the sarcophagus. Everyone, including Michael, moved to look inside. Just like the Abbot's tomb back in Tinker's Grove, thought Jace. The grave was empty except for a cloth wrapped package tucked in the base of the coffin. Sure that it was the wooden box pictured in the mosaic, Colly and Jace gently lifted it out and removed the cloth.

A smell of cedar wafted over the group and Scatha spoke for them all, "It is beautiful," she said. "As perfect as when it was carved many centuries ago."

"Do not tip it or shake it in any way," said Michael. "Colly, open the box carefully, and Jace, remove what you see."

There was a simple gold clasp on the lid and Colly opened it easily.

"Oh, my God," said Jace, "not a Cauldron, but the Grail."

Jace looked at Michael, "Maybe you should touch it." But the angel simply nodded at Jace. The Champion lifted out a golden cup, inlaid with a circlet of rubies around the lip and another smaller circlet around the base. As beautiful as it was simple, that is not what caught the eyes of those who saw.

"It contains drink!" said Scatha. "How can that be? After all these years?"

"Do any of you know the real legend of the Grail?" asked Michael.

Jace nodded. "I know what it means to Western civilization. But it has a strange tale behind it that maybe Ita would know better than I."

"Or perhaps the Morrigan would know," cackled the old crone. "It belonged to the Old Ones first. We were marvelous metal workers and a people of great power. The pathetic humans called us the *Tuatha de Danaan*, and thought us gods. To them, I suppose we were. One of us, the Dagda, the greatest chief among us created the Cauldron. It was the Cup you see before you. It became one of our most treasured heirlooms along with the Sword and Spear, not because it was beautiful but because it had the power to bestow life to anyone who had died or was near death. It was always full with a sacred wine—we revived armies with it when we conquered the land. And then we lost it, taken by a thief whose name we never knew. But we know where it went. To Egypt. To Pharaoh. To Meritaten who brought it back to us. In time, another thief stole it away and took it again to the east to another meddlesome people."

"Perhaps that thief's name is also lost to memory," said Ita, "but you know as well as I where and when that Cup appeared again. On a night, long ago, at a rabbi's feast with followers and friends. Strange words were said, not really understood in the moment. All present drank with the rabbi who identified the drink as the Blood of the Lamb. Not a sacred wine anymore, nor a Cauldron of rebirth, but a Chalice with the gift to heal, a Grail of everlasting life. Anyone who drank of it with true faith would not simply renew their physical life but have it for eternity."

"We knew when it was used by Him," said the Morrigan. "The earth convulsed; there was an eclipse and a great emptiness filled our hearts. It had been given a higher purpose. Now, it no longer belonged to us, but instead belonged to the world. That is when we knew we were no longer gods."

Ita laughed, "You were never gods. Talented, powerful beings, yes, but never gods. And yet, the Grail came back to you."

"So it is said," mused the Morrigan. "But we never found it. Those meddling monks must have brought it back, because I recognize it. And they kept it; took it to their graves. Now, what will you do with it?"

"Help Conor," said Jace. "We need him for what is coming."

Michael moved and took the Grail out of Jace's hands. "You've all seen something no one has seen in centuries, and now it will be used for the first time since Arthur sipped from it long ago in Avalon."

"That's true too?" said Jace.

"Indeed," said Michael. "Conor's wounds are like Arthur's. Slain by the evil abroad at their time, they are placed outside the realm of the living, not quite dead, but still not really alive. What Ita and I did for Conor was preserve his body so he can act in both this world and the Otherworld. To drink from the Grail will heal him and bring him back to us."

Michael cradled Conor's head in his right arm and dripped the contents of the Grail into the boy's mouth as he spread his wings over the suffering lad.

Jace whispered, *"And he who drinks ... will live forever. Shield him from death under the shelter of thy wings, O Lord, shield him under the shelter of thy wings."*

Conor swallowed instinctively and then coughed several times.

"Look," said Scatha, "his bleeding has stopped and the wound is closing."

Troubles whined but came for a sniff where the wound used to be. He barked and then licked Conor's face enthusiastically.

That's when Conor awoke. He was weak and so was his smile, but he opened his eyes, looking at everyone and said, "Thank-you. I'm getting used to walking roads of darkness, but it sure is good to see all of you again."

Even the Morrigan joined in the celebration. But the smiles and laughter faded when Conor tried to stand. Jace caught him as he sagged to the floor. "My legs don't work!" he said.

"You took severe wounds, lad," said Ita, "wounds that would have killed an ordinary man. The Grail is healing you but it will take time for you to recover fully. You will need to recuperate away from all this trouble. Do we have any ideas where he can go?"

"My island," said Scatha.

"Excellent choice," said Michael. "Can a *faerie* track carry them there, wisp? Time is of the essence, even though the threat from Balor remains real."

"Of course," said Lettie, "if the boatmen agree."

Jace and Colly replaced the Grail and secured the sarcophagus. Colly reluctantly handed the key to Michael. The angel picked up Conor and the little group made its way back to the boat landing. The sailors were waiting for them and Michael asked the favor.

The captain nodded and spoke, "I've sailed the seas long ago as you know, Ranger of the Heavens," said Brendan to Michael. "I have been tasked by Ita to take Conor wherever he needs to go, and I do it willingly as do my friends, and we place ourselves under Scatha's guidance."

"Then to Skye you go," said Michael. "Speed bonny boat."

"Like a bird on the wing," whispered Conor as he opened his eyes. "Good song. Are we going somewhere?"

"Aye lad," said Michael, "to a place where you can finish healing, hidden from Balor's gaze. Much is still expected of you, but you must be well. Now get you all gone. And I charge you, hound of God," said Michael bending down to look into the huge dog's eyes, "to guard this boy as I would, and let no harm come to him. I do not leave him willingly, but if he is in your care, I rest secure." Troubles' eyes flashed in acceptance and he licked the angelic hand that petted him.

"Good thing angels aren't bothered by dog spit," said Conor weakly. A shimmer of laughter rang throughout the cove as Michael lifted Conor up and set him back into the boat.

"Go now, Scatha. Take him to your island. Hide him there while he recovers. We will have need of him soon."

The boatmen quickly rowed the ship out of the cove. No one noticed the Morrigan. She remembered what everyone had forgotten and she backed away from the landing hiding behind a makeshift shed used by the student archaeologists. There, she shifted into her crow form, flying low and unseen across the waters back to the mainland. Michael turned to Lettie. "I'll need you as a wisp. We need to check Ballinskelligs and then do what we can to stop the plague from overrunning the land."

"Ah," said Colly, "exactly how do Jace, Ita and I get back to the mainland?"

Michael smiled. "I had Philomena call your father when you landed here and told him you got marooned by some feckless friends. He is on his way. Ita, I expect you to have an excuse why you need the same ride back."

"Don't worry," laughed Ita. "Mr. Roddy will remember me. I scared him half to death when I visited his 'newborn son' all those years ago. He won't ask too many questions."

Lettie morphed back into the glowing blue ball of light and tucked herself into Michael's cupped hand. He mounted Brian and the three took off over the sea towards Ireland, intent on seeing how much damage Balor had caused.

They landed on a beach still in chaos. Moira and Phil were checking over the remaining tourists and townspeople for anyone suffering from any kind of illness. Ita had suspected the remnants of the plague, weakened by her prayer and Conor's effort, while not sufficiently strong to kill anymore, were still able to cause terrible sickness. She had told the two how to stop the progression of the illness and cure any others who were sick.

Both of them, as well as townspeople and tourists left on the beach, saw Michael approaching from the sea. The wisp was tucked into the hollow where his crimson cloak was pinned to the shoulder of his tunic. Though awestruck, few were afraid, for in the heart of the people of Kerry was a long memory of the archangel. Though they had never witnessed him in angel form, their forebears had and interacted with him down through the ages. Now, when Brian landed on the beach and Michael dismounted with two wings arching and trident in hand, golden armor glowing, those that could knelt in welcome and he laughed.

His voice, now more human, boomed across the beach. "Rejoice! The demon of darkness, Balor the Terrible, has been defeated for now. But he will return. The people of Kerry have suffered a grievous blow tonight. Balor was not alone. He nurtured an evil from the other side of the world who has spread contagion and pestilence over this blessed land. Even now, that plague seeks to contaminate the whole island. It has been stopped here and I will do what I can to halt its spread, but when I do, I will reveal myself and all shall know that these are days both of despair and hope.

"You have known the Otherworld, at least your forebears did. They were much more familiar with it than you are. Your memories have clouded over the years, but remembrance of things past may find you again. What will be clear from this night forward, first to the powers of good and evil and then to those who dwell in this time and place, is that the Earth is made up of two realities, two worlds now sundered which seek to re-unite. The reality known as the Otherworld is on the brink of merging with this one. It will be a time of tumult and great anxiety. Evil will walk abroad like it has never done before, but there is still good in this place and you must make a choice for one or the other. Everyone must make a choice, for how the worlds reconnect matters. If evil has the upper hand, all will be darkness. But if good prevails, then a new dawn is coming. After this evening, no one will be able to stand aside and simply observe. You must choose."

With that, Michael mounted Brian again and took to the sky. He circled Ballinskelligs several times so that everyone could see him, and then he flew off to the northeast on his business to stop the plague.

The wisp stayed behind, and took the form of Lettie again, saying to Moira, "Have you seen my pipe? I could use a good smoke … and a shot of whiskey after all I've been through." She blew some air from her lips to dislodge a few displaced strands of hair and then looked expectantly at Phil and Moira. "Well? I'm powerfully parched!" They laughed and led her back into the pub.

THE SCOURING OF KERRY

Saturday Evening, 11/7, County Kerry

THERE WERE OTHER residents of County Kerry who saw Michael and his winged horse Brian flying high above the land. After all, only Tralee and Ballinskelligs had yet felt the direct force of the plague. But the 'Night of Cherry Blossoms' had released a pestilence in the land that threatened all human life in Ireland.

Nothing about the plague had crossed the media yet, but Kerry folk, seeing the angel in the skies, felt deep in their souls that something was terribly wrong. Their minds searched the rusty pathways of unused memories looking instinctively for ancient beliefs and traditions. They could not Google an answer to unspoken questions and, stressed with everyday life, they could not put a finger on what it was that troubled them so, only that they feared the darkness around them. The Hand of God nebula, so beautiful in nights before, now seemed a portent of disaster from a divine hand. People knew something was coming and so they didn't close their eyes. Instead, they gathered their children, few as there were, to their sides in an ineffective effort to protect their families.

Michael saw the plague as two misty outreaches, one pouring north from Ballinskelligs, the other streaming northeast from Tralee. The mists of pestilence were moving slowly so Michael simply flew several miles ahead of the contagion and pointed his trident to the ground and began tracing a boundary, first north and east of Tralee, then south and east toward Ballinskelligs. Beams of energy burned into the earth so deeply that people felt it throughout the south as a *faux* earthquake. Buildings actually shook and a few windows shattered. Once the angel had made a boundary line from north to south several miles from the advancing pestilence, he hovered his horse high in the air, clasped the trident with both hands and shouted,

Igne natura renovatur integra.
(Through fire, nature is completely healed).

Everyone on the Kerry Peninsula felt the angel's cry, but many interpreted it differently. Shiro Ishii, driving his Mercedes north as swiftly as possible, clearly heard the old magical alchemical spell—*Through fire, nature is restored in purity*. Ordinary folk heard something like—*Nature is completely healed by fire*. Jace and Ita's ears heard the words but they sparked a vision in their minds—an acronym, on a plank of wood, suspended above a twisted body—INRI, the acronym of the Galilean proclaimed by Rome as King of the Jews, by others as Savior of the world. Neither said anything to the others.

All were close to the truth for Michael intended his words to cleanse a land tainted by an evil that had once tried to kill the Light. And as he spoke, he shouted the final command: *Crema! Crema! Crema! (Burn! Burn! Burn!)* From the deep trench he had blasted into the earth, flames rose nearly a mile high. Nothing burned but the particles of plague that drifted into it, but so bright were the flames that they could be seen throughout the island and across the Irish Sea to the United Kingdom.

A GRAVE IN THE GLEN AND THE HARROWING OF TRALEE

Saturday Evening, 11/7, Near Tralee

THE NIGHT WAS quiet once again when the Morrigan took wing from *Skellig* Michael. It was a short but peaceful flight back to Meritaten's Glen just south of Tralee. Her conscience niggled at her since she was not attending the plague dead of the city, but this task could not be delayed. Landing on a dying willow tree, she hopped to the ground and shed her avian form deciding to adopt her warrior garb once again. She had to admit to herself that she looked beautiful in her crimson robes and golden battle gauntlets, her lustrous red hair shining in the moonlight.

She walked to the ancient stone with the glyphs proclaiming that Meritaten, the warrior princess and Pharaoh of Egypt, was buried in this glen. Striding to the middle of the rock, she turned to her left and counted out fifty paces. She turned right and walked another thirty in amongst a grove of beech trees that nestled next to a small hill. Reaching the base of the rise, the Morrigan stretched out her arms, holding high her hands. Even the sleeping birds heard the snapping of the bones of her fingers as they lengthened into sharpened claws. Kneeling down, she thrust them into the side of the hill and began to tear out the sod and rock. Marvelously efficient, she had dug three meters into the earth when she struck metal.

Swearing softly, she muttered, "There, I've gone and broken a nail."

"Works better with a shovel," said a voice.

The Morrigan stood up suddenly but did not turn around. "Priest," she hissed, "however did you get here from Ballinskelligs on this fine evening?"

"An evening of death, I'm afraid, not a fine one at all," said Fr. Greavy. "I figured you might come here, after the death of the Red Thirst. I found the remnants of the revenant. Just got done burying her ashes. Even the damned deserve that."

The Morrigan turned to face him. "Again, I ask you, what are you doing here?"

"I'm a Walker of Worlds and you aren't the only one who knows the secret of this place. Legend has it that Meritaten, the mighty warrior princess who founded the Irish nation, was killed here in the fight with the *Tuatha de Danaan,* your people. But there is so much more to that story isn't there?"

"They were heroic times," said the Morrigan, "and I knew her before she died. She was so brave that a truce was held so her people could bury her here. My people honored her as well, enemy that she was, and were present to pay homage to her courage and battle skill.

"What a funeral; what a burial!" continued the Morrigan reminiscing. "It never ceases to amaze me how my people, known for their love of ancient places, never bothered to study this hill closely or visit it again down through the ages."

"It's man-made, like Newgrange to the north," said the priest, "and it encloses the most sophisticated burial chamber outside of Egypt."

The Morrigan barely raised her voice above a whisper, "She was Pharaoh once, an Egyptian Princess who became a Celtic Queen."

"Forced to flee Egypt during terrible times with her Greek husband and her hundreds of followers. They made it all the way here and founded a nation," said the priest.

Their reverie was interrupted by Michael's heavenly cry. The Morrigan and the priest heard the massive whoosh as the very atmosphere ignited where the archangel directed his trident.

"What is that meddlesome creature doing now?" hissed the Morrigan.

"Collecting the plague, I imagine," said Fr. Greavy. "As the particles drift into the wall of fire, they will be destroyed." Both felt the heat of the flames as they shot up through the eastern horizon more than a mile high.

"Listen to him now," snapped the Morrigan, "he's doing my job for me."

A haunting cry came out of the flames, and they could see Michael and Brian emerging like a new born star, shining on the land. It was the angel singing, and he held up his trident as it changed into a huge and shining scales of justice. Now, he was the harrower of the dead, the one to lead them to their eternal reward or punishment, and he was singing them home.

The Morrigan and the priest knew what was happening on the streets and byways of Tralee, and they saw what ascended to the heavens. A wind picked up and swept through the town and over the many bodies of the dead. From their poisoned or charred hearts spiraled the souls harking to Michael's call.

The Morrigan could not help herself. She twisted grotesquely into her crone shape and began keening for the dead, a wail matching in minor counterpoint to Michael's call assembling the departed. Even Fr. Greavy, fell to his knees in wonder, for it was as beautiful in the skies as the previous hours had been terrible on the streets of Tralee.

Motes of light swirled high towards Michael and the flames, darting about in the air before the Ranger of the Heavens. A startling thing actually, thought the priest much later. As they gathered, only one side of the scales tipped, as if every soul weighted that end of justice. Perhaps a mysterious mercy, perhaps a purgatory already suffered, but there were no damned before Michael. He sent them all through the purifying fire. Fr. Greavy could have sworn they were aimed in the direction of the Hand of God nebula, but he knew Michael had a flair for drama. None the less, the priest breathed a sigh of relief. It would not slake the grief of survivors who had not seen this part, but at least The Red Thirst and the necromancer who drew her forth possessed no soul from this night. Michael had made sure of that.

The haunting wail of the Morrigan and Michael's gathering cry ended abruptly as did the flames scouring the land. For a long while there was a silence that stretched throughout County Kerry, as if the land was holding its breath. Then the insects started to sing in the night once again.

Fr. Greavy looked over at the Morrigan, sunk to her knees on the ground, head bowed, stringy white hair falling over her face to the dying meadow grass.

"Come," he said, lifting her up, "we must do what we came to do."

She grinned a toothless grin at him and stood on shaky legs, running her gnarled hands on withered arms through her greasy hair. "Oh," she said, "I must look a sight. Can't meet a princess like this." With surprising speed she threw off the priest's grasp, and grew young again before his eyes, a battle maiden once more.

THE WORLD TAKES NOTICE

Saturday Evening, 11/7, County Kerry

WHEN THE ANGEL lit the atmosphere on fire, NATO satellites quickly picked up the disturbance, and without asking permission of the Irish government, immediately scrambled Great Britain's RAF jets for a quick look see. As they approached the barrier, their engines died as if an EMP blast had sucked the energy out of them. Their planes crashed into uninhabited countryside, but all pilots ejected safely. The International Space Station and several military satellites continued to focus their lenses on the phenomena and saw a further peculiarity that frightened all the military minds.

The fire was clearly visible as was the alien being who seemed to be directing it, but where County Kerry had been, there was now nothing, as if it had been removed from Ireland entirely. It stayed like that for several hours and then, near dawn, the fires died down. As the flames were extinguished all satellite and space station cameras focused on that area began to recognize the outlines of the once absent southwestern section of Ireland. As if it had never disappeared, the land was clearly visible again. But running north of Tralee to the southeast of Ballinskelligs, a scar had been carved into the earth, a plague barrier marking where the flames had been. Barely 500 meters wide, it made a dark valley for miles, and only a few knew the real reason it was there.

Michael and Brian looked at their work and the angel turned the steed back to Ballinskelligs. "Good work, my friend," he said. "There is no more pestilence abroad in the land, though many have died this past night. Tralee is a city of the dead, and the morning to come will be one of worldwide grief. All creation will groan with pain, like a woman in childbirth. But the souls have been sent on; their suffering ended. A prelude of things to come, it remains to be seen what this new heavens and new earth shall look like. Will it be one of woe, or one of wonder? We have much to ponder, my friend."

Far off, he could already see the line of ambulances and military vehicles approaching the town. The news would be everywhere soon. Sensing a new resolve in the angel, Brian flew with haste back to the beach where the battle earlier that evening had taken place.

Things were much calmer there. As Michael settled Brian on the sand, he touched the horse and transformed it back to old Malby, and Michael appeared once again as the young fisherman in his white woolen sweater. All of the wounded had been attended; those seriously hurt, evacuated. As he caught up to Ita, she brushed her hands together saying, "Well you didn't do that quietly. Everyone will know something great and profound has happened to the land."

"Could not be helped," said Michael. "I have never seen such a virulent pestilence before. Had that escaped from us, more of the population would be dead by now and the globe at risk. Yet, my curtain of flame has created a rift through which the Otherworld and this world may touch. It is much like the same rift in Conor's homeland. There will be no keeping secrets from the powers on either side, in this world or the Other."

"I suppose you are right," said Ita. "We are as ready as possible. Conor's wound is a setback, but I trust Scatha. She will take him beyond time and let the Grail's healing restore the lad. His absence will be brief, for us at least." Looking out on the beach at the rest of Conor's friends, she said, "We have all the others necessary to accomplish our appointed task. They only need direction. Your direction. Did you find Shiro Ishii?"

"No," said the angel. "He was not within the boundaries I cleansed. I expect him to flee the land with his master defeated."

Ita looked at him skeptically. "I believe Balor has slunk away somewhere to lick his wounds, but his absence will be temporary at best. He has shown his hand, and we are weakened. You may have stopped the plague, but it killed thousands this night. He will strike again, and soon."

"Perhaps you are right," said Michael.

Jace had just arrived with Colly from the *Skelligs* and overheard part of the conversation as he was walking toward them. "I don't mean to be disrespectful, Michael. But weren't you the one who once drove things like Balor into hell?"

Michael smiled tightly, "Indeed, but there are no gates on hell. The demons defeat was terrible, but they revived. In times past, the goodness of people or at least their fear of demonic beings was enough to keep those evil things at bay. But this is a time when few believe in anything but their own interests. In their mockery of places like the Otherworld or a hell that could hold a demon, humans weaken the laws of reality, and the demons feel free to walk abroad again. Not many, but some like Balor and *Piasa*, in your own homeland, have been encroaching and seeing how much they can infiltrate once again. I fear they or others like them will continue to be successful."

"Do something, then," said Jace. "Drive Balor out again like we did with *Piasa*."

"I cannot, or rather I am not permitted. I am the guardian of this world, not its master. You humans have free will and all the power you need to keep the Dark out. But you choose not to do that. I cannot overrule your freedom. Your choices and their consequences are yours to accept and endure."

"None of us want them here," said Colly coming up beside Jace. "None of us can make the rest of humanity ... and those of us allied with humans ... follow our direction."

"Not yet, maybe," said Michael. "But that is where Conor and Jace, you and the others come in. Prophecies are strange things. They exist for a reason, to let humans know there are higher powers that can help them if they seek them. Humans, and you and your kin, Colly, have a chance because you care. But so many do not. I can assist you, but I cannot fight your battle. It is an awful thing that the worlds are colliding as this struggle is occurring. It means that the battle will be fought on two fronts. And neither you or Jace, Conor, Scatha, Moira or Phil, or any of your friends really have the skill to captain this fight. But you do have abilities and I will help you."

"Well, you can clear something up now," said Jace. "What happens when there's more than just incidental contact between the worlds? I heard you talking to Ita. There's a rift in Wisconsin and a big one here. Worlds are touching. What does that really mean, and what happens to our world? Are we just going to cease existing, swallowed up by a bigger cosmic amoeba?"

Michael smiled at Jace. "Your scientists often talk of many alternate realities. They will examine what happened tonight because my intervention has left very strange readings on their instruments. They will soon question whether another dimension or reality is intruding on this one. I will give you a head start on them, Jace. There is no multiverse as your scientists claim. There is one cosmos, only one, though it is far too huge for you to truly comprehend. But this cosmos has different reality depths. Like I said once before, Earth is made up of two realities right now. That is unnatural. They were not made to be separate; rather, they once were simply different sides of the same existence. What's happening now is a re-fusion of this reality with its deeper partner. Once, that union produced a world of incredible beauty, but then—"

"We blew it," said Jace.

"Not just humans," said Michael, "other beings as well."

"The so-called War in Heaven," said Jace.

"It goes by other names in other cultures, but basically, yes. The result, if not the name, was the same—a sundering of this reality with its deeper manifestation. The Otherworld kept much of the wonder and beauty, but even it was tainted by evil and rebellion. Only now is there a possibility of closing the breach uniting both realities as one again."

"So, do it," said Jace.

"As I said before, I do not believe I have the power, and I certainly know I do not have the authority."

"Then who does?" asked Jace, a defiant scowl on his face.

"I think you know the answer to that question, little one," said Ita not unkindly. "But it is not as simple as it seems. Events were put in motion long ago, and we are at a point now where the actions of a few might turn the tide toward the Light and save many unparalleled suffering. Conor is the unifying force between the worlds. The One who saved creation guaranteed the victory of the Light, but the Dark refuses to accept its defeat. It is powerful and still can cause untold destruction."

"Then God, or the One, or Whoever ought to just stop it from happening."

"Simple boy," said Ita patting his cheek. "We all wish that, but if such a thing were to happen, we would be mindless drones enslaved by the One who created everything. And the One makes no slaves. Free will means creation gets a say how this victory is won. Whether the Creator is aided by his creatures, or must pull victory out of ashes and rule himself alone, an apocalyptic nightmare can become reality. Neither angels or saints, champions or kings, well-meaning young people or," and here she ruffled Colly's hair, "other creatures allied with humans, will succeed on their own. Only together, only united, only of one purpose, and committed to fighting with our last breath can we win."

She walked away a bit from them and said, "I have waited so long, and now the time is here. Already we have begun, and it is as I have feared. We are balanced too equally with the forces of the Dark. And I cannot see what even tomorrow brings."

"Nor I," said Michael. "But we have made a start in these past days that I think bodes well. And we had a victory tonight."

"But all the ones who died …," said Jace, his tortured gaze looking over the bloodied beach.

"Did you think there would be no cost?" said Michael, a sad smile on his face. "Death will stalk this world, because the stakes are so high. Save the beauty and see a new heavens and new earth, or give the One ashes and dust, blood and bone to simply start anew, this effort a failure. I know not what will happen except there is a choice to be made. We are here to make sure beauty does not disappear from this earth, or wonder from the hearts of humanity."

They fell silent then, as the first rays of the rosy red dawn touched the wine-dark sea, and the crashing waves sent currents of uneasiness in the hearts of all who stood on the sand.

THE TOMB OF TRUTH

Sunday, 11/8, Meritaten's Glen, Southwest of Tralee

ABOUT AN HOUR before dawn, when all was quiet in Meritaten's Glen, Fr. Greavy and the Morrigan had succeeded in uncovering the door to the ancient tomb. It was small and covered in hieroglyphs.

"I did not take time to learn her language," dismissed the Morrigan.

"Fortunately," said the priest, "I did. Give me Russian or Chinese and I look like a fool way beyond my depth. But give me ancient Egyptian or Akkadian and I'm a veritable Middle-Eastern Shakespeare." He grinned with pride.

"What does it say?" said the Morrigan. "How do we open the door? Few doors keep out my presence, but this one does."

Greavy was silent for a while looking closely at the cartouches with a flashlight. "Well," he said, "it tells of her death and burial."

"I can save you time and speak of that. First it will say who she was, namely, the daughter of Pharaoh Akhenaten the Heretic who sought to destroy all gods but Aten, the Sun God. She ruled as Pharaoh after his death, but only briefly. Plague wiped out her family and the other royals. The priesthood of Amun rose against her and the strange religion her father foisted on the country. She incurred the wrath of the priests by marrying a non-Egyptian, the Greek prince of Tyre. She had to flee with what loyal followers she had. Traveling here by ship, they successfully conquered this land. The last battle against our people was fought here. Riding a horse that final day, she led her cavalry against our infantry. This is a small place, this glen. She could not get many of her soldiers in here and neither could we. Only dozens on either side, actually, but the battle was fierce. She led her stallion over there by that hillock and she made it leap the rise. It stumbled, she fell and was stunned. One of the *de Danaan* soldiers, stabbed her with a Spear. A mortal wound, her fall should have turned the tide, but it did not matter. They were fierce in their anger. We lost that skirmish and the larger battle at the base of the mountain behind us. It was the end of our reign."

"And of her," said Greavy.

"And yet not," said the Morrigan. "I sensed death on her, but something was not right. Her Egyptian priests came immediately to her aid. They had spells and gods they prayed to that I did not know and they changed her. I could sense it, but I told no one. We were so enamored of her courage—we were a foolish people—that we stopped the battle so she could be honored and buried. Both sides agreed. And we buried her here in this tomb, where death is supposed to reign, but does not."

"What do you mean?" said Greavy.

"Get the door open, and I shall show you."

It was not difficult to figure out the instructions on the glyphs. Putting five fingers on separate cartouches with one hand and pushing, the door moved instantly inward. The Morrigan scampered in and Greavy followed.

There were torches in the entryway to the tomb and the Morrigan had them lit immediately, how the priest didn't really want to know. But the light was a welcome relief. The priest wondered if anyone had been here since the tomb was sealed.

"I know my way," said the Morrigan, "I saw it built."

"Why did you never come back?"

"Because," she shivered, "something was not right here, and it was beyond my ken to figure it out. I and others left it alone."

"But the boys found the Seven Sleepers on *Skellig* Michael this past morning. And you think there might be a connection. It's impossible though. Two millennia separate those monks from this woman."

"Maybe, maybe not. I told you something was strange here."

"Is it good or evil?" asked the priest.

"You are asking me?" smirked the Morrigan. "My apologies, I think it is neither. It is just strange, and it is something I have never encountered."

They walked through a passage with paintings of Pharaoh Akhenaten's rule, his death, his daughter's brief reign. Meritaten, she was called in Egypt, and she was beautiful. Nefertiti was her mother and a bust of the princess outside another chambered door testified to her inherited beauty. Greavy saw this door had a simple handle to be pressed downward. There was a place where a key could have hung but the door bore no lock.

"There are no traps," said the Morrigan. "We need not fear."

The priest opened the door.

The Morrigan absently waved her hand and torches in the room immediately lit. Both stood still in awe at what lay before them. Every wall was brightly painted with scenes from Egyptian life, except for the far wall facing them which chronicled the events of Meritaten and her husband's life in Celtic lands. This wall was inlaid with gold and lapis lazuli tile—it was breathtaking.

Greavy thought it would take archaeologists years to decipher the events and meaning behind the artwork.

Beautiful as the walls were, they were overwhelmed by the sarcophagus that lay in the center of the room. Later, Greavy would deduce it was a precious wood, perhaps cedar or acacia, overlaid with gold. The lid encompassed a carved body of a female, presumably Meritaten herself, yet the image was of no Egyptian Pharaoh or princess. Celtic in style, it seemed totally out of place in the room.

"She was unique, unwilling to discard her past, anxious to succeed in her new role as founder of the Celtic nation." The Morrigan rested her hand upon the bier.

"There is a deep disconnect here," said the priest. "The strange sarcophagus destroys the balance that should be here."

"You can feel it, can you not?" said the Morrigan. "There is no peace in this place. It is the abode of the restless dead."

"We must open it," said Greavy.

"I think not," said the Morrigan shivering slightly.

"I've never seen you show fear," said the priest.

"It is not fear that makes me reluctant. Open this tomb, and the future will be changed. I prefer to make changes, not experience them."

"Well," said the priest smiling slightly, "this must be a particularly difficult time for you to walk the earth."

The Morrigan did not answer. She simply sighed, put both her hands on the lid and gently moved the carving to the right.

Both of them heard a sigh as the lid moved, and Greavy felt a breeze waft against his cheek.

"Help me with this," said the Morrigan, and Fr. Greavy assisted her lifting the lid and placing it on the floor. It was much lighter than he expected.

The tomb was empty, not even a shroud or a dust mote to be found. "She was never buried here," said the priest.

"But something was," said the Morrigan. "Look over there, against the wall."

In the corner of the room, darker than the shadows cast by the flaming torches in their wall sconces, something was slowly moving.

"My God!" said Fr. Greavy, "Another Changeling?"

"No," said the Morrigan. "Something else. It is what I feared. Neither flesh nor spirit, and yet, it is Meritaten."

Slowly the form was coalescing into the figure of a female. "Ah," said the priest, "now I know what you mean. It's called a *ka*, a sort of *doppleganger* or double. It contains her life force, not really her spirit. You were troubled because if this is what I believe it to be, her spirit still resides in her body, wherever that may be."

"Unnatural," said the Morrigan.

"Now who's calling the kettle black?"

"I do not know what you mean, but is this thing intelligent?"

"It's like downloading a consciousness into a computer," said the priest. "You get thoughts, memories and emotions, but not the person."

"What is a computer?" asked the Morrigan.

"Never mind," said Greavy, "let's see if this double of Meritaten will talk."

By this time, the form looked like a real person. Meritaten's *doppleganger* was dressed exactly like the figure on the sarcophagus—a white toga, belted with leather, a golden torc on her neck and black hair cut to shoulder length. A red cloak pinned to her shoulder wrapped around her. On her head a golden crown of a hawk with wings folded back in flight.

"Who disturbs my tomb?" spoke the figure.

"She speaks English!"

"Celtic," said the Morrigan. "But if you hear her in your tongue, then it is powerful sorcery, indeed."

"First," said Fr. Greavy, "who are you?."

The figure stood and walked towards them. "I am the messenger of Meritaten, queen of the Celts." Turning to the Morrigan, she said, "You, I remember, are some type of goddess of death who led the enemy's army."

"I have missed you, too," smiled the Morrigan.

"My name is Greavy, and we are here to speak to Meritaten—or her representative."

"Why?"

"There are things happening in her lands. The graves of seven visitors from her birthplace have been discovered, an ancient cup ..."

"The Chalice of Life," said the figure, "This I know. This was why I awoke."

"What do you mean?" asked the Morrigan.

"You may call me Meritaten. For all intents and purposes, that is who I am. Years of sleeping and I have only been awoken twice before, once for the Chalice, once for the Chair."

A distant expression crossed her face. "Long ago, in Egypt, I was Pharaoh."

"You jest," scoffed the priest.

She smiled. "Only for a few years. It was a time of crisis. Before my father died, I was called Meritaten—beloved of the Sun God Aten. But plague and rebellion were his gift to me, not the throne. That was by accident. I married the prince of Tyre, and he immediately knew our days were numbered in Egypt. So did my uncle, Horemheb. He was general of our armies and also High Priest of Aten. One day he came to my husband and I with a Chalice of gold, brilliant rubies around the Cup and base. Inside swirled a dark wine. He said to us, 'Egypt's gods wage war against one another, but there is one thing the priests of Aten and Amun agree on—this ancient treasure, the Chalice of Life. It is older than our people. We have been only caretakers', he said, 'but it carries a powerful magic. Whosoever looks into this Cup with deep and true desire will see the wine of life. If they drink, they shall be healed, and if they drink, they shall have their years lengthened far beyond the normal span of life. It is not eternal life, but it is a great boon. Drink now, for time is short and you both must leave.'

"We worried it was poison, but it was not. We drank deeply and felt refreshed. I was still young but felt younger. But my husband, he was quite older and I watched the years depart from him and both of us were young again. My uncle said, 'Take the Cup with you, because Egypt faces dissolution, and bestow it on a worthy people. Now go.'

"Our escape had been planned. We and several hundred of our followers sailed west across the Middle Sea, through the paths of the Narrow Rocks, and then around the coast of Spain where we spent several years at rest.

"Setting out again, for we were a restless people, we founded colonies in northern Britain and then moved to the farthest island west we knew. Ireland. A strange and sorcerous people held the land." Here she looked severely at the Morrigan. "We were not many, but the Chalice of Life healed our warriors and we lost very few. Here in this glen began the last battle, and the one in which I lost my life."

"But you didn't lose your life, did you?" said Fr. Greavy softly.

Her head fell forward and tears fell from her eyes. "I did not. I had instructed my Egyptian priests to treat my death differently from other Pharaohs. They knew spells to put my life in stasis, for in the years of traveling I had begun to see that the Chalice was essential to the survival of all life, though I did not know how. I had bequeathed it to no one, and if I died, it would be lost and seen as plunder. So, I had them change me, trap my spirit in my body and create this double which could wait in stasis for the true heir."

"Why did the Chalice not preserve you?" asked the Morrigan. "You had drunk from it. Was it all a lie?"

Meritaten gave a small smile. "It preserves life, but life still may be violently taken. I was mortally wounded. My drinking of the Cup preserved my existence long enough for my priests to work their wonders. The Chalice is precious. It was worth the sacrifice I made."

"But you let the Celts have it," said the priest. "They used it for their armies for hundreds of years."

"On loan," said Meritaten. "Till it was seemingly stolen by an Egyptian merchant who then sold it to a Jewish scholar and seller of foreign wares."

"Joseph of Arimathea," said Fr. Greavy, his hands beginning to shake.

"It was as I planned. I knew it had a task near my former country, so I had it returned. I knew not what that destiny was until one night, my tomb trembled, and the torches lit of their own volition and I knew the Cup had helped weave a new story for life on this earth, something remarkable, and then I slept again. Until seven holy men from Egypt, now belonging to a new religion, brought the Cup back to this island, disturbing my rest once more. I knew it would return, but I knew not its purpose and none was revealed to me. They found me here, just as you did. They showed me the Chalice, but it was dry. After all, I am not really her. I told them what I told you and asked them to keep it till the day a key unlocked one of their graves, a key that would hang on my chamber door until that time. That key is gone now. I sense its absence. Tell me where it is, and I might possibly let you live."

"Before we do," said the Morrigan. "tell this man what your people told mine during the truce to hold your funeral."

"I instructed my people to end the war, to merge or seek peace with your people, to be a light to the nations, and a vanguard against all evil. Have you done that? The holy men from my country were unclear."

"With very modest success, and more often failure," said Fr. Greavy. "But the Cup has made itself known now to the Children of the Light, the ones who fight evil. When it was returned to this land, it came back with a greater power than before. Tonight, it saved a king's life, a king who will unite this world and the Otherworld to defeat evil and usher in a new heavens and a new earth. The Chalice you so carefully guarded is now called the Grail. Long ago it was given new purpose, granted a new destiny. It is one of three weapons we have to fight the darkest evil in existence. Already this night we have been stricken, but prevailed. The King Who Shall Be, who could have perished this past evening, is destined to be the force around which the people will gather, just like you were. Only his people will not be of one race but shall be the people of the world."

"My husband had a name for this," said Meritaten. "He called events, such as you mention, apocalyptic times. Times of great upheaval and death."

"But also times of hope," said Fr. Greavy.

"You have given us much needed information, Meritaten," said the Morrigan. "But nothing we could not have eventually figured out on our own. What else did you tell the Seven Sleepers—what is it you are keeping from us?"

"I cannot say."

"Cannot or will not?" asked the priest.

"You know this creature you are with, human, plays the Dark and the Light against one another. She is a feckless and utterly untrustworthy companion."

Greavy glanced at the Morrigan. "Feckless, perhaps, but I do not call her untrustworthy, nor companion. She has her own agenda."

Meritaten laughed, "That is one way of shading the truth. But my knowledge is not for her."

"Then for whom?" snarled the Morrigan.

"For the boy king. I am *ka*," she said running her fingers over the priest's bald head, startling the man so that he backed away. Her falling hand dislodged his wire rim glasses. "This human's mind is open to me like papyrus sheets rustling in the wind."

Quickly picking his glasses up, Fr. Greavy took out a kerchief and began polishing the lenses, all the while blushing deeply. Both the Morrigan and Meritaten laughed lightly.

"At least the two of you seem to enjoy putting me off balance. But you should know, Meritaten," said the priest slipping his glasses back on, "that this 'boy king' as you call him, holds the power to bring two realities back together that were sundered long before you first walked this earth."

"I see that in your mind," said Meritaten. "All the hopes you have placed on him. He is not simply human," she said as she walked around the priest again concentrating deeply. Suddenly she turned and shrieked at the Morrigan. "You! This man's mind tells me the boy is tainted with the blood of your kind! What twisted sorcery did such a thing?"

"No sorcery," sighed the Morrigan. "It was love. Something you once knew when you married the Greek king, also tainting your blood."

Meritaten's face softened. "I remember. I was young then, and foolish. I could have lived out my life as Pharaoh, but I risked everything and lost my throne when I married my prince."

"But you gained a nation," said Greavy.

"Barely barbarians were they when we landed on these shores, ruled by the Morrigan's people." She strode over to the Morrigan, glaring at her. "You made them worship you as gods. You could have shared your knowledge, helped them know the secrets of the earth and the heavens. But you lorded your superiority over them, making them slaves. That's why I and my followers freed them from their vassalage."

"After your death, we did share much of what we knew with the people you adopted."

"But not all," said Meritaten. "I cannot read your mind as I can the human's, but your face tells me enough. You still hold secrets within secrets, veiled from them."

"Enough," said Greavy. "What you say is true, Meritaten, but that does not help any of us. The Morrigan and I represent forces that want the boy to succeed. Indeed, he must, for the merging of this world and the Other must happen in the Light, or destruction will follow as surely as night follows morning. If you know something that will help, tell us now."

Meritaten looked intently at Greavy. "There is a Spear and a Sword that I see in your mind. They are ancient to this land and even when I lived they were the stuff of legend. They have been found. What's more, they have been used. And now, you have the Chalice of Life, what you call the Grail. These three were once bound together here on this island, forged here originally, made to be physical carriers of the power of the Light. Then they went their separate ways and were changed again, made even more powerful. Now they have returned to this land, but for one purpose only. To enable the boy king to find the fourth sign. First discovered near my birthplace, it has traveled much. But once it rested here in this land with the other sacred objects, for many centuries. It must be found again, if the boy king and companions are to have any chance at success."

"What is it—this fourth object?" said the priest.

"Let us go," snapped the Morrigan. "I know what it is. We do not need her or her supposed wisdom to find it. I have seen it."

"Seen it yes, but you did not know what to do with it. Neither you nor your people," hissed Meritaten.

"What is it?" said Fr. Greavy. "Stop your bickering and out with it."

"She and her other divine usurpers," said Meritaten pointing at the Morrigan, "knew it as the *Lia Fail*, the Stone of Truth. Her people are more than human, but even her kind, if they sat on the Stone, not only had to tell the truth but also had to listen to its judgment. For it could speak."

"It was a treasure beyond price," said the Morrigan. "Until it too was lost or stolen from us when our power slipped from this world."

Meritaten laughed and said to the priest, "They only thought of it as a speaking piece of rock. But it is so much more. It had the ability to ennoble the truth that was in a person. Find it, human, and you will gain an advantage over the Dark, over the Evil that seeks to rise. Wake the Seven Sleepers and listen to their wisdom for they know much more about the Stone than the Morrigan does."

"Yes," said Fr. Greavy, "but what else does it do?"

Meritaten shimmered in the torchlight. "My ability to keep this form is fading. You know enough. Now go. Let me rest." She moved toward the tomb and as she approached it, her form dissolved into the dark mist she was before. It settled on the floor of the sarcophagus and both the Morrigan and the priest approached carefully. Once again, they heard the sigh, like brittle leaves across a stone pathway, only this time something else appeared.

"She was there all the time," said the priest.

"As she was when we buried her."

Both of them viewed a wrapped Egyptian mummy solidifying before them in the tomb. A golden death mask encased the face, but the rest of the body was shrouded in linen wrappings.

"Why now?" asked the priest. "No one has seen this before. Unless her *ka* is truly gone."

"Egyptian sorcery again," said the Morrigan.

"In this case you might be right. The *ka* was placed here to give messages to those allowed to enter this burial chamber. I think we were the end of the visitor's list. Meritaten was in stasis before. I think her body was simply wrapped and not embalmed. Her soul never departed."

They felt a trembling shudder shaking the chamber. "Until now," said the priest. As they looked, the body of Meritaten, Pharaoh of Egypt, known as Meritaten of the Celts, crumbled into dust. But the tremors only increased.

"We must leave," said the Morrigan.

"Couldn't agree more," said Fr. Greavy and moved to leave the chamber, but another tremblor knocked him to the floor. The Morrigan moved swiftly and picked him up in her arms.

"Don't get used to this," she said, "but I can move faster with you in my arms than simply having you try to keep up with me."

As the walls fell, she moved like a wraith through the tunnel, leaping the last several meters out the exit as the passageway collapsed behind them.

Both of them were coughing on the ground as the dust continued to pour out. As they looked back, the entire hill seemed to heave and then settle much lower than it had before.

"Thus passes Meritaten, Queen of the Celts," said the priest making the Sign of the Cross.

"And good riddance," muttered the Morrigan.

BREAKFAST AT BALLINSKELLIGS

Sunday Morning 11/8, Ballinskelligs

MOIRA AND PHIL cobbled together an Irish breakfast for the tired company. By the time the beach had been cleansed and the injured either headed to hospital or home, the sun had risen far above the horizon.

No one said anything as scrambled eggs and bacon, juice and coffee began their work of driving the horror of the night away. Popping in through the window came a blue glowing ball swiftly orbiting the table and stopping close to a seated Jace who mumbled into his coffee cup, "Oh look, Tinkerbell is back."

With a zap like a broken electrical wire, a spark hit Jace's ear and the blue ball disappeared leaving a glaring Lettie holding on to the young man's earlobe. "I'm more than a Disney sprite, lad," said Lettie, twisting her fingers.

"Ow!", said Jace, "I didn't mean any disrespect ... really, I didn't!"

"I've listened to my share of men in my time, and you're all the same. Quick with the lip and slow with the brain. Now, get me a chair and fill me a plate. I'm just as hungry as you."

Jace hustled to accommodate, but the exchange had loosened everyone's tongue and after piling on Jace for what he said, conversation turned to the absent Michael.

"Did you hear RTE this morning?" said Phil referring to Ireland's morning news broadcast. "The flames we saw were a mile high, and the news readers were saying that for a while the whole of Kerry was blotted off the map. They're showing pictures of what Ireland looked like from space last night. Where we should be is just a black hole, darker than North Korea. And the pictures showed the fire made a plague barrier. And they showed Michael, though nobody could really say what he was."

"What about the military?" asked Colly. "Do they have any reports on the flying horseman?"

Phil nodded, swallowing a piece of toast. "I think so. NATO and the Royal Air Force aren't saying much about a UFO they spotted near the flame wall. Do you know the British bastards violated our air space? Whatever it was they saw, it is being studied."

"Let's hope not too closely," said Jace.

"Oh, it's worse than you think," said a voice near the doorway. Everyone looked, and there was Fr. Greavy, a little muddied and tired, looking longingly at the food on the table.

"Here now," said Moira standing. "Get yourself over to this spare place and sit down. Food will revive you and you can tell us the bad news."

Ita smiled, "In all the bad news I've ever heard there was always the faint echo of hope. Out with it, Fr. Greavy."

"Well," said the priest, "what has happened here is not so secret anymore. Tralee was basically destroyed; its citizens killed, the town practically burned to the ground. Right now, the government is picking over what's left and they are going to want answers. Nothing we have to worry about except keeping secret whatever we decide to do next. They'll fixate on Michael, but he can handle himself, maybe even run a little interference for us. The government's involvement is bad news, but the Morrigan and I discovered something that might be helpful."

"Where is she?" asked Jace, looking around.

Fr. Greavy looked blankly at him. "She left me at Meritaten's Glen and went ... wherever it is she goes. But before she did, we found the grave and opened it."

"Meritaten's Grave?" shouted Colly. "Magnificent! What did you find?"

The priest described their discovery and told the story of Meritaten. "As wondrous as all that is, she left us with a mystery and a task. Ireland has four great talismans and we have three of them: The Sword of Light, the Spear of Destiny, and the Holy Grail. But there is one more, and Meritaten thinks it's absolutely necessary that we find it."

"The Stone of Truth," whispered Ita.

"How did you know?" said Fr. Greavy. "It just doesn't seem to fit anywhere in the stories and prophecies now."

"It does if you're British royalty," said Phil. "You're talking about the Stone of Scone, the Stone all British monarchs are crowned on. It's in Edinburgh Castle, surrounded by enough Scottish security that it would be easier if we would try to steal the Crown Jewels, which, by the way, are also there."

Greavy said, "Meritaten told us that the Stone speaks when a king sits upon it, and when it speaks, the truth is made known. Are you sure it's the same as the Coronation Stone?"

"Good question," said Ita. "Of all the sacred objects of this land, the Stone's story is most shadowed in myth. They say it first appeared in the Holy Land, when Jacob used it as a pillow to sleep on when journeying to his uncle Laban. When he slept, he dreamed of angels ascending and descending a ladder that stretched from earth to heaven."

"Or a ladder that bridged the gap between this world and the Otherworld," mused the priest.

"Exactly what I was thinking," said Ita. "Then its story fades and comes clear again when the Stone appears at Tara. It is found on the hill where High Kings were crowned. The candidate for the High Kingship had to sit on the stone, speak the truth of his name and herItage, and it would cry out, 'Chosen!' or it would remain silent if the candidate lied. Silence was rejection. St. Columba moved it to Iona, and there it stayed, on the island itself or near enough, until King Edward Longshanks stole it down to England. But I know for a fact that he took a fake, because Robert the Bruce of Scotland, his mortal enemy, was crowned sitting on the same stone. Then it disappeared. But the British claim they truly have the Coronation Stone. They use it still today, but that particular stone has never spoken or revealed any heavenly truths in a dream state. That's how I know it is a massive forgery."

"How do you know so much for a sixth century nun?" smiled Jace.

"I have had a lot of time to read," she smiled sweetly.

"Whether or not it is the Stone, it is the only lead we have. We have to steal it, in order to know for sure … no offense Ita," said Colly.

"None taken, Changeling. You hardly ever listened to me anyway." Her merry smile took the sting out of the words.

"And do what with it?" said Phil. "How could it possibly help Conor? Maybe Michael would know?"

"Don't be too sure," said Lettie. "He's a seraph and while he puts on a good show of being human before us, it's an act and difficult for him. Our concerns are not always his."

"You're not human either," sniffed Colly.

"But I'm like you," she said. "An ally, and certainly more useful than you." The company laughed as Lettie twitched the insult away with a purse of her lips. "I agree with Phil, though. I'm not sure of what use it would be for us."

"Doesn't matter," said Fr. Greavy. "Meritaten thought it important enough to hang around for a couple of thousand years to tell us. That's good enough for me."

"How should we get it?" said Jace. "I'm a football player, not a thief. I'm too big to walk into Edinburgh Castle unnoticed."

"Leave that to me," said Colly. "I've got an idea."

SCATHA'S ISLAND

Sunday Morning, 11/8, Isle of Skye, Scotland

BRENDAN AND HIS boatmen rowed along the *faerie* track without uttering a word. Here in the Otherworld, the sea was calm and distances were short. A fog, however, arose and set a shroud of silence over all those on the vessel. Troubles laid across Conor's legs, trying to give his master some warmth and Scatha stood by at the prow anxiously looking down upon Conor's still face.

Absently, brushing a stray lock of his hair from his forehead, she said to him, "Perhaps you can hear me, even in your sleep, but we take you to my island where you may recover. Your people will be there, all those who love you. You will rest and you will gain strength and I will teach you what you need to know to be king."

Her strong words gave small comfort in the mist and Troubles whined with concern. He had been out of touch too long with the heart of his master.

Conor's body was still as the boat slipped through the sea, but his mind was not. The moment he drank from the Grail, he felt his awareness expanding. Abbot Malachy had told him to see the bright mountain behind the mountain, and at this moment he had no trouble grasping the existence of the world of humans and the Otherworld. Surrounded by stars, the Hand of God shimmering high in the cosmos, Conor hovered above the earth he loved. It rotated beneath him and it looked beautiful—mostly. Here and there he saw dark shadows obscuring the land and the sea. Not clouds, but something else, a pall perhaps. Seeing Ireland below him, he gasped. Where County Kerry should have been, only a dark hole remained. When America appeared, he sought out the Great Lakes and saw Wisconsin. A similar blackness appeared right where Tinker's Grove should have been. He remembered the cancer his mother suffered from. That's what this looked like, a cancer eating at his world.

Sensing movement, he looked up and saw the Hand of God nebula swirling closer. A starry finger pointed toward the earth and he saw his home planet dim, and a new halo of light surrounding the sphere, cradling the globe. The light hardened and Conor looked upon another earth, almost exactly the same but somewhat larger and, from the parts he could see, much more beautiful. That's what Malachy meant, thought Conor, when he talked about the bright mountain behind the mountain. Not another planet, not another dimension, but a deeper world that holds my little earth—the Otherworld. He saw the moon similarly wrapped by a larger satellite that shone like luminescent pearl.

Separate but together somehow. Motes of light encompassed him, as the Hand of God seemed to grasp him, lift him and hurled him toward his world. Conor fell much like the comet seen days ago. But he did not hit the surface. Instead, he plunged through space swiftly, blacking out momentarily. When his eyes opened again, he gasped, thinking he had just passed through the earth. Now, he was held in stasis between the worlds.

He felt the two realities trying to merge, immense forces competing. He was caught in the middle. Knowing he was a nexus linking them together, he didn't understand how or what it really meant.

He puzzled over the problem for a little while but then felt a whisper, a tentacle of dark thought invading his consciousness. It had the cold feel of an enemy and he grew suddenly afraid.

In the boat, Conor made a gasping noise that Scatha clearly heard. In fear, she touched his forehead to see if he had contracted a fever, but her eyes caught a movement just off the port side of the *faerie* track. Something was surfacing from the depths of the dark sea and snapped a tentacle towards the boat.

Scatha was thankful that the *faerie* track existed as more than just a two-dimensional road. It had height and depth as well and the probe was rebuffed. Whatever sought entry onto the boat could not overcome the barrier. Then she saw the behemoth surface, and on its massive body a single, huge eye opened, glaring balefully at her. Balor! He had found them again.

She moved to grab the Holy Lance off Conor's chest, but Brendan cautioned her. "Milady," he said, "do not be afraid. This thing cannot harm us now. It knows it is forbidden entrance to the *faerie* track. It is here for something else. We can prevent its physical molestation, but it uses its nearness to Conor to try to enter his mind."

Just then, Conor moaned again. Within himself, Conor turned and twisted trying to evade the grasp of Balor. Darkness enveloped him again— the vision of the worlds was gone.

He felt so weak from the wounding he had received from the demon. He shivered at the touch of the tentacles, felt them again tightening around his neck. When he thought he could not escape and would be captured, a light pierced the darkness, and it burned the demon, driving him away.

"Mom?" said Conor, disbelieving that this vision of a lady in shimmering white could be Finola. The figure smiled at him, coming closer. Gently, hands cupped his face and she spoke.

"Conor, my son," she said. "You were not made for the Dark, but for the Light. So many depend on you. I cannot let you be prey to that thing that seeks your life. When it tries to attack your heart, I am able to see you through the storm."

"Why haven't I seen you before? Do you know what's been happening?"

"Yes, and I have been near. But you see me now because you have drunk from the Grail when your very existence was in balance. Your life is much brighter than before. You were made from the dust of stars and now you shine like them in the sky. Even the Hand of God can hold you. You see more deeply and clearly."

"I've missed you."

"And I, you. But you have a chance to learn even more now. The Grail has deepened your awareness of all things, and though you are just coming to perceive, you now can sense the One who conducts the symphony of the stars—the music of the spheres."

"Amergin made me Bard of the West. I don't even know what that means."

"You will, because the best way to describe what has been happening to you is with the music that you love. Amergin became the song of his people. I heard him pass and his song falter. But I also heard when the land and the sea bequeathed that music to you. To be the Bard of the West is not some glorified version of your time at the *DerryAir* in Chicago. You embody part of the song of Creation, and that is one of the reasons why so much hope rests in you. Amergin lived one foot in this world and one in the Otherworld. He was a nexus and now you are but in an even more special way. You are human and *Roan*. You are in this world and the Otherworld as well. The bards of old could sing of the Otherworld so that people could feel its presence. You can also but you have the added ability of singing that magic into existence, of bringing both worlds together."

"How?" said Conor. "I feel like those suits, those middle managers who came to the pub for Happy Hour, weighed down with all the responsibility they had and angry that no authority went with the expectations put on them. I don't know how to do all this. I don't think I can."

Finola smiled gently. "You will. Scatha will show you some of the ways. You will learn the rest from the people and creatures you meet and help. Trust her. You have been through much. The son of Madoc and Finola has proven himself over and over to be the match of any prophecy spoken about him. Do not worry overmuch about the lore, or the rumors, or the expectations anyone or anything has of you. Be who you were born to be."

"And what is that, Mom?" said Conor, feeling a tear running down his cheek.

"Be my son, Conor. Be my good, generous, open hearted son like you have always been. You held me as I passed. As hard as that was for you, behold, you made it so easy for me. I am at peace and so proud of you."

"Mom, where are you going?" said Conor, reaching for her as she seemed to fade. Their fingertips touched.

"I cannot stay. I will be watching and protecting you as I am able. My love, my son. You shall always have my love." Her luminous figure disappeared into the starlight as she faded from his sight.

"Look!" said Scatha, to the boatmen. "He weeps!"

Troubles moved up and licked Conor's face, nuzzling his neck.

Brendan gazed on Conor's face as he and his companions rowed along the track. "He is grieving, and that is good. A heart deeply touched is a heart protected from that loathsome serpent we saw in the sea."

The sun now raised its head above the waves and Scatha could clearly see her island in the distance. "There," she said to the boatmen. "Head for the Cuillin Hills. We will make for *Loch na Cuilce* and the River *Scavaig* with its landing behind the Roan Rocks."

Conor began to rouse as the Isle of Skye came closer. The sound of sea birds calling in the air and gannets diving into the waves for morning fish woke him.

He was about to speak when he heard something else. Actually, a lot of somethings—barking and hooting, growling and yipping. And he knew what they were. The sounds of seals basking on rocks. He had heard them at Ballinskelligs but had hesItated to go and see them. Time and events plotted a different course.

Now, as he woke, he was curious. He opened his eyes to see Troubles on his chest looking at him. Turning his head, he saw Scatha smiling. "Your people are greeting you. Do you feel like sitting and setting eyes on those you intend to rule?"

Conor smiled back but said nothing. As he sat up, he saw dozens of seals on a rocky island in the bay at the base of the Black Cuillin, the mountains of southern Skye. "It's like a still life of Middle-Earth," he said, awestruck at the surreal craggy peaks and the sea life all around him.

"It is a beautiful but strange land, even in this present reality. But you cannot recover in the ordinary world. You are healed of your immediate injuries, but sorely in need of rest and replenishment—a kind of convalescence you can only get in the Otherworld. So, behold my island as it really is, in all its majesty."

It seemed to Conor that reality contracted swiftly and then expanded again. The *faerie* track disappeared, majestic hills grew taller, the land sloping down to the sea became covered not with rocky scree but with green meadow, the sky shone more azure blue. But the biggest change was in the seals before him. They now looked more like humans who grew up in the sea, but they were selkies, *Roan*, the sea people that he belonged to. Different than human but much the same. He felt himself changing as well and was surprised when Troubles tipped him into the ocean. The dog cast off Michael's glamour, resuming his 'Otherworldly' size. He barked once and laughed, jumping into the sea as well. Scatha, clad in her majestic gown of seaweed executed a perfect flip off the boat and joined Conor as they swam to the rocky island.

Amazingly, the *Roan* turned and bowed as they came ashore. They said nothing to him but smiled in welcome.

Scatha said, "In time they will greet you by name, but they know your need and will let you rest for now." She turned and waved to the boatmen.

"Fair weather to you friends," she said to Brendan and companions. They raised their oars in salute and then departed the bay.

DUN SCAITHA AND
THE BLACK CUILLIN

Skye Time in the Otherworld

THE LITTLE ISLAND in the bay was called Green Island, though when they had approached, it looked like any other rocky outcropping on the Hebridean shores. But when Scatha cast them into the Otherworld, the island manifested itself in all its glory. Scotch Pine crowned the center of the little isle and grass grew outward mixed with tiny flowers, yellow and lavender. Conor remembered that November in the Otherworld was not the bleak desolation in his reality. Here, the autumnal weather was warm and glorious.

But as beautiful as the island appeared, it was the *Roan* who captured his attention. The roly-poly, waddling, and always awkward looking seals were transformed into magnificent selkies, men and women who looked remarkably human until one started noticing the differences.

First of all, thought Conor, as he and Scatha walked among them, the *Roan* were taller than humans. Unlike their animal appearance in his reality, they had little fat on them and were lean and muscular. Their skin and their hair were dappled shades of green or grey. Some were bipedal but the ones closest to water had legs that morphed downward into appendages that looked like fins. Their hands were webbed, and when Conor looked at his own, he found he had changed as well. He was one of them and he began to smile. These were his people, and he immediately felt he belonged with them.

Scatha led both he and Troubles to the center of the island where a small table was set up. Three cups and a pitcher of some type of golden liquid were placed on it. One of the *Roan*, a male, stepped forward and poured the fluid into the cups. Conor, Scatha, and the stranger took them in hand. Conor imItated Scatha and raised his in greeting to the stranger. Scatha said, "This is Calador. He represents the *Roan*. In their name, he welcomes you with mead. Drink now, and be at peace."

Conor had tasted mead before. His mother had some excellent vintages they drank for special occasions. This mead, Conor thought, was out of this world—'Otherworldly', he laughed to himself. As he drank, he felt himself warm and he looked around at all those who had gathered.

"Come with me," said Scatha, and she led both the boy and the dog swiftly to the shore. "It is just a few hundred meters across this bay to the River *Scavaig*, and our adventure begins." She leapt into the water and he followed, amazed anew at his abilities to adapt to the ocean. Swiftly and strongly all three swam, and, together, they climbed out where the River *Scavaig* flowed into the ocean.

"Geez," said Conor, "this has to be the shortest river in the world." He lifted up his head and gasped. Before him lay a freshwater loch, the first of many on the isle of Skye, and on the horizon the Black Cuillin mountain range rose up stabbing the blue sky.

"That's where we are going?" he asked.

"Indeed," said Scatha. "We will go to my home, *Dun Scaitha*. It means the Fortress of Shadows, but it is not as dark or bleak as it sounds. The name was given because it is invisible to those who idly seek it. Only those with courage and strength can see it. Take my hand, Conor Archer, lest you miss it." She laughed gaily in the warm morning sun and Conor blushed as she said, "As you humans are often saying, I am just kidding you."

Walking alongside the loch, Conor noticed the landscape gradually lifting upward. Unlike its ordinary appearance in his world, the plain below the Black Cuillin was beautiful and fertile. Beech and pine, oak and hawthorn grew there freely.

"Look!" said Conor. "Waterfalls!"

"Those are called the *faerie* pools, a series of waterfalls with crystal ponds at the base of each fall. You can swim in them, and if you are lucky, you will see creatures that never walk your world but will charm you with their beauty and grace."

She didn't let him linger long. Conor could tell she was anxious to reach her home. He didn't know how much time passed, but one moment he was stepping through a golden grassy meadow mountain pass and the next he looked up and there on a high rise at the base of the largest of the Cuillin was a castle, a fortress not of heavy stone, but of red quarried granite. In front of *Dun Scaitha* was another beautiful loch, its clear water reflecting the deep blue sky.

"Long ago," said Scatha, "my ancestors took rock from the Red Cuillin to the south east and brought the granite here, erecting this castle. We had few enemies, and it was built as much for beauty and comfort as it was for protection."

"In my down time at Ballinskelligs," said Conor, "I found a book of folklore at the hotel and read about you. You have been around awhile and taught the greatest heroes of the Celts martial arts and the ways of battle."

"It was my purpose for many centuries, and I made many warriors. But their bravery has passed into time and dust. They were the men of old, the heroes of renown. When I sent them back to their world, they did great deeds that spawned countless legends. You've heard their names, Cuchulainn, Finn MacCool, Brian Boru, and many others. They would feel out of place now, so weak have you humans become."

"What of me?" asked Conor. "Why did you really bring me here?"

"You must recover from your battle with Balor. He wounded you grievously and though Ita and Michael kept you alive and the Grail healed you, your strength is depleted. You will recover here and learn the ways of Celtic battle and lore. Though you were magnificent in your struggle with Balor—do not look so surprised; I have learned that men must be flattered—you are not skilled with the Spear of Destiny or even know how to use your own body as a weapon. I can teach you, and you must learn, if you are to be a leader of men and the king of your people."

Conor laughed and his words were heavy with sarcasm. "I am not even in college yet, and you want me to be like Brian Boru. I don't think that in this age of terrorism and cyber warfare, your skills will be terribly helpful. No offense."

She slapped him then across his face. It didn't hurt much but it startled him. "I'm sorry," he said. "That didn't come out right."

Scatha looked at him scornfully. "You know nothing of combat. For that matter, you know nothing of me. I am not some relic of a forgotten past. I know your world well with its armies and armaments, its technology and cyber abilities. I am Scatha, always the warrior queen, and I will teach you how to make your body into a weapon, and how to unleash the power of the Holy Lance. If you learn from me, you will be unbeatable, unstoppable, unconquerable."

"Oh, I think Jace will still be able to whip my ass."

Scatha's anger quickly passed and she laughed again. "Perhaps. He is the Champion and I believe the Morrigan will teach him things he does not know about himself and the power he possesses. We will need both of you to succeed in the days and years to come."

SHIRO ISHII PLOTS HIS NEXT MOVE

Sunday Morning, 11/8, North of Tralee

SO, THEY THINK I'm a wizard, thought Shiro Ishii. He was driving his Mercedes back from Limerick. He had sped there after the disaster in Meritaten's Glen, but he still felt fiercely proud that he had hacked the leg off that insufferable werewolf. But that was the only good thing that happened. He couldn't save the Red Thirst, and he had more plans for her than simply wiping out Tralee. Yet enough people had seen her and probably survived that he felt she would somehow live on in the retelling of the story of Tralee's destruction, a nightmare to frighten both children and their parents.

The plague had worked to perfection. He still felt a momentary loss in his heart, thinking of what it would have done to Washington, D.C. back in the spring of 1945. The Emperor could have won the war with his weapon. But who was he to question his god? Hirohito must have had a reason for not releasing it on an unsuspecting America. That was long ago. Ishii knew that the Emperor's sons no longer possessed divine status, if they ever had it. That, the Emperor had bequeathed to Shiro with the potion the ruler made him drink, there in the throne room so long ago. A wizard, indeed, thought the terrorist. More like a god.

He didn't know what possessed him to flee to Limerick, but he was glad he did since it put him outside the barrier of flame that the strange being in the sky had inflicted on the land. He felt the fire's power. If he had been caught behind it or actually in it, he would have feared for his existence. It actually caused him pain for the time it flared in the sky.

No matter. He lived, and though he had not heard from Sir Hugh he was not overly worried. He knew Sir Hugh was a Celtic godling, perhaps more powerful than himself. But they had planned. The seraph's intervention and the constant meddling of the companions of Conor Archer were troublesome, but they could be handled.

All in all, the 'Night of Cherry Blossoms' was a success. It would put this world on notice that change was coming, that death, darkness and destruction were in the air. Long ago, Shiro had learned that a frightened people are a weak people. He wanted the people of this reality weakened so that, when the worlds merged, Balor, Ishii, and those allied with them could unleash the power of the Dark Otherworld and release those things that abhorred the Light. The people would not be able to resist them.

Over the years, Shiro had come to sense the Otherworld just outside of this reality. He had felt it moving closer and was grateful to Sir Hugh for instructing him on the finer points of what would happen if the worlds merged. He appreciated the knowledge, but it didn't change his modus operandi. What was valued in someone like a car mechanic, who liked to take engines apart to see how they worked, was actually an appalling talent in a being like Ishii. The doctor liked unmaking things. He had spent the years before and after World War II learning how to take apart humans. He had expected the Japanese war machine to praise his efforts to develop better and more effective killing techniques, but no one, excepting the Emperor, ever offered him praise. Even his countrymen thought him a monster, though they had no problem using his techniques against the allied nations.

When Balor rescued him after his shipwreck at Bull Rock, he found a kindred spirit in whatever it was that disguised itself as Sir Hugh Rappaport. Sir Hugh was delighted in Ishii's past exploits and as he revealed his plans for the merging of the realities, Ishii knew he had found new meaning for his life.

"It's going to happen, Shiro," said Sir Hugh over dinner one night. "The worlds are coming together again, and we can't nor should we stop that event. My people were so powerful back when reality was one united existence. It will be so again. We bring the coming of the Night, a darkness so terrible that everything that manages to live through the event will wish for true death."

Ishii thought of this again as he drove back through the outskirts of Tralee, stopping at the new military roadblocks. Pretending to be a confused and bereaved citizen of the town, he was easily waved through all barricades.

He thought of the fear on the soldiers faces as he drove past them. All of this was out of their experience. He gathered from the radio that the events here in Kerry had reverberated throughout the island. The always despairing young were turning to the new supplies of RAGE that he had farmed out through his associates to the various towns and cities. It wasn't exactly the plague, but similar enough that outbreaks of the drug's use brought new fear into the populace of the land.

South of Tralee, there was less military traffic, and Shiro found himself alone on the road towards Meritaten's Glen. Parking on the shoulder, he made the short walk back to the tiny glen. He saw the remnants of battle, the new grave where the remains of the Red Thirst lay, and he noticed the collapsed hill, wondering how that ever happened. Much had occurred, obviously, after he had left.

Hearing a skittering in the grass, he glanced off to his left. The bracken was moving and more than just one thing was rushing through it. Springing into the clearing, dozens of *drocs* surrounded Ishii. These had escaped the ravening wolves. Hungry and without a mission, they thought Ishii might make a good meal.

He simply laughed at them. They were primitive, but they would understand. "Friends," he said, "you are welcome to come with me and help me in my quest. If you join me, I will find food for you."

They clicked and hissed in their reptilian way. They didn't attack and Ishii felt that must mean they understood him. He turned his back on them and started for his car. Hearing them chittering behind him, he smiled again, breaking out with a jaunty whistle, imitating the tuneless cry the Red Thirst sang when she hunted. Like some ghastly pied piper, he led the little *drocs* to his car, opened the back door to his Mercedes, and sang them all into the back of his automobile.

A PLAN OF PURSUIT

Sunday Morning, 11/8, Portmagee

HE DROVE SLOWLY south, deciding to head to Portmagee. He couldn't very well visit the hotel tavern where he first saw the priest, that American boy, and that despicable werewolf thing. Hoping that the whole area was off balance because of the previous night's excitement, Ishii thought he might stop by the cleric's house and coerce a little more information out of the pudgy priest.

The *drocs* had other ideas. He heard them whispering in the back seat, and he could almost make out the words they were trying to say. Turning his head, he asked, "Sounds to me like you little balls of mischief are hungry. Want to stop for something to eat?"

The whispers died away and Ishii felt the expectation roiling off their bodies. "Eat it is, then. Be patient for a few more minutes."

The area around Portmagee was not heavily populated and he found a crofter's house and barn far enough from the main road that it would suit his purposes. Smoke was coming from the chimney so someone was at home. He didn't even get out of his car. Simply rolling down the windows, he chuckled as he said, "Meat's on the table; go and get it boys."

Chittering excitedly, the *drocs* scrambled out of the car and bumped and jumped toward the house. Ishii thought they didn't even slow down as they smashed through the windows. For a moment, all was still, and then the screams began. A high-pitched wail—the woman of the house no doubt, and a deeper cry of pain—the crofter himself, home enjoying a hearty Irish breakfast. The screams cut off almost immediately and it could not have been more than five minutes later that the *drocs* came barreling out of the house, leaping back into the car.

"How was breakfast, lads?" smiled Ishii. Slurps and burps, that's what he heard. Guessing it was a sound of contentment for the creatures, he put his vehicle in drive and headed for Fr. Greavy's home.

Ishii parked some distance away and rolled up the windows. He didn't want his new friends to distract from what he was going to do. Finding the door unlocked, he quietly let himself in. Seeing no one, he thought the priest might be gone, but then he heard sounds from the kitchen. Creeping forward, he hazarded a look around the corner. There he was, that cretin who stabbed his hand tight to the table days before. Ishii held up his hand. All better now. He was truly blessed to be able to heal so swiftly.

"Might as well come on in," said the priest, not turning his head to look at the intruder. "Just making a spot of tea. I find with all the excitement it settles my nerves. Like a cuppa?" The priest turned toward Ishii with a smile.

"Of course. Why not?" said Ishii and sat down at the table.

"I see your hand is much better. I wonder how much of your soul you had to sell to get that wondrous power. Don't mean to be disrespectful; it's just that I sense no good in you, so whatever allows you to heal can't come from anything dealing with the Light."

"You don't know me, priest."

"You are correct," said Fr. Greavy. "But I've read about you, and Amergin told me about his experience with you. I doubt Balor could have accomplished so much last night without your expertise. The plague was your idea?"

"Yes. It's been a plan of mine since the war."

"Ah, yes," said Fr. Greavy, "'The Night of Cherry Blossoms' you called it—the biochemical plague you were going to release on Washington, several months before Truman sent the nuclear bombs that ended the war. I read about that too. Knowing what I know now from last night, you truly might have won or at least brought the war to a stalemate. Too bad your Emperor didn't allow it, right?"

Gritting his teeth, Ishii said, "He had his reasons. I didn't question him. Had he not forbidden me, you and I should never have met."

"Is it good that we are meeting?" queried the priest. "Because I can't imagine any reason to converse with you since you plan to kill me anyway. That's why you are here, isn't it? Strike another blow for Balor and all that."

"Perhaps," said Ishii, sipping his tea. "Or perhaps I just want to know what the bigger plan is. I thought I'd only have to deal with the Archer boy and his friend. But then you show up, with all your companions. Like you've been expecting me."

"Not you per se," said Greavy, "but we knew that evil forces were gathering. The island you see has been ill."

"What do you mean?" said Ishii, cocking his head.

"The land is sick. I walk through the fields and it feels like I'm walking on asphalt. No life in the earth. People loved this land because of the way the light played with everything on it and above it. Dirt and stone reflected that light and Ireland actually seemed to glow with vitality. It was a thin place with glimpses of 'otherness', of what this reality once was. I believe that is what made this land special. The light is still here, but the earth is dull and unresponsive. So are the people. I watch families here for generations forget their lore and their ancestry. We're a people that live on stories, Ishii. We're not telling them to each other anymore. We are in love with tech, money, and supposed freedoms that only seem to enslave us to our own selfish needs. The land is dying and we with it. The people just don't know it yet. But I think last night has got most of Ireland thinking a bit more deeply."

"And you blame me and Sir Hugh?" Ishii twisted his face into a smile.

"You? No. You are just a tool. But Sir Hugh? He is Balor the Destroyer, bane of this land for thousands of years. He is not the only evil thing in Ireland—after all we have you as well. But he is either the source or the conduit to the Darkness within this earth of ours. Don't get me wrong. You are dangerous enough and evil in your own right. Your actions of last night have pushed you farther into the Dark. But you will never be master of evil. Even after you kill me."

"You think I want you dead?"

"Oh yes, indeed, and the sooner the better."

"It's on my mind, but I thought I'd make a final decision after I heard what you had to say."

"About what?"

Ishii leaned forward, arms firm on the table. "About your next move. What have you got planned? Your friends are a bit too troublesome to be allowed to interfere again. So, tell me, and you might live."

"You think to torture it out of me?"

"I have never failed to extract the information I have needed."

"Well, I hate to disappoint," said Fr. Greavy, "but I've lived longer than you and gone through things that would even shake your decaying soul. I think I won't be telling you anything."

Ishii didn't know why he was wasting time bantering with the priest. He felt like cleaving him in half with his katana. But something was niggling at the edge of his thoughts.

On a whim, he said, "Tell me, priest, just as a favor, why now? Why are the two realities merging now?"

"You truly do not know?" asked the priest. "All things come to an end. Some of those endings are planned. Some are not. In the beginning, the world was bright and one. When things like Balor and his minions rebelled against the Light, the battle was so great that the world was sundered in two. That reality, called the Otherworld, took much of the heart and soul of creation with it when it separated. This reality, the earth you know, retained much of the corporeal substance of the once united world. One world more ethereal and beautiful, the other more substantial. But it was a split that signaled an entropy—a vast winding down of both realities. That was neither planned nor set in motion by the One. Both realities slowly decayed, until a crisis was reached, fairly recently as history is marked. Both are dying. As I said, just witness this land you call your adopted home. People like you, and the man known as Drake you sent to America, hasten that decay. Things like Balor and the river demon *Piasa*, have broken through from the Otherworld to assist corrupt beings like you that stifle the remaining life force in this reality."

"But the worlds are coming together," said Ishii. "I sense they are trying to re-unite. I long for that. The closer they come, the more I feel my power growing. My Emperor must have known. That is why he prepared me, and gifted me with power."

"You are correct in that the realities are moving back together. But that shouldn't happen if an entropy is occurring."

"True, so what is causing it?"

"I break my own promise in telling you, but perhaps the truth will cause you to hesitate and stop your infernal plan. The boy, Conor Archer, he is the cause of the merging worlds."

Ishii snorted and then began to laugh. "I cannot take you seriously priest. I know he is involved but he is just a boy, albeit one with important gifts."

"He is the nexus, the catalyst if you will. I tell you this because you have already tried to use him and also attempted to destroy him when he did not bend to your will. He will not be used. He will not bend. He is a messenger of the One. You sense the weakness in both these realities, but I tell you it is not time for Creation to be destroyed. The One put forth a plan to merge the realities so that the completed, whole world would be able to fulfill its destiny. The One wants a new heavens and new earth. And Conor is to achieve that goal."

"You are a fool to tell me."

"Not really. You would have eventually figured it out. Better you know now so you can turn from your path. Redemption is offered even to your kind and after the deeds you have already done in the name of the Dark.

"Besides," continued the priest, "I have not told you the most important things and will not. The One wishes to give you a chance. I, however, am not as merciful, bounded as I am by my own human frailties. Conor must be given a chance to succeed. You could abandon your alliance with Balor and assist him."

Shiro Ishii felt anger grow within him. He had come to twist information out of the priest and here it was Ishii himself that was being manipulated. He looked at Fr. Greavy weighing him with his grey eyes of judgment behind those prissy wire rim glasses. Ishii fumed. So Conor was more important than he had originally thought. Greavy hadn't given him much. He wanted to know the how, the why, the plan.

The wizard stood up slowly, walked around the table and approached the priest. Grasping Greavy's throat, he started to throttle the man.

"Tell me what you know," he shouted, his spittle striking the priest's face. "How is he going to do it? How will he bring about the merger of the worlds?" He threw the priest to the floor and bent over him. "I already have seen the Sword of Light and I know about the Spear of Destiny. But those are weapons. What else does he need to merge the worlds? Balor won't tell me."

Fr. Greavy began to laugh. "All that magic. All that power. All that infernal knowledge that you and Balor possess. You are allied but you don't trust each other. Your minion Drake knew all of this as well and look how that turned out."

Ishii raged above the priest, kicking him in the ribs as he stormed out of the house. Fr. Greavy slowly got up, rubbing his throat and trying not to breathe too deeply. He really thought the wizard would have sliced and diced him with his katana. Hearing a distant car start its engine, he figured that Shiro was leaving. That just didn't make sense. Getting some water from the kitchen faucet, he thought he heard something outside.

Whispering, it sounded like, and then a higher pitched chittering. Fr. Greavy turned pale and found a rosary in his pocket. Grasping it in his hand, he was already moving when the windows crashed inward. Damn that Ishii, he thought. He's sent in the *drocs*. Rushing up the stairs on his fat little legs, Greavy mused that he could afford to lose a little blood and flesh, but if they caught him, the *drocs* would drain him dry.

Halfway up the stairs, he felt the first claws pierce his legs. The pain caused him to scream but doubled his speed. He shook off the two *drocs* that clutched at him as he turned the corner around the upstairs banister. He rushed to his room, slammed and locked the door. He pushed the dresser against it as he heard several more *drocs* smash their bodies into the barrier.

He knew he didn't have much time. He doubted the little vampires were super intelligent, but it wouldn't take much cogItation to figure out another way to get in, namely, hurling themselves through the upstairs windows of his room.

Fr. Greavy knew he was beginning to panic. Just when you needed holy water there wasn't any around. Nervously, he glanced around the room and threw open the door to the bathroom. There on the floor was an empty spray bottle that the housekeeper had left after yesterday's cleaning.

Maybe, he thought. Maybe it would work. He turned the faucet on and filled the bottle with water. Closing his eyes, he wracked his memory for the traditional blessing to make holy water. For a moment his mind went blank, and then, unbidden to his lips came the familiar words as he made the Sign of the Cross over the water:

To the Maker of All I cry:
Pour down the power of your blessing into this water.
May it drive away evil spirits and free us from every harm.
May the wiles of the lurking Enemy prove of no avail.
Let whatever might menace our safety and peace
Be put to flight by the sprinkling of this water,
So that we may be made secure against all attack.

Screwing the sprayer on the top of the bottle, he knelt by his bed and pointed it toward the windows. Already, he heard the *drocs* smashing the outside of the house. Higher and higher they threw themselves until they started hitting his bedroom windows. Several hit at once, smashing the panes of glass and rolling into the bedroom.

Immediately, Greavy sprayed the water, and he found he was a good shot. Whenever the blessed water struck a *droc*, the creature screamed, smoked and burst in a bundle of gristle and blood.

To the priest, it seemed he went at it for a long time, and it was a losing battle. As effective as he and the holy water were, more and more *drocs* were penetrating into the room. Then, something worse happened.

Screaming came from downstairs and, then, a pounding up the stairs. Something was trying to push itself through the door. For a moment it suddenly went silent and then the door exploded inward causing the priest to slide out of the way of the falling dresser.

But it wasn't something worse. It was Jace and Colly. They had been coming up the drive to see Fr. Greavy and saw the *drocs* bopping and hopping toward the rectory. Hearing the priest scream inside they doubled their efforts but found themselves fighting the vanguard of the approaching *drocs*.

Neither was in much danger for Jace had his Sword which cleaved through the beasts with ease. Colly simply made his hands into ferocious wolf claws and disemboweled any *droc* that attacked him.

"Nice trick," said Jace. "Your shapeshifter talent comes in handy at a time like this." He ducked as a *droc* launched itself at his head. The creature sailed harmlessly over him only to be dispatched by a swing of Colly's wolf claws.

"We have to get into the house," said Colly. "The priest isn't going to be able to fight them off."

They plunged into the residence but couldn't find him anywhere on the first floor. Then they heard the breaking of glass upstairs, so they screamed his name rushing up the stairway. Trying to force their way into the closed bedroom, they found the door blocked. Looking at each other, they simultaneously threw themselves at the door, breaking it inward and pushing whatever blocked their entrance away.

Quickly taking in the scene, Jace saw the priest bleeding on the floor, spritzing three *drocs* on his torso with some kind of spray. He gasped as they blew up on top of the priest spraying blood and matter everywhere. Neither he nor Colly had time to say anything. They simply went ahead and attacked any *droc* they could find, dispatching each one that came through the windows.

Then it was done. There was nothing for the Sword to slay or Colly's claws to dispatch. Both of them looked at the priest and seeing he was alive, they began to laugh.

Jace said, "You spritzed them, Father?"

The priest blushed saying, "It's holy water made on the fly and it worked pretty well against these things of the Dark. What a mess though."

"Better a mess than death," muttered Colly.

"Where did they come from?" asked Jace.

"It was Shiro Ishii, again," said Fr. Greavy. "He came for information and to kill me. Wasn't going to let him carve me up with his Ginsu carving knife, so I strung him along with a little info. He gave me more than I gave him."

The boys looked at him, not understanding.

"He and Balor don't know everything. They discovered the worlds were merging. That was always foreseen by the One, but what made them act was the knowledge that both realities were corrupted. They knew that instinctively, but then mapped out a plan to take advantage of the weakness of the separate worlds. If they act decisively, they could ensure that the merger would usher in one reality of darkness and despair where they might rule and subjugate. They know Conor is crucial to the merger. That's why Ishii tried to co-opt him first and then tried to kill him when he did not cooperate. They fear the Sword and the Spear, but they know those objects are not enough to allow Conor to succeed. Ishii doesn't know our traditions, but Balor must be aware of the two other treasures sacred to Ireland—the Grail and the Stone of Truth. Neither of them is aware we already have the Grail. They will search for that in vain. But they could reach the Stone before we do. We must find it first."

THE DARKENING OF THE WORLD

Sunday Afternoon, 11/8, South of Tralee

SHIRO ISHII WAS furious. He should have just killed the priest with his katana, but Fr. Greavy warranted the slower death the *drocs* would give him. Suck his blood and leave his corpse to rot. He deserved no better. As far as he was concerned, the *drocs* could ravage the countryside around Portmagee. At this point, the more chaos the better.

He headed back up to Sir Hugh's mansion in the hopes that the Chief would have returned. As he drove, he saw the land was empty of people. Clinging to homes and family, he thought. Humans were so predictable. The fear he produced with his plague would far outweigh the actual physical toll it took. The media would run with the story and simply provoke more outrageous actions by people, like the RAGE orgies occurring now across the country. Perfect for destabilizing the society.

Such were his thoughts as he traveled. Pulling into the long driveway, he was surprised to see normal activity occurring. Sir Hugh's servants were bustling about, and he could see the fresh RAGE product delivered by the service trucks—even a plague couldn't stop those deliveries—now being loaded onto other trucks for distribution throughout the country. Sir Hugh was back and clearly in charge.

Ishii strode through the huge foyer and walked into the office where he found the dapper gentleman looking no worse from last night's struggles.

"Where have you been, Sir Hugh, and have you been injured?" asked Ishii, looking the man up and down with a critical eye.

"Well, since you asked," said Sir Hugh, puffing on a cigar, "I've had better nights, but apparently I survived. I woke up in my bed, a little bruised but none worse for wear."

"You truly don't remember?"

"I do, I do," he said. "But it's almost a dream to me. After my ship sank, due to that meddling spirit, I was cast free into the ocean. It was glorious. I felt whole and powerful. Unbeatable. Undefeatable. I know I visited Ballinskelligs, and Shiro, I believe I killed that wretched Archer brat."

"I'm not so sure," said Ishii, thinking of the chittering *drocs*. "There were whispers that I heard in the wind. I believe he was badly injured, but he has disappeared."

Sir Hugh seemed not to be listening. His head was cocked to the side as if he was in discussion with someone or something else.

"That he has, that he has," spoke up Sir Hugh, though whether to Ishii himself or to another, the Japanese wizard could not decide. "I remember now, swimming in the sea and there was a boat. He might have been in there. I think I touched his mind. Still, badly injured at least, I believe. Yes, badly injured indeed."

"We succeeded with Tralee," said Ishii.

"I've already been on the phone with the *Taoiseach*—the Prime Minister is most concerned and hopes I take an active hand in the recovery since I am so close. I assured him I was already on top of the matter. I've sent supplies to buttress the Ministry of Defense response to the unfolding human tragedy. Thousands have lost their lives, and everyone is seeking an explanation. The sheet of fire in last night's sky has people talking about some kind of alien intervention."

"Well, then," said Ishii, "'The Night of Cherry Blossoms', has accomplished its purpose. Death and dread, fear and flight will begin to overwhelm the people's sense of civilization. The chaos you wished has begun."

"Indeed," said Sir Hugh. "You have done well."

Ishii leaned over the desk, blowing away the cloud of cigar smoke hovering over its surface. He glared at the gentleman in front of him. "You never told me how important Conor Archer is. I had to learn details from that meddlesome priest, and even he did not tell me everything."

"What do you mean?" asked Sir Hugh with a placid look on his face. "I am in the dark about him as much as you are. He is important, but exactly how, I do not know. I tried to kill him last night because something deep in my bones tells me that he will try to obstruct us somehow."

"No, no," said Shiro. "You know more than that. What's this about a prophecy? Why do the Tinkers hold him in such esteem? How could he and his friends have been so disruptive last night?"

"Bollocks!" said Sir Hugh. "We accomplished what we set out to do."

"We did well, true, but we did not do everything. The plague was supposed to spread. I think he and his friends stopped it. They had help from the Otherworld. Did you know about that ahead of time? There is a force, bigger than a bunch of kids and a few representatives out of legend and story. Something is opposing us."

For a long moment, Sir Hugh sat staring at Ishii. A few drops of drool cascaded over his half-open, pendulous lips and he was mouthing words without speaking. Then his hand slapped his desk and he stood up, spittle flying as he shouted at Ishii. "I don't have to tell you everything. We are not equals. I know of the prophecy about the Archer boy. I've known about it for years. It's one of the reasons why I sent Drake to investigate. But I don't know specifics. What Drake found in Wisconsin was something much bigger than I imagined, a plan laid forth in ancient days, as if someone expected me to do as I have done. And yes, that bothers me, but it does not stop me." He glared at his partner. "I was not sure, so I did not tell you. Even if we knew Conor Archer's role exactly, it wouldn't stop what we are doing. You knew enough to try to kill him when he would not cooperate."

"I know a bit more about his role now," said Ishii. "He is a nexus between the worlds. I don't know how, but he is the one pulling them together. He is the catalyst and the key. Whatever plans we have had best be adjusted to take in these facts."

"I agree. He and his friends kept us from accomplishing everything we sought for last night, but it is only a minor setback. However, there are two things I have not told you about. You are not one of us, Shiro. You are one of the most powerful humans I have ever met, but you know little of the Celtic Way.

"Our myths and stories are not organized very well, and there are many variations among them. You can be forgiven for not seeing the hidden clues our lore gives us. Jason Michaels carries the ancient Sword of Light and Conor carries the Spear of Destiny—two artifacts crucial to the Celtic mindset. How they ever ended up in those children's hands ... Powerful in themselves, the artifacts never act alone. Yet, it's not simply symbiotic, for there are two other objects that weave their way through song and story intimately connected with Sword and Spear. Whenever our history changes greatly, all four artifacts are found to be involved. The two you don't know about, though you may have heard of them separately, are the Grail, also known as the Cauldron, and the Stone of Truth, the Coronation Stone of Celtic Kings down through the ages. Their histories are long and full of power even if less well known. If Conor and companions have already used two of the objects they will try to get their hands on the other two. I know they don't have all of them yet, because once all are possessed by them, they will have a power that could defeat us. I would feel it. We must get those objects first."

OFF TO EDINBURGH

Sunday Evening to Tuesday Morning 11/8–10, Edinburgh, Scotland

IN THE END, Colly convinced the group to split up. He and Phil would go to Edinburgh and, as he said it, "scope out the Stone of Scone." Two could travel more swiftly. He suggested Jace, Ita, Lettie and Fr. Greavy head for the *Skelligs* and see if they could find out anything more about the Seven Sleepers.

"And what do you expect the rest of us to be doing?" said Moira with a frown. Kevin and the Shandyman nodded vigorously.

Jace said, not unkindly, "Moira, you've done so much, and you've got a business to run. Your pub can be the center and clearinghouse for all activities. We all report to you. Kevin, someone has to fill in the Travelers with what's happened. They'll be spooked but they'll listen to you and your wife. And take care of that little one—Laura's too cute to be put into danger."

"Tomorrow, I'll drive Colly and Phil to the airport, and come back and stay here with Moira," said the Shandyman. "Don't think there will be any more trouble, but you never know. Strange times and all that."

"Right then," said Jace. "We've got our marching orders so let's get a good night's sleep and then get to it."

Monday dawned overcast. Colly and Phil had never ridden with Tom Shandy and they doubted they ever would again. He drove like the Great Hunt was after him. They made it to Shannon Airport in record time and hopped a Ryanair flight to Edinburgh.

"It's like riding a metro," said Colly. There weren't even seats for them, he and Phil having to stand in the aisles. Of course, that was against airline regs, so the flight attendants let them sit in their seats while they walked the aisles serving refreshments.

"Wonder how they get away with it, flight rules being so strict?" said Phil brushing the streak of pink she had dyed through her blond hair after a morning shower.

"No matter," said Colly, "it's not that long of a flight." But it was an uncomfortable one, their seats being one step better than metal folding chairs. By the time they reached Edinburgh, their legs were cramping. That pain all went away once they took a cab into the city. Even from far away, the castle built on top of a volcanic cone looked fantastically impressive.

"We're back in the Dark Ages," whispered Phil.

"Just the Stone Age, Phil," laughed Colly. "Forgot to tell you almost everything here is made out of rock, hard, dense, volcanic rock. It was a brilliant place to set a city."

Climbing up the Royal Mile to the castle was a walk back into medieval times. Lots of tourists still at this time of the year, but the overwhelming effect was age.

"This place is just really old," said Phil.

"Yeah," said Colly with a shiver.

"What's wrong?" said Phil. "You think we're being followed?"

"By that flaky wizard?" said Colly. "Not a chance. He skedaddled back to Sir Hugh where they are probably hatching some new nefarious plot. But we are being watched. Can't you feel the eyes?"

"You're spooking me Colly Roddy." Phil looked up and down the street. "I don't see anyone watching us."

Colly pulled her towards him tightly. "Don't mean to be forward, lass, but I told you this was an old town. Those who passed long ago don't sleep deeply here. The restless dead are all around us. Not *sluagh*, just ghosts. There is a whole abandoned city underneath this one, medieval as shit. Plague, murders, thugs, robbers. Long ago stuff happened beneath us and those that did the dark deeds haven't gone away. It's only because it's daylight that we can't see them. I feel them though, staring at us with hungry eyes.

"Once, on one of my infrequent trips to the Otherworld, I met my Uncle Ned. He'd been around a long time. Knew everything about this place. 'Good thing they built Edinburgh on top of an old volcano. At least the fires of hell were of some use keeping them spirits from causing shenanigans topside.' That's what he told me, one night long ago."

Colly was silent for a moment as they walked and then he continued. "They envy us you know, we the living. You'd think they would have gone on by now, but they can't cut their ties to this place. I've been to Edinburgh once before, at night. I saw them all. They left me alone, being as how I wasn't human, but they didn't like me much."

"You're scaring me," said Phil, reluctantly leaning closer. "I've gone to school with you for twelve years and I always thought you just an ordinary guy. Kind of a putz, actually."

"Putz?"

"Yeah, just getting by, knowing that Daddy was going to have a job for you when you got out of school."

"Really?" said Colly. "I get a superior for my acting ability."

"Don't think it was much acting," said Phil with a smile.

Colly laughed, and they walked the rest of the way to the castle in companionable silence. As they wandered past St. Margaret's Chapel, the oldest building on the palace grounds, both Colly and Phil talked about the history of the place. Kings and queens, wars and coups, the weathered rocks had seen them all. It didn't take them long to find the entrance to see the Crown Jewels and the Coronation Stone.

Phil snorted. "We have to pay the bloody English for the privilege of seeing our own Stone which they stole right out from under Robert the Bruce's nose. So they say. But maybe not if we get a little Irish luck." The sign over the ticket booth described the prices, and Colly dug into his pocket for some euros.

"Remember, Ita said it was a fake," said Colly. "If we can prove it, the tickets will be a small price to pay."

There was no line, and the lady selling the tickets was talkative. Phil did the ordering and the lady looked straight at her. "Irish are we now? Did hear about the other night's tragedy over in your land?"

"No," spoke Colly, lying with a smile. "We've been in Scotland for a few days."

"Well," said the lady, "I can't see how you haven't heard of it. It's all over the news. Plague in Tralee, fire in Kerry, dead all over." She looked around as if she was afraid someone would overhear her. Lowering her voice, she said, "I can tell you this much. The government is worried. Castle police told us this morning to look out for anything strange or any sick folks. As if the contagion had traveled here right over the Irish Sea. They're worried I tell you." She plunked two tickets down in front of them and smiled. "There you go. Museum and castle close in two hours. Happy touring." ˌ

Glad the conversation ended without requiring a response, Colly hustled the both of them down the hall towards the exhibitions. "That's how Balor and Ishii are going to do it," said Colly. "Fear. They're going to cause chaos and let the people do the violence themselves. Those two caused thousands of deaths the other night, but that's all they needed. Fear will do the rest. We've got to get this Stone or find out where the real one is as soon as we can."

"Colly," said Phil. "We can't just waltz in and steal the rock. Too many people, too heavy a stone."

Colly just smiled. "I've been lifting a lot of weights."

Phil cocked her eyebrow in disbelief.

Laughing, Colly said, "I'm not human, Phil. I can pick up that stone and carry it under one arm if I have to. Eluding law enforcement will be easy. I just have a bad feeling that others will cause us more problems."

Phil thought it best not to ask. Enough difficulties for the moment. Get the Stone first.

"It was taken once before," said Phil.

"Yeah, but nearly a century ago. It didn't come out unscathed. The college kids who took it dropped it and cracked it."

"So, why," asked Phil, "is Ita so sure it's a fake?"

"The archaeologists studied it. It's the same kind of rock that's all around the abandoned Abbey of Scone," answered Colly.

"Not surprisingly," said Phil.

"Actually," said Colly, "quite a bit of a surprise. The archs thought it was a fake too. The original stone, if you buy the Meritaten story, was a meteorite black as the Ace of Spades. Jacob slept on it on his way to Uncle Laban and had those mighty dreams. Then the Egyptians got it from Joseph and Meritaten absconded with it to Ireland. Somebody had carved Celtic symbols all over it and it didn't look a bit like the Stone of Scone that rests in this castle."

"So maybe not stolen under Robert the Bruce's nose," mused Phil.

"I think King Edward got fleeced when he captured the Stone, but because almost everybody since accepted the imposter Stone as true, there still may be a clue here. I am going to take it, at least to have a little look at it." Colly grinned impishly at Phil. "And you're going to help me get away with it."

When Phil saw the Stone resting in its protective translucent case, she wasn't very impressed. They were in the Crown Room where the Honors of Scotland also were. Colly was looking at them, part of which were the Crown Jewels. Much more interesting, thought Phil, than this piece of gravel, gazing at the rather boring artifact. Looked just like every other rock she had seen. She closed her eyes and harrumphed quietly. Couldn't even 'feel' the history beaming out of it, she thought.

"Come here," whispered Colly. "Something's not right."

"What do you mean?" said Phil following Colly's pointing finger.

"You see the precious stones all around the Crown? Look at the ruby here. Notice anything?"

"It seems dull?"

"Yeah, that, but there's more. There's a glamour on this ruby."

"You mean a spell."

"Kind of," said Colly. "The jewel is more than it appears. I can feel it pulsing with power. Since the rock over there is probably not the real Stone of Truth, maybe this is more important."

Phil raised an eyebrow. "Don't worry," said Colly, "we're still going to look at the Stone. As soon as closing time comes. But I think I want to take a closer look at that ruby. Come on. We've got to find a place to hide."

It didn't take Colly long for him and Phil to take refuge behind a door just off the entrance to the Crown Room.

"The cleaning closet, Colly? Really? Security will have to be lobotomized not to look for us here."

Colly had a hurt look on his face. "You know, girl, I am a Changeling. We know things and can do stuff. I'll keep us safe."

"Don't 'girl' me you sexist pig, just do your 'stuff' so we don't get caught."

In the end, Security did look in the closet. In fact, the guard looked straight at Colly and Phil and promptly shut the door again.

"Hey," said Colly to Phil's unspoken question, "I'm a shapeshifter so all he saw was a broom—that'd be me, and a waste bin." He pushed her out the door saying, "That would be you. I can throw some shade and disguise you too." She fumed while he laughed. "Don't worry about the security cameras either. We've got some thievin' to do so we'll step sideways into the Otherworld. Take my hand; they'll never pick us up."

Strangely, at least to Phil, the Crown Room in its Otherworld manifestation didn't look all that much different. Brighter perhaps, but all the stuff looked the same.

She and Colly approached the Stone and without any ceremony, Colly shapeshifted his arm into its Changeling form, broke the glass and grabbed the Stone as if it were made of Styrofoam.

"What are you looking for?" said Phil as Colly ran his elongated fingers over the rock.

"When this Stone was stolen years ago and then recovered, Bertie Gray, the stonemason who repaired it and made several copies, inserted a metal tube with a message in the 'real fake'. I'm just looking to see if we have the real fake here or one of the several copies."

Colly looked the entire Stone over and ran his fingers over every fissure in the red sandstone. He saw where the break had occurred when the Stone was stolen by the renegade students back in 1950. He didn't want to do it, but he felt he had no choice. He had to know if the metal tube was in the mortar that held the Stone together. For a moment, he gazed at the pointed nail on his Changeling hand. Then, accompanied by a gasp from Phil, he plunged the nail into the mortar and dug a gouge out. The mortar parted like butter and halfway through the Stone's depth, he struck metal. He waggled it out of its mortared tomb and it dropped to the floor.

Phil picked it up and stared at the brass tube. "Looks like this Stone was the real fake. And you've seriously weakened that rock again. How are you going to get it back into its case?"

"I don't think it will break again," said Colly. "I didn't dig that deep or wide. Let me put it back in its display case and do a little magic and see if we can cover up our meddling for a few centuries."

Fortunately, the Stone did not break, and as soon as Colly returned it to its resting place, he held out his palm over the mortar dust on the floor. A few Celtic words was all it took for the dust to float onto his palm. Cautiously, he poured the mortar back in the gouge he had dug.

"I would make a terrible burglar," he said as he smiled at Phil.

Frowning, she shook her head. "Colly, anyone can see that's been tampered with."

"As I told you, a terrible burglar. But not a half bad mage." He touched his fingers to the dust and it merged seamlessly with the old mortar. "Unless, someone suspects and delves more deeply, this will hold for the next few centuries. Let's take a look at the metal tube."

Phil opened it easily and shook out a little parchment into Colly's hand. He unfolded it and said, "It's written in *ogham*, the ancient Celtic language. I know it looks just like a lot of vertical lines, but it is writing. Very simple writing, but I can actually read this. Here's what it says:

Storied stone, never here,
Jeweled stone, over there,
Minus the stone, kings shall fear,
Take the jewel, find the chair
Stone shouts destiny's dare.

"The ruby," said Phil.

"Exactly. Come on, we actually need to take something now."

They hurried over to the Honors of Scotland. Once again, Colly broke the safety glass and looked at the Crown. "Gotta take that ruby. It's been glamoured by someone for some reason. Best take it with us."

Colly snatched the ruby and gave it to Phil. "Hold this, while I take one of these fresh-water pearls—the Crown is dappled with them. They'll figure a pearl has been taken, but they won't know it's actually the ruby gone, because this pearl is going to take its place." He positioned the pearl where the ruby had been and touched it with his Changeling fingers. In a moment the pearl looked exactly like the now absent ruby. "If a jeweler ever examines this, even he will think it's a ruby unless he does a chemical test on it." Colly sighed. "No one will know."

"I will," said a voice. "Now don't you thievin' shites move a muscle."

Colly and Phil would have jumped in abject fear if the voice hadn't of been that of a young girl. They looked to the entrance and saw her standing there in a white shift, one of her hands clutching a ragged doll.

The girl looked about ten years old and somewhat transparent as shadows rippled over her body. Colly smiled, mostly to buy some time, and said, "Now, who might you be, little one?"

"My name is Annie," she said and took a few steps closer to them.

Phil took Colly's hand and pulled him backwards. "I don't like this," she said. "Who do you suppose she is?"

"Abandoned Annie, that's who she is. Read about her on the plane, but I also remembered a few things my Uncle Ned said. She's one of the restless dead I talked about, a ghost from the plague times four hundred years ago. She got sick, and her parents, fearing the plague itself more than loving their daughter, walled her up in her bedroom. People still see her, but only there, never this far from her home." Colly looked at the little girl and said, "What are you doing here, lass?"

He couldn't believe it, but she actually snarled a little, her teeth growing long and her fingers sharp. "Stopping a robbery. You stole from the Crown."

Colly swallowed hard. "Yes, but what difference does it make to you?"

The specter shook its head again, once more a little girl. "Doesn't I guess, but Ma and Da say never to take what's not our own."

Phil looked with a little more compassion at the girl. "And where are your mommy and daddy?"

"Haven't seen them since I got sick," she said. "They barricaded my room and went away." She started crying and clutching the doll to her chest. "I got real sick and then the Birdman came. I need to touch you." For a moment her eyes flashed green and she again took tentative steps toward them. This time, both Colly and Phil noticed the shadows swirling around her.

"Look," said Colly. "What looks like shadows are not. They move around her neck, her upper arms, and her legs. She has the plague, and it's like it's alive!"

"I want to touch you," she said again, moving ever more closely, this time dropping her doll and moving forward with her arms stretched out, fingers clawed again.

"Can she hurt us?" asked Phil.

"Don't know. Don't want to find out either. Come on." He grabbed her hand again and rushed her around the display just as Annie lurched forward with surprising speed. She stopped at the Crown and reached in to touch it, giving the two a chance to put a few more castle artifacts between them and the ghostly girl.

"I want the ruby," she said. "It will make me feel better."

"You could have taken it any time," said Colly. "Why now?"

"Can't you feel it?" she snapped looking around the room. "I've been trapped in my bedroom forever, but tonight, the barriers that kept me a prisoner are gone. Something's happening. I've seen others like me freed as well, walking the streets of Mary's Close."

"I feared this was happening when we came up the Royal Mile," whispered Colly to Phil. "These are the things Ita warned me about when I was a kid, what I had to be watching for. It wasn't just Conor or Jace that I had to find." He looked at her with dread in his eyes. "I had to look for signs that the boundaries between your world and the Otherworld were collapsing. Until Jace and Conor showed up, everything was fine, mostly. And what wasn't, me and the wolves took care of. Now, we've got the real walking dead amongst us."

Abandoned Annie laughed a soulless chuckle. "I want the ruby. Give it to me now."

"Think not," said Colly. "Go away. You're dead and not supposed to bother us anymore."

"I have to touch you, though," said the little girl, puzzlement on her face. "Just like I touched Ma and Da before they walled me up. They never came back. Do you think I did something bad?" She giggled again, but moved, albeit this time slowly, towards Phil and Colly.

Suddenly, the outside door was flung inward with a loud crash. The apparition turned toward the noise and gasped in what Colly and Phil could only later describe as terrible fear. "The Birdman," she screamed. "He comes for me again!"

Phil felt her heart pumping even faster as all three of them gaped at the empty entrance to the museum. A rhythmic thump broke the silence and the dragging of some heavy cloth or garment accompanied the sound. Into the entrance of the museum walked a figure from hell. It held a torch and in the light of the flames, Colly and Phil could see that whatever it was, it was tall. The figure was dressed in a flowing cloak of leather covering black leggings and waistcoat, with a broad-brimmed hat on its head and in its other gloved hand a wooden staff surmounted by a winged hourglass. But that was not what struck fear in Colly or Phil. It was the footlong beak that curved downward from a masked face, making the stranger look like some vulture from the pits of Hades taking a break from lurking over the damned.

The ghostly girl screamed again but did not move. "Annie," whispered the Birdman. "Whatever are you doing out of your room? You cannot wander these streets."

"You," she spat, "you killed me. I remember. You broke down my door, said you would heal me, but you didn't. You tried to burn the sickness out— look, look where you touched the hot iron to my arm. I should touch you, and make you feel what I felt. You left me alone, and I died without my doll. I was cold, and sick, when you came back. You walled me in again, and no one heard my screams."

"I did," said the Birdman. "As you say. But I could not allow you to infect people with your sickness. All of you were the same, wanting to touch those who lived. And all you did was spread the contagion. Little girl, I am so sorry."

The ghost looked petulant in the flickering light. "Why are you here now?"

"Because you are not supposed to be here. I have spent much of the night finding others like you and giving them rest."

"What do you mean?" said Annie, backing up again.

"Take your doll," said the Birdman. He bent down and grabbed the figurine and held out his hand to the girl. She reached out and took it from his gloved hand. Clasping it to her chest, she bent her head over it, not seeing the Birdman spread wide his cloak as he raised his wooden staff, bringing it down and striking her head.

Colly and Phil gasped again as the silver hourglass ignited Abandoned Annie when it cleaved through her ghostly form. She was, for a moment, a flame of green light flashing in the night, a hollow wail echoing in the ancient room. Then she was gone.

Unfortunately, Phil took that moment to back into a suit of armor, knocking it loudly to the floor.

"Who else is here?" said the Birdman. "What poor soul seeks release?" Neither Colly or Phil said anything as the figure moved forward, stopping suddenly to look at the Scottish Crown. Its beaked face came close to the regnal honor and it hissed in fury. "Who has taken the jewel. Where is it? Where is the ruby?"

"Here," said Colly, managing to stifle the quaver in his voice. "I have it, and I don't think I shall be giving it to you."

The Birdman glided around the Honors of Scotland and found the two huddling on the floor. Holding the torch high, its beaked face gazed silently at them. Then it said, "Give it to me now, mortals, and I shall leave you. Resist, and I shall send you to a hell worse than the plague that little sprite died from. You do not know what you possess."

"Have you ever noticed, Phil," said Colly, saying in the most nonchalant voice he could muster, "that every demon, ghost, monster that we've met lately speaks like a B-movie character actor? Just so pompous and self-important."

He stood up, pulling Phil to his side and as the Birdman struck with his staff, Colly morphed his arm and grabbed the stick with his Changeling form.

"Sorcery!" cried the Birdman.

"Not really," said Colly, "but I'm not human either. And this lovely lady by my side, mortal though she may be, is far more precious than either the jewel or you."

The Birdman uttered a wordless cry and swung the torch at Colly. Morphing his other arm, Colly easily struck the torch aside and for good measure backhanded the Birdman across its beak. He must have struck it hard because the beak or, what appeared to be the entire face, was ripped from the head of the stranger. Colly and Phil found themselves standing before a rather stunned man.

"You're human!" said Phil. The man was speechless, but Colly pulled the staff from his hand and threatened to hit the man with it.

"Who are you?" he said. "And what the hell are you doing here scaring us half to death?"

The stranger spoke in a halting voice with a heavy Scottish accent, but both of them caught the gist of what he said.

"My name is George Rae. I am the plague doctor for this city. It is a terrible night for you to be in my presence."

"Told you Phil," said Colly. "Talks just like they do in B horror movies. You know Vincent Price perhaps? Peter Cushing? Christopher Lee?"

"What?" said the baffled doctor.

Laughing, Phil said, "Show him a little mercy, Colly."

"Mercy?" said Colly, not smiling at all. "He was about to, as he said it, send us to the bowels of hell."

"I'm sorry, lad and lass, but I thought you were plague victims."

"What?" said Colly. "You thought you'd use your vaunted healing capabilities on us like you did on that poor girl?"

"She's a dead girl," said the doctor. "Tonight, all the ones who died and were never buried, all of them that were walled up in Mary's Close—all of them are walking tonight. I don't even know if they are human anymore, but I can't let them survive the night."

"See," said Phil to Colly, "one of the good guys."

"Maybe," he said. "But doctor, you are out of time and place. Or we are. The plague has been over for nearly 400 years."

"What sorcery is this?" sputtered the doctor.

"You already said that," smiled Colly. "I'm not sure how you got here, but I have an idea. Are you familiar with the Otherworld?"

"Of course, I am a Scotsman, and though a Highland Catholic I am not a superstitious idiot. I know it exists, but the Otherworld doesn't usually come calling."

"You're right," said Phil. "Tonight, however, in Edinburgh and all over the islands, it is."

Colly looked at him sympathetically. "You're just going to have to believe us. Two worlds are meeting again for the first time in thousands of years, and weird things—like your presence here—are happening."

"I've seen things in my time," said Dr. Rae. "The plague killed nearly 100,000 people here and I lived through it. But I saw death, like no one sees death. The things I've had to do."

"She called you Birdman," said Phil.

"Aye," said the doctor, "that the wee thing did. She never saw my face. I wore the mask with the beak because there's herbs and spices in there that protect my lungs from the miasma in the air where the plague dwells. She wasn't so lucky. I could not cure her though I did cure others."

"You are famous," conceded Colly, "but you are wrong about the plague. You lived because your whole body and skin are protected from flea bites. Remember the rats? They carried the fleas that bit the people and spread the plague. You had the right idea, just the wrong reason."

"Truly?" said the doctor.

"Truly," said Colly. "That doesn't answer the real question though. You did cure others. History shows that. Though you lost many, you cured more. How? Nobody ever subdued the plague before modern medicine, except you. Again, how?"

Dr. Rae grimaced, "I suppose you must know since you are taking it with you. The jewel you steal. The ruby. It is part of the Honors of Scotland. They consisted of the Crown, the Sword and the Scepter that are over there. But there was also a Ring with a ruby jewel. It was worn last by Robert the Bruce, but it was passed down secretly and came to me through my family. The Chancellor of Scotland, my uncle, gave it to me. It possesses a power so that anyone who wore it would be able to heal the land and even people. Whenever in my possession, I was able to cure many more patients. I do not know how it worked, and sometimes it did not work well. But many were still healed. When Queen Mary was 20 years of age, I gave it to her and she had it placed in her Crown. There it has remained. Why do you take it now?"

"Actually, I don't know," said Colly. "But I think it is more important than that Coronation Stone we were supposed to fetch."

Rae laughed, "Coronation Stone? Hardly important. It is a fake. Everyone knows that."

Phil and Colly smiled at each other. "Not everyone in our time."

"The ruby, however, is real," said the doctor. "But if you take it, Edinburgh will fall."

"It will not," said Colly. "In my time, a new king is coming, and he needs it. His power is such that even Edinburgh will be preserved. I promise you this."

"But you're a demon!"

"Am not!" said Colly, seriously offended. "I'm a Changeling from the Otherworld but baptized just like you."

"This is all so strange," said Dr. Rae.

"We could tell you things that are stranger," said Phil.

"Look," said Colly. "We have to get back. So do you, doctor. You need, you must, take care of the plague dead. You would be doing us a favor. As you said, this is a strange time and we can't have them wandering free. They will cause too much trouble."

"A new king?" said Dr. Rae. "You swear this on the jewel?"

"Aye," said Colly. "A king that will make sure the terrible things you have had to do will never happen again. You can be of great service to him, if you settle the streets of Edinburgh and make sure the memory of the great plague will be put to rest."

"Maybe," said Phil, "he could help us with the current sickness."

"What?" said Dr. Rae, "There is another pestilence ravaging your lands in your time?"

"Yes, but it is new," said Colly. "We stopped a huge breakout the other night in Ireland, but those who spread the sickness will not stop till the whole world is infected."

The plague doctor wiped his hand over his sweating face. "The plague I fight, or fought, at least according to you, was so terrible. When it struck Edinburgh this last time, it had already punished us for two hundred years. But this was the worst. I can help you rid your world of this new sickness."

"How?" said Colly and Phil.

"The ruby you take. It truly helped me heal people, but it was as if something hindered it, keeping it from being fully functional. However the ancient kings came by it, King Robert the Bruce was the last to wear it. I was just grateful it helped me in my time."

"It has been 'powered down' so to speak," said Colly. "Someone, some powerful mage, cast a glamour on it that hides its beauty. Perhaps, it hides its power too."

"Twasn't a mage that cast the spell," said Dr. Rae. "It was the last Cardinal Chancellor of Scotland. I watched him pray over it before he gave it to me. There was a spark of fire between his fingers and the ruby as he blessed it, and I thought the jewel duller when he gave the ring to me. But I haven't thought of it since. If you could find a way to erase the glamour, it would be a mighty weapon against any plague, new or old. It would not just heal individuals but destroy the contagion itself."

"So, you won't rat us out when we take this?" smiled Phil.

A tentative grin crossed the doctor's face. "Nay," he said. "Provided it is wielded by the true king. Now I must go, and so must you." With that he turned and walked into the darkness beyond the hall. Colly and Phil ran after him, but when they got to the hall, no one was there, and the exit door was shut and locked tight. Sirens could be heard in the distance.

"Guess we're out of the Otherworld," said Colly. "Come on. We have to get out of here before the police or soldiers raise a hue and cry."

Thankfully, the exit was one of those doors that let you exit and relocked automatically. The two raced down the Royal Mile, stopping in darkened doorways when police cars shot by. They found a cabby still awake and idling at the base of the hill. Catching their breath before they hailed him, they then walked slowly forward like two lovers out for the night and asked for transport to the airport. There, they found a room at a small hotel and tried to get a few hours' sleep. Their plane was scheduled for seven **Tuesday** morning.

Neither slept nor did they breathe a sigh of relief until they their plane took off. Security was heavy and everyone was searched, but Colly hid the jewel well and it was not discovered. As soon as he lay his head back on the headrest he fell into a fitful sleep. Phil could only envy him. Too wired to even close her eyes, she nervously looked around the cabin for anyone taking too much notice of them. Finding herself and Colly wonderfully anonymous, she stared out the window as they flew across the Irish Sea, her fingers twisting a few strands of her hair, her teeth biting into her lower lip.

THE SEVEN SLEEPERS

Monday Morning, 11/9, Skellig Michael

WHEN TOM SHANDY left with Colly and Phil for the airport Monday morning, an oppressive silence settled over the remaining group. Moira absently twisted a strand of her hair in her fingers, while Lettie tapped the stem of her pipe against one of her teeth. Ita and Fr. Greavy looked taken up in prayer, while Jace studied the floor. It was Kevin who broke the silence.

"I'm going," he said. Glancing around firmly at the group, he said more confidently, "I'm going to touch base with all the Travelers I can find and bring them back. I think we are going to be needing them in a few days."

"Might not be a bad idea," said Moira. Nodding at Mary, she said, "Besides, your wife and little one will be safer away from here, and you'll still be doing work we need done."

"Aye," said Lettie. "I approve. Ask the nun over there what she thinks. Seems she's communing with her God."

"Wisp," said Ita, without opening her eyes, "every once in a while you are just too free with the cynicism. Do not mock me. We are going to need all the help we can get."

"I want to go back to *Skellig* Michael now," said Jace. "We need to find a way to wake those monks and find out what they know about the Stone of Truth."

"If it is true that they are only sleeping," said Fr. Greavy. "There's always a chance that they're eternally sleeping." They all just gaped at him. "Just a thought," he said in apology.

"All right, then," said Jace. "We each know what we are doing so let's get at it. Colly's boat leaves in a half hour, so get yourselves ready. Moira, are you sure you can handle this place by yourself?"

A ghost of a smile stole over her lips as she said, "Jason Michaels, I've been handling crowds and quelling arguments and dealing with all the strange stuff this island can dish out since before you were born. I think I can handle a few hours on my own."

Sheepishly, Jace nodded and headed out back. Needing to be alone for a few minutes he strode out to the shed. Hearing a cry, he craned his head to the old oak shading the building. There she was; the familiar black crow cawing at him again.

"Actually," he said, "I'm awfully glad to see you. Where have you been?"

By the time the crow glided from the tree to the ground, it had shifted into the Morrigan. No armor now; she wore a simple flowing white gown, a circlet of gold around her lustrous red hair.

"Miss me, did you?" she cooed, stroking the stubble of Jace's blond hair.

He couldn't keep himself from blushing. "Don't do that," he snapped. "It embarrasses me."

The Morrigan laughed. "I do think I am captivating you, my Champion. Perhaps we should be seeing more of each other."

"Look," said Jace, "I wanted to talk to you to see if you had any ideas about those seven Egyptian monks and the Stone of Truth. We need to wake them and see what they know."

Bitterly the Morrigan hissed, "Apparently, according to that Egyptian witch, I know little about the Stone, but I know enough of its history to be able to tell whether the priests who sleep will tell the truth when they awake."

"Okay, I'll bite. What do you know?"

"The Stone of Truth was brought here by Meritaten. The *Tuatha de Danaan* used it along with the Grail. When the monks arrived nearly two thousand years later, they took the objects and guarded them. The Grail they kept, but the Stone was gifted to a great man named Columba—Ita or the monks could tell you more about him—so that he could use it as a Coronation Seat to crown the first Irish king of Scotland. A worthy gift to a worthy man. He was the last Champion I knew till I found you. Every Scottish king afterwards was crowned on it till the man you know as King Robert the Bruce. He was the last. It disappeared after he was crowned. They say he hid it and only he knew where. I don't see how the Egyptians are going to know anything that will help us. They had already been asleep seven hundred and fifty years when it disappeared."

"Point given to the Morrigan," muttered Jace. "Maybe they know nothing, but they are not dead for a reason. Just like Meritaten, maybe they are waiting for us. I need you to come with us to *Skellig* Michael. Please."

"You need me?" said the Morrigan running her tongue over her lips and smacking them hungrily. "Why, Champion, do I detect a yearning for me?"

Jace wanted to say no, but he couldn't speak. She was beautiful and he did want her to travel with them, and he was thinking it might not be for the purest of reasons. There was just something about her.

"I know," said the Morrigan, "you don't have to say anything. You are finding me irresistible, as do all men." She stretched languidly and planted a kiss on his lips. "You will be mine you know. Fate has arranged it."

Jace turned swiftly and stalked back into the pub, saying, "Come on, Morrigan, we've got work to do and our ship sails in five minutes."

Once again, the Morrigan laughed and changed into a crow, alighting on Jace's shoulder as he went to find the others. They were waiting by the boat for him. As they boarded, Jace took a look out to sea and was pleased the water and sky were both a deep blue. Fair sailing on an autumn day. Fr. Greavy took the helm and placed Colly's captain's hat upon his head.

"What?" he asked the astonished group. "You think I can't pilot a twenty-footer out to *Skellig*? I've done it before, once or twice—seriously."

He watched them as they didn't respond. Each of them however grabbed a life vest. He laughed as he started the engine and pulled away from shore.

It turned out he was a good sailor, and forty-five minutes later, they were pulling into Seal Cove where the waters were serene. There was even a seal bobbing there, raising a flipper in greeting.

"Do you know my friend, Conor?" whispered Jason, and to his surprise the seal fixed his round-eyed gaze upon him and he could swear he heard the seal purr almost sub-voce a sibilant "Yes."

Only Ita noticed, and she gave Jace a small smile as she lightly jumped from the boat to the beach. She sidled over to him and whispered, "It is a beautiful thing to be able to know the speech of creation. You have been given a great gift."

He nodded and said, "If only it could help Conor."

She patted him on the back and said, "Come on, we've got some sleeping monks to wake."

Fr. Greavy was steadying Lettie as she got off the boat, but she shook him off saying, "I don't need your help, you dear little man. I've been scampering about the rocks of the Emerald Isle longer than those monks have been sleeping."

Fr. Greavy chuckled and tied the boat off. Together they all entered the cave. It was so reverently quiet there. Even the birds seemed to call more softly out in the cove. Again, they saw the ruined ship the monks had sailed to Ireland over 1500 years ago. The Morrigan seemed content to perch as a crow on what was left of the main mast. The others, steadying themselves on the slick stone carved steps, ascended to the flat escarpment that lay before the chapel.

This time, candles were burning in the holy place, casting shadows on the altar and the gravestones beneath. It was bright enough that the light illuminated the mosaic in the apse with breathtaking colors.

"I used to come here often back in the day when I walked among the living," said Ita. "It still is an awe-inspiring place. In our haste the other evening, I had no time to re-experience its beauty. Each of these monks I knew." She pointed out first monk standing on the prow of the ship pointing out the nearby *Skellig* Michael. "That's Serapion, the Abbot. Notice how they are all clean shaven? More Greek than Egyptian, but that's the way things were, back in 459 A.D. when they arrived here to help Blessed Patricius in his final years. Wise man. Back there at the helm is Malchus. Holy in his own way, but a brute of a man, more muscle than thought I'm afraid. And there in the middle, those five from left to right are Maximian, Marcian, Dionysius, John and Constantine. Dionysius could sing like an angel. The other four muddle in my mind, but my memory is of men well spoken, chaste and charitable. The work of Blessed Patricius would have foundered had it not been for them. I met them thirty years after he died. They wandered the land preaching and teaching. Then, they found Meritaten's tomb and woke her. They brought her the Grail—she told them it was the Chalice of Life and was one of her treasures returned to Egypt many years before. They told her what had happened to it, and she let them keep it with the new information that there was another treasure they should acquire—the Stone of Truth. She had brought it as well from Egypt two thousand years before. It had been given to her as tribute by the Hebrew foreigners who dwelt in her lands. They said it was a stone from the stars, black as the night sky, and it had pillowed the head of their ancient forefather Jacob, and it made him dream.

"Serapion told me that Meritaten had sat upon it and saw a vision of a line of kings crowned, of the Stone shouting its affirmation for each one of them, of the rock speaking the truth of the righteousness present in the crowned kings. Serapion asked how they could find it, and she told him, but he nor the others ever told me. When I came of age, they sailed away, not back to their Egypt but here, to the *Skellig* where they lived for several years. I was present on their last day. They had summoned me, and my boatmen rowed swiftly here. I found them in this chapel and it was exactly as you see it now, except the graves were open. Each of them stood at the foot of a grave except for John and Constantine. They stood together by a slightly larger grave, the sixth as you see. As for the seventh, I already saw the Grail was placed reverently there.

"I was a cheeky thing back then. Instead of being sad at their approaching deaths, I chirped at them, 'What John, what Constantine? You have not yet earned your own eternal resting place? You must share a grave?' They laughed as well, for they were an uncommonly cheerful lot. I grew somber then, for I knew they were leaving this world. They said they were going to sleep but would return when the land and people had need.

I watched each enter his tomb and they lay on their right sides, looking towards my country, their adopted homeland. I blessed them and prayed *'Sleep now and rest and so fade sorrow.'*

"They closed their eyes and slept. As they did, the chapel was filled with an unseen presence and a voice echoed, 'Arise, rock of the earth and blanket these men with your embracing strength.' Each of the tombstones raised in the air and moved over each of the sleepers. Down they gently descended, and not a sound was made as they nestled into the earth. I did not see who spoke, for I had not yet met Michael face to face."

She moved her eyes from the mosaic and looked at each of them. "That would be another story."

Jace walked up to Serapion's grave and tried to move the covering stone. Unlike the Grail burial spot, this slab did not move. "I think we're going to have a little trouble here," he said.

"I have found that, in times when strength is needed, a little prayer goes a long way," said Ita. She knelt, and so did Fr. Greavy, but Jace inched his way backward until he could exit the chapel unseen. He wanted to explore some of the rooms that were locked to him the other night. Lettie was as curious as he and followed without his knowledge, popping herself into the wisp she was.

The rocky passages looked much as they did last night, and on second observation, there were not as many doorways as he thought. But he tried each one. None opened. A branching corridor led slightly upward, but it was a narrow path that swiftly ended. Fortunately, there was a door. This time, the latch turned easily, and the old oaken door, aged by time so that it looked turned to stone, creaked open. Jace slipped in; the wisp close behind.

He could only take three steps inward before he stopped and gasped. He could never have imagined a space this large under the mountain. It looked not like some damp cave, but a vaulting cathedral bright with soft light. The walls were rock and full of polished amethyst and white geodes which made the chamber sparkle with a muted brilliance. The top of the room was vaulted stone, but no man could have chiseled such massive, sweeping beams hundreds of feet in the air. Whoever designed it kept the huge space undivided by support pillars. Jace thought the space should have felt heavy, but, instead, all was light, airy and gave forth an atmosphere of joy.

"Oh boy," thought Jace, "I've entered where I shouldn't be." Before him lay treasures of gold and silver, ruby and sapphire—piles of them. All were polished and arranged, as if one was walking through a garden of living stone, for they pulsed as if breathing. It was the earth in all her beauty. As he walked further in, he said again, "Nobody should be here. There is enough wealth here to tempt a million souls and enough beauty to make one stay forever."

"You are correct," said a voice. "No one should be here. It is a temptation best left untried."

Jace gulped and looked ahead down the hall. Over a floor of polished gemstones, he walked toward a towering figure on a massive throne carved from the wall of the mountain itself. No clumsy chair, it arched and wove in untold directions to encompass the huge form sitting upon it.

"You have come, Jason Michaels. Ever curious, ever probing." The figure paused a moment. "Not all curiosity is forbidden. Come closer."

Jace wasn't sure he should. He knew it was Michael, but he marveled again at the fact that the figure didn't look like any angel in the books he had studied at school. No tiny, fluffy wings or cherubic face. No softness or welcoming visage that took away fear and gave peace. No. Here was power, beauty, wisdom and judgment. As before when he first met him down by the cave entrance, Michael was beams of light woven into substance. Human in form, barely, but that was all. Twelve feet tall, a face that moved and changed like starlight exploding from the massive orbs of fire. And wings, six of them moving all at once and covered with pinions of light rather than feathers. Michael was seated with a trident across his knees and in his right hand, a scepter of judgment with the globe of the earth swirling upon it. In this hall of mountain stone, he was the incarnation of the poet's verse, 'The angels keep their ancient places; turn but a stone and start a wing.'

There on the throne, the figure spoke, "I am the guardian of this planet; the Watcher of the Heavens. I judge the living things upon and within it and utter the doom the One proclaims. Few are privileged to enter. Why have you come?"

"Yes, why?" said a higher voice as the wisp whipped around Jace and floated before his face.

"You sneak!" said Jace. "Following me like a little mouse."

"Had to see what you were up to. Why not stay with the others?"

"They can pray all morning, but that's not going to open those tombs. I thought Michael might have some ideas."

"Hoom, hoom, hoom," rattled a sound through the chamber, and Jace at once knew the angel was laughing—first time he ever heard of that happening. "He has you there, little wisp. Only I can wake the Sleepers. That was our covenant when I first shut their eyes so long ago. I have only wakened them twice since."

"So, you will do it?" asked Jace. "Please, we've got to know how to use that Stone of Truth and find Conor."

"Please?" said the angel. "Why human, you have more manners than that Changeling friend of yours."

The seraph seemed receptive to Jace's request, but paused in mid thought, gazing upward. "I am to watch and see, advise and dispense wisdom, but not overtly interfere unless real doom is upon us. What I did the night before last was unprecedented since before time, when I drove the Betrayer from the heavens and he fell like lightning from the sky. I had no choice then, and I had none the other night.

"What Balor and his wretched companion tried to do was nearly successful. Having to reveal myself to a modern world that has cameras and satellites everywhere will eventually change things radically on earth. I am no shadowy Loch Ness monster on a grainy film, or some supposed alien who crash landed in the Arizona desert long ago. The people will experience me as a real being and already, having seen the little they saw last night, they are afraid."

"They will not fear you once you let them see you in a … more familiar form," said Lettie.

"I do not mind appearing in human form, little wisp, but when I act with full possession of my power I must appear as I have been made. Trust me, they will fear me. Already in the halls of power, the whisperings have begun around the world. Brief though the appearance was, I was very visible last night. They wonder what I portend."

"But you saved us," said Jace.

"Yes, but a broken world, already beset with factions and quests for dominion will frantically try to figure out what I am and who controls me. I do not fear their search for answers, but I am not the only knowledge they will recover. Balor and Shiro Ishii will exploit their thirst for understanding. They will act more openly and move more swiftly to merge the worlds to their liking and destroy the good they cannot abide. There will be many who will prefer their way of accomplishing that task."

"Well, then," sniffed Jace, "you've got a lot to do, so if you could just help us move a few stones, we'll wake the monks and get on our way."

Michael laughed, "Ah, a human of the practical sort. Come, let us go see your friends."

The huge figure stood, walking surprisingly smoothly down the pathway towards Lettie and Jace. As he walked, reality expanded around him so by the time he got to the little entrance door, it looked like a castle gate and he moved easily through the opening. He strode into the chapel followed by his two retainers, and Jace heard the praying stop. Ita give a little gasp.

"Haven't seen you like this in centuries," she said. "I must say you improve on the eyes every time I view you anew."

Michael let out a small laugh again, "That is because, holy one, you continue to grow in wisdom and knowledge and ever see more of that of which I am made."

She inclined her head to him. "Yet always the gentleman. In all the rush yesterday, I forgot to tell you how much I have missed your presence. But here you are and all will be better. I have foreseen it."

"Then let's get to work," said Jace. "Times a'wastin', and we have the Stone of Truth to figure out. Let's wake these monks up and see what they know. Michael, if you know how, then get the blood in these old ones moving so they can help."

Without another word, Michael strode forward. On each of the sarcophagi, there was a carving of the Tree of the World beneath that of a carved Tau cross. Michael's hand of light gently touched each carving on every stone. Like liquid gold, the light filled in the etched spaces on the Tree and Tau, until every shape glowed brightly there in the chapel.

"Brilliant!" said Fr. Greavy. "Some kind of sensor activated by photons. Simply brilliant!"

"Or miraculous," said the seraph sarcastically.

There was a sudden snapping of stone and Jace could see the seam that held each slab to every sarcophagus break apart and the top stones quiver in movement. He could see they were now loose. He ran to one and tried to lift it, but it was too heavy. Michael gently pushed him aside, and easily picked up the slabs, setting them against the walls of the chapel.

Those who watched barely noticed, for they were consumed with curiosity at the figures placed reverently in the tombs. Their bodies were incorrupt, lying on their left sides, facing away from Ireland. Remarkably young, their faces were stern and though eyes were closed their brows were pinched as if they were glaring at something or someone.

"Not good," said Ita. "They should be facing the land. That's how they were buried and the fact they have turned means sorrow and woe."

"Indeed," said Michael. "I have not opened these tombs since we made the island secure when the local monks took off back to Ballinskelligs seven hundred years ago. They were at peace and right-lying then. Something has disturbed them, and we all know who or what that might have been."

"They turned for a reason, Michael," said Ita. "There is nothing to the west but ocean. They look for something else."

"Maybe they gaze at something closer. Look," said Jace, "the last body in the farthest vault." Jace pointed to where the two monks lay together in the tomb. The one on the left seemed relatively at peace, but the other was contorted, and Jace could see his eyes were half open, as if he was trying to awake and flee.

"What's wrong with him?" said Fr. Greavy. "It looks like he wants out of the box. Like Jace said, the others seem to be glaring at him."

"It's Constantine," said Ita, "the youngest of the group. There is an illness gripping him. He is not himself."

"We must awake them all," said Michael. He moved among the Seven Sleepers and touched each one on their brow, hesitating as he came to the last monk.

Jace noticed their chests started moving, but something was still wrong with Constantine. Despite not being touched by the angel, his chest was heaving and his arms started stretching out, hands trying to clutch the edge of the tomb. Getting a grip, his eyes opened and he lunged over the edge falling upon the chapel floor. Jace raced to help him, but Ita caught his sleeve.

"Do not touch him. Some fell thing has him in its grasp. Wisp, check out the lad."

The wisp floated over to the young monk seizing on the floor and hovered above him. The monk looked up, a feral grin creeping over his face, and he snatched at the wisp. She was too fast for him and swept back towards Ita, transforming into Lettie as she did so.

Lettie, a little out of breath herself, gasped, "I saw into its eyes. There is no Constantine there. The poor youth is gone. What remains, I do not know."

Jace muttered in a sardonic voice, "We haven't done zombies yet this week. Must be a zombie."

Ita swatted Jace's head. "Show some respect. Constantine was able to commune with the One as are the other six. If he is truly gone, his loss is devastating."

"Not a zombie," said Michael, "but, instead, a ..."

"Demon," said Jace. "Look, it's trying to talk."

The monkish thing was working its jaw as if it were trying out a new tool, but finally managed to croak out a few words. "A message from my master," it said.

"Where is the monk?" interrupted Jace. "What have you done with him?"

The demon gave a twisted sneer. "Dead for at least many of your centuries. When the tomb was last opened, I crawled in as a spider, sent by Balor of the Evil Eye. I wove a web in the monk's ear and spent years tunneling into his brain. I learned everything he knew, and as the monk began to die, I assumed his body. He passed long ago after exquisite suffering."

"The message," said Lettie. "What's the message from Balor?"

"A wisp," said the demon. "Will wonders never cease? A handsome old hag at that. Tell me, have you betrayed them yet? Your kind always do."

"Oh, pish posh, little insect," laughed Lettie. "Your lies can't offend me. The message. Get to it. What does Balor say?"

"Ah," said the demon. "The Lord of the Dark says the Stone you seek no longer exists in this world. It belongs to him and he has taken steps to protect it. Seek for it and choose death." The thing started crawling on the floor like the demon spider it once was. "Delivery of that message was my last task. I'll just make my way out to find my master." Then it dashed for the chapel entrance.

Michael barely moved. He lifted what passed for a seraph's foot and brought it down upon the back of the hapless monk. With a squeal the monk thing twisted but Michael snapped the bones with his graven sandal and ground the demon into the chapel floor. As it sunk into holy ground, it screamed and burned to ash.

"Guess it was his last task," said Lettie, "but not much of a message."

"More of one than you think," said a voice.

They looked back at the altar and there stood Serapion with the other five monks looking serene with hands folded and shadowed faces barely seen past their hooded heads.

Jace stepped forward. "I'm so sorry about your friend … Constantine. What a terrible thing to wake up to."

Serapion smiled gently. "Ah lad, a kind wish from you is gratefully accepted, but we do not grieve. We did when he passed many years ago. We all felt it, there in our graves, and that is when we turned our bodies to gaze upon the usurper. He was a powerful demon but not more powerful than six monks of the One. Our gaze held him in thrall and he could not possess any more of us. If we had been vigilant, we could have saved Constantine. But our attention was elsewhere."

"Tell them what happened," said Michael gently.

The monks as one looked up at the seraph and then bowed together as Serapion spoke. "Well met, Ranger of the Heavens. You were there when last we woke and bid farewell to the monks of *Skellig*. It was not a propitious time. The weather had deteriorated; the rock was too cold to eke out a living. They wanted us woken to ask our advice. We told them to go to Ballinskelligs and set up an abbey there. We would then be the ones to guard this place.

"I remember the day they left," continued Serapion. The sun followed them across the sea to land and then a storm came up out of the west. Balor came with the wind. Him, we had not seen since Columba did battle with him at Loch Ness. There was a true saint and druid. He was a wielder of miraculous magic. We had joined him in Scotland to bear the Stone of Truth to Aiden's coronation. It had been a truly holy event, the first King of Scotland crowned on the same Stone where Jacob had beheld the One. The King could not be everywhere so we carried the Stone throughout the land, showing the people and having them take an oath to the new King.

"We were on the shores of Loch Ness when it happened. The waters swirled like Charybdis, the whirlpool that bedeviled Ulysses. And out of the maw of the whirlpool arose a beast who's like I had never seen, but I knew what it was. Most saw only a reptilian serpent, but I saw the Eye.

So did my brothers. So did Columba. All quailed at seeing this beast, and sad to say, even I shook, so fearsome was the sight. The others, too, feared the monstrous visage. I saw the demon within, for I knew it was Balor and I knew what it wanted. It wanted the Stone of Truth."

Serapion halted his voice and it echoed ringing in the chapel. He looked at each one present, and he bent down in his tomb and grabbed his Acauldronbbot's crozier shaped like a Tau Cross.

"This was Abbot Columba's staff. He held it high as Balor approached the Stone. He did not fear one of those who fell from heaven. Michael, you would have been so proud of him. He stepped forward and said to the beast, 'Balor of the Evil Eye, this Stone you shall not have today. I foresee you possessing it in the future, but you shall not touch it this day. The very day that comes when you seek it again shall not be a day of victory for you, for the day you touch it your doom is wrought, and the King Who Shall Be will pursue you to snatch it back from your hands, from your arms, from the sight of your Eye.'

"So powerful was the voice of Columba, that the serpent stopped, turned and fled, and for many centuries the Stone was safe, until the last time we were awoken. The beast had discovered where we were entombed and sought to rob of us of the Grail we guarded. But the Fallen did not think of whose territory it trespassed upon. Balor was surprised to see the enemy that caused his first demise, and thank the One you were here, Michael of the Shining Blade. For he certainly would have killed us with an eternal death. But neither was he afraid, for he had already done the thing prophesied of him by Columba. He had the Stone, and he had come to the island to gloat and to steal the Grail."

"Too true," said the voice of Michael. "I remember well the vision Balor showed us, of Robert the Bruce being crowned upon the Stone, of the celebration of the Scots, and in the midst of happy chaos, the thieves of Balor came and stole the Stone. The holy Stone. The Stone of Truth. How dare they? And they carried it away."

"Where is it then?" asked Jace. "Conor needs it."

"Patience, Champion," said Serapion, "the story is not over. Michael sent us to recover the Stone. We took Robert the Bruce with us to the Isle of Skye. The Stone was in a portal tomb on that island surrounded by an enchanted spell. No one, not even those who dwelt in that land knew it was there. We lifted the enchantment, and King Robert, a guest with the Lady of the Island, came back one night and hid it away in a cave on that island. It rests there now."

Serapion paused and looked at Jace quizzically. "You mentioned someone named 'Conor'? Is that the name of the King Who Shall Be?"

"Yes," said Jace, setting his face like flint, daring anyone to object.

"Be at peace, warrior," said Serapion smiling. "We can shed some light on where to look for the Stone. That may be enough for Conor to find it."

"Though we did not see where King Robert finally placed it at rest, we do know it is underground, in a cave near the sea, in some kind of grotto where the Tree of the World manifests itself, guarded by were-beasts. That means it rests in the Otherworld. Michael can better explain."

"Yet I will not. Conor shall soon seek the Stone. It will be your task young friends to find him on Skye and help him in his search. Scatha will supply whatever direction is needed."

Fr. Greavy spoke up, "Then we travel to the Isle of Skye. It will be a bitter place this time of year. Is there no other advice you can give us?"

"No advice but some assistance. Go back to Ballinskelligs. Prepare swiftly and when you are ready Brian and I will be there to take you swiftly to Skye along the *faerie* paths. This part of the world is descending into chaos and travel will be dangerous. Besides, you must look for Conor in the Otherworld. That is fortunate for you because there, Skye is a virtual paradise."

"Now that they are awake," said Fr. Greavy, "may the monks accompany us?"

"No," said Michael. "They were awakened not only to give you information, but to assume their last and perhaps longest, most important duty. Have you ever heard of the Sword of Michael?"

"Yeah," said Jace, "I'm looking at it at your side."

"That's a trident he carries, and he means a metaphorical Sword, little one," said Ita, not unkindly.

The seraph continued, "The Sword represents a straight line on a map. It begins on Mt. Carmel, Israel, where I first battled the fallen Light Bearer here on earth, and it continues through six other geographical spots in a straight line from the mountain in the Holy Land to this, the farthest peak to the west in Europe. All seven places were sites of battle with the Fallen and it culminated and was won here on my *Skellig*. Each monk now goes to one of those places to guard the site and guide the pilgrims who will come in greater numbers now. With the death of Constantine, this place shall be guarded by myself."

The monks bowed in acknowledgment of their task and Michael shimmered out of the chapel presumably back to his hall. For a moment everyone was silent but then there was a croaking at the entrance to the tiny church.

"Is he finally gone?" said the crow.

"Morrigan," said Jace, "where have you been?"

"Listening to him pontificate. You could hear him out in the cove."

"You don't like him much, do you?" smiled Jace.

"I am uncomfortable with his kind, and with this type of place. We each have our tasks. Come, let us go. The sooner to Skye, the better."

They slept that night at the hotel, knowing that Phil and Colly would be back in the morning. They had heard nothing from them but didn't expect too since Jace was being more paranoid than usual, insisting that cell phones were forbidden while the government was no doubt spying and Balor was as well.

THE DOCTOR WILL SEE YOU NOW

Tuesday Morning, 11/10, Shannon Airport

TOM SHANDY WAS doing his duty, waiting in the car park of Shannon Airport for Ryanair Flight 74 to come in from Edinburgh. As soon as it landed, he'd go to reception but for the nonce he wanted to listen to a few tunes and wrap his head around all that had transpired in the past twenty-four hours.

Never had so much excitement invaded his life. Though he'd never admit it out loud, he rather enjoyed the cloak and dagger aspect of this mission. He didn't think the young ones would get in much trouble at Edinburgh Castle, but one never knew. He had listened to the news, but there was nothing from Scotland about any theft, break-in, or, as the police would call it, hooliganism reported. That meant success in the Shandyman's mind.

The chance that something went wrong was another reason he wanted to stay in the car park till the last moment. If customs gave the kids trouble, he'd book it back to Ballinskelligs fast for some reinforcements. The governments of Ireland and the U.K. were on edge right now because of the plague scare. It was a wonder they let the airports open, but the news had said not a trace of the virus had been found outside Tralee. Scientists and medical officials were puzzled, but the Shandyman knew Michael had snuffed the bad stuff out of existence with his wall of flame.

The Shandyman was fiddling with the radio when he heard a knock at his window. He expected it was the car park attendant wondering if he was going to get out and get a ticket or just going to loiter around. But when he turned, he sat looking at the face of Shiro Ishii grinning at him. He heard Ishii's muffled voice saying, "Roll down the window," but he shook his head no and made to start the engine.

In a moment, Ishii had a ballpeen hammer out and smashed the glass. "I said, 'roll down the window' idiot, and I meant it."

"What do you want?" said the Shandyman, his voice quivering in fear.

"Where are they?"

"Who?"

"Don't make me waste my time, you pathetic Irish dumbfuck. Where are the boy and girl? Has their flight arrived?"

The Shandyman didn't know where he got his courage, but he pursed his lips and made to shift the car and drive away. As he did so, he felt a blinding pain in the right side of his head as Ishii's hammer slammed against his temple. He felt nothing after that since Ishii didn't stop. The hammer rose and fell at least ten times until what remained of Tom Shandy's face was unrecognizable.

"Should have rolled down the window," muttered Ishii as he tore off his blood-spattered coat and used his scarf to wipe away the blood on his face and hands. Looking at the driver's side mirror, he felt he was presentable enough. His cream-colored sweater was still spotless and his dark pants hid any droplets of the Shandyman's blood. Throwing the hammer onto the passenger seat, Ishii strode away toward the arrival area, hoping he hadn't missed his two targets.

Colly woke when the wheels hit the tarmac and he felt refreshed but looking over at Phil, he saw what a wreck she still was.

"No sleep, huh?" he said sympathetically.

"None whatsoever," she said. Clearly, she was still on edge.

"Don't worry," said Colly. "The Shandyman will be there to pick us up. We'll have the ride from hell back to Ballinskelligs and a late breakfast waiting for us. You'll see."

She gave him a nervous smile. As they deplaned, they walked through the arrival hallway looking for any sign of Tom Shandy. At the actual arrival area there were a lot of people. Tourists didn't seem to be scared away by a little plague, and Colly figured the government wasn't trying to broadcast its fears since no contagion had showed up any of the tests the past twenty-four hours. At least that's what the people around him were saying.

Suddenly, he spotted a sign saying, *Welcome Colly and Phil*. It was being held by a smiling Shiro Ishii. Jolted with fear, he yanked at Phil's sleeve and said, "We're in trouble. Follow me!"

Trying not to catch the attention of any of the security folk milling around, he hurried Phil towards the right side of the arrivals' exit, trying to put the American tourists in between themselves and Ishii.

"What is it?" said Phil with fear in her voice. "What did you see?"

"Ishii," said Colly. "He's waiting for us, with a sign and everything."

"But the Shandyman?"

"I don't think we'll be meeting him, Phil. Ishii wants us too badly. No doubt he's taken care of Tom Shandy."

"What do you mean, 'taken care of'? You don't think he killed him, do you?"

"I love you, Phil, but I wish your soul would sometimes be as cynical as your wit. This is the man that set loose a plague and tried to kill Fr. Greavy. I doubt he just slapped the Shandyman around. Come on! We've got to move faster."

They burst out of the building and headed for the taxi stalls. Colly corralled one and ordered the driver to take them to Ballinskelligs.

"Cost you dear," said the cigarette smoking driver. "Got to show some euros first."

"Dammit all," swore Colly, jamming his hands into his pockets trying to find some cash.

"Here," said Phil, "taking out a wad of euros from her pocket. Will this do?"

"Sure will, ma'am," winked the cabby. "Always listen to your girlfriend," he said to Colly who was gaping at Phil.

"Me mum gave it to me, Colly, just before we left, in case we had any problems."

"God bless, Moira," said Colly. They got in and locked the doors as the cabby drove away. A thump on the boot made Colly look around and he saw Ishii trying to hit the trunk again with his hand in frustration.

"You know him?" said the driver.

"Yeah, and you don't want to," said Colly. "Now go, as fast as you can."

Both Phil and Colly decided the ride to Ballinskelligs was smooth sailing compared to the Shandyman's driving, but both were worried. Tom Shandy had been nowhere to be found and both of them feared they would never see him again.

THE RANGER OF THE HEAVENS

Tuesday Morning, 11/10, Shannon to Ballinskelligs

THE CABBY HAD been whistling a tuneless warble for a while when Phil and Colly saw the signs for Portmagee. Colly had wanted to skirt the Kerry Way highway in case of traffic. Most of the parts of Kerry they had traveled were deserted and this was no exception. Except for the one car that followed about a quarter mile behind.

Colly's sight was better than most humans. He saw it was a Mercedes and feared that Shiro Ishii had not yet given up the pursuit. He urged the driver to go faster but 50 kph was as fast as he dared. They sped through Portmagee, but the Mercedes caught up with them when they were just past the town. It hugged their bumper for a few kilometers and then started playing chicken with them. Colly could see the mad doctor laughing at them through his windshield.

The cabby started swearing both at the driver and his passengers, wondering what made them so important that someone was trying to run them off the road.

Neither Colly nor Phil answered. They just craned their heads to see what Ishii would do next. It was disaster. Right by St. Finan's Bay, Ishii made his move. He came up beside the cab and jerked the wheel left. The cabby did what was natural and steered left as well, but as Ishii braked, the cab bounced off some stone abutments on the left-hand side of the road. The driver compensated too much and began to skid to the right. Braking too hard, he sent the cab into a 180-degree spin going right off the road down an embankment towards the Bay. The car flipped several times. Phil, who for some reason had not buckled her seat belt was thrown through the side window. Colly stayed with the car till it stopped fifty feet from the Bay. A small fire erupted in the engine, and Colly, who had not lost consciousness, unsnapped his belt and crawled out his broken window. There was no sign of Ishii, but what concerned Colly at the moment was the driver. He wasn't moving and, quickly, Colly gauged he would never move again. His neck was twisted at an obscene angle, his dead eyes fixed forward.

Colly could do nothing for him, and as the fire spread, he began looking anxiously for Phil. He found her just up the hill, bruised and bloodied. Bones were broken. That he could tell. Tears filled his eyes and he crawled to her, touching her face and pleading, "Please, wake up. Please. Don't die on me now." She said nothing, and he let out an animal cry to the sky. He looked down at her face and wiped the blood away saying, "I told you on the plane I loved you, but you thought I was just being a smartass again. I wasn't. Ever since school, I've noticed you. Seriously. You know I was always around. We always had fun. Just couldn't tell you what I felt about you. And then, when you found out who I was, what I was, a few days ago, I thought there might be a chance, because, because you didn't walk …"

"Colly Roddy!" roared a voice from up by the road. "Where are you now? Did you survive my little trick? Ah … there you are, with that bitch with pink hair. Looks dead to me. I'll leave you alive if you give me whatever you found in Edinburgh." Shiro Ishii made to walk down the gradient.

"Nothing!" screamed Colly. "We found nothing. The Stone was a fake!"

"I know that, idiot. Always have known it. But I'm thinking you found something, something that will help that Conor brat. Maybe a clue to where the Stone can be found. Maybe something that will help it work. I know where it is. You could have simply asked me, or my Master. Come with me. We'll find it together." Ishii beckoned to him.

Colly was out of options. He looked out towards the sea and he saw *Skellig* Michael looming eight miles away. He didn't have a choice. The seraph hated him, or at least mistrusted him, but he didn't have any options left. Phil was still breathing. Ishii would put a stop to that no matter if Colly went with him or not.

His body ached and he was powerfully dizzy. Knowing that Ishii wouldn't wait forever, Colly said what Ita once taught him. He had been bullied by some of the bigger kids in school. Ita was making one of her rare visits to see how he was doing and found him hunched up at the docks, a welt under his eye and his knees skinned. "Lad," she said. "Next time this happens, here's a prayer that you can say. Someone guards this land and the folks in it. Here's how it goes." She taught him. He memorized, but the next time never came. He grew too fast and nobody messed with him then. But next time was now. He looked again out at the *Skelligs* and said,

Come, Ranger of the Heavens,
Warrior of the King of all;
Put round about me now,
The shelter of thy shield.

Drive from me every temptation and danger;
Surround me in times of confusion and weakness;
And in my waking, working, and sleeping,
Keep safe my life; guard me always.
Be a bright flame before me,
Be a guiding star above me,
Be a smooth path beneath me;
And be a kindly shepherd beside me,
Today, tonight, and forever.
You of the white steed,
And of the bright brilliant blades,
Nothing can harm me,
'Neath the shelter of your wings;
Nothing, 'neath the shelter of your wings.

Then came the Ranger of the Heavens, Michael the Victorious, upon Brian the winged white horse, from across the sea. Colly could see a flashing trident in one hand, a golden shield in the other, but a cry from up the road caused him to look and see Ishii slipping and sliding down the hill. He was almost upon them.

"Give me what you found, you Changeling bastard!" Drawing his katana from the scabbard on his belt, he raised it high. "First, I'll make sure your girlfriend is dead—beheaded, I think. I rescind my offer to take you with me to the real Stone. You are as dead as she is."

For Colly, time slowed. He saw the raised katana begin to descend, but a huge shadow overwhelmed the scene. A horse's scream pierced the silence and Michael, his seraph wings beating, leapt to the ground with his shield coming between the flashing blade and Phil's head. There he stood between Colly and Ishii.

He held the trident at the throat of the wizard. "Kill him now," whispered Colly, "he's too dangerous to leave alive."

"I cannot," said Michael, not looking at Colly but gazing in Ishii's hateful eyes. "I am the guardian of this land, not the murderer of its inhabitants. I am limited at the actions I can take, even if it would be, as you say, for the greater good." Brian landed by Michael's side, baring his teeth at the doctor of death.

"Fine," snapped Colly. "Then let me do it." He began shifting to his wolf form. Snarling, he could barely be understood, "I'll rip out his throat. Put an end to his madness. He wants to kill us all."

"No," said Michael, "he doesn't. He wants to rule over all. Something he has not yet shared with his master. Is that not right, wizard?" Ishii simply shifted his eyes refusing to look at the seraph. "Besides," said Michael, turning to Colly, "should not your first care be to Philomena? With your help and my aid, we can save her."

Colly spit blood from a bruised lip onto the ground as he shifted back to human form. "I thought you were limited in what you could do, angel."

Michael's features softened. "I treated you poorly, lad, when we first met. In haste, I judged you from the experience I have had of your kind. That was wrong of me. You are not like them. I can bring healing to whomever I chance upon. What say you? Can we try to save her together?"

Shiro Ishii chose this moment to raise his blade again and strike at Michael. The trident swung snapping the katana in half and breaking Ishii's wrist. "Fool," said Michael, "you seek to battle me? You are weaponless for the moment. Get you gone, back to your master, and tell him he shall not succeed, for though I cannot battle him openly yet, I have friends who can." Here he looked at Colly. "Good and faithful friends. Brothers and sisters in arms. Tell Balor they are coming. Tell him to beware." He spun Ishii around with a massive hand and used his trident to push him up the hill.

Without a second glance at the wizard, Michael turned to Colly. "Help me with her." Colly looked to see if Ishii was gone. He heard a car speed away. "Fear not, little one. That spawn of a demon shall trouble you no more this day. Now, lift Philomena's head up, and let me get to work."

Colly said, "I thought you needed my help."

"I do," said the seraph. "You need to bring her back from the darkness of death. Tell her what you told her before."

"You heard that?" said Colly blushing.

Michael smiled gently. "The earth and sea heard you, Colly. It is no secret anymore."

In a moment, he transformed into the being of light Colly had witnessed on *Skellig*, and he saw light surround all of them. He heard music, beautiful and sad, like the wind through falling autumn leaves. And a voice spoke, of love and loss, of suffering and healing, of death and life, brief though it was in this world. Colly bent down to Phil's ear and said, "Come back to me. Please. We need you. I need you. I ..."

"You love me," she said, her eyes still closed. "I heard you the first time."

As he kissed her on the lips, the light grew brighter and then with thunder echoing in the skies, Michael and his steed were gone.

"Are you okay?"

"Fine, I think," she said. "You know, he could have given us a ride back to Ballinskelligs."

"Somehow, I don't think his mind ever goes in logical directions."

OVER THE SEA TO SKYE

Tuesday Noon, Ballinskelligs

A RICKETY CAR, muffler failing, drove up to the *Skellig Pub*, braking with a squeak. They were lucky a neighbor who knew Colly loaned him his auto. Colly, bruised and disheveled and Phil, slightly worse for wear, tottered out the back doors and up the steps into the pub. Stares of horror greeted them.

"Phil!" cried Moira rushing to her daughter's side. "What in the Blessed Mother's name happened to you? Are you alright?"

"Yes, Ma," whispered Phil, still groggy from the wreck and the healing. "Colly will tell you what happened."

Jace got up and helped them both into chairs while Moira got them something to drink.

Colly began. "The Shandyman—he's dead, I think. Shiro Ishii killed him, just like he tried to kill us." Colly filled them in on what happened at the airport and on the way back. For a moment all were speechless.

Then Fr. Greavy said, "I'll call the airport. If something happened to him it won't be on the news. Too much else is going on."

"What else?" said Phil.

The priest continued, "There's been riots in several cities in Ireland. Authorities are blaming it on that designer drug RAGE, and no doubt it's true. Balor and Ishii weren't content to spread just the plague. This must have been their backup. What you and the government don't know is that the more civil disturbance there is, the more it attracts things from the Otherworld. There are fractures in the boundaries and chaos is like fish bait to the darker denizens of the Otherworld. The *drocs* we saw a few days ago—they're just the first of many things this land has not seen for thousands of years."

"We have seen those other things before," said Lettie. "Where do you think the old stories come from about things that go bump in the night? And then, there's me—the wisp from beyond." She curtsied a little.

Fr. Greavy smiled, as he punched in the airport number on his phone. "Granted, Lettie. But seldom could those things get through the thin places—it didn't happen all that often."

He was talking to some official at Shannon Airport, so Jace broke in. "What did you guys find out about the Stone of Truth? Is it the Coronation Stone?"

"No," said Colly. "The Stone is fake, but there was a message in it from the stonemason who repaired it when last it was stolen." Colly then told them of their adventures in the museum.

"Did Ishii get the ruby?" asked Jason

"Not a chance," said Colly. "I've got it here." He pulled it out of his jeans' pocket and let it gleam before them. "Conor needs to use it to banish this new sickness forever. Plus, it apparently does other things. That's what the Birdman—I mean Dr. Rae—told us before we left. It only works with the true king and he won't be king till we get him proclaimed one on the real Stone of Truth. If we can find it."

Fr. Greavy gasped and everyone looked at him. His face was pale as he talked into his phone. "Thank you. Officer. I'll be in touch." He ended the connection and turned bleak eyes to the group. "Tom Shandy is dead. They found his body in the car park. His head suffered blunt force trauma. He was murdered in the front seat of his car."

Phil burst into tears. The others just hung their heads.

It was Jace who broke the impasse. "He was a good man. But what's done is done. We've got little time left. If Ishii and Balor are still intent on bringing the worlds together in such a way that evil wins, then we have to stop them."

Ita stood and spoke. "I do not know Shiro Ishii except what you have told me of him. But Balor, I know. He is one of the Fallen, an evil beyond imagination. He ruled this land thousands of years ago, a reign so terrible that even in my time his name was used to scare children into good behavior."

She gave a bitter smile. "I've seen darkness. I've witnessed terrible deeds. Even now, when I walk the Otherworld, or this one in my few excursions from the Summer Country, I see evil growing at a pace unaccounted for in dozens of generations. Perhaps it is the end of all things. Or perhaps it is a test for a weary world and a people who have long ago lost their ability to sense the grace, the power, the goodness that pervades creation.

"Maybe we are being given one more chance. And your Conor, this young lad whom prophecy whispers should be a king, is the catalyst that can make it so. I say we go find him, and search for the Stone and stop all this nonsense we see around us."

She looked her regal self for just a moment there as she stood before them. Then, with a sigh, she sat herself down. Only Jace saw her hand tremble as she slid it into her lap.

"It's settled then?" said Jace. "We all go?"

"Not my Ma," said Phil in the strongest voice she had used since her return.

"Why ever not, child?" said Moira. "I am as capable as anyone for this task."

"No, you're not," said Phil. "You're my mother; it will be dangerous; and you are all I have. I won't risk you."

"Moira," said Colly, "she's right. Besides, Kevin will be coming back, probably bringing caravans of Travelers and they'll need to be cared for. They have a stake in this too."

"Neither can I go," said Ita. "I am tied to the land here. With you gone, no one will be around to deal with the Otherworld if it breaks into here again. Michael will be preoccupied with Balor, and if not, Colly has made it clear that Michael is restricted on how much he can actually intervene. No, my place is here."

"And I will be welcome for it," said Moira. "How do you Americans say it, Jace? We will 'hold the fort.'"

Jace laughed and said, "I'm sure you will. But we don't even know how to find Conor. Where exactly did Scatha take him?"

"She took him far away, on a journey longer than any of you can appreciate," said Ita. "Yet, I think you will find him on her island, the Isle of Skye. It's named after her."

"You're kidding me," said Jace. "The Isle of Skye? 'Speed bonnie boat' Isle of Skye?"

Ita's eyes twinkled. "Indeed, but not the Isle of Skye in this reality. She would have taken him to the Otherworld version. In this world, Skye is incredibly beautiful. But in the Otherworld, it is the borderland of the Summer Country, a land beyond all measure, Scatha's land, where kings to be have been trained for thousands of years."

"You've got something up the sleeve of your habit," said Fr. Greavy. "How exactly are we getting there?"

"Well," she smiled, "Michael promised to take you, but there are too many of you. However, Brendan and my boatmen have returned. They're docked by the ruined abbey even now. It will be a tight fit, but they can take you immediately. It will be a faster trip on the *faerie* track with them then if you flew back to Scotland on a plane, and a safer one I think."

"Good idea," said Greavy. "The airport rep said they were thinking of shutting down the airport because of all the violence in the country. We don't need that."

"Hopefully," said Ita, "you'll be safe. But Brendan told me they were tracked by some sort of serpent on the way there the last time. Just make sure Jace has his Sword ready—in case of trouble."

THE FLIGHT OF THE DOVES

Monday Morning To Tuesday Evening, 11/9–10, On the Way to Doolin, North of Shannon

KEVIN, MARY AND Laura were the first to leave on that Monday, even before Phil and Colly took off for Edinburgh. Caravans don't travel swiftly, but the wagon made good time. Malby knew that speed was of the essence, so he set out in a brisk trot.

Kevin skirted Tralee and its environs as much as possible. The smell of death and burning was unmistakable, and he was acutely conscious of little Laura's reactions.

"Da," she said, wrinkling her nose, "make that terrible smell go away!"

"Well, that I will, darlin'," he said to her, affectionately putting his arm around her neck and hugging her close. "The smell of the sea will be in our nostrils soon."

And so it was. Just south of Limerick, near the sea, they parked for the night. But not before they took quite a scare. They were off the major highway, but the side road they were on climbed a little hill and they could see down onto the four-lane roadway. Cars were abandoned on the shoulder and roving gangs of people, not large groups, but still four or five to a gang, were bounding around them. Some had sticks or clubs and were bashing windows out. Some were attacking the fleeing passengers. It was violent, and to Kevin's mind a terrible break down in order. If they were seen, they would be set upon. Travelers were not liked and in the best of times were oppressed.

Mary looked worriedly at her husband. "It's RAGE isn't it? That wretched drug worse than drink is possessing the lot of the people."

"True, that," said Kevin. "Never saw this much of it though. Got a feeling Shiro Ishii and Sir Hugh might be behind it. I heard those toughs say when they attacked us last week that the Chief was expecting some shipment. Didn't think he made all his money from oil and Saudi sheiks."

"I'll get off the road," he said, "so they can't see us. Don't be too worried though. They seem to have enough to do down on the roadway."

That's what led them to a small caravan park close to the sea southwest of Limerick. Surprisingly, it was deserted. After they made a fire and had eaten, Mary packed Laura off to bed and she sat by the warming coals and said to her husband, "What's your plan, Kevin? Where are we going and what are we doing?"

He stretched and lit a pipe. He seldom smoked but with Amergin gone, he had taken to imitate his departed dad in this respect. "I'm thinking, Mary of going up to Doolin in County Clare. Travelers—ones we know well—are there this time of year with all the tourists gone. I'm thinking of asking for help. If we get there tomorrow night, perhaps I can get them to send out a call for a Gathering, back down at *Staigue* Fort this coming Friday. Conor's going to need us. I don't know where he is now, but whatever happens is going to have its grand finale near Ballinskelligs. *Skellig* Michael is the key. We can't all go there but we can be near. *Staigue* Fort is the best gathering place for us."

"You mean to send out the doves."

"Our clan is in charge of communication. The birds will get to everyone Wednesday morning, plenty of time to make it to the Gathering if everyone hustles."

"Mommy," said a voice from the caravan, "will Conor be coming back to visit soon?"

"Soon, honey," said Mary turning to see Laura's tiny face peeking out the doorway. "But not if you don't get some sleep first. He's sent us on an adventure, and you don't want to disappoint him do you?"

They could hear the thump as she jumped back into bed.

"I'm worried, Kevin. What we saw today and days past—it's not natural."

"Well you welcomed him, Mary. This all started with picking up a hitchhiker from Shannon Airport."

"What would you have had us do? It was the hospitable thing. It was the right thing to do."

He kissed her on the cheek. "I know, I know," he sighed. "It's just that since he came every bogart, leprechaun, wight, ghost, and whatever has popped up at crossroads, city and towns. You'd think, with the Otherworld come crashin' in, some good stuff would be visiting us as well. It's only the bad I see."

"It's a fight," said Laura. "A battle really. And we're a part of it. I know we didn't want to be, but, somehow, we're necessary. If your Da were here, he'd be singing of it already. We're going to be a part of the story of this land, however it turns out. Right now, it looks bad, but tomorrow will be better. Just you wait and see."

"That's my red-haired Mary," smiled Kevin ruefully. "You keep me tracking right, you do now. Let me feed Malby. Go get ready for bed. I'll be in, in a moment."

She watched him go into the dark up to where Malby was tied to a fencepost. She could barely see him in the shadows, feeding the horse and brushing him down. Mary thought about how blessed she was to have a husband like him. She only hoped her wish for a better day was true.

It was not. The weather wasn't bad on Tuesday, but as they rounded Limerick the tension in the air grew. They heard far away blasts of gunfire and even saw a few outlying homes ablaze. They had no radio but it was just as well they did not. As they passed an untouched home close to the tiny side road they were on, a radio was blasting away. Some newsreader was sounding slightly hysterical, claiming that the army had come marching into Limerick to put down riots in the streets. As best as Kevin and Mary could hear, the rioting was not contained to Limerick. Violence was reported in Galway and Dublin as well.

Kevin clicked Malby into a faster trot, wishing that Michael was around to jumpstart the old horse into that beautiful stallion with wings he had seen a few days ago. Figured he could use a good guardian like that about this time. He glanced up at the horse only to see Malby turn his head and fix one eye on him and whicker, as if to say the horse had his back whether he was a brown nag or a white steed.

Things seemed calmer past Shannon, and Kevin breathed a sigh of relief as they came into Doolin as the sun was setting. They had made great time, and the Travelers came out to greet them as they rode into Nagle's Caravan campsite just northwest of town on Doolin Beach. About 50 caravans were gathered there and the people had made a great bonfire in the center of the camp with smaller ones here and there for cooking. A clean-shaven man, big and burly came up to Kevin and embraced him. "Well met, cousin," said the man who turned out to be Eamon Joyce. "So sorry about your Da. Couldn't make it to the funeral, but some of us, drank to his memory that night. What brings you amongst us this evening?"

"You know what's been happening?" said Kevin. "Down south and maybe hereabouts?"

"The world's going mad, I think," said Eamon. "Witchery is about as well." He looked out into the dark. "There are things at night. We see the shadows and hear the cries."

"That's why I'm here. A boy, a young man really, from America has come. Conor Archer's his name. He's one of the People of the Sea."

Eamon sucked in his cheeks. "It's been awhile since we've mingled with them."

"Some say he's to be their new king and ours as well. They, like we, haven't had one for ages."

"True, that," said Eamon. "What do you think he wants?"

"Look," said Kevin, "he landed on these shores and stuff starts happening. He says the Otherworld is coming for more than just a visit. From what I've seen, he's got some powerful enemies who are dead set on seeing him destroyed. You know Sir Hugh Rappaport?"

"Bastard," said Eamon, "drove me and mine off his 'supposed' land last year and busted up several of our caravans."

"Well, he's not really Sir Hugh."

"What do you mean?"

"I saw him, Eamon. He's Balor of the Evil Eye, just like our grandmothers used to tell us to scare us into good behavior."

If it hadn't been so dark, Kevin could have sworn he saw Eamon turn pale as a ghost. Eamon coughed to cover his fear and said, "If this Conor is what you say he is, we have a pact we must keep with the People of the Sea. They've never asked us to fulfill it, but you and I both know if there is a king or one to be we have to help him."

"I know, that's why I'm here. Are the homing doves in good shape? Can we reach the Travelers throughout the country?"

"When? I mean they're fine, but how soon do they have to fly?"

"Tonight."

"Kevin Bard, you know our doves don't fly at night. We'd lose them all to owls. Too much of a risk."

"It has to be tonight," said Kevin. "They must reach the Travelers throughout Ireland by morning so all can rendezvous at *Staigue* Fort by Friday."

"Can't happen, cousin. Won't happen. Earliest they can fly is tomorrow noon. Besides, what message do we give?"

"Here," said Kevin. "Mary's been at it all this day. Seventy messages for the scattered clans, rolled and ready for your birds, calling for the pact to kept at *Staigue* Fort, Friday night."

"Busy lass, hasn't she been? Still doesn't change anything. Wednesday noon at the earliest. Now get yourself and your family something to eat and park that caravan down there by the water for the night. We'll talk in the morning."

Kevin was more than merely perturbed. He remembered just how much Eamon pissed him off when they were kids. Always knew better, always had to have his way. He complained to Mary as they ate. She tried to placate him. "Something will come our way, Kev. You know that. Help always seems to come Conor's way, and I have a hunch his luck falls on us too." This time, she was right.

The bonfire still burned high, but most the caravan folk, after they had greeted Kevin's family had gone to bed. Kevin stayed outside his wagon listening to the sea and hearing the doves cooing in their coops near Eamon's caravan.

He was dozing lightly when he heard the song, coming from the ocean. The crescent moon and the stars shone brightly over the water with the Hand of God nebula in the heavens. The waves were luminescent, giving enough light for Kevin to see the bobbing heads of seals not far from shore. They were the source of the song, and it was beautiful. He saw a big grey lumber out of the ocean, gazing at him from the sandy beach. His dappled coat shone with the sheen of the foam. Once Kevin's eyes had lost the fire blindness from gazing at the bonfire, he could see the intelligent eyes of the seal staring at him. Raising his voice over the lilting song from the seas, he said, "What do you want of me? I'm trying. I know the need. You need our help, but Eamon, my stubborn cousin is just a piece of horseshit sometimes. You could be king of the *fae* and he wouldn't change his mind."

The seal barked twice at him, as if it was commiserating with Kevin's problem, and then it did the strangest thing. It lumbered toward him, moving awkwardly across the sand and up into the grassy *machair*. Coming beside Kevin, it barked quietly at him. Kevin couldn't help himself. He reached out to touch the head of the seal, and it let him. So smooth he thought, and, then, it moved forward. Kevin jerked his hand back, thinking he had offended it, but it stopped, looked at him again and barked softly. Kevin reached out his hand a second time, and the seal led him forward towards the bonfire.

As they came closer to the flames, the seal started singing with his mates in the ocean again, and this time, the Travelers heard and poked their heads out of their caravans.

"Look, mommy," said Laura, leaning out of the wagon, "a seal and daddy!" Mary took Laura's hand and with others pouring out of their dwellings, joined Kevin and the seal around the fire.

"What is this? What is this?" snorted Eamon, his hair a little wild from sleeping. "What's this seal doing here in the midst of all of you?"

"Asking for help, it seems," said Kevin.

Even Eamon's face softened at the wonder of the scene. "Look," he said, actually addressing the animal respectfully, "I told Kevin they cannot fly at night. I won't risk it. They're my pride and joy, and frankly, income. You can't expect ..."

Just then, a soft neigh and whicker were heard from the other end of the camp. Kevin thought later that he had to hand it to Malby. Never a better time for a transformation. Into the light of the bonfire walked a winged stallion amidst the gasps of the people. Some could be heard saying, "The seraph's steed! The stallion Brian!"

But it was Laura who was heard the loudest. She clapped her hands and said, "Da, let me ride him!"

Surprising himself, Kevin picked her up and set her between the wings of horse. At that moment, the seal rose up on its hind flippers and barked at Eamon, and Brian whinnied loudly at the man.

Eamon snorted in resignation saying, "Who am I to fight the animal kingdom?" ordering the people to each come and take a dove and affix the messages that Mary had made for them. It was chaos for several minutes and everyone heard Eamon complaining. "They won't fly you know, and if they do, I'll lose them all." Yet, in a few minutes the job was done.

Since Eamon wasn't going to commit himself to sending his own doves to their doom, Kevin did the honors himself.

"It's our Pact with the People of the Sea we honor tonight. Each of you came to me this evening, and I told you what we have planned. We must get to *Staigue* Fort by Friday if we are to help Conor Archer. It's a beautiful evening on this beach. The song of the seals surrounds us, and a magical horse is amongst us, but not far away the Dark is rising and taking hold of people's minds, corrupting the land, and blighting the spirits of men and all creation. This is our chance, we Travelers, to play a part for the Light, and for the King Who Shall Be. Now, on three, send these birds on their journey."

As the doves flew, they circled first the campground, and then the seals, and as they came back for a circle of the people again, Brian spread his wings and lifted his front hooves crying out into the night. The flames of the bonfire grew brighter and the birds each flew down to touch the nose of the horse and fly just above Laura's reaching hands. Kevin and Mary gasped at the perceived danger, but Laura sat tightly on the stallion laughing at the dozens of birds passing her by.

When they were gone, the horse folded his wings and Kevin took Laura from his back. A startled Eamon saw the horse moving to him and gently lowering his head to Eamon's shoulder. Tears sprung from Eamon's eyes. The stallion whickered softly and then walked back out of the campground. Those who saw said, as the light dimmed on him, the horse seemed to shrink back into the brown draft animal that Kevin called his own.

"Well, I'll be," muttered Eamon, wiping the wetness from his face.

"Satisfied, cousin?" asked Kevin. "I think your birds will be safe this night's journey."

CONOR

'Otherworld' Time, Isle of Skye, Scotland

CONOR PERCHED ON the summit of *Sgurr Alisdair*. It was a beautiful morning and the whole of the southern Isle of Skye was open to his vision. To the east, he could take in the golden meadows and Caledonian forest of the Trotternish peninsula with farmland close to the sea. To the west, Conor could gaze down on *Dun Scaitha,* Scatha's Fortress of Shadows and the beautiful loch beside it. Further down the slopes, he could see the *machair* plain with the *Faerie* Pools and, further still, the beautiful white sand beach that bordered the turquoise water of the ocean. His sight was keen and he spotted someone far down the strand walking by the waves.

Conor stood and stretched his arms. Rubbing his face, feeling his close-cropped beard, he willed himself to change into his Thunderbird shift. Normally, he could only morph into animals native to the island. He suspected that would be true anywhere, but the Thunderbird and seal forms seemed to be a necessary part of him and able to be accessed at any time.

Not waiting for the complete shift to happen, he launched himself off the peak and fell like a stone until the change was complete just above some lower jagged peaks. He had done this before and it was a thrill. His wings opened in the dive and with a searing cry he went soaring above the highest Cuillin. He headed for the *machair* and beach, and the lonely figure down on the sand.

Conor cried loudly again, diving for the strand. The figure heard him and glanced backward. Seeing the pursuing Thunderbird, he began to run swiftly but not fast enough. Conor glided down till he was wingtip to Troubles' shoulder, and his laugh was another Thunderbird cry. The dog barked joyously and ran more swiftly with Conor pursuing. Suddenly, Conor pounced on the dog, resuming his human shape and the two went rolling over the sand till they landed in the water. Troubles jumped up and bounded like a pup through the waves back to Conor and shook himself over his best loved human.

A shadow fell over the two of them as they wrestled in the foam. Scatha looked down on them sternly and said, "Both of you cease; it is time to get back to your training." But even her grim gaze faltered, and she burst out laughing at the two, Labrador and human, inseparable as always.

They were walking on the beach after Scatha had given Conor a tunic to clothe himself. Absently petting Troubles' head, Conor said, "Scatha, it's been a long time. Surely I must be close to the end of my training."

"We shall talk about this when we reach the tent and speak with Amergin." They were headed for a canvas tent set up near the waves. Someone had started a small fire just outside the tent flaps.

"Amergin!" cried Conor at the bearded figure exiting the tent. "A good morning to you!"

"And to you, Bard of the West," said the older man. Normally, Conor would have been shocked to see a dead man walking around, but Amergin had graced their presence many times in the past, 'On leave,' he said, 'from the Summer Country', expressly to help train Conor.

They were about to sit down for breakfast when Conor asked again, "Surely, both of you know my training is nearly completed. It seems like we've been doing this for an awful long time."

"We have been at your education for nearly five years," said Scatha.

"Five years?" said Conor. "Impossible! It can't be that long. Maybe a few months, but five years! What about my friends, what about my supposed destiny, what about Aunt Emily and all those back in Tinker's Grove?"

Amergin looked carefully at Scatha and said, "I'm surprised he hasn't questioned this before. Why today?"

"This morning," said Scatha, "as he was waking, I removed the *geas* upon him. He only now is remembering."

"What's a *geas*?" asked Conor, "And what am I only now remembering?"

"A *geas* is a binding put on a person to do or not do something. In your case, when we arrived at my island after your wounding, I put a binding of forgetfulness upon you. Do not start. It was only a binding to forget the passage of time, not any other memory."

"Almost five years?"

"Yes," said Amergin. "Look at you. You have become a fine young man. I like your beard, close cropped with only a short width, just like the Ancient Greeks and the *Tuatha da Danaan*. You look like a hero out of the past."

"Yeah right," smiled Conor, "but what of the crisis we were in when I came here?"

Scatha said, "You are in the Otherworld, Conor, and time moves differently here. Your friends are on their way, and for them, mere days have passed."

Conor sat down so fast that Troubles barked in concern. "Just a few days? Still, I've let them down."

"Nonsense," said Amergin. "Your training here has made you even more of an asset to them. Look at what Scatha has accomplished with you. Tell him, lady; refresh his memory."

"Year One," she said, "Remember the training of the body. I and others helped finish the healing the Grail had begun. When you had recovered, you ran the meadows and scaled the mountain paths of my land. Your body hardened with the effort and Niall, the *Ealaiona comharaic (martial arts)* master taught you *Dornalaiocht (boxing), Coraiocht (wrestling), Speachoireacht (kicking), and Batadoireacht (stick fighting)*."

"Yeah," said Conor, "my body remembers it well. I think I still have the bruises."

"Year Two," said Scatha, "Remember the weapons training, where you learned to fight with knife, Sword and Spear."

"You taught me that," said Conor. "I don't know how many times I was beaten by a girl." Scatha laughed out loud and Conor continued, "Remember, I asked you why I just couldn't use a gun."

"I told you why," said Scatha. "Knife, Spear and Sword are extensions of yourself. Bullets are not. No doubt you will have to learn to use them, but not on my island. We keep the memory of our ancestors."

"Year Three," said Amergin, "was the memorization and practice of lore. You learned to heal with herbs and potions. You learned the power of your own body to transmit its healing energy to others. And you learned the lore of our people, for in our stories and tales much wisdom exists."

"Year Four," continued Amergin, "you learned the full use of your powers as a *Roan*. Scatha taught you the ways of your People of the Sea, and I taught you the runes of nature, the power of shifting, the ability to conceal oneself and manipulate the reality others experience."

"But you didn't teach me magic," said Conor.

"Because," said Amergin, looking over at Scatha, "in that, we do not keep the memory of our pagan ancestors. Blessed Patrick taught and St. Columba demonstrated that prayer and spirituality are more powerful and better at doing good and fighting evil. The ancient spells and incantations have real power but can only be used by you when they are heartfelt prayers to the One above all. It is how you access the *neart*, the life force, the grace of the One that is in everything—his power, his presence, his love. Every night of year four, while you slept, I whispered the words you would need to use to make your prayers a reality should the One grant them. They will come to your tongue in your need and be more powerful than any druid magic."

"Year Five," said Scatha, "the present year. It is only months till Christmas but your time here has come to an end. This shortened year saw the combining of the wisdom of years one through four. We have taught you all we can, but it is enough. You are ready."

"For what?" said Conor. "Tell me plainly."

"Ready," said Amergin, "to meet and help your friends, something you would not have been able to do had you remained in their reality. Throughout these five years, I have taught you the music of the land, Scatha has given you the music of the sea, songs to bind all the disciplines we taught you together into one whole. You were formidable but untrained before. Now you are schooled in the Celtic arts and your powers have found a home. You are a worthy foe to Balor and Shiro Ishii and to all who try to bring the Dark to humanity. Come, you must graduate this evening. Already, the People of the Sea have been summoned and those of Scatha's land informed. They shall be at the castle to feast, to sing, and to give you courage, Conor Archer. For their existence depends on your victory over the Dark. Let them honor you this evening, so that when you meet your friends, you may show them that you are the King Who Shall Be."

That evening in the fortress, she gave him clothes like a Celtic hero of old—white tunic, trousers, leather boots, a cape-like crimson *brat* fastened with a gold pin on his right shoulder. She even cut his hair and trimmed his beard. She was like that, Conor thought. Scatha had cared for him these past years and he had grown more than fond of her. He thought he was starting to love her.

Of course, that scared the hell out of him. She was so powerful and magical. He remembered now. The first time she took him out of her fortress into the Cuillin Mountains, she looked him up and down saying, "You are like him."

"Who?" he said. "Who am I like?"

"The man for whom these hills are named, Cuchulainn—the Hound. One of the greatest heroes the Celts have ever birthed. I trained him here, so many centuries ago. He was like you—intense, alert, a fast learner, impetuous, quick to act before he thought. Brave as well, prone to mistakes but quick to repent. I loved him for a while, but he could never be mine. He belonged to the ages. But of all those whom I trained, and they were thousands, he was the best. Until you came along."

"I am not Cuchulainn, or any of the other Celtic warriors. I'm just Conor Archer from Tinker's Grove, whose genes are a little mixed up I guess with your people." He laughed at that.

"Did I tell you Cuchulainn had a sense of humor?" smiled Scatha those years ago, long in time, but passing swiftly for Conor. "I compare you to him on purpose because never have the times been so dangerous. He had many adventures, and what he did set history on its course until today, but he did not have to face what you must. Balor was a myth to him just as the demon is to the people of this age. But you have met him and fought him. A brave thing. You will meet again, but you must be better trained, or your destiny will die with you and so will your world and that which we call the Otherworld."

Conor remembered that talk and the years of hard training. As he was dressing, he looked at his hand—the scar still present where Rory had bit him, initiating him into the secrets of the People of the Sea—the *Roan*. He touched his side where Drake's dagger had pinned him to the Tree of the World, and he twinged from the remembered pain he and his friends, especially Beth had to endure. Lastly, before he put the tunic over his head, he saw in a mirror the faded blast mark from Balor's Eye in the center of his chest. It had healed into a red sunburst contrasting brightly with the dark tattoo winding around his torso. He remembered when Balor had struck him, piercing him deeply. Conor felt his insides nearly burst. But the pain had ended when he had drunk from the Grail. People would envy him in later years, but to Conor, the Grail had brought back a familiar feeling. It was not the first time he had tasted the contents of that Chalice. It was just that even though the Presence was there in the Cup the Savior had once used, it was the same Blood that had healed his soul before in times of distress, that had healed his body and spirit from the encroaching death with which Balor had struck him. Again, Conor had cause to thank his mother for implanting his spiritual vision. It was the anchor that kept him stable in all these trials.

His tunic on, he glanced at Troubles who cocked his head to one side. "What, don't I look cool, or is it something else?"

"Little Master," said the dog's voice in his mind, "you look like you belong to another time and place."

"We are in another time and place, you big lug," laughed Conor.

"Indeed," said Scatha, entering to pin on his crimson *brat*. "You are ready to assume the duties of King, if that is the destiny the One has set before you."

"That's what you mean by graduation?" Conor smiled at her, knowing all along what the evening was going to bring. "I can't thank you enough for what you have done for me," he said, a warmth beginning to beat steadily in his heart. "If I succeed in what people expect of me, it will be you who gets the most credit. You were ... brutal in the training, but I could not have learned any other way. That's what Amergin says."

"And he would know," said Scatha, a glint of mischief in her dark round eyes. She walked up to him and placed a warm hand against his cheek. "You are ready, my prince, and I am proud of what you have become."

Conor could never say later why he did it, but he took that moment to bend down and kiss her full on the lips, embracing her for just a moment.

He pushed himself back, an embarrassed smile on his face, saying, "I'm sorry but I had to thank you, and … I don't know why I did it that way."

Scatha had brought her fingers up to her lips and touched them. Gently, she took his hand saying, "I welcome your thanks, Conor, may we grow in the knowledge of each other in the years to come." With that, she smiled a warm smile again and left the chamber.

"Well done, little master," said Troubles, leaning up against him, chuffing in what passed for a Labrador retriever laugh.

"I don't know. I'm kind of surprised she didn't rip my face off. What do you think she meant by saying we would grow in knowledge of each other?"

Troubles yipped and Conor could swear his eyes were dancing in mischief as he reached up and licked the boy on his face, then trotted out the door.

There was a huge front palazzo that stretched out from the entry doors of the castle. Large steps descended down to the loch. When Conor stepped out from the interior of *Dun Scaitha*, he gasped in awe. Torches were placed throughout the forecourt and down the steps. Everywhere, there were people and other creatures filed in ranks across the piazza and down the steps to the loch.

Conor stood in disbelief at the entrance of the castle with Troubles by his side. Amergin and Scatha came forward to welcome him, each taking him by an arm. Turning to the crowd, Scatha cried, "Behold the King Who Shall Be over the land, under the sea." The crowd burst into cheers.

Conor could see the ordinary farmers of the island dressed in their finest, but he also saw many of the *Tuatha da Danaan* present, their tall, graceful bodies bowing in welcome. Over the years, he had gotten to know some of them. Now, they were a shy, retiring race of people, hardly the brash and impulsive heroes of old. Still, they possessed a grace and power that often stunned Conor whenever he met them. Creatures were there as well, *kelpies*, water horses, griffins, hobgoblins, *bodachs*, wisps, sprites, *naiads* and *dryads*. All very beautiful, thought Conor like a bestiary from mythological times. But as they walked past these shining people and creatures, Conor began to wonder where the *Roan* were. They were his true kin. Surely, they would be here, but if not now, when?

Amergin and Scatha led Conor down the steps to the beach by the loch. Some magic had flattened the shingled stones into a cobbled pavement, easy to stand on. Conor heard the quiet movement of the water and began to get a little nervous as his two escorts simply stared out over the fresh waters of the most beautiful lake on the Isle of Skye.

The pause gave Conor a chance to look around. The stars were out as was the waning moon, but so was the *Aurora Borealis*, just charging up for the evening. There, high in the western sky was the Hand of God, a symbol of his destiny that had often provoked troublesome dreams. Suddenly the curtains of light from the *Aurora* began to move and sweep up to the center of the sky. That's when Conor heard the music. It was the People of the Sea singing as they rose up out of the depths of the loch. Seldom did they ever take their true form, but tonight was different. Conor remembered the one time when he first came to the island, but he hadn't seen them do it often.

They were tall and dappled with grey and green skin. He wished he could describe them better because it would sound as if the *Roan* were dull colored and odd, but it was not so. In fact, they were dressed in the garments woven from the plants of the sea and their clothes of green and red, yellow and brown meshed beautifully with the almost luminescent skin of their bodies. They could be mistaken for human until one looked more closely. Their arms and legs were longer with lean but strong muscle. Though their eyes were round, their heads were slightly elongated. Any more than what they were and Conor thought they'd look a little like the aliens from Area 51. He wanted to slap himself for thinking that because these were handsome and beautiful people, their hair long and dark, in waves like the sea they sprung from. Of course, their hands and feet were slightly webbed, just like Conor's.

As they rose from the loch, they stood on the surface singing their haunting melody. Calador, a prince of the People, now a close friend, led them in song. Conor thought for sure he had heard it before. He remembered the plaque above the bar at the *DerryAir* in Chicago, "Who knows where we go when we listen to Celtic Music, and we are left a little while alone?" Then, he had it. The song they sang was an ancient hymn from 6th century Ireland.

"It is your Coronation Prayer," said Amergin to Conor. "They sing it now to remind you who you are and what you are to do."

Be Thou my Vision, O Lord of my heart;
Be all else but naught to me, save that Thou art;
Be Thou my best thought in the day and the night,
Both waking and sleeping, Thy presence my light.

Be Thou my Wisdom, and Thou my true Word;
Be Thou ever with me, and I with Thee, Lord;
Be Thou my great Father, and I Thy true son;
Be Thou in me dwelling, and I with Thee one.

Be Thou my Breastplate, my Sword for the fight;
Be Thou my whole Armor, be Thou my true Might;
Be Thou my soul's Shelter, be Thou my strong Tow'r,
O raise Thou me heav'nward, great Pow'r of my pow'r.

High King of heaven, Thou heaven's bright Son,
O grant me its joys, after vict'ry is won;
Great Heart of my own heart, whatever befall,
Still be Thou my vision, O Ruler of all.

Conor took out his whistle and played along with them. He soon stopped and joined his voice with theirs and found that Scatha and Amergin had returned to the crowd, leaving him and Troubles alone on the beach with the People of the Sea. As they sang the hymn again, the other guests joined in and soon the mountains echoed with the song of the *sidhe*, singing a welcome to their prince, their King Who Shall Be.

That was startling enough to Conor, but when the song ended a second time, there was an expectant silence, broken suddenly by the sound of a bird crying in the night. Then he saw it, a dark shadow flying across the waters, hovering just at the edge, then landing and morphing at the same moment into the beautiful warrior maiden, the Morrigan in long crimson robes upon which cascaded her lustrous red hair. Conor could see how she could have been mistaken as a goddess in the past. Beautiful beyond anything he had ever seen, she was totally other and possessed of an identity far stranger than any human. Yet, she was not intimidating tonight. She was regal, and he saw she carried something in her hands. Then he knew. Everyone present tonight was meant to be here; every moment of this event was specially choreographed by Scatha and Amergin.

The Morrigan held in her hands a circlet of gold. Nestled in the empty center was a gold torc. She walked slowly toward Conor holding out the marks of royalty and power.

"Approach me, Hound of Conor," she said to Troubles. Silently, Troubles did, and she rested the circlet of gold on his broad back. Taking the gold torc, she easily bent the shining metal into shape and placed it around Conor's neck. Then she took the crown from the dog and set it on Conor's brow. Finely wrought filigree, it rose in the center into a Celtic Cross, though its center had an empty opening. Both the torc and circlet gleamed in the torchlight.

The Morrigan looked beyond Conor and spied Scatha in the crowd. "Now, you say the words, Scatha. It should be you and not me."

"As you wish," she nodded, turning Conor to the crowd and saying in a loud voice,

Here he stands among you now,
Kingly crown upon his brow,
Torc of power yoked to him,
Strengthens when the times are grim.

One thing missing you cannot see,
What shall in the center be,
Of the circlet that he wears,
A missing jewel the kingship bears.

It is the sign of rule begun,
Shouted from the Stone of Coronation.
Stone is hidden, yet is found,
Without the gem, an empty crown.

One last test, O future King,
Pass it now the bards shall sing.
Wear the jewel of which we told,
Sit upon the Stone of old.

Hear the cry the Rock shall give,
Then the crown will truly live.
Thus, the King begins his reign,
Searching, finding evil to chain.

Balor of the Evil Eye
And his henchman, both draw nigh.
Who shall help you in this fight,
Who will stand against the night,

If not your friends these days of woe,
On their way if you must know.
So be at peace my King to be,
Many are those who stand with thee.

Friends who are coming, we who are here,
Stand together to banish fear.
If good prevails, prophecies say,
Evil then shall lose its sway.

Worlds will merge and peace shall stay.
So claims Scatha, here on Skye,
She the enemy of the Evil Eye,
Presents to you the future King.

Swear the oaths that now you bring
To this storied gathering,
So this Roan shall now go forth,
To his fate upon this earth.

On the other side of the loch, a huge bonfire burst into blaze as the crowd cheered, and for the next hour, the gathered throng came forward to pledge their fealty to Conor. Scatha handed him the Spear of Destiny, and as each approached, they kissed the Spear in honor of the One who died for them so long ago and in expectation of Conor's faithfulness to that sacrifice. Far from filling with pride, Conor felt deep humility in his heart because of the hope these trusting souls placed in him. The once angst-ridden teenager was gone, the fearful heart replaced by a peaceful confidence that, grace be given, he could achieve the goal destined for him. The worlds must be brought together for good, not evil, and if he was the one chosen to do this deed, then do it he would.

As the hour drew to a close, the crowd felt the ground begin to shake, so strongly in fact that scree and small stones were jostled from the slopes of the lower hills. An opening appeared on the side of a small rise and a vaporous cloud from the revealed cave passed through into the valley. There in the mist appeared several figures, and the size of one of them told Conor who they all were.

"Jace!" he cried, "You made it!" Conor and Troubles dashed over the cobbled and shingled stone beach toward the group and embraced them all. Colly, Jace, Phil, Lettie, and Fr. Greavy looked in wonder at the assembled throng and marveled at what Conor was wearing. Colly saw the empty space in the circlet crown on Conor's head and started to speak of the gem he carried, but Scatha, who had just joined them gave him a stern look to keep silent. Now, apparently, thought Colly, was not the time to share Phil's and his Edinburgh treasure.

Conor led them back to the piazza in front of the castle. Everyone was eating and drinking, and many came up to greet the new arrivals. Not one of Conor's friends were able to ask him what all of this around them meant. For several hours, the celebration carried on and then, just before midnight, invited guests began to take their leave.

Scatha was busy with the farewells as the rest of the group gathered around Amergin and Conor. The ancient bard led them all to a more private alcove near the entrance of the fortress.

"Here," said Amergin, "sit yourselves down and rest. Plenty of time for questions now."

"Excuse me," said Colly, "but aren't you supposed to be dead?"

"Always the tactful one," said Jace, punching him on the shoulder.

"No harm in an honest question," said Amergin. "I have passed on from the reality you came from, but as you can see, this is not the Isle of Skye in either your time or in your world. This is Scatha's land and her realm borders the Summer Country. Let me see ... how would you best understand it?" He cocked his head and smiled, "I've got it! This version of the Isle of Skye is like a suburb to the Summer Country. I can visit it for a while and have done so ever since Conor first arrived."

"Amergin," said Jace, "he just got here a few days ago, though he didn't have a beard then, and he seems larger and a little older to me. How does that work here in Scatha's land?"

Conor blushed deeply saying, "Ah, Jace, I've been here quite a while ... a guest of Scatha's for five years."

Everyone gasped except the old bard. "It's true," said Conor, "time flows differently here. I've had a whole college education while you guys were busy mopping up the mess I left you."

"It had to be this way," said Scatha, joining the group. "Conor could not hope to fight Balor as a seal pup king. He had to learn the arts of battle, the lore of the People of the Sea, and how to use his many gifts. Amergin and I have taught him these many years. Yet, though he has matured, he has not truly aged, nor will he for many years to come. The *Roan* are long-lived and Conor now bears the title of Bard of the West. Ask Amergin, the title granted him thousands of years of life."

Fr. Greavy let out a sigh saying, "I'm so sorry, Conor."

"What do you mean?" said Colly, "We Changelings live long as well, but I'd gladly choose to live longer if I could."

"It seems," said Greavy to Scatha, "that the young of humanity and *faerie* never understand."

"Understand what?" asked Conor

"Understand that death is a gift given by the One," said Lettie, puffing on her pipe, "and life prolonged is not always a blessing."

The priest touched his face and the others swore later that he was wiping a tear from his eye.

No one said anything more for a moment and then Jace softly said, "How long have you been alive, Fr. Greavy? You said you were like Abbot Malachy—a Walker of Worlds."

The priest gave a rueful smile. "I remember Scatha when she was just a wee lass playing here on her parent's island. I remember Amergin when he first came to Ireland and charmed us all with his song. But I also remember the wars, the friends I lost, the sundering of the worlds, the split between *faerie* and humanity. So many wonderous and beautiful things have I seen, but none of them soothe my soul, for my heart breaks for those who died and went on before me. I love and care for you all, but living as long as I have ... well, it is terrible to be alone, and when you live long enough, loneliness is your mistress, your spouse, your constant companion."

What could anyone say to that? Lettie shifted into her wisp form and hovered over the priest's heart, trying to let him feel her care. Several attempted to speak, to comfort the priest, but the words died on their lips.

Then Scatha took charge. "Stand up, all of you. Come with me into the fortress, into my study, and let me show you why you were led here. Come now, step smartly. The sooner I can explain, the sooner you can take leave for a night's rest."

They followed her into the fortress. Phil was taken with the beauty inside the thick walls of the castle. "Scatha, your home is fantastic. The artwork alone would keep me busy studying it for years."

"Actually," said Conor, "it only took me four months."

Phil stuck out her tongue at him and then laughed, "Seriously, Scatha, the place is beautiful."

Pleased, Scatha ushered them into her study. Before them on an oriental carpet set the strangest object they had ever seen. It was a black stone bench, concave in the center for one to sit on. The pillars that held it up had beautiful Celtic knotwork and spirals carved into them.

"Phil," said Colly, clasping her hand, "it's the Stone of Truth, the *Lia Fail*. But how did it get here?"

"It is merely a replica, Shifter," said Scatha. "But you need to know it by sight and what its powers are, for tomorrow all of you shall play a part to rescue it from captivity."

Questions erupted from the group, but Scatha silenced them all. "By now, you know that the stone in Edinburgh is a forgery. The real Stone of Truth disappeared after Robert the Bruce was crowned on it in 1321. Rumor had it that he took it and hid it in the Western Isles."

Jace said, "The Isle of Skye is one of the Western Isles."

"So some say," said Scatha. "Robert the Bruce surely believed it, for it was on this island that he rescued the Stone from Balor's clutches and hid the Stone again, and here it has remained ever since, not in your reality but here in the Otherworld."

"You've had it all along?" said Colly. "You let us risk our lives when you knew what we were looking for was a fake? The Shandyman gave his life for the stupid ass farce you put on us! What kind of a witch are you?"

Scatha's face clouded over in fury, "I will let those comments go, because of your grief, Shifter, and the peril you and Phil found yourselves in. But it was not a pointless trip. You found out valuable information and led

Shiro Ishii to focus on your travels, giving us a bit more time to be prepared and delaying his arrival in my land."

"He's coming here?" croaked Phil. "I mean, let's just take the Stone now and go."

"It's not that simple," said Amergin.

"Indeed, not," said Scatha.

"You can't rescue it, can you?" said Jace. "It's here but you can't touch it. You said it was in captivity. How did that happen?"

"Seven hundred years ago," began Scatha, "Robert the Bruce found a cave on this island that suited his purposes for hiding the Stone of Truth. Unfortunately, it was a cave that suited others' purposes as well. Had I known he chose that particular cave, I would have forbidden it, but he went by himself with one of my ponies carrying the Stone. He chose the largest cave on the island. It descends deeply underground, even below the level of the sea. At the end of the cave there is an astonishing sight. A pool of fresh water lies beneath a mound upon which grows a Tree, bathed in the reflected light of stalagmites and stalactites that grow from the ceiling and base of the cave. Where the light comes from originally, no one knows, not even I, Scatha. The Tree is something more powerful than me, and I am not permitted in its presence. The Tree is thickly trunked but made of two substances twined together—dragon bone and oak wood."

Conor gasped, "It's the Tree of the World! But I saw it at the Crossroads in Tinker's Grove. How can it be here?"

Amergin sighed, "The Tree of the World holds up all reality. It appears wherever it is needed. It is neither good nor evil."

"Or perhaps it's both," said Jace to bewildered looks from the group. "We've had more current experience with it. The Worm that gnaws at the roots of the world, that gave birth to *Piasa*, the river demon, is as evil as evil gets. Half of the Tree is made out of discarded parts of the body of the Worm and its bones are death. But the living wood of the Tree comes from the life force of all things, and it permeates both the Otherworld and ours. Life and death intertwined. It can cast a powerful spell. I have a hunch Michael knows more about it than any of us. Touching the bones of the Tree saps one's life force, but the eternal oak part of the Tree is life always reaching upward and outward, spreading fruitfulness and energy wherever it goes. The Tree wars within itself, with the bones of the Worm that Gnaws the Roots of the World seeking to destroy all life."

Scatha took over from Jace. "In front of the Tree stands the Stone of Truth. Robert the Bruce placed it there, and thank the One he was a fearless man. For the Tree contended with itself for possession of the Stone. Branches and bone whipped forward to grasp the Stone of Truth, but Robert slapped his Sword upon that Stone and the *Lia Fail* cried out:

Cease for now this fruitless battle,
Death and Life together wait
Let the King decide my fate
With his judgment both must grapple.

According to Robert the Bruce, the Tree stopped fighting itself. A fragile peace was restored."

She turned her face to Conor, "You are the King Who Shall Be. The Stone's location has been my burden to bear. To never tell anyone where it was through all these long years has been terrible. It could have helped so much down through the ages. But Robert the Bruce swore me to secrecy. I could only reveal it to a promised King in times of great danger. There has always been much danger, but only one promised King. The Stone belongs to the King Who Shall Be.

"Hear me, Conor. The verses spoken by the Stone of Truth foretell conflict and war, death and destruction before there will be any peace. One or both parts of the Tree will war with you, and that will be a grave danger for you, one I might add, for which you are prepared. While you strive with the Tree, the same battle will continue throughout your world and the Otherworld, for the Tree is everywhere and everywhere it touches reflects its struggle."

Phil said, "Why would the Tree of the World want the Stone?"

"Excellent question," said Amergin. "The Stone has real power. It must tell the truth about anyone who comes near it, much less sits upon it. If it accepts the man as King, then it gifts that King with the steadfastness and courage to make right decisions all his reign if he but listens to his conscience. The Tree perceives that whichever part of that Tree possesses the Stone will be victorious over the other. Hence the conflict. Each will try to influence Conor's decision."

"Why can't I just go in to snatch the Stone?" said Conor.

"Because," said Scatha, "the Tree will not let you take it without a decision to be for the Light or for the Dark."

Conor laughed, "That's easy then. I choose the Light."

"It will not be that simple," said Fr. Greavy. "Whoever approaches the Tree sees things, of one's life, of what is to be, of things that are past. Then, the person is offered a gift. In your case, Conor, it will be the Stone."

"I won't have to fight? It will just give it to me?"

"Not exactly," said Greavy. "You will make a choice based on what it shows you, and the choice is never easy."

"I said I would choose the Light," Conor said between clenched teeth.

"I am so sorry, Conor," said the priest, "Sorry for the second time this evening. You will choose what you think best at that moment, and it may be for the Light or for the Dark. Either way, the Tree will rejoice. You will feel it to be the right decision and at peace with yourself. But you walk in two worlds, the reality most of these friends of yours come from, and the Otherworld—both realities seeking to merge again with one another. Your choice will help determine whether good or evil shall dwell at the heart of the merger.

"If your choice rests with the part of the Tree made up of the Worm, then evil wins a dramatic victory and you will call it good. You will believe till the end of your days that you made the right decision. But if you choose Life, the living part of the Tree—well, even then, good will not triumph. You will merely give it a fighting chance, for Balor and Shiro Ishii will try to wrest the Stone from you and complete what you could not finish. No matter your decision, all roads for you will end in sorrow. Choose the death tainted part of the Tree and the Dark wins with you as its ally. Chose the living part of the Tree and you buy yourself some time to battle Balor later."

"What's so wrong with that?" said Conor in a quiet voice.

"Because in the battle with Balor and his allies, all will not survive. And in your fight with the One-Eyed demon, you may not survive. The Dark may win still. You see, the Tree has one more surprise. It is guarded by the cu sidhe."

"What is that?" said Conor.

"'They', not 'that'. The *cu sidhe* are the original hell hounds, monstrous, dog-like things with dark green fur and bodies the size of a horse. Troubles and Colly, in his wolf form, would barely match them in size. They are the last line of defense for the Tree, if it is unhappy with your choice."

"So, the deck is stacked," said Jace. "Doesn't seem very fair. I take it we get no help?"

"All of us here," said Scatha, "are the help the One gives to this fight. It is within us to win."

Lettie blew a prodigious smoke ring into the air. "But also within us to lose. I know how this goes. Seen it too many times. The long twilight struggle. We win a few—we who fight for the One—but the march toward darkness goes on. The odds are against us. We don't usually win."

"The stakes are very high," said Amergin. "To choose Life and Light as Conor wishes is to walk a road of sorrow. The only thing promised is that, for those who survive, peace waits at the end. But be warned. The road to darkness is not without a destination. It too is a road of sorrow, and its ending is despair. We approach the final conflict, both realities do, and losing this time will be catastrophic."

"Enough," said Scatha. "Tomorrow is already here. Sleep now, and what will be shall be. Conor must be accompanied by all of us to the cave. We will assist as needed, but this part is his battle alone. The Tree recognizes he was crowned tonight, but this test before the Tree is part of the ceremony. The Stone of Truth will not cry out the new King's reign until the test is completed. Now go to your rooms. I will awake you when the sun rises."

TO SLEEP, PERCHANCE TO DREAM

Tuesday Evening, 11/9, Isle of Skye, Scotland

THE SKYE BRIDGE was a brilliant addition to the island's attempt to be a tourist draw. It connected the mainland to this largest of the Hebrides. Important as it was, something older beneath its span held a greater claim for the future of the Isle of Skye. A pile of stones lay on the Skye shore under the pylons holding up the bridge. Conveniently forgotten by the bridge's builders, the roots of those rocks reached deep into the earth. The stones were the remnants of an ancient portal which could, when used properly, send someone from this reality to the Skye that existed in the Otherworld.

The Morrigan knew this well. There was a day when she ran the hills of the Otherworld Skye rejoicing in its beauty, knowing that was as close as she would ever get to the Summer Country. She was at the portal as the sun was setting Tuesday evening. She was waiting, and not for long. Her keen sight saw the Mercedes on the other side of the water, creeping forward to pay the toll. She watched it trundle over the bridge and park in the small car park. People gathered there looking at the horizon. Sunsets here were spectacular and tourists often stopped to witness the evening glory.

Not this person. He got out of the car, climbed over the abutment, and started down the gentle slope. The Morrigan sat by the stones in her crone form, blending nicely in with her grey rags and oily white hair. She didn't even look at him. It was enough just to hear the man slip and stumble on the scree that mounded by the water's edge.

The man came to the pile of stones and didn't even notice her. He walked around the mound, trying to figure out how the old portal tomb originally faced. Deep in concentration, he started when he heard her voice.

"Shiro Ishii," her voice scraped, "what brings you to this place of the dead?"

He glanced around until he finally saw her, tucked with her back up against a large rock. "You!" he said, "you must be the Morrigan. I've heard so much, but we've never actually met. You were waiting for me."

"Yes," she hissed coyly, like a senile old woman with a supposed secret. "I knew you would come. Balor had to tell you of this portal. It is the only way for someone like you to reach the Otherworld version of Skye." Her lips moved in a circle as she mashed her gums together. He could barely understand her.

"It's a tomb portal," said Ishii. "The dead used to be buried at the entrance so their spirits could exit the other side."

"Precisely," said the Morrigan, smacking her lips. "And it was but a mere hike to cross Skye and reach the Summer Country, the ultimate goal of the dead. Fortunate were the ones who made it this far."

"That's what Balor said."

"Did he also tell you that one has to be dead to be transferred through this portal to the Otherworld?" The Morrigan cackled with the sound of challenge.

"Ah," said Ishii, "that's why you're here, to make sure I'm dead enough to travel."

"Well, since you put it that way," said the crone, and she leapt up morphing into the battle maiden, hair now lustrous red and flowing, a bone knife in her hand. "I cannot let you pass and cause mischief to my Champion and Conor, his best friend."

Ishii laughed, "You are so mistaken, you worthless excuse for a goddess. I don't have to be dead to pass here. I am no ordinary human, and you shall not be able to stop me. I serve no master in this land, but only my Emperor. Balor and I have similar agendas, but he does not rule me. I have magic of my own, enough to see me through and you dead at my feet."

The Morrigan's blue eyes flashed and she lunged for him, but Ishii had his katana out in a moment and blocked her slashing swing. She was relentless and swift, parrying, cutting, swiping, and stabbing. The Morrigan landed a few superficial blows, blooding the wizard, but he only laughed the louder. It was over in less than a minute. The Morrigan leapt forward punching Ishii in the face and sweeping the knife up toward his abdomen. But the knife never made it. Ishii took the punch but with his katana he stabbed her in the heart.

She slumped onto his shoulder, her head lolling against his left ear. Gasping she whispered, "Nicely played, wizard. I have not been outfought in millennia." Then she slid off the Sword onto the scree where she moved no more. Ishii looked down at her with contempt, stepped over her body to the collapsed portal. It only looked ruined. Balor had told him how to activate it. He said the words, a faint blue light shone, and he stepped forward into the stone and vanished.

Minutes passed and the Morrigan moaned. She sat up and looked at the blood dripping from her chest. "My best dress," she said. "Ruined!"

She looked at the deep wound, then tossed her head of lustrous red hair and laughing, said, "Good thing I do not have a heart; I would be in real trouble."

She morphed into her crow form, and, dripping blood flew directly into the portal tomb and vanished in a flash of blue light.

Ishii walked out the Skye side of the portal tomb into the evening twilight at the foot of the Black Cuillin mountains. He was not pleased. "Really?" he exclaimed, "They couldn't have built this thing on the other side of the mountains? Idiots. Stupid, Celtic idiots. Now I have to navigate these hills and find Conor Archer."

Ishii could not shapeshift. That was not one of the powers his Emperor had given him in that special elixir he quaffed so long ago. But he did have the ability to lessen his mass which made it easy for him to jump and run and most especially, climb. What would have taken a full day, now took him a mere hour and much less effort. Still, he was angry at the delay, and as he climbed his mood worsened.

He reached *Dun Scaitha* after sunset just as the festivities began. Hiding himself in the low foothills under *Sgurr Alisdair,* the highest peak on the island, he watched and pondered. He saw Conor crowned by the Morrigan and couldn't imagine how she had lived through his Sword thrust, much less without a stain of blood on her dress. There was much magic in her and in all the people down below around the fortress. He could feel it. He had never seen so many of the denizens of *faerie* gathered together and was impressed with the *Tuatha de Danaan* and the other fascinating creatures he beheld.

There was power in the stately human-like *sidhe* and he lusted to have some of it. It was different than his and would be a good addition to his talents. All he needed was a blood sacrifice, and he could absorb that power within himself. Balor had shown him how to do so countless times with the lesser *fae*. To actually take within himself the power of the rare *Tuatha de Danaan* would be a marvelous addition. And the night was still young.

None the less, that was not his main task. He returned to observing Conor and noticed that his crown was missing something in the center. That wretched jewel the Changeling boy and freaky girl had stolen from Edinburgh Castle must belong to that crown, but for some reason, they had not given it to Conor. Balor had talked about the jewel quickening Conor's kingship and personal power. Shiro Ishii laughed at the sham king down in the piazza. He may be crowned but he could not rule until that jewel worked in tandem with the Stone of Truth to inaugurate his kingship.

The Stone! thought Ishii. Where was that? Fruitlessly, he searched the gathering but it was nowhere to be seen. Perhaps it hadn't been located yet. It was too late for Conor to journey tonight. As he was pondering the problem, he saw the side of a hill not far away slide open and a mist pour out to gather around the fortress proper. From the opening in the hill, marched the friends of Conor through this portal, obviously one Balor did not know about nor make Ishii aware.

Surprisingly, Ishii felt relieved. They were all together now, all that mattered, and he could dispatch them at his leisure. He felt fairly certain that they would search for the Stone in the morning, so he settled himself for the night in the cleft of a rock to await the dawn.

His rest was short-lived however. Laughter, near him, startled him out of his dozing. *Tuatha de Danaan!* He heard their musical voices almost upon him. He cast a glamour of invisibility, hoping they would not be able to pierce its veil. He saw them then. Three beautiful people in long flowing robes, moving swiftly upon the rocks, chattering exuberantly. Even the *fae* folk could imbibe too much, thought Ishii.

He thought them gone, but his ears picked up a straggler—a tall older male, moving more slowly, also inebriated. It was Ishii's chance. Casting off the cloak of invisibility, he rushed toward the figure. The old one saw him immediately, and with a fierce cry made ready to meet the onrushing wizard. Ishii slammed into him hard, throwing them both to the rocky ground. The wizard took out his katana and slashed the *fae's* neck. Deep blue blood, almost black in the dark, flowed swiftly out and Ishii plunged his face into the spurting artery. He knew what to do. He swallowed thrice and then stood up, wiping his mouth on his sleeve. The *fae* silently bled out, and when the flow stopped, the body caved in upon itself and turned to dust. Even the blood on the ground dried and flaked away.

Ishii noted that with surprise but was much more preoccupied with the change inside of himself. His vision cleared. He could see perfectly in the dark. And hear? His hearing was vastly improved. Of the guests who remained, he could pick out some of their conversations. He even heard and understood the voices of Conor and his friends until they moved inside. The gift of the *Tuatha de Danaan* was the gift of awareness, and for that, Ishii was grateful for the *fae's* sacrifice. He settled back into the cleft of the rock, to await the dawning day.

***

Just as Conor was taking off his tunic, a knock came at his door. Opening it, he found Jace ready to knock again.

"Sorry for bothering you," said Jace, "but my room isn't ready yet. Some short little girl with dragonfly wings and a tall butler looking guy in green were bringing in towels and stuff. Thought I'd see what you were up to."

"Come on in," smiled Conor. "It's great to see you again, Jace."

"Man, it's only been a day or two."

"Not for me, it hasn't," said Conor. "It's been years."

"I'm having trouble wrapping my head around that," said Jace. "I mean, I can tell Scatha must have a great gym somewhere in this place. You look ripped, and the beard thingy doesn't look so bad. Just tell me you're okay."

"I'm more than okay. What I've gone through here has been amazing. I know I'll never be as smart as you, but I think I could fight you now and even win." Conor grinned hugely at his friend.

"Dream on. No matter how well she taught you to fight, I'll still Bruce Lee you all over the mat. I'm the Champion, you know. Or hasn't the Morrigan informed you in a while?"

"That was one good thing about the last five years. I didn't have to see her."

"Lucky you. She sticks to me like glue. I think she wants me for my mind."

"Ah ... no," said Conor laughing. "I remember how she looks at you. Your mind is the farthest thing from her thoughts."

"Seriously, though," said Jace. "how can I help tomorrow?"

"I don't know. Scatha could have shown me the cave anytime but she kept it secret. I confronted her on that earlier. She actually seemed sorry but said that, had I known, I would have done something stupid like lay siege to that cave right away. She was probably right, so I gave her the benefit of the doubt."

"Speaking of Scatha," said Jace.

"It's nothing," said Conor swiftly. "There's nothing between us. Hasn't been and never will be."

"Right," said Jace. "You're just saying that because you think I'd be pissed if you liked her—because of Beth and all. And I would be ticked, if it had been just a day. But it hasn't. For you, it's been five years, and I'm fine with that. All this just amazes me. Geez, it's like you've graduated from college and everything, and I've not even gotten you a present."

Conor smiled, "It's okay. You're here. All I know, is that I can't succeed in bringing worlds together—however that's supposed to be done—without you. Tomorrow, I want you by my side. Whatever we face won't be easy, and whatever it is, I want us to face it together."

"Sort of 'all for one and one for all'," said Jace. "By the way, did you learn to sing better these past five years? I heard Amergin was teaching you and now you might be able to carry a tune."

Conor punched him in the shoulder, but just as he was about to usher Jace out of the room, they heard a barking howl from somewhere deep in the mountains. Rushing to an open window, they peered into the darkness.

"What was that?" said Conor.

"Remember what Scatha said, about the final defense the Tree of the World possesses?"

"You mean the *cu sidhe*?"

"Yeah," said Jace. "The feral hell-hounds. The legend says that they are silent hunters. They will bark or howl three times. Once, to warn their prey to flee. Twice, to let their prey know they are coming. And on the third howl, to let their prey know that death approaches."

"So," said Conor, "this is their only real warning. Still want to come with me in the morning?"

"Wouldn't miss it," said Jace, as he walked out the door, headed for his own room.

IN THE CAVE OF
THE TREE OF THE WORLD

Morning, Otherworld Time, Isle of Skye, Scotland

SCATHA SERVED UP a breakfast spread that would be the envy of any guest in a five-star hotel. The sun was barely breaking over the horizon when they all sat down to eat. Even though they had slept only a few hours, those few hours in the Otherworld had totally refreshed them.

When they were finished, Conor said, "Scatha's going to lead the way. She says it's not far, and we'll follow. When we get to the cave, I'm taking Jace in, Troubles too, and no one else." Protests erupted but Conor was firm. "I can't risk all of you. If something bad happens in there, you will at least be left to do what you can to stop Balor and Shiro Ishii."

No one had an answer to that. Silently, they got up from the table and walked out into the morning dawn. At the end of the loch, they stopped and looked at the view before them. A wide slope descended gradually down to the *machair* and the beach. Scatha pointed out that once down on the *machair*, they would be taking a right, going north/northwest toward the cave.

It turned out to be a two-hour hike. The ocean was always to their left and near the end of their journey they came down upon the beach. As the sandy beach disappeared into flat slates of rock, the ocean waves became higher and footing more slippery.

"There," said Scatha. "Around that outcrop, there will be an opening. We are here at low tide and it is only now that the opening is accessible from land. Go. We will wait as long as it takes, but remember, at high tide, you will not be able to come back. You will have to wait. Do not worry about us. We shall keep vigil and let no one accost you unawares."

There were no real goodbyes, but a sudden set of howls and barks broke the uncomfortable silence.

"There they go again," said Jace.

"You heard the *cu sidhe* last night, then?" said Scatha.

"That we did," said Conor. "Now we know they meant their warning."

"They are fell beasts," said Scatha. "We can stop them if they approach this way, but I fear they will find another entrance to the cave."

"That's why Jace and I are taking Troubles along. Nothing will get past him." Conor ruffled the fur around the dog's throat while Troubles glared up into the hills, growling a challenge.

Without another word, Conor, Jace and the huge dog turned and marched up what remained of the beach and onto the rocks, disappearing around a tall pillar that blocked the view forward.

Their first sight of the cave was anti-climactic. There was a small entrance with water lapping near it. Conor found it hard to believe that much could be hidden within, but he sighed and went forward. He was happy to have his staff with him because the rocks were slippery. Jace, however, was having no problem walking. Neither was Troubles, who bounded in and out of the water, clearly in Labrador heaven.

"Guess Scatha didn't teach you much about balance," laughed Jace looking at Conor. "Just slip-slidin' away."

Conor glanced back and frowned, "Laugh all you want huge man. It's your weight that keeps the waves from making you lose your footing. Don't forget, I can swim like a seal—no wait, I am a seal. You, on the other hand, will sink like a stone if the water gets deeper."

Jace just laughed again as the three entered the cave. Surprisingly, they had to angle upward for about a hundred feet.

"Now we know how the cave escapes flooding," said Conor. When they got to the edge of the rise, a downward slope began. As they stepped forward, sections of the cave wall began to glow. "Those are geodes," said Conor. "Scatha told me they'd give us enough light to see by."

"Let's hope they are charged up for the next few hours," said Jace. "I'd hate to have to navigate this place in the dark."

They walked for what seemed like an hour, always heading gradually downward. The cave was unremarkable. Just a passage so far, free of damp and any of those stalagmites that would make their transit difficult.

All that changed when the passage leveled off. Suddenly the ceiling, never more than ten to fifteen feet high, soared upward, followed by geodes sparking into light. Once the ceiling, almost a hundred feet in height, was illuminated, Conor and Jace gasped in wonder. Colored stalactites hung from the roof of the cave, sparkling in the light from the geodes. And from the floor, stalagmites rose up like alabaster traffic cones. To Conor and Jace, the 'mites' and 'tites' made the cavern look like a mineral forest, beautiful but alien. Troubles licked one of the stalagmites and shook his head at the alkaline taste. Surprisingly, the floor was not really wet. True, the stalactites did drip occasionally, but not that often.

"I can't even begin to guess how many thousands of years it took to create this," said Jace.

"Great," said Conor. "Jeopardy Man has run out of questions for the answers in front of us. Let's get through this and find the Tree."

The huge cavern ended in an arch and as they walked through the passage they descended yet again, though not for long. As it leveled out, they found themselves in another hall, this time free of any mineral encrustations.

"Someone has been here, long ago by the looks of it, and cleared out all the hanging stuff," said Jace. "But I smell water."

"Spoken like a true river rat. I knew I brought you along for a reason." Conor hiked ahead and then stopped suddenly.

By now, they were used to the geodes lighting their way before them, but this time, the lights revealed a small lake with an island in the middle. The water was still as glass, not a ripple on its surface. As the illumination grew, they saw the Stone of Truth standing at the edge of the water. Behind it, looming around it and far above was the Tree of the World. A most unusual tree. Half of it was alive, a flourishing oak, thought Jace. The other half was bone white and dead. But the parts were intertwined together in a very visual demonstration of life and death entwined with good and evil contending.

Conor and Jace stood looking at the forbidding Tree, until Conor whispered, "I hung on that Tree, Jace. Drake crucified me there. It sounds crazy, but it's the same Tree. I feel it."

"I know," said Jace in a low voice, his hand on Conor's shoulder. "Don't let it freak you out. We're just going to get the Stone."

Suddenly, the Tree began to writhe and as the living and dead parts scraped each other, a high-pitched wail was heard. It pierced into the minds of the two young men, and they found themselves flat on the ground in front of the lake. Troubles howled in pain and rolled around on the barren dirt.

"O God," yelled Jace, hands over his ears, "my head feels like it will burst." Just as he finished saying that, he went completely still.

"Jace!" yelled Conor, scrambling over to him. He could barely see his friend, so blinding was the sound in his mind. He managed to drag himself over to Jace's body and cover his friend's head with his arms hoping that would shield Jace enough from whatever the sound was doing to him. Troubles tried to reach the two, but collapsed just a foot away.

The sound grew ever louder. As Conor lost consciousness, all he could think of was that he failed before he even got started.

SPLINTERS FROM THE TREE OF THE WORLD

Morning To Afternoon, Otherworld Time, Isle of Skye

CONOR DIDN'T KNOW how long he'd been out, but when he came to, he had fallen over Jace's unmoving body. Getting up on his knees he peered down at his friend, looking for injuries. Dried blood encrusted Jace's ears and nose, but at least he was breathing. Out like a light, though. Troubles was unconscious beside him but breathing normally. No visible damage to him.

Conor got up and looked across the water at the Tree. No sound was coming from it and its branches were not moving. Making Jace as comfortable as possible and checking to make sure the dog was okay, Conor took out a little leather pouch that Scatha had given him earlier in the morning. It contained some of the same dust that Ita had used to reveal the *faerie* track across the sea. He threw some onto the water, and sure enough, a golden, sparkling path whisked its way across the lake to the island. Tentatively, he stepped onto it and it held his weight well enough. He turned and looked at his companions, saying, "Got to go over there, guys. I think you'll be okay, but you know I have to do this."

It took only a couple of minutes to reach the island. He walked over to the Stone of Truth and touched it with one webbed hand. He could feel it vibrating. Wondering whether the sound had come from it, rather than the Tree, he put his ear to the Stone. Hearing the same resonance as before, though at a much lower volume, he still stepped back in wonder. It was harshly metallic sounding, and he remembered that Scatha had told him the Stone had originally come from the stars, perhaps even from the Hand of God nebula that still hung in the heavens over Ireland and Skye. A meteorite, he thought. Otherworldly, too. No wonder it had some unusual powers. If it was the source of the sound that had knocked them unconscious, then it must have been a warning about the writhing of the Tree.

Conor approached the Tree with trepidation. After all, he had hung on it for what like seemed forever when it had masqueraded as the Crossroads Oak back in Tinker's Grove. He could almost feel the binding on his one wrist, the nail in the other, and his side ached where Drake had plunged in the dagger. No, this Tree was not his friend.

Stretching out his hand he touched the live oak part and was immediately rewarded with a splinter in the center of his palm.

"Crap!" he exclaimed. "Stupid ass Tree just can't stop hurting me." He pulled the wood out and, without thinking, laid his palm on the nearest patch of bone that wound around the live oak. Just as promptly, he was rewarded with a bone splinter in the center of the same hand. Plucking it out, he was amazed at the amount of blood the two small splinters had caused. He wiped the blood on his jeans and absently leaned his palm just where the bone and oak twined together in the center of the Tree. He felt a slight suction on his hand. Then he realized the awful truth—the Tree was absorbing his blood.

Feeling the Tree move again, he jumped back, looking at his hand. It was smeared with blood and a bloody print remained in the center of the Tree, half the handprint on bone, half on live wood. And still the Tree was moving, writhing again as the Stone of Truth began its wailing once more.

"Enough!" cried Conor, slapping his palm once again on the twisting Tree. Movement stopped and wailing ceased. He touched his nose and wiped away the drops of blood that fell from it. He thought to himself the damn island was going to kill both him and Jace.

Suddenly he shivered. Something was very wrong. He tried to move his hand on the Tree, but it was stuck tight. In fact, he was being pulled into the very trunk of the Tree. Not able to wrench it free, he looked back across the water and saw Jace sitting up, Troubles at his side. Stretching out his other hand, he yelled for help, just as his entire body was pulled within the Tree of the World.

Conor was on the island one moment, and then he was not. He found himself in some dark twilit room which he quickly realized was inside the Tree itself. Half the circular room had walls of wood; half had walls of polished bone. A geode embedded in the floor emitted what light there was and behind it, on some sort of thronelike chair sat a figure.

As Conor's eyes grew used to the dim scene, he could see the figure more clearly. It was staring at him and it blinked. That's how Conor knew it was alive. But he had never seen such a strange person.

The figure looked carved out of both bone and oak twisted together but forming the entire body. Not only that, but the body was clothed as well, though the clothing looked molded to the skin and was the same peculiar mix of supple bone and wood.

Then Conor gasped. He recognized those clothes—biker gear. My God, he thought, it was Rory. But last he saw him, Rory was prone on the Wisconsin River beach, neck slashed by Dr. Drake and dissolving into mist.

"It's me, nephew," rasped a voice. "You have guessed correctly. What was it that convinced you? My stylish biker look or the slit in my throat where the wretched doctor sliced me with Piasa's scale?"

"Clothes, I think," whispered Conor automatically. But his eyes were drawn now to the slashed neck still leaking fluid.

"Rory, is it really you?" he asked. "I know it's hard to kill the *Roan* but you dissolved away to mist."

The figure smiled, those even white pointed teeth looking mighty familiar to Conor, making the hand bitten by Rory ache with the memory.

"Oh, it's me little nephew. And I knew you would come."

"What are you doing here?"

"I'm a prince, am I not?" said Rory, stepping up off his throne. "Now, I finally have a kingdom to govern, though there's not many live folks here with me. Damn, I could use a beer!"

He began to move around the geode and Conor matched his every step as they walked around in a circle.

"Don't trust me lad?" said Rory.

"I've never trusted you," said Conor. "You brought a lot of pain and confusion into my life."

"But look at you," smiled Rory, "all grown up now. That Scatha who rules outside of this cave where my … kingdom … dwells, has been educating you hasn't she? More ways than one, maybe?" He smiled a lascivious grin.

"Always a smutty bastard, aren't you Rory?"

"Well, shade though I may be, I do still get the itch now and then."

"You look real enough to me," said Conor, still matching Rory step for step.

"Only here, I'm afraid. Only real inside the Tree of the World. Outside of the cave, I would just mist away, like I did when Drake slit my throat. You seem afraid of me. Don't like my avant-garde look? Bone and wood, it's all the rage here under the shade of the Tree."

"What are you now, Rory?" asked Conor. "What have you become?"

"Nothing good; nothing bad," he said. "I'm the living, breathing voice of the Tree of the World. Do you know how I claimed this kingdom? Of course, you wonder." Rory jumped a little closer to Conor. "I'm just like the Tree, such a mixture of good and bad. Isn't that right, little nephew? I hurt you; I help you. I piss you off; I save your life. I show you wonders I take your choices away. I know you don't really hate me. You'd like to trust; but I ruin that trust every time. Just like the Tree of the World. Just like reality as you find it in your world and in the Otherworld."

"What do you want of me?"

"I want to make sure you are ready," said Rory. "The Tree wants to make sure you are ready."

"For what?" said Conor, suspicion dripping from his voice.

"To be King. King of the People of the Sea. King of the *Tuatha de Danaan*, what remains of them. King of the World, though what that would look like remains to be seen."

"They crowned me last night," said Conor. "Outside Scatha's fortress. Sorry you missed it."

"I miss nothing," snarled Rory suddenly. "The Tree sees everything and shows me. Did you take a close look at your crown? Didn't you notice it was lacking something?"

Puzzlement crept over Conor's face. "What do you mean?"

"Right in the center, where the circlet mounds up into the shape of a Celtic Cross. Right in the center of the circle where the Cross beams connect there is a space."

"For what?" said Conor.

"Indeed, for what?" answered Rory. "Something is to rest there. A symbol of your power, a catalyst for your abilities, something without which you will only reign but never rule."

"Something that Phil and Colly found in Edinburgh," said Conor with finality. "They mentioned they had found something besides a fake Stone of Truth, but with things so busy, we never got to talk much about it. Must be a jewel, because they said it was part of the Honors of Scotland."

"Perceptive little kinglet," said Rory. "But just knowing about it won't help you much. You have to possess it and know how to use it. I can show you how. Then, of course, there is the Stone of Truth. You have to learn how to use that too. The Tree can show you how. For a price."

"I'm not selling you or this overgrown bush anything," said Conor. "I'll not be taken in by you or it again."

"Not even for the life of your friend?"

"Jace?" said Conor. "What do you mean? I saw him sitting up on the beach."

"Only briefly, I'm afraid. The sound you heard from the Stone affected him more deeply than you. He has a brain bleed now. What do you call it in your reality—an aneurysm? He'll die unless you let me teach you how to use the Stone. Oh, and you have to give your allegiance to the Tree of the World."

And if I don't?

"Jace dies."

"Why do you do this, Rory?" screamed Conor. "He's done nothing to you. His sister was killed by Caithness McNabb's wretched sons and Drake did nothing to save her. No, he crucified me on this Tree; stabbed me in the side with a dagger, made from this Tree. I couldn't even rescue her. Now, the Tree is going to kill her brother. Why? For what purpose?"

Rory began to laugh. "Naïve little nephew. Tiny little fool. The Tree could care less about Jace but cares deeply what he means to you. It judges rightly that you value your kingship very little, but his friendship highly. That's a wrong placement of values, in the Tree's opinion. But it needs you as King, and needs your loyalty. It knows it can only get that commitment if it threatens to take from you something of more value. Hence Jace and his brain bleed. Get it? Got it? Good!"

Rory stopped for a moment and cocked his head, like he was listening. "Grand," he said. "Don't keep your part of the bargain, the Tree gets Jace, dead of course, and I get the dog—always wanted a pet. That's the deal. Conor, you are less stupid than before. Time on the Otherworldly version of the Isle of Skye has served you well. So, what's it going to be? Loyalty and power beyond imagining? Or a friend's death and me getting a rescue dog?"

"You are as perverse as always, Rory." Conor clenched his fists and raged impotently inside himself. But wait, he thought. Did his uncle just wink at him? No, it couldn't be. Rory's face was as smirky as ever. He had to have imagined it.

"I don't have a choice," said Conor. "I'll not have Jace die for me too. And I sure as hell won't let you have my dog. It's been a while, Rory. I'm not the little kid I was when you first met me."

"Good man," said Rory, finally close enough to put his arm around Conor's shoulder. "Let's get started then. Sooner to work, faster to rest. That's what I always say. This won't take long. It's a mind thing, lad. Scatha's and Amergin's training will have helped you far along the way. I'll just put in the finishing touches."

"No," said Conor. "Not till Jace is healed. Not till I see that he and Troubles are alright. That's the deal."

"Oh," said Rory, pinching Conor's cheek, "you truly are part of your uncle's family, so preciously tricksy. Ah, well, if that's what it takes. Let me check." Rory turned his head to the side, again as if he was listening to someone or something. "Done," he said, looking again at Conor. "Done and done!" He pointed over to a section of the room, and Conor saw a body lying on the ground. Outside of the Tree, he heard Troubles howling.

"Jace!" he cried. Rushing over, he bent to look at his friend. The blood had been washed away, and Jace's breathing was normal. "How do I know he's healed?"

"Trust me," said Rory and held his hand up for silence as Conor began to reply. "Seriously, you have to trust me." Conor could swear Rory winked at him again.

"All right," said Conor, "but he lives no matter what. Even if I fail at whatever you are trying to teach me. I'll keep the bargain, but my failure is not his death sentence."

"Deal," said Rory, "but you will not fail. You are the King Who Shall Be."

Later, when Conor reflected on what happened, it seemed so simple. All Rory did was sit him on that throne-like chair and help him focus his thoughts towards a pin-point place in the upper center of his forehead, just where the middle of the circlet of gold he was crowned with last night would rest. He had no trouble focusing. Amergin had taught him well that the power of song rested not only in the singer's ability to carry a tune, but in his ability to focus the power of words towards his listeners. It was in a real way 'throwing his voice'. Thinking a thought meant just moving that focus up his face, away from his mouth to the center of the forehead.

But Rory also taught him a phrase. It was said like one word but it meant, "May it be so." In Celtic it was *biodh se amhlaidh* and Rory taught him to say it as one word, "bee-uck-say-owla" and then push with his thought. He said that when the gem was in the crown it would focus the thought and channel the energy Conor possessed as the King. "Now," said Rory, "you cannot create something from nothing, so your power is limited to moving energy and shifting the shape and position of matter. That should sound familiar to you since you can already do this within your body. The gem simply allows you to free that power to affect other things. You will have to practice, and you will get stronger with its use."

"Seriously?" said Conor. "That's it? That's all there is to it? You want me now to sell my soul to this Tree for the power I already possess?"

"That was the deal."

"And if I don't take it?"

"Then Jace's brain bleed begins again."

"Asshole," said Conor.

"It's not me," said Rory, and Conor could swear he looked sorry about all of this.

"How am I supposed to pledge my loyalty to the Tree of the World?"

"The old-fashioned way," said Rory. "With blood."

"I've already bled enough on this Tree," said Conor, the rage building in him again.

"True lad, but you didn't make your blood do anything. Now you'll be shedding blood with the pledge of loyalty to the Tree and what it wishes to accomplish in time to come."

"What is it really, this Tree? It's not the One. It doesn't feel right."

Rory looked at him sympathetically. "Do you remember when Emily taught you about *neart,* the vital life-force of all creation? Another word for it is 'grace', divinely infused life-force. Take away the grace and what you have is energy without a higher purpose, an existing life-force without ethics, as it were."

"My God," said Conor, "you're getting all professorial on me."

Rory laughed, "That's me, the Harley-Davidson philosopher. But seriously, lad, the Tree is ambiguous, ambivalent, and duality personified. It is both good and bad, amoral to the extreme, capable of acts of death and life. Left to its own devices, it causes chaos, not order."

"Just like you," said Conor, already regretting the snarky comment.

"True," said Rory without a hint of apology, "a lot like me. That's why it chose me as king of this realm."

"So, I would be pledging loyalty to Chaos itself."

"In a manner of speaking, yes."

"You know I cannot do this, even for Jace. He wouldn't want me to."

"Oh, nephew of mine, you are most difficult to raise. You cost your mother her best years and now you will cost me what's left of my life. You see, I agree with you. You cannot waste yourself on Chaos."

The moment Rory said this, something changed in the room. Conor felt it first within the chair and he leapt off of it. It was morphing, twisting and twining. He could swear he saw something like a snake or a worm wrestling with a vine of feral and unhealthy green. The ends of the twisting snakelike or vine-like things met and then focused outward like two protruding eyes looking at him. An open maw appeared beneath and it spoke, "You promissssssssed, Conor Archer, and we shall make you keep your promise."

"Time to go, I think," said Rory. He clapped his hands and the body of Jace just disappeared. He pulled Conor to the section of wall where oak and bone met and like Samson of old, pried the edges apart and stood with arms cruciform holding an opening to the outside wide enough for Conor to get through.

As soon as he stepped outside, Conor turned to Rory and said, "Come on, we've got to go." For a moment it looked like Rory might take Conor's hand but then the two ends of the twining Tree struck Rory's shoulders like fangs on a viper, and Rory screamed in pain. Troubles, who had been waiting impatiently for Conor to reappear, dashed forward and grabbed Rory's leather jacket, trying to pull the biker forward. Conor stretched out his staff for Rory to grasp.

"Go," Rory cried, "I will hold bone and wood, death and life here. You cannot help me. This is my kingdom after all, and I will deal with them."

Conor doubted that. Already, he saw Rory diminish and wither. A last whispered shout from the poisoned lips of Rory, and Troubles let go and immediately set his mouth on Conor's tunic to drag him away from the Tree. The snaky vine-like appendages dragged Rory backwards and the trunk snapped shut. A scream from within was abruptly cut off.

For a moment, all was still, but then, branches swept down toward the ground as if to grab Conor and thrust him inside the Tree again. He used his staff to bat away the moving branches and backed away on all fours with Troubles till they rested by the Stone of Truth. There, Conor felt safe with the branches unable to grasp him. He saw Jace on the other side of the stone and heard him groaning as he came to consciousness.

"Jace," cried Conor, leaping over the Stone, "are you alright?"

"Yeah," I think so. "Had an awful headache but it's better now. Where've you been?"

"Inside of the Tree, with Rory," said Conor.

"That bastard Rory? Doesn't anybody stay dead anymore?"

Conor was so happy to hear his friend's voice that all he could do was hug him tightly while Troubles lavished licks on both of them.

They stood and looked at the Stone, wondering how they were going to get it back to the beach. Jace said, "How do you even use this thing?"

Conor said, "I don't know. Rory was going to show me, but we got interrupted by this Chaos Tree. That's what the Tree of the World is. Rory somehow got put as ruler of whatever realm exists inside of it, and he said the fact that it was balanced between good and evil made it a force for Chaos because there was no overarching good to control it, or evil for that matter."

"Rory's a king?" said Jace. "Figures it would be here. A Chaos King for a chaotic realm. He is just bad news."

"Yeah," said Conor, "but he planned to save me all along, and he went through with it. Maybe not so bad."

Jace grumbled and tried to lift the Stone. Surprisingly, he had no trouble. Conor tried the other end and lifted it with ease.

"Man," cried Jace, "we are a bodacious team. Pumped up and everything." Troubles barked his agreement.

The *faerie* track was still visible and they had no problem traversing the water nor carrying the Stone of Truth. They turned to look once again at the Tree of the World and it was actually shaking—Conor thought probably with a lot of anger.

Their brief rest was broken by a thunderous growling that rose screaming to a howling bark. From beneath the branches of the Tree of the World stepped three of the *cu sidhe*. The hell hounds were huge and their rank fur was a deep green as if it were covered with luminous moss. They wasted no time taking off from the island on the *faerie* track, intending to run down Conor, Jace, and Troubles on the beach.

Conor reached for the dog, but Troubles had already bounded for the track. Before he could even call off the dog, Troubles had made it onto the path and threw himself at the monstrous canines. They met in the middle of the lake. Though he was not quite as big as the feral hounds, he was amazingly more balanced. He wove in an out of them on the *faerie* track, leaping, slashing, and biting. Each time he struck, he wounded and the *cu sidhe* could not lay a fang on him. He was too fast.

Troubles was able to throw two of them into the water and they were unable, at least for the moment to climb back up on the track. He engaged the last hell hound and found himself overmatched this time. Troubles could not hope to outmuscle his opponent. On shore, Conor could see that the Labrador was tiring and sustaining painful wounds.

Then the unthinkable happened. The last *cu sidhe* managed to straddle Troubles and pin him down on the track. Conor saw the maw of the hell hound open and he knew that if the beast struck, Troubles would be fatally wounded. Without thinking, he pounded his staff on the ground, got a grip and then threw it as hard as he could. In the air, it transformed into the Spear of Destiny and sunk into the chest of the *cu sidhe*. The hell hound leapt into the air, mortally pierced and fell into the water. A snap from Troubles' jaws caught the Spear and yanked it out of the fell beast. Bleeding from superficial wounds, Troubles trotted back down the *faerie* track into the arms of a grateful Conor. Jace dragged them both back onto the beach and then used the Sword of Light to sever the path's connection to the shore. It immediately winked out of existence.

"I thought I lost you," said Conor, tears streaming into Troubles fur.

"Never, little Master," said the huge dog, turning to lick Conor's face.

"They're gone," said Jace. "The other two hell hounds must have drowned. I don't see them anywhere and they would not give up their prey willingly. Nice job, Troubles." Jace ruffled the fur on the dog, threw out his arms saying, "Whoozagoodboy!" laughing as the dog spun happily in circles.

Conor, however, was quiet and looked back at the now silent Tree of the World. He doubted he was done with it. Jace broke into his thoughts and wanted to know exactly what happened "inside that stump", so Conor related the story as they walked. Their journey took a while because the Stone, while not heavy for them, was cumbersome, but the three soon heard the waves and saw the exit back out towards the beach.

CORONATION

Evening, 'Otherworld' Time, Isle of Skye, Scotland

THEY WERE A bedraggled lot when the three of them rounded the rocky outcrop and stepped onto the sandy beach. Stopping in amazement and almost dropping the Stone of Truth, Conor and Jace stood openmouthed at what lay before them.

No empty beach awaited them. Instead, a tented pavilion surrounded by torches burning in the twilight was filled with all manner of creatures and people. They had been gone for two passages of the tide. *Roan*, seals, *Tuatha de Danaan*, farmers from the fertile plains on the other side of the island, dogs, wolves, eagles, sprites and wisps, *naiads* and *dryads*. There were many more than the evening before at *Dun Scaitha*. Scatha, herself, strode forward to welcome the adventurers.

Conor wryly said, "What would you do with all of them if we hadn't succeeded?"

She smiled broadly, "I knew you would pass whatever test the Tree of the World would place before you."

"You have no idea," muttered Jace.

Troubles woofed and plunged ahead to see the canine newcomers, while Scatha directed Jace and Conor to place the Stone of Truth in front of the stone pillar they had just circumnavigated. Her voice and directions were gathering attention, particularly when guests noted that Conor and Jace had returned.

Scatha stopped and said, "Get you over to that side tent and change those filthy clothes. Conor, we must complete what was begun last night, and Jace, your presence is mandatory as well. You both will find there what you need to wear. And use the baths that I prepared."

For Conor, it was pretty much a repeat of what he wore the previous night—a white tunic hemmed in Celtic embroidery and a crimson *brat* pinned at the shoulder with a seal brooch, trousers and boots to match. He had never taken off his gold torc.

"You've got to be kidding," said Jace. "I can't wear this stuff. They'd laugh me off the football team." He was holding up a similar tunic and a blue *brat*, to be pinned also with a seal brooch. "And what's with the plaid trousers? Although the boots are pretty cool."

Conor laughed, "When on Skye, do as the Skylanders do. And promise to tell Scatha thanks for making you look presentable."

Jace groused all through putting on the clothes.

Scatha called to come in, and Conor pulled back the tent flap. "How do we look?" he said.

She pursed her lips and looked both of them over saying, "Amazing how mature you both look in decent dress." Scatha went to the entrance of the tent and met a *Roan* carrying an ornate chest carved with a seal rampant on waves. Opening it, she first took out the circlet Crown which graced Conor's brow the previous night. With great care and dignity, she placed it on his head. It glinted gold in the candlelight. Next, in silence, she took from the chest a silver torc and snapped it around Jace's neck. He squirmed a bit with the unfamiliar metal. Next, she took a silver circlet with a blue sapphire shining in the center. She walked over to Jace and lifted up her arms to place it on his head.

"What's this?" he said rather sternly grasping her hand.

She looked him in the eyes and said, "You are the Champion, the one who sits at the right hand of the King. He will need you in times to come as he has in times past. Will you not accept your destiny?"

Conor looked over at Jace and grinned, "Will you not?"

"Oh, all right," said Jace, "but only because I promised Abbot Malachy I wouldn't let you get in trouble by yourself."

Scatha placed the silver circlet on his head. "Not bad," said Conor. "Actually, you look pretty cool, Jace."

"At least I have a sapphire to break up all that silver," he said.

"I have a feeling," said Conor, "that the missing part of this gold circlet is what tonight is all about, right Scatha?"

She nodded her head. "Correct, Conor. Your crowning last night began your reign as King Over Land and Under Sea, but the jewel missing from your gold circlet must be joined with the crown in order for you to rule. You are not only a symbol, you are the power that will join this Otherworld with the world of your birth."

"That's what Colly and Phil brought back from Edinburgh," said Jace, "and I've got a feeling the crown jewels of Scotland are missing a gem."

"Right enough," said Colly entering the tent. "Well, will you look at that. The both of you, all King Arthured up and everything. All the females," and here Colly cocked his head back towards the pavilion, "of whatever species, are going to find the both of you very fetching."

Scatha lightly smacked his cheek saying, "Hercules Columba Roddy, go get yourself cleaned up and muster the rest of the group. They will be in the front when Conor inaugurates the Stone of Truth."

After Colly departed, Conor suddenly got serious and said to Scatha, "I don't mean to make light of this. Just nervous is all. You've spent so much time preparing for this moment—years in fact. I only hope I don't disappoint all those who are putting so much faith in me. It's not that I don't feel ready. Five years of prep is enough, I think. It's just that perhaps I'll fall short of accomplishing the task that's been given to me because what you all really need maybe isn't in me."

Before Scatha could say anything, Jace turned to his friend. "Conor, listen to me. We've only known each other for half a year—at least in our time. But one thing I've gotten to know about you is this: there is a depth and fullness in you that I've never seen in a person. You've got your quirks and God knows you have your failings, but all your strengths, the blessed talent that is just in you, makes up for anything you might lack. I used to be just a football player, now I'm an amazingly smart football player, so I think you have to trust me on this one. You're the man for this. As Scatha keeps saying, 'You are the King Who Shall Be.' Now let's get out there and make you the King Who Is."

Scatha smiled and had Conor on her right and Jace on her left as they exited the tent. This time all eyes were focused on them and the crowd erupted in a mighty cheer.

Conor stood in front of the Stone of Truth; Jace at his right hand. Scatha turned to the crowd and said, "Before you stand they who fight the Dark. Personified by Balor and those who serve him, the Dark seeks to corrupt the realities that bind us together. The world of Conor Archer and Jason Michaels seeks to reunite with our world, known to lesser beings"—and here she winked at Conor and Jace—"as the Otherworld. For those of the Light to prevail, we must have a King. Conor Archer is that man—three times pierced for the sake of us all. Jason Michaels is the Champion, the right hand of the King. Together, they promise hope for all." Then Scatha spoke:

Bring forth to me the Sword of Light,
Bestowed upon this Champion Bright,
Bring forth now for all to see,
The Ancient Spear of Destiny,
Bestowed upon the King Who Shall Be.

At that moment, two *Roan* came forward, tall and noble in their grey and green dappled skin, their round eyes gazing at the two young men before them.

The *Roan* with the Sword placed it in Jace's grasp, and the *Roan* with the Spear did likewise place it in the hands of Conor. Scatha spoke again,

Armed as heroes of old are they,
Given to lead us on the way,
Forth the Light to battle Dark.

One thing more, the jewel we seek,
I call upon the Crow to speak,
And bring forth to me the ruby red.

She of the battle, she of the grave,
Washer of wounds, blood of the brave,
I call her now to say her peace.

From the dark skies above, came a cry, a bird cawing a sound of triumph, and sweeping down, it flew through the pavilion above the heads of the assembled guests and touched down as the familiar battle maiden of old, the Morrigan brave, the Morrigan bold, holding in her hand the ruby red.

Here I am, I have answered your call,
With the ruby red, the Dark's downfall,
Place it now, within the crown.

Its glamour removed, the shadow gone,
The jewel gleams, its power dawns,
Place it now within the crown.

Once done, the worlds can touch,
Merged together, gently crushed
Place it now within the crown.

So says the crow who flies above,
So says the prince in the barrow down
So says he who walks the twilight bound.

Reaching out her hand to Scatha, the Morrigan placed the jewel in her palm. The ruler of Skye turned to Conor. Reaching up she placed the ruby in its designated spot within the center of the Celtic Cross in the middle of the gold circlet.

For Conor, all went black for a moment. Then a flashing pain rippled through his head. He heard himself cry out, and sensed, rather than saw, Jace and Scatha reach for him. But he was already falling back. The joints on his knees smacked the Stone of Truth and bent. Conor sat heavily on the Stone, and then his sight gradually returned. Everyone was staring at him. The red jewel was glowing, and though Jace couldn't see it, his sapphire was shining as well.

Before Conor could speak, a tremendous boom thundered three times across the beach as lightning flashed in the west. The Celtic swirls on the pillars of the Coronation Stone flashed brightly in movement. Conor felt the skin tattoo that encircled his body begin to luminesce brightly enough to be seen through his clothing. The crowd murmured in awe, and indeed, Conor and Jace with Scatha looked incredibly impressive, but once again, three loud booms resonated across the beach as the lightning flashed closer.

It began as a slight pressure on Conor's shoulders as if invisible hands were pressing down upon him. Then from the pillars upon which the Stone sat, beams of light coursed up above Conor and it appeared to the crowd that some kind of being with wings raised up behind King and bent over him touching his shoulders in benediction.

"One of the Dominions," gasped Scatha and she knelt to honor the visiting angel.

"What does that mean?" said Conor. "I feel it, or him, or whatever it is."

"A Dominion, Conor," said Jace. "It's a member of one of the choirs of angels called Dominions who deal with justice, and order in the One's creation. It's here to bless you, all of us I think, in what we are about to do."

Everyone gathered on the beach had taken a knee, but all was not yet over. For the third time, three loud thunderclaps boomed across the beach and just off the sand, in churning waters, lightning struck three times. Human and *fae* together saw something never to be seen again. A white horse manifested out of the waves and on its back the Ranger of the Heavens, Michael the Victorious came riding. Across the whitecaps he galloped, trident in hand, wings outspread, with his shield born high engraved *Quis ut Deus*— Who is like the One. Once he arrived on shore, he dismounted and walked to Conor at the Stone of Destiny. Though he did not kneel, he deeply bowed and presented his trident to Conor saying,

In your service am I,
Ranger of the Sky,
In service to King Over Land, Under Sea.

What I can do, I shall do,
To aid you, advise you, guide you.
My presence shall always be nigh.

He touched his trident to Conor's brow and then turning, walked to the edge of the beach and mounted Brian who opened wings and whisked the angel away. No more sound from the ocean, nor lightning from the sky, and everyone present was struck silent for the longest time.

The Dominion grew brighter over Conor and a not unpleasant humming was heard that resolved itself into a beautiful chord of music. Then the Stone of Truth spoke:

> *Upon this Stone sits the King*
> *Prince to Rule; Bard to Sing*
> *He the King Over Land, Under Sea.*
>
> *Righteous One, Healer be.*
> *Merger of Worlds, Destined He.*
> *Destroyer of Dark, Peace He brings.*

Like the star-bright sun rising over the ocean, the Dominion burned more brightly, encompassing Conor until no one could look directly upon the Stone of Truth. In a flash of light and booming thunder, the angel departed and all was quiet once again.

Until Colly said, "O my gosh, Scatha, my stomach is as loud as the thunder. Do you maybe have something to eat?"

And with that the celebration began.

BALOR PURSUED

Evening, 'Otherworld' Time, Isle of Skye, Scotland

SHIRO ISHII WATCHED the coronation celebration with barely concealed contempt. It took all his personal discipline, not to march down upon the beach and behead the upstart King. Conor Archer, boy wonder, pathetic princeling. As if Balor would have to lift the lid of his eye more than a mote to wipe this pretender off the face of the earth.

Yet, Balor had been precise in his words to Ishii: "Watch only; do not engage; gather information and hasten back to me so we can respond appropriately." That was probably best, for he had seen the irritating wisp bobbing through the crowds and up the hills no doubt thinking she was some sort of guardian. But Ishii was well camouflaged with his new abilities. Sighing, he made ready to leave.

As Ishii made his way back to the portal on the other side of the Cuillin Hills, he wondered how disrupted society was back in his own reality. They had certainly given it a push toward chaos. Then, there was the unmistakable mystery of Balor's last comment to him: "On your return, I may have a new ally for you to direct and mentor, one for which you are peculiarly well-trained."

Ishii couldn't begin to guess what that was, but he was growing tired of Balor keeping back knowledge that could easily benefit the both of them. Why Balor should be in the least bit jealous of him, Ishii couldn't fathom. Unless the Emperor had gifted Ishii with magic more powerful than Balor possessed. If so, then Balor would deem the Mad Doctor of Unit 731 disposable. Just like the old movie said, "In the end, there can be only One." Ishii intended to be that One if Balor had already decided he was a hindrance rather than a help to Balor's plans.

When he reappeared at the portal, it was Friday morning November 13 in his world. He grabbed a newspaper at the car park where he left his Mercedes and was pleased with the pictures of riots in Dublin and Galway. Many deaths as well. The *Gardai* were having a hard time keeping up with all the mischief going on throughout city and countryside. No longer a slow decline into anarchy, Ireland was rapidly approaching non-governance.

The buzzing of his cell phone caught his attention, and he sat up straight in the driver's seat when he recognized a text from Sir Hugh. It seemed that the mysterious ally had come forward and Shiro Ishii began to smile as he read the details. He had a lot to think about as he headed back to Ireland.

***

Conor looked over the celebration on the beach and said to Jace, "Do you feel it?"

Jace smiled and said, "You mean that 'There's a monster in the wilderness just begging us to come and find him' type of feeling?"

"Yeah, I guess," laughed Conor.

"Balor is a genius at playing this game," said Fr. Greavy waving a drink of mead over the assembled throng. "He could have appeared here and slaughtered us all, but he wants you, Conor. You as well, Jason Michaels. You are the only two who could put a serious crimp in his plans, so he'll wait as long as it takes to flush you out. To him, the rest of us are superfluous—not worthy of his effort."

"What about Shiro Ishii?" said Phil, sitting over by the fire still burning brightly. "Where does he really fit in all of this chaos?"

"Ishii," said Fr. Greavy, "is a potent player in the merging of the worlds. He has his own agenda, I believe, but right now it is parallel with Balor's. Yet, this doctor; indeed, I think we can call him a sorcerer now that we have seen what he is capable of, is a power in his own right. We must get both. To let Ishii live to see another day, means the battle will go on. No doubt about it, though, Balor is our first concern."

"Balor wants us," said Conor, "so let's draw him out. But let's pick the battlefield. We'll come to him halfway, and then choose where we fight. Let's go to *Skellig* Michael."

"Lovely place in the autumn, I hear," said Jace. "Sounds like a plan to me."

Colly was bringing back food but overheard the proposal. "Not a bad idea. I feel the fur coat of my were-beast growing as we speak, eager to keep me warm on those wind-swept peaks." Colly laughed, "O my gosh, I'm chanting werewolf poetry."

"Well, think about it," said Conor. "*Skellig* Michael is a holy place, and we're the good guys, so that's got to count for something. We'll be highly visible there, and he can come to us. God knows what he's going to look like this time. Maybe Michael will even show up if he gets over his, 'I'd like to help but I can't intervene' mood. But this time, it's just Jace and me that will go. We've got weapons that can fight him; no one else does."

A strong "woof" from the darkness beyond the fire objected, and Phil and Fr. Greavy stood up and began talking at once. Colly dropped his food and started vigorously protesting. Lettie even deigned to pop into her human form and began arguing. Scatha noticed the disagreement and came over.

"What is the problem?" she asked. "The celebration is wonderful. Conor, you should mingle among the guests."

"I will. I promise," said Conor, "as soon as we finish this, ah, discussion. All I said was that Jace and I should be the ones to go and confront Balor on *Skellig* Michael. And we should go alone."

"I think Conor's right," said Jace. "Before we left, I had a talk with Kevin and he plans on bringing the Travelers to *Staigue* Fort to await whatever crazy plans Balor and Ishii have dreamt up for our return. Phil, Fr. Greavy and you, Scatha, with the help of the *Roan*, should aid Kevin in whatever is coming his way." Jace turned to Colly, "You've got to stay with them. Shiro Ishii isn't going to be with Balor. They'll split up. The group will need you in case he shows. Besides, you've got a beef with him; he took your arm last time."

Colly made to protest but then fell silent. Scatha didn't even speak; she simply quirked her brow in a withering stare that made Jace break eye contact. It was so apparent that Conor laughed out loud.

"No laughing matter," said Phil. "We've been with you all the way, and we're not about to desert you now."

"No weapons," said Conor, rather softly. "No training."

"I don't need weapons," said Colly. "Neither does Troubles. We are weapons."

"Do not worry, little King," said Scatha, not unkindly. "I have been training warriors for centuries and my battle hall is full of weapons that do not take much skill to handle. Besides, we each carry the most potent weapon of all. Friendship. Our actions together already show we pledge our lives to you. In this fight, martial skill is not the only thing that will help us win. Balor is evil and he seeks to isolate his enemies. The easiest way to weaken you, Conor, is to deprive you of your friends and deepen the loneliness that rests in the heart of every human."

In the end, Conor and Jace were persuasive enough to win the argument—mostly. It was decided that Lettie and Troubles would accompany Conor and Jace to *Skellig*, while Scatha and the others, along with the *Roan* would head to *Staigue* Fort to deal with whatever Ishii had planned. Not everyone was happy with the decision, but all had eventually seen the wisdom in it.

They decided they would set out in the morning, using a ship piloted by the *Roan*. Scatha motioned for Calador to come over, and the prince agreed to the plans, bowing to the King and assuring him that the *Roan* would rendezvous on the beach near *Staigue* Fort. They plotted strategy and then, Calador led Conor through the crowd to meet the people who had seen him take his throne.

"Come, Your Highness," he said, "your people wish to meet you face to face."

"What's with the 'Highness' stuff? Don't call me that," said Conor.

"But," said Calador, confusion clouding his face, "it is what you are."

"No, No, No! That's ridiculous! Really! Can't you all see that?"

Scatha came up to him and pecked him on the cheek, "Of course, Your Highness," smiling as she stepped away.

Phil and Colly bowed together, totally enjoying Conor's embarrassment. Even Troubles came forward and bent in a huge Labrador bow.

But it was Jace that smoothed things over. He went up to Conor, hugged him tightly and said, "Listen to me for once. Whether you like it or not, you're a King. Don't know how, barely understand why, but I feel it in my gut that you are not just your own person anymore. It's like being captain of a football team. You are the team's spirit, cheerleader, master planner, and most of all, leader. You don't get to decide whether people call you captain or not. They've got the right to do that. And everyone here wants you as King. So, let them call you whatever they wish. Hear me? Don't be a douchebag about it." Phil was about to say something but Jace shushed her, "I know, I'm a sexist pig too; sorry for the language but he's got to know what I mean. So, do you get it, Conor?"

Conor looked at his friends and just nodded. Then, Calador led him away.

Jace looked out over the crowd. "What about the others who are here?"

"The *Tuatha de Danaan*? The creatures of the *fae*?" said Scatha. "Their time for marching in armies is over, and they know it. They diminish, sad as it is to say. They will never truly disappear, but they keep to themselves now, and are dependent on us to win the day. So many times in the past they protected us. Now, it is our time to do the same for them. They will still police the Otherworld, but the coming battle is ours, not theirs."

TINKERS AT THE FORT

Friday, 11/13, Staigue Fort

KEVIN WORRIED HIS hangnail down to the cuticle. He was standing outside *Staigue* Fort in the afternoon, looking down the road towards Castlecove, counting the caravans as they trundled up the way. Good thing the *machair* was wide here, for hundreds of caravans were parked from the fort down to the sea.

The Flight of the Doves had brought miraculous results. After hearing the horror stories of the Travelers, Kevin was amazed that so many had been able to make the trip at all. They came from all corners of the land, but their trips were terrible.

The violence that he had seen on the roadways and the surrounding countryside just a week ago had spread throughout the country. Roving gangs of RAGERS continued to be reported everywhere. Mostly composed of the young and unemployed, the numbers were increasing as was the scale of violence. Many deaths were reported, and horror was sweeping through the populace as those who used the drug recovered from one dosage only to find out the despicable things they had perpetrated while under the influence. This only added to the despair in their souls and they quickly dosed again, adding exponentially to the disaster spreading through the land.

Riots and breakdowns in the social order throughout the cities did not abate. Adding to the fear of human violence were reports of legends coming to life. These were not the real-life appearances of heroes of old, but demons from the nightmares of humanity down through the ages. Kevin and Mary were able to decipher the descriptions from news reports and Travelers' tales, noting that the *sluagh* were abroad again, as were *kelpies, pookas, cu sidhe*, and assorted ghostly apparitions—all causing death and destruction among the populace.

Amazingly, all the Travelers and their caravans escaped the violence, but they kept their eyes and ears open. There was one rumor sweeping throughout Ireland that seemed to have its start in the northwest, near Lough

Derg, a barren lake that, according to a medieval legend, housed an entrance to the netherworld.

As best as Kevin and Mary could understand, something had arisen from the depths of those waters and now strode throughout the countryside dealing death and destruction to whomever and whatever it met. No real description had been given yet, though, like many of the other demonic manifestations, waves of fear and hysteria preceded its appearance. So powerful were these emotions in people that they often could not describe what they experienced, leading the authorities and medical personnel to surmise that some sort of mass hallucination among the people was occurring.

Kevin suspected that nothing could be further from the truth. With the passing of Amergin, his father, Kevin had somehow attained a status as a leader among the Traveler clans. That kind of leadership was not usually heredItary, but Kevin's foresight and advice in the past weeks had seemed eminently sensible to the Travelers. He was consulted more and more, which allowed him to put together the tales told and make some sense out of them.

"Mary," he said late Friday afternoon as they sat outside their caravan waiting for new arrivals, "the smart folk say there's a powerful correlation between the appearance of these so-called hallucinations and the breakdown of the social order. My Da never put much stock in what those elites said and neither do I. I think correlations are like coincidences, but I don't believe in them either.

"Something powerful, though, is happening throughout the nation. Amergin had been saying for a long time that the people had lost their tether to the land. They had become soulless."

"He was right, you know," agreed Mary. "I know what you're going to say, because I've thought about it too. A broken spirit in the heart of a person shatters the barrier that holds dark things at bay. If that happens to a whole lot of people, then the things that go bump in the night break loose and folks discover there is such a thing as hell, and its denizens are loose in the land."

"Don't forget that we have this world and the Otherworld coming together as well," said Kevin. "Unseen boundaries have been breached and these evil things have crept abroad. Mary, I think they are as real as the things we've seen these past weeks, only worse. I fear what has crawled out of the depths of that lonely lake in the northwest. You know what it is, don't you?"

"I do and neither you or I will speak its name. St. Patrick put it there a long time ago and we've heard hide nor hair of it since. The people were strong once and their faith kept it at bay. That's gone now. We still keep the old ways, but they treat us with prejudice and suspicion. While they laugh at us, they have forgotten to lock their doors and something has come creeping back that was long gone."

Kevin embraced his wife and whispered in her ear, "That's why I called all the Tinkers together. The people may despise us, but we've never forgotten. We know the Dark and what it can do, and we've kept the doors to that evil closed to our caravans and our folk. We're not and never have been saints, but we've not been eejits either. We're the last best hope for the land and those who live in it. The others have lost their minds, and darkness clouds their hearts. For some reason, we've been left untouched. I've talked to all the elders that are here so far. Tonight, we'll meet and plan. No one else is coming to help Conor and his friends but the Travelers. And there's not many of us. Better say a prayer that we'll be enough." In the pale November afternoon sunlight, they held each other close until they warmed each other's hearts.

***

It had crossed into County Kerry earlier in the day and now hunkered down in the heather near St. Finan's Bay. Feeling the call of the sea, it had ceased its predation on any life it came across. Something was beckoning it forward. It had been alone for so long, there in the depths of the lake where the being of light had driven it centuries ago. That fiery human, named Patricius, with the Cross topped staff had been relentless, chasing it the length and breadth of the land till it cornered it by the shores of Lough *Derg*. It remembered the slashing force with which the holy man had smashed it into the waters and sent it down, down, down into the rocky bottom of the lake. He had cast boulders over it, huge, heavy stones that it could not lift. He had taken away all chance of escape, banished all hope.

There it lay for centuries, bereft of any contact with things like itself. It could not feed and so slowly starved through the years, alone, with the gnawing Dark in the pit of its stomach its only companion. It was a being attuned to despair. When last it walked the earth, it had fed on fear and on the chaos so often present in the lives of humans. Its very presence deepened the violence in the land and the hatred present in human society. An elemental creature, it did not process the meaning of all this, but exploited the existence of that chaos none the less.

Now, deep in the dark waters of the lake, it began to feel that chaos again. Something was happening in the world above that it perceived as an opportunity. It could do nothing for many years but slowly regain strength. Only now, had the chaos grown swiftly stronger. It reveled in the warmth of the despair plunging into the depths of the lake. An ordered society would not fear it. Reason and faith, love and hope could pierce it as sure as an iron pike. Last time it walked abroad, there was little reason, love or hope, but there was a holy man's blinding faith, and that proved the creature's downfall.

But the holy man was gone, and it sensed that those left behind were not of his stature. So, the creature tried to move, first slightly and then with greater purpose. Stones tumbled off it, and soon it ascended from the depths to the surface of the lake and thence to the land. Terror ensued and it fed. Wherever it met a well or standing water, it spat and vomited into the liquid. Its spew was a potent collage of bacteria and disease, spoiling the waters with which it came in contact.

The creature angled south. It was large but fast on its two feet, strong but skilled in movement and stealth. Killing viciously, it disappeared swiftly from the scene, and was never more but a nightmarish blur in the eye of victim or survivor.

Through its wanderings, it heard the constant call, like a beacon piercing its vile heart. The closer it headed toward the sea, the more it could feel the pulsing signal beckoning it to come nearer. That's how it found itself finally on the shores of St. Finan's Bay. Plunging down the sloping *machair*, it stopped in front of Shiro Ishii, wearing his black duster coat, brandishing a katana in a distinct samurai pose, just in case.

"Welcome," said the doctor. "You beautiful thing. You are a living, breathing contagion. I've been waiting for you. So glad you heard my call. What my plague could not finish, you have helped restart. It is indeed an honor to meet the *Caorthannach*—so tell me dear, do you have another name or do I just address you as the Devil's Mother?"

THE *CAORTHANNACH* COMES

Friday Sunset, 11/13, Staigue Fort

"OUT WITH IT now, Kevin," shouted Eamon Joyce. The bonfire had been lit in the center of the old stone fort and all the elders were gathered inside the roofless ruin. The rest of the Travelers moved restlessly in a circle around the ancient fort, grabbing what bits of the conversation they could.

"I'm ten feet from you, cousin," said Kevin. "No need to strain those pipes of yours." The elders hummed a low laugh.

"Seems to me you used my birds and hastened us all here for a might powerful reason, though besides what you and Mary whisper about late at night, no one else seems to know. Now like I said, out with it now, or we will be taking ourselves back on the road."

Kevin sighed. He had already told Mary getting Travelers to agree to anything was going to be next to impossible, but she had assured him he was up to the task. "Listen to me, all of you. I wouldn't have called out a Gathering if it wasn't an emergency. You saw what you saw on your way down here. You know it's bad throughout the land. Folk have lost their minds. We have hours, not days, to lend a hand toward fixin' things before everything falls apart."

"Spit it out," yelled someone in the crowd. "Tell us plainly what you think is happening."

Kevin took a deep breath, prayed that his father would send a little help from the Summer Country, and began, "It's like this. First, you know as well as me that each great immigration of peoples into this land over thousands of years was traumatic. Each time it happened, though, the newcomers learned the stories and the lore hidden in the everyday around them. In our lifetime, strangers have been coming to our shores in droves, for over a generation. We've never minded because we are a land of immigrants, and everyone becomes Irish eventually, even we Travelers. But this time, it hasn't happened. The old folks lost the stories and the lore. Couldn't teach the newcomers even if they wanted to learn, which they don't. The land is sundered from the people.

"Second, that'd be just like every other country on earth, but here, it has greater consequences. The Otherworld, which everyone in Ireland used to know something about, is merging with this world. People sense something momentous is happening, but they can't name it, and nobody knows what to do. You can see it in the chaos around us—riots, loss of control, violence— you name it and I bet you've experienced it. That means good might get the upper hand, but as you've seen, there's a better than even chance that evil might win.

"Third, one man and his friends are all that stands between the Dark and the Light. I've told you all about Conor Archer and that he's good, decent, and dedicated to the Light. But he's also young, inexperienced, and only one person. He's only been here a little while, and he sure has caused a lot of problems. He has a few friends, and I'm one of them, and I think you should be his friends too. Because we Travelers aren't tainted. We believe. We know the old stories and the lore; we've kept the old ways. There's power in us yet. We've got to stand with Conor." Pain in the ass that he is, he muttered to himself.

The elders agreed, surprisingly. That brought about a huge sigh from Kevin. But just as he took a breath, wood fell in the bonfire and started up a flash of sparks into the air which seemed to have a mind of their own. They swirled for a moment and then flashed off to the walkway at top of the circular fort, coalescing into figures from of old—ancient Celts in leathered armor with fixed pikes and Swords at their sides.

Kevin knew who they were. Conor had told him what he had seen at his father's funeral. Kevin saw them now, and a quick glance showed him that everyone else could see them as well. The captain of the guard lifted his pike and pointed down at Kevin.

The ancient warrior spoke, "You sir, seem to lead here, but you cannot see what we glimpse from our post. Out on the *machair,* near the sea, two figures walk. One is a man, but he must be a sorcerer, for he walks with a monster out of legend, out of time. The *Caorthannach* walks abroad, dragging with it the pestilence of hell. It knows of your presence here and it seeks you. You have found your task. The Mother of Demons must be defeated, or the King Who Now Is will be sorely tried and most likely killed. He cannot defeat both this and Balor of the Evil Eye."

"Conor is King?" said Kevin. "Are you sure? This would be fantastic news!"

"Even now," said the chieftain, "he lands at Ballinskelligs with his friends to try to destroy the power of Balor."

"Do you hear that?" said Kevin to the elders. "Conor has come and the battle is given to us. We are the ones to defeat the *Caorthannach*—bitch that it is. Send the mothers and children to the hills, and those women and men who can fight meet me at the entrance to this fort in five minutes."

The chieftain and his men began drumming their pikes against the hollow stones of the parapet. Above the noise, the chieftain's voice was heard, "We will join you, Kevin, son of the Bard of the West, for it is this we have kept watch for these millennia. Let me tell you how to fight this thing and the sorcerer who wields the monster like a weapon."

Kevin climbed the steps to join the chieftain, and as he ascended, reality shifted as the Otherworld embraced him. The night brightened, the soldiers could be seen clearly, and Kevin's vision was so sharp that he could see down to the sea and quickly identified the two monstrosities that were marching toward them.

He turned to the east and saw the mothers and children quickly rushing toward the hills. They would be safe, at least for now. He had positioned the caravans between the sea and the fort earlier in the day, thinking instinctively, that if evil came it would come from the sea.

"What are we supposed to do?" he asked the chieftain. "Just tackle the demon and disarm the sorcerer? We have no weapons."

"But you do have magic," said the chieftain.

"Do not," said Kevin, feeling the instinctive resistance toward magic stiffen his spine.

"Why do you resist what you are? Your ancestors from the continent had no difficulty realizing the existence of magic. They used it well and for the good."

"We are Tinkers. For centuries it has been beaten out of us, if it ever existed in the first place. What little we may have had took refuge in our skills with metal. We are a nothing people, even if we have kept the old ways."

"What of your relationship with the People of the Sea?" said the chieftain. "Why do you think they have kept that connection alive?"

"I do not know, and I do not care. We only get into trouble when we associate with them. I like and support Conor and all, but he's one of them and sure enough, we make friends with him and 'poof' we are in trouble again."

"Because you are like them," said the chieftain. "Look at that thing," he said pointing at the approaching *Caorthannach*. "It is red with fire and pestilence. Let me tell you a secret and how we shall defeat it." Kevin bent his ear to the ancient one, and gasped as he listened.

Three minutes later, Kevin was rushing down the steps and out the door of the fort where he stopped and looked at his little army. Less than five hundred elders and fighters, but it would have to be enough.

The crow landed on his shoulder as he moved out of the fortress. The Morrigan whispered in his ear, "Not so weak as you thought, Tinker? You have it in you to win, but it will be a victory precious bought. You and your clan will be powerful but not powerful enough. I shall go and bring friends to help you."

Kevin barely heard her or noticed her leaving so intent was he on addressing the elders. He stepped up on a pile of stones and was assaulted with questions.

"What are we going to fight with, Kevin?" they all began to shout.

Because of what the chieftain had told him, tears were running down his face. He stifled the sobs as best he could, and though his voice broke, it carried throughout the gathered crowd.

"Travelers all," he said, "can you believe the evil that is facing us? Nobody has ever asked us to do what we have to do now. Before us approaches the greatest catastrophe this land has ever faced. Defeated once before, it roams abroad. Do you know why? Because the faith of the people is dead. The demon feeds off their despair. They stopped telling stories to their kids. They don't even bless their kids at bedtime. They died inside. And this thing out there, it lives on hopelessness and that dead, empty space in each person's heart. What's worse is that it is led like a dog on a leash by one who is not of us yet possesses great power. He would like nothing better than to see us wiped off the face of the earth. He killed my mother, your nieces and nephews, uncles and aunts, and he caused my father, the Bard of the West, to die of a broken heart."

"How can we stand?" shouted cousin Eamon. "How can we hope to defeat what approaches? We can't even utter its name for fear it will hear and tear us apart."

"You saw the men on the ramparts," said Kevin. "You know they are the ancients. What you don't know is that they are kin."

"You can't be serious," said one of the younger elders. "How could you possibly know that?'"

"I can and I do," said Kevin, "for the chieftain just spoke to me. I have always known I am Amergin's son, and I loved him for the great Da he was to me. But I only knew what he was, not who he was. He was my father. Oh, he could sing, and weave a magical spell that took us to times past so we could face the future. But that's the 'what he was.' 'Who he was,' I have only now discovered. You know your history. How this land was invaded by the sons of Miles—the Milesians they called them. They did battle and won victory over the *faerie* people, the *Tuatha de Danaan*. One of the sons of Miles and Pharaoh's daughter, Meritaten, was Amergin, my father."

"Impossible!" yelled some. But Kevin quieted them with a raised hand.

"Believe what you wish, and yet it is true. He walked the world for thousands of years, and his blood flows in all of you. And that's the secret that chieftain just told me." They all looked up the rampart and saw the wizened one bow his silent head. "We are what's left of those ancient ones, and that means magic flows in our veins. We have what is necessary to defeat the *Caorthannach*." Here he screamed out toward the sea, "Do you hear me Devil's Mother, breeder of demons? We have what it takes to defeat you!"

A distant scream was the only answer. Eamon stepped forward and said in a lower voice, "How do we do that Kevin; how can we accomplish such a thing?"

"My cousin wonders if it be so that we can defeat these two monsters. We've only used our God-given power to tickle tin and other metals to do our bidding. People marvel at our creations. Yet, all we really do is bring the power of the Otherworld to affect the things of this earth. What if we brought the power of the Otherworld here to fight this beast? There's a reason it's not galumphing around that reality. Fear and violence do exist there but not in the amount found here. Here, the *Caorthannach* can take shape, gather substance, and kill living things. It can poison life, here in this world. Though it can physically kill, it works better by poisoning emotions, feelings, sucking up what's left of hope, vomiting despair, breathing forth nothingness."

A moan of hopelessness swept over the people. "Don't you see?" said Kevin. "Already, its outward whispers touch your souls. All we have to do is bring the Otherworld here, and then take what that demon mother gives us and do what we do best—mold and shape it into something else. You know how to do this with metal; the only new thing is to surround our whole selves with the Otherworld, not just our hands. So, do it now, before it is too late, before the Dark comes to destroy the last best hope of this land. Do it for my father; do it for me; do it for the Travelers, we the last of the ancients!"

The chieftain and his soldiers on the ramparts cried out as one, and the Travelers found themselves shouting as well. They turned to the sea and saw the *Caorthannach* and Shiro Ishii almost upon them. They held their hands out, much as they did before they bent tin and metal to their will. Only this time—perhaps it was because they did it in unison, or perhaps it was the dead Amergin himself guiding them—they were able to extend the Otherness around the entire group. As one, they began to hum to themselves as they did individually when they tinkered with metal. As they did so, the soldiers on the ramparts marched down the steps and through the crowd to be the first phalanx to face the monsters that were upon them.

But what is this? Kevin lifts his head. A whisper in the wind carries the voice of Amergin to the ears of his people. They hear him say:

Weaving the Otherworld around them,
The hands of the Travelers sing.
Faerie embraces the fort, the machair, the sands down to the shore of the sea.
Beaming intensely gleams the crescent moon;
Sharply shine the brightest stars,
While in the dark spaces between the lights,
Swiftly sails the Hand of God.
Bright are the heavens this night.
Bold are the hearts of the Tinkers.
Strong is their courage.
Great is their hope.
Sing now my friends, for the Dark is rising.
Shrink not from the song that will strip this hate from the earth.
Sing now my friends of the Light that comes!

The humming of the Tinkers grew greater as Kevin raised his fist out towards the approaching evil, and Kevin smiled, "Thanks, Da," he whispered. "We're ready now."

CONOR'S COMPANY
ENTERS THE FRAY

Friday Evening, 11/13, Ballinskelligs and Staigue Fort

THE SHIP CARRYING Conor and friends by way of the *faerie* track landed in Ballinskelligs Bay as the sun was setting in the west. Calador and the *Roan* crew bid them farewell.

Calador said, "The ship will stay here, but we will follow the *faerie* track on the sea to White Strand Beach just south of *Staigue* Fort. The King has asked me to lead a contingent of *Roan* there to be of any help the Travelers might need. I, too, sense what the King feels; namely, that the ancient fort will be a crucial site in the upcoming battle." Conor nodded his thanks as Calador and the crew slipped overboard, quickly shapeshifting into seals.

"If we are going," said Phil, "aren't we supposed to follow them?"

"No," said Jace. "Ita knows of a portal here in town that can take you to the fort and us to *Skellig*. We apparently couldn't use it before because of the Red Thirst …"

"But that problem dried up and went away," said Colly laughing at his own humor.

"Yeah, right," said Conor. "Look, Scatha has some weapons for you, Phil, and for Fr. Greavy, if he's changed his mind?" Conor looked quizzically at the priest.

"No," said the priest, softly. "I have my dagger and that will be enough."

Scatha gave Phil a similar weapon, slightly longer than the priest's knife, saying, "It's for stabbing and you don't need much skill for that."

"She doesn't need it at all," said a voice from behind them. They hadn't noticed Moira and Ita walking down to the dock, and Moira was fuming.

"What do you think you are doing, Philomena? Whatever these people have planned is not going to include you. You lost every fight you ever had in school, and you think you can take on Balor and that renegade Japanese doctor? I think not."

"Your mother's right, girl," said Ita. "I certainly won't be a part of having you throw your life away."

Fr. Greavy nodded his head in agreement, but it was Colly who spoke up in favor of Phil. "A lot has changed in the past few days. She's not the same girl. You didn't see her in Edinburgh when she saved my life from that plague waif who wanted to hug me to death. She's also walked the Otherworld and been at the coronation of a King."

"By the way," interrupted Moira, looking at Conor, "you look absolutely ridiculous in that outfit, like you're dressed for some renaissance festival. You, too, Jace."

"Told you," said Jace, punching Conor in the arm. Both looked mightily embarrassed.

Ita stifled a chuckle and said, "Don't worry Conor, I can fix all that in a moment. I've had to wear disguises for the past 1500 years when I've walked this world. But back to the matter at hand. You simply can't go Phil."

"As I was saying," resumed Colly, "she's different now. We need her and it's not going to matter much if her life is in danger here or there. If we lose, the bad guys will find us sure as the sun shines and kill us, so we might as well fight on our terms."

"Eloquent, Colly," said Jace, "and you have a point."

"Ma, I have to," said Phil, not the rebellious little chit that she could be, but with the firm voice of one who had found a bit of a purpose.

Lettie finally chimed in, "Moira, dear, I've known you since you were a wee one. Phil is your child and you love her so much, but sometimes love has to let go. It's her time. If you make her sit out this momentous event, life will pass her by and her destiny will pass to another. She was meant to be here with these her friends. Meant to be right here, Moira."

"I don't like it one bit," said Moira.

"Didn't think you would, Ma. But I will be alright."

"And if you are not?"

"It won't matter, because the world as we know it will pass away and we won't be a part of it anyway."

Troubles moved slowly towards Moira and sat before her. To the surprise and delight of everyone, he spoke within their minds. "It is an uncertain time, Matriarch, but even in times like these, you must let the pups grow up."

He put his huge head on her shoulder and licked her face. She gave him the sternest look possible and made to speak, but he licked her again and again, until she and everyone started laughing.

"Okay," she said, "but I'm entrusting her to you, Hercules Columba Roddy, so you better bring her back in one piece."

A cawing in the sky drew their attention as a huge crow alighted on the beach and transformed into the Morrigan. She was in her glory as the battle maiden, golden gauntlets shining in the twilight, crimson robe and lustrous red hair shining like the blood-red setting sun.

"Make haste!" she said. "The *Caorthannach* has come!"

"The Cornerknock?" said Phil, not understanding.

Colly gasped and said to the Morrigan, "It can't be. Nobody has seen that thing for 1500 years."

"Yet, it comes," said the Morrigan.

"What is it?" said Conor.

"Ah, the King," said the Morrigan. "I had to leave before I could officially bend the knee in your presence, Your Highness," which she did in front of everyone, and seemingly meant every bit of it.

Jace look bemused.

"What troubles you, Champion? Did you think I would not honor the new King? He pleases me and is necessary for what is to come. Besides," and here she walked up to Conor and stroked his face and crown, "what's not to like?" She laid her face on Conor's shoulder and looked demurely at Jace, "Jealous yet?"

Conor burst out laughing, "I told you, Jace, you are more than just a mighty intellect to her."

The Morrigan swirled over to Jace saying, "Indeed, I appreciate a man whose body has as much brawn as his brain."

"O my God," said Phil, "can she go away now? Please? Fr. Greavy can't you like exorcise her from our presence?"

"I could if she was a demon, but she's not, just a mighty nuisance sometimes," said the priest shaking his head.

"Enough," said Ita. "Back to Conor's question. The *Caorthannach*—and Phil, we pronounce it qweer-ah-nock, has been called the Devil's Mother, the Mother of Demons and many other terrible names. St. Patrick himself chased it throughout this land till he buried it under stone in Lough *Derg*. It is the only one of its kind, and though it is physically mighty, its strongest power is its ability to sap the hope and joy from a human heart. It gives only despair and draws new strength from the collapse of civilization around us. You must go. Now. I fear for Kevin and the Travelers if it and Shiro Ishii are together. They will be potent foes. There is a portal behind the *Skellig* Pub. With the Red Thirst gone and no *drocs* around, it is safe to use again. It will open at a small standing stone just outside of *Staigue* Fort. Now go, for doom is upon us." Suddenly, her staff appeared in her hand and she transformed from the non-descript pudgy old lady into the imposing habit-coiffed nun and Abbess of the Kerry territory. She looked more regal than Conor as she raised her crozier and blessed the group saying,

"Go with God,
The Blessing of his power,
The Blessing of his love,
The Blessing of his hope
Be upon you in the task to come.

"Now take them, Moira, and show them where to go. I bid you Morrigan, go with them. I cannot command you, but you represent everything ancient in this land. We need your help."

"Why Ita, that's the nicest thing you've ever said to me. I would not miss this battle for the world. So much blood and suffering. I love the smell of death in the darkness of the night." She changed into a crow and outpaced the group to the portal.

Ita shook her head with a slight smile. One could never understand the Morrigan's motivations, but her help was needed. Hopefully, she would hold true. Ita, with her arms spread wide bid them farewell as they walked up the beach to the portal behind the pub.

Turning to Conor, she smiled and said, "I am rather good at disguising things. Let me see what we can do with you. You and Jace must look like you belong to this place and time." She settled on outfitting them both in their contemporary jeans and boots.

"The torcs stay for there is power in them to give you strength," she said. "They will have to be enough. Too much more battle gear and your movement will be impaired. You have the Spear and the Sword. Use them well. They respond to your will and can do things beyond their stated purpose. Conor you have your crown, and you have this beautiful hound who will fight to the death for you. Look also for Michael. Though he has been absent and fears to intervene, I think he will not be able to stay away. If you hold firm, he may decide humanity has cast its lot with the Light and elect to help you over his own objections. The wisp will seek him out."

She took out her bag of dust and cast it on the sea. A brilliant *faerie* track curved round the bay out towards *Skellig* Michael. "Conor, you have chosen to battle Balor in the best place possible in this reality. He will not be able to resist coming to you, yet the very battlefield is one dedicated to the Light. Never has he prevailed there. Go now, for the time is nigh. You must win, if we are to survive. All that is beautiful, all that is good, all that is fair rests with the King and his Champion."

"Geez," said Conor, "nothing like dumbing down what we have to do. I feel so super-confident now."

Jace laughed and winked at Ita, "We'll take care of one another. We're the underdogs in this battle, but we've got a great team and a great captain. How can we lose?" Troubles barked his agreement and they were off.

THE TESTING OF JACE

Friday Evening, 11/13, Skellig Michael

LIKE A SMALL Viking ship slicing through the waves, Jace, Conor and Troubles were speeding along the *faerie* track on Calador's vessel across a placid sea towards *Skellig* Michael. Lettie was in her wisp form floating above. The dog was standing up, front paws on the prow, enjoying himself immensely, and in minutes, the mountainous island loomed in front of them.

Conor aimed for Blind Man's Cove, docked and had just ascended the concrete steps of the landing when he gasped in horror, almost knocking Jace into the water. There, in front of them, sitting in a deck chair, was Sir Hugh Rapapport, casting a fishing line into the waters of the cove. Flicking the lure into the sea, he turned his head, acknowledging the newcomers. "Welcome, lads, I've been waiting for you. Rather boring really; I haven't caught a thing. Only three of you? I thought I caught a glimpse of that precious wisp following you."

Conor looked around but couldn't see Lettie, for which he was grateful. Hopefully, she was hiding somewhere.

"What's the matter, boys? Cat got your tongue?"

Troubles started growling.

"Get over here, you big galoot," said Sir Hugh, "and let me have a look at you. What a fine specimen of a Labrador. What could you hunt for me, if I put you up to it?" He stretched out his hand gently beckoning, but the dog felt himself being dragged against his will over the dock towards Sir Hugh. Conor made to grab him, but Rappaport said, "No need, just want to look at him more closely." Troubles tried to open his jaws but something like an invisible hand seemed to be clamping them shut.

"Beautiful dog, lovely animal, faithful companion," cooed Sir Hugh. He looked up at a seething Conor and said, "Can't be having that in a beast." Almost faster than Conor could see, Sir Hugh made a fist and smashed it into the side of Troubles' face. The dog flew off the dock and crashed into the sea below. As Conor ran to the edge, Jace drew his Sword. Conor leapt out to dive in and retrieve his dog, but Sir Hugh's arm lengthened into a tentacle and caught him around his waist.

"Let me go!" shouted Conor.

"Touch me with that Sword," said Sir Hugh to Jace, "and I'll squeeze the life out of him. You'll have more than a dead dog with which to deal. Your precious King will have had a very short reign."

Without flinching, Jace walked up to Sir Hugh and placed the blade against his neck. "I think I'll call your bluff. You won't hurt him with this next to your neck. It's the Sword of Light, and I'd guess you are rather allergic to it."

Sweat beaded off Sir Hugh's forehead as he laughed and set Conor back on the dock. "Just joking lad. No harm done."

Finding himself free, Conor leapt into the ocean to find Troubles.

"No harm except to the dog," said Sir Hugh. "He'll not find him. I sank the bloody cur deep and hid his body well."

Conor surfaced yelling, "He's nowhere, Jace. I can't find him." Running up the steps, he began to throttle Sir Hugh, water spray from Conor's wet clothes drenching him. "What did you do with Troubles? Where is he?"

Sir Hugh was growing red in the face as Conor choked him. Then, to Conor's horror, Sir Hugh's head began to swell. Wormy appendages, rapidly growing, began to appear around his mouth, snicking around Conor's hands. Disgusted, Conor let go, and Sir Hugh's elongated arms smashed him backwards into Jace. Catching Conor, Jace dragged him away from the morphing man.

Little was left of the human Sir Hugh. Like some mutated cephalopod, he writhed and grew there on the concrete dock. Mucus sloughed off him in a disgusting green goo. His two eyes merged and formed one giant ocular opening, closed at the moment though movement could be seen underneath the huge lid. Arms were tentacles now, with more of the wriggling bastards appearing by the moment.Two of them twisted out and snatched Conor and Jace. Jace's Sword of Light clattered onto the dock near to the Spear of Destiny which Conor had dropped to rescue Troubles.

Neither of them said anything as they were lifted high. Terror had shut their mouths tight. Conor futilely struggled, trying to make another attempt to find the dog, but then he found himself gasping for breath.

A voice snaked inside his mind saying, "Leave the dog be. He is gone. It is not the only sorrow you will have this evening. Do not even think of using that gemstone in your little invisible crown. I have blocked the part of your mind that links with it. Just as well. You lads have far more important deeds to do for me. I arrived here this evening to find the ruler of this rock gone. He abandoned his post, it seems, so I have taken over. At least for the moment. I do not fancy his return, so let us see what we can do to make it difficult for him to come back. Then, I'm going to take this rock apart piece by piece, mine the gold that is here, and find some of those living gemstones that rumor has are deep within this island rock. Sound like a plan?"

"What are you?" said Jace, barely able to squeeze the words out of his lungs and mouth. "Are you the devil?"

Hollow laughter ran through the minds of both boys. "Well, thank you for the honor, but no, I am not. I am something else entirely. Just as bad, I fear. But enough about me. Did you know the ancient Celts who lived around here thought I was both the source of drought and rain? Wet or dry, it does not matter to me. With either, I bring blight and pestilence. However, I think we need a little storm tonight. We need to be alone, you and I for just a little while. Watch and be amazed."

A massive tentacle stretched upwards as Balor began to chant in some obscene sounding language. The wind kicked up and even in the twilit darkness, Jace and Conor could see huge storm clouds forming in the sky. (Radar in Ireland and Great Britain would suddenly pick up the disturbance and record a well-formed eye of a small hurricane settling over *Skellig* Michael giving the island comparative calm but setting a raging storm around its boundaries. The hurricane didn't even reach to the mainland, but cast its impenetrable, swirling force six kilometers out into the ocean effectively walling off *Skellig* Michael.) Balor chuckled saying, "That will do for now. Come, let us go to my new home. I have renamed it the 'House of Pain'. I want to show you why."

He dragged them to the hidden doorway where Michael had them enter days ago. The geodes embedded in the walls of the passageway glowed as before but their light was dimmed considerably. Along the path stood *sluagh*, like guards lining a military parade route. There was a hissing undertone from them like an obeisance to Balor, and the darkness emanating from their darkling robes sucked the light out of the cavernous corridor. Balor, his captives tightly in tow, slithered between his gruesome honor guard making for Michael's Throne Room.

Conor had not seen the hall before, and he was shocked at its size and grandeur. Balor left a trail of ooze between the *sluagh* and the piles of Otherworld living gemstones that were in that place. He perched on Michael's Chair and set his captives down to stand before himself. Lest they run off, he kept them tethered to his tentacles. Though Jace noticed, Conor could not know that the brilliant luminosity of the room was much diminished by the creatures of the Dark that now inhabited it.

"What do you want with us?" snarled Conor.

A moist tentacle caressed his cheek as Balor said, "Worship from you I think. You are just so hard to kill. I blasted you with my Eye; in fact, I saw your beating heart, but you just would not die. I am sure I could accomplish that goal, but it bores me now. You have already seen the death of your beloved dog—shattering isn't it to lose someone for a second time? And now you will watch your best friend die. That should soften your mind up for the brilliant re-education plan I have for you. And then, King that you are, you shall reign by my side as we pull the worlds together and begin the Rule of the Dark."

Conor said, "I'll never worship you, you loathsome sack of jelly."

Balor laughed. "Oh yes you will. You have seen what has happened to the Emerald Isle. The people are in revolt. They kill one another. That's not all that's dying. Nothingness rests in the heart of the people as their values die, their traditions die, their hope dies. And that, young King, is what it means to worship me. And all that has happened to the people will happen to you. It will happen to Jace as well, but death will come as a welcome end to that pain. Both of you will, at the last, open your arms wide to despair."

"Don't listen to him, Conor."

"I won't." Looking at Balor, Conor sneered, "You have no power over us."

Balor laughed again, "Of course I do. Again, watch and be amazed."

They heard a series of clicks from the mouth of Balor and the door to the hall opened. Two *sluagh* entered and came forward. They bowed to Balor and then turned, facing Conor and Jace. Balor's tentacles released the two and they crashed to the floor, but before either could move, the *sluagh* opened their wing-like robes enveloping them, embracing them both.

Conor heard Jace scream, but then realized he was screaming as well. But from sudden fear, not pain. He could feel nothing. He was floating in darkness. Realizing that he wasn't going to plummet into the depths of that black nothingness, he fell silent, but Jace did not. He sounded like he was being tortured.

"He is being tortured," spoke Balor in Conor's mind. "I am flaying his skin with the hooks on my tentacled arms."

"Why?" said an anguished Conor. "What do you gain by this?"

"Nothing," laughed Balor. "Do you not get it? Nothing! I gain nothing! There is absolutely no purpose in what I do other than that I can cause him pain. Of course, there is the fact that you can do nothing to help him either. My *sluagh* have you both immobilized. Now, I am not sure how much your friend will be able to pay attention, but I grant him the boon of seeing what you shall see—my complete and total victory over your friends, including both the Travelers and the *Roan*. Watch and be amazed. Watch and then despair."

Conor's vision cleared and ahead of him he could see a white beach and hundreds of seals. They were the *Roan* coming in from the sea. Once they were on land, they transformed into their true form. Graceful and tall with grey and green dappled skin, they were singing as they walked up the *machair* towards *Staigue* Fort. Between them and hundreds of Travelers, were Shiro Ishii and the huge bulk of the *Caorthannach*.

As far as Conor was concerned, both were demons and though they ignored the *Roan*, they looked about to engage the Travelers. Conor could not believe how big the demon mother was. Twenty feet tall, if not larger, its form was constantly morphing but never really varying from a serpentine, almost dragon-like appearance. Conor saw great movement on its broad back and then gasped as it seemed to be shedding parts of its body. Conor's vision resolved and realized that what he was seeing were hundreds of *drocs*, leaping off the *Caorthannach's* back, rushing ahead to attack the Travelers and behind to assault the *Roan*. Shiro Ishii shouted with delight and Conor felt a sinking feeling in the pit of his stomach. How could a bunch of Tinkers resist this evil? Despair gripped his soul as the screams of Jace turned up a notch. Balor was not distracted by the battle; he intended Jace to suffer as much as possible so that wherever Conor turned, his vision would perceive only pain.

THE DEATH OF INNOCENCE

Friday Evening, 11/13, Staigue Fort

THE WISP HAD hidden while Sir Hugh spoke with Conor and Jace, but when that husk of a man swatted Troubles into the sea, she dove as well but could not find the dog either. It was as if the Labrador had just disappeared.

Surfacing, she hugged the air above the waves and darted off to the other side of the island hoping to find Michael. She quickly determined he was nowhere to be found on the rock, so she skimmed over the surface of the ocean towards *Staigue* Fort, hoping against hope that she would find him watching over the Travelers. No such luck. She didn't sense him anywhere, but she did feel the ancient standing stone by the fort start a high-pitched hum that only she could hear. Curious, she darted over to it and watched the stone reveal an opening which disgorged Conor's friends and the Morrigan. No doubt they were here to help the Travelers, but the wisp still had one last place to check for Michael before she'd assist them. She went to find Kevin's horse, Malby.

Sure enough, he was pasturing up towards the hills and he wasn't alone. A figure sat in the heather, watching over the upcoming battle. To the wisp, it looked like just one of the shepherds of the area, but she knew it wasn't so. She was pretty sure she could see past any disguise the seraph could devise.

Indeed, it was Michael, and he looked up to see the wisp speeding down to meet him, erupting in the heather herself with her the folds of her dress fluffing in the air and her smoking pipe clenched tightly in her teeth.

"Where have you been and why aren't you doing anything?" said Lettie, fiercely puffed smoke circling around her head. "Can't you see what's happening? These people are about to be destroyed!"

"You know the *geas* that lays upon me. Guardian though I be, I am tasked not to intervene directly in the affairs of humanity or *fae*."

"But you've already done so. Was that just a charade with you and Brian in the air, seemingly destroying the power of the plague?"

"No," said Michael, "but the plague was unnatural, and no one but me could protect the land and its people from that."

Lettie pointed down towards the fort. "What you see down there is natural? That demented little sorcerer and his pet demon are natural?"

Michael stood up. "Yes. The *Caorthannach* is the most natural thing I have seen in the past several weeks. It walks among the people of this land only because it personifies the despair in their hearts. They embraced nothingness freely and let loose the likes of the demon mother and individuals like Ishii to walk the land."

"The Travelers didn't do this, nor did the *Roan*," said Lettie. "They are making a stand down there for this world and the Otherworld. Could you not aid them? They did not release this darkness upon the land. They have remained faithful. Act for them. At least for them, do something!"

Michael stood and looked at her. Oh, I've made him mad, she thought. But he spoke to her with kindness. "Go now, Lettie. Help them as you can. I was considering what you said even before you spoke to me. The land and the people are in my care, but I have to respect the choice all the people have made. The Dark is rising because of them. I can neither interfere with their free will or the consequences of their decisions."

"Then let the Travelers and *Roan* speak for the weak. They are the few who have remained true. There was once a bargain between the One and another great man to save a city if only ten good people could be found."

"I know" said Michael. "I was there."

"Then you know that ten people couldn't be found, and the city was destroyed."

"Exactly. My point exactly."

Lettie pointed her pipe down the hill. "Look down at the fort. Conor's friends are there. The Travelers are there and the *Roan* are down by the sea. That's far more than the ten that would have freed a city so long ago. Let them be enough, for their hearts are pure and their courage strong. Do not let the strength of humanity and *fae* vanish tonight in a slaughter arranged by demons of the Dark. Do not let goodness perish from the face of this earth. Do not let hope die. Or else when the worlds merge, as they will soon, the Dark will have won and all that is good, and true and beautiful will be lost, and you will be guardian of nothing. Then, as you look over the desert of evil's mighty works, you will despair, and hope will vanish from the world."

"Oh, my brave wisp," said Michael, touching her wet cheek. "Go now and do what you can, as will I. Go with the blessing of the One." He turned and walked toward Malby. Lettie watched him for a moment and then started down the hill. She thought to herself that she might get a few licks in against the *Caorthannach* before that wretched demon won the day.

As Lettie took her wisp form again, the Morrigan, Scatha and the others made their way to the fort.

"I can get you past the demon and the sorcerer," said the Morrigan to Scatha.

"No doubt," said Scatha sarcastically, "but I am quite capable should I wish to have passage to my people. But I prefer to stay here. Kevin apparently has found courage and purpose, but he is suspicious of the People of the Sea. I will help him get over his fear."

"As you wish, said the Morrigan. My place is not here. It is with the Champion on *Skellig* Michael. Balor is a fierce foe and the King and the Champion are young and inexperienced. They will need help."

Scatha grabbed the battle maiden's red robes and whispered into her ear, "If you harm Conor, or push the young Champion into doing something foolish, I will have your head. Meritaten should have taken it millennia ago."

"She could have tried," sneered the Morrigan. "Do not get your seal skin all bunched up. We have not always been united in purpose, but we are tonight. They will be glad of my presence. This I assure you." She pushed Scatha away, assumed her crow form and vanished into the night toward *Skellig* Michael.

Phil and Collie had already joined Kevin, and Fr. Greavy was making rounds amongst the elders giving blessings when asked and encouragement when needed. Kevin looked at them all gratefully and then raised his voice again above the humming of the Tinkers. They were doing well in facing what was to come, but he could sense their fear as the *Caorthannach* and Ishii approached.

"Here's what we're going to do," he shouted. "When my father and his brothers landed at Ballinskelligs Bay so long ago, they claimed the land from Balor and his awful band of misshapen monsters. He had a chant he used to tie himself and his brothers to the land forever and with that link forged, they defeated their enemies. We shall do the same. I am not a bard, but I represent you. I can lead you to do what Amergin did and if we act as one, we shall forge a new bond with the land." He looked over to Scatha. "If we do such a thing, what will the *Roan* do; what will the People of the Sea say?"

Scatha's voice rang out over the assembled crowd. "We have always been tied to the Travelers, ever since you came to this shore. We will act as one with you, in our own way. But we will be one and together be unbeatable, undefeatable."

A cheer went up amongst the gathered, as Kevin spoke again. "You know the wave the fans do at the games? Fun, huh? But it could be more than that if we want it to be. It can be a thing of power that will hinder the ones who wish to do us harm. It is the motion of the air and the sea. It is the motion the rocks make in the earth. Start it now and match your voices with mine, for our enemies are almost upon us."

The *Caorthannach* had started running on its reptilian legs, and its morphing body disgorged hundreds more of the *drocs* that had clung to her back. Only the parked caravans and then the ancients with their pikes stood between them and the Travelers. Little though the *drocs* were, their fangs were sharp and their claws like whirling scythes if they should connect with human flesh. They spread throughout the *machair*, intent on setting their tiny fangs on whatever living thing moved. Even though the ancients had placed themselves in front of the Travelers, the Tinkers closest to them felt their knees knock in terror at the approaching *drocs*. The chittering sound the nattering demons made as they skittered across the *machair* sapped the courage of even the hardiest of men.

Fortunately, the first wave of the deadly creatures were skewered on the pikes of the clansmen. They had made an effective shield wall that repulsed the first onslaught. The *Caorthannach* was occupied tearing the caravans apart.

That gave Kevin time to get the gathered elders swaying and moving in the rhythm of the wave. For just a moment, he absently thought that if someone threw a ball into the crowd a great game of sport would start. Shaking his head, he concentrated as he lifted up his voice. As the elders moved, Kevin chanted and had the people repeat,

> *We are the wind that breathes in the sky,*
> *We are the breeze in the trees that sigh,*
> *We are the breath moving clouds on high,*
> *We are the air and the gale.*
>
> *We are the rocks that move in the earth,*
> *We are the stone that gives the world birth,*
> *We are the mountains shaking with mirth,*
> *We are the mud and the clay.*
>
> *We are the waves strong as the sea,*
> *We are the waters meant to be free,*
> *We are the rivers and lakes that be,*
> *We are the rain and the snow.*

And it happened that as the Travelers echoed back Kevin's chant, arms upraised with bodies swaying in the evening breeze, a new sound was heard above them all. It was the song of the People of the Sea repeating what the Travelers had uttered but in a new key with the voice of the ocean behind the *Roan* singers.

All saw the storm form out to sea surrounding *Skellig* Michael. They could almost taste the salt spray in the air. All felt the earth begin to quake merging its motion with the swaying of the Tinkers. All bent to the force of the wind that picked up and buffeted everything alive there on the *machair,* in front of *Staigue* Fort, running down to the sea.

Suddenly, *drocs,* demon and sorcerer bounced backward as if they hit an invisible wall. The chanting had united the Travelers and the *Roan* and they expanded the Otherworld to fill the space between them. For several minutes, they were able to hold their enemies in stasis. But then, the *Caorthannach* screamed a cry of defiance. Ishii's hands moved in a sinuous flow, and a snap of thunder was heard. The reality of the ordinary world snapped back into place. The *drocs* broke through the shield wall of the ancients. Shiro Ishii plunged into the crowd, ignoring the people but heading straight for Kevin and Conor's friends. And the *Caorthannach* could move again. Whatever the demon mother touched withered and died. More of the Travelers would have met that fate if the ancient clansman had not been present. Though their shield wall could not keep out the pestilential *drocs,* who bit and clawed their way through the ranks, it was strong enough to repel the demon if only briefly. No doubt the iron on the tips of their pikes caused the *Caorthannach* great pain, and as it screamed aloud, it withered the courage of men.

After the thunderous boom, Kevin felt a diminishment in the shaking of earth, the blowing of wind, the roaring of sea. He yelled again to the assembled Travelers, urging them to hold firm and repeat the chant again and again. They did and the first to feel the new energy were the *drocs* who had made it past the clansman. The *drocs* were their own worst enemy. Barely sentient, they were creatures of hunger and stopped to feed whenever they blooded anyone or any creature. Gross and disgusting as they were, they caused many injuries but could have caused even more death had they not indulged their hunger.

That was not true of the *Caorthannach.* It screamed again, and pressed the invisible wall back, finally breaking it with another thunderous roar. Its reptilian dragon mouth dripped a pestilential poison that burned like acid into the flesh of anyone it fell upon. The ancients, out of time and out of place, touched by the Otherworld, were still susceptible to the damage the demon mother could cause, and they died a second death there on the *machair* before their ancient fort. Their screams were heard and mourned by Michael, who witnessed their deaths from his place near the hills above *Staigue* Fort.

This cannot stand, he thought. He had weighed what Lettie had said and had decided the Travelers and the *Roan* deserved whatever aid he could give. He could not take their place, for then they could not achieve their own victory, but he believed he could help in situations to keep the brave alive, to aid the steadfast, to assist those whose courage did not fail.

He turned to Malby and said, "It is time once again." The horse transformed instantly into Brian, but Michael kept his own disguise as the Irish shepherd with a staff. "Take me down to the fort," he said, "and drop me there. Wait for me, for I believe something is happening on *Skellig*. Balor has come and is causing great evil. Look at that storm; he seeks to keep me out of my own island, fool that he is."

Brian lifted Michael up and in seconds was over the fort. Michael had him circle the swaying Traveler elders and Michael, himself, shouted out a cry of encouragement over the crowd. Coupled with Kevin's chant, their gathering cry strengthened again, forcing the *Caorthannach* to pause.

Not so Shiro Ishii. His own spells blunted the chant and he slipped through easily. He had almost made it to where Kevin was directing the crowd. He could walk amid people unseen and though many of the Travelers had the ability to pierce through any disguise the Otherworld presented, most could not. Those that did were able to see Shiro Ishii and tried to stop him. They got a katana in their gut for their efforts, and, soon, a string of bodies littered the ground where he had walked.

Ishii was enraged. This should have been an easy victory, and it angered him that Balor was not present. Another promise not kept and he wondered what the delay could mean. So fierce did he feel that he no longer avoided killing those who did not hinder him. He simply scythed them all down and that's how Kevin noticed that something was approaching him. He looked at bodies falling, and, suddenly, from out the corner of his eye, he caught a glimpse of Shiro Ishii in the crowd. Their eyes met and Kevin knew he was a dead man. He had no weapon to wield. Phil was next to him and she had her dagger pulled and ready. She swiped once at Ishii, and he stabbed her in the shoulder. She dropped the knife as Kevin pulled her back and shoved her away while Ishii struck at him. But the katana never hit Kevin. A rock-hard rapier blocked the thrust and metal clanged on metal as Scatha threw back Ishii's attack and saved Kevin's life.

"I told you we were one," she grinned at Kevin, before her attention was fixated upon Ishii again as he renewed his attack.

Colly was not by Phil's side when she was set upon. He had seen the death of the ancients and quickly morphed into his wolf form. It took him only moments to reach the *Caorthannach* and because he was not human, the virus it carried could not infect him. But its strength could. He had managed to claw out a huge hunk of what passed for flesh on the beast. The demon grasped him around his neck and threw him over several Travelers to crash into another group of them, all of them still answering Kevin's chant. *Drocs* were everywhere and as Colly got up he stamped and bit and crushed as many as he could as he made his way back to the demon. This time it struck first, grabbing him again around the neck and lifting him high. It tried to crush his windpipe, but Colly was incredibly tough. He took his arms and smashed his claws on both sides of the creature's neck making it drop him. As he fell, he watched the thing lift up its leg to crush him under its foot.

That's when Michael appeared. The seraph looked just about like any other Traveler, but he had no trouble grabbing the demon's foot on its downward motion and tossing the *Caorthannach* into the air. It traveled about a hundred yards down the *machair* and dug out a trench in the stony earth as it fell.

Colly burst out with a wolf-like howl of laughter and grabbed the offered hand of Michael who hauled him to his feet. To his surprise, Michael winked at him and then ran down the *machair* to engage the demon mother again. Colly thought one good turn deserved another so he bounded after. To his surprise, he heard the singing of the *Roan* and noticed they were not staying at the beach. There were hundreds of them and they were moving forward up the *machair* incline intending to join with the Travelers in a pincher movement against the *Caorthannach*.

They looked strong, but Colly thought they could be torn apart by the monster as easily as he could. He felt fearless though and bet himself that he could stop the bitch before they got to it. Michael was simply punching the thing when Colly arrived barreling into the beast. It was like striking the side of a mountain. Colly bounced back and was thankful he was in his werewolf form. He landed prone on the ground and suddenly found himself looking into the maw of the demon mother. She dripped poison from her mouth and it smoked on his fur. As expected, its contagion couldn't hurt him, but from the burning pain he felt, he discovered its corrosiveness could. He screamed in pain and then saw Michael tackle the beast to the ground.

Colly gritted his teeth as Michael saved him again. He was going to owe that arrogant angel several times over before this battle was done.

Shiro Ishii had recovered from Scatha's parry and was harrying her with brilliant swordplay. Incredibly, she found herself pressed as she had not been challenged for many centuries. He was a master swordsman. She was not that familiar with samurai swordplay and found herself measuring the man and his movements, reluctantly admiring his skill.

Suddenly, he managed to knock her rapier away. A feral smile crossed his lips and he backed her up against the stone fort. Raising the katana, he meant to bring it down on her neck, but he was distracted by a cry. The little pudgy priest was hurling his body toward him in an effort to give Scatha a chance to break free. Scatha saw what was going to happen and she screamed to distract Ishii, pushing herself off the fort into the sorcerer himself. But she was not quick enough. Ishii had switched the katana to his other hand at the last moment and thrust the blade into the onrushing priest. There was a sigh from Fr. Greavy as he was impaled on the katana, and he slipped to the ground as Ishii was hit by Scatha, the impact ripping the katana out of the priest's body.

For Scatha, as for many warriors, time had slowed and she saw Fr. Greavy look at her with a small smile before she knocked Ishii aside. As she fell, she yelled in horror at what happened to him, knowing that he was dead before he hit the ground.

Furious with Ishii, she picked herself up and went for him again but he was nowhere to be found. He had slipped away in the chaos. Though the chant continued, it was weakening as Travelers fell from the onslaught of the *drocs* and the *Caorthannach*. Even the *Roan* were suffering from the predation of the *drocs* upon them. No deaths yet among the People of the Sea, but grievous wounds were inflicted. The whole earth seemed to groan in anguish as Kevin sought to gather his decimated Tinkers together again.

IN THE HALL OF
THE MOUNTAIN KING

Friday Evening, 11/13, Skellig Michael

THE WITHERED AGE spotted hand slapped onto the dock steps
that descended into Blind Man's Cove. A head with bedraggled white hair
bobbed above the surface and the mouth moved incessantly.

"Every … time … we … have … a … battle," gasped the voice,
drawing in a deep breath, "you get yourself in an impossible situation and
have to be picked from the jaws of death."

The Morrigan, in her crone form, hissed even more loudly, smacking
her lips against her toothless mouth as her one arm hauled the body she had
recovered from the sea. "And you weigh more than the great Dun Cow. Just
because you are nigh near death doesn't mean I excuse your laziness in not
helping me."

The hand still underwater hauled forward the body and pushed it onto
the steps. Climbing over it like an emaciated sea crab, she dragged it up to
the dock itself. Looking down upon the very still form, she shook her head
and muttered. "I cannot do it. I wash the dead; I keen their passing; I do not
give life; I grieve its passing from the world."

Silently she looked over the drowned body of the Labrador. She was
stunned when a tear leaked from her eye and fell upon the dog. "I do not
weep for beasts. But the dog is his. And he loves the thing. And he is the
King." She bent over the head of Troubles. Her withered lips hovered over
his face. She puckered them over her toothless gums, willing the breath to
come that might still give the dog life. Then she snorted, lifting herself up
while on her knees. "I cannot do it this way. I look such a fright." With a
wave of her hand she transformed herself into the battle maiden, gold
gauntleted wrists helping fingers smooth her red lustrous hair and crimson
robes. "There," she said. "Much better."

She bent back over the dog, and without hesitation pushed on the
beast's chest, once, twice, and thrice. A huge gout of water cascaded from

the dog's mouth, but he did not breathe. She cried her frustration to the skies and then bent over the Labrador's face again. This time she cradled the head. Clamping the jaws shut, she placed her mouth over the dog's nose and began to breath in air, again, once, twice, thrice. She counted that in her mind. Lifting up her head, she watched, and suddenly the dog's body shivered, and he opened his mouth to suck in air on his own.

The Morrigan stood and crossed her crimson robed arms. A faint smile stole across her face, a glimpse of brilliant white teeth showing. The dog made to get up and turned his head to the Morrigan. Into her mind he spoke, "I thank you, lady. I was lost beneath the waves and I could not find him. He is nowhere to be found."

"You drowned, or nearly so," said the Morrigan. "I had to haul your furry carcass up from fathoms below, and let me tell you I was the worse for wear because of it. I've romped in the beds of many warriors and come out looking better."

The dog did not laugh. His dark eyes were pools of pleading, and the Morrigan knelt down and took his face. "I should not jest. Your heart is as great as any hero I have ever met, and I fear the King has need of you. But you are the first I have ever brought back from so far down Death's Road."

Solemnly he licked her and she suddenly rose, sputtering, "Oh, you kiss like a brute you brazen beast." Then she threw her head laughing to the skies. But her joy was short lived, for at that moment, Balor's micro hurricane manifested itself and surrounded the island with walls of clouds. Only the eye of the storm directly above them let in the starlight and the light from the Hand of God nebula.

"Look hound. Even Balor cannot keep the heavens from shining through. The storm is bad, but I have decided the stars and that Hand are a good omen. Let's go find the King, your Master. While we are at it, we need to find the Champion—I'm missing him more and more these days. Here, take the Spear of Destiny—I'll shrink it into a more manageable size for you." She then bent down and took the Sword of Light and slung the scabbard carrying it on her back. The dog cocked his head and sighed, following her to the hidden door that led inside the mountain.

The *sluagh* were gone. The geodes still lit the passageway, but it was deserted. Once the door closed, they both could hear the screams coming from far away. "I know that voice," said the Morrigan. "It is my Champion and he is in agony. Quickly, follow me. We run to Michael's Hall." She picked up her long crimson robe and stuck the hem in her teeth. Barefoot, with nails matching crimson, she pounded the rock floor with her *faerie* feet, just as she had gone into war many times before. Her eyes filled with battle rage as a muffled scream came from her lips. By the side of the once upon a time goddess ran the hound, and from his throat came a howl of vengeance. Together they sought the entrance to the hall, and when they found it, they slammed their bodies against the door crushing it inward.

She stood with arms out, looking for anyone or anything that hurled themselves forward toward them. Both of them dropped the weapons they were carrying, still looking for attackers. The danger, however, was behind them. Troubles heard the whispering of robes in the hallway, and in a moment the sibilant hiss of the *sluagh* rose to a fever pitch as they entered what Balor now called the House of Pain. The Morrigan heard them come and she gave herself time for a brief thought. She simply did not understand the *sluagh*. Like her, they dealt with the dead, but they were foul. She was there at the passing of people; she sang the dirge for the dead; she washed the blood from the battle garments of warriors. Her celebration of Death was a rejoicing in their lives. That was not the way of the *sluagh*. Everything they did was to suck the last energy of life from those who were passing. They had no purpose in their actions, other than to bring the Dark. And she hated them for it.

That's why she unclasped her robes and revealed the white battle garments she often wore in combat. As the crimson robe fell, she reached for the knives strapped along her legs and struck them together, making them ring like the death knell of a funeral bell.

Both of them attacked, she with her daggers, the dog with his teeth. Because they both now walked in the world of humankind and *faerie*, those weapons had real power against the *sluagh*. A passing wail like the sigh of dying breeze through the leaves was all that was heard as the hound and the Morrigan cut a path through the oncoming wraiths. They suffered no wounds for the *sluagh* carried no weapons. They only sought to smother the two in their embracing grasp in order to bring despair in their minds and souls as they died from fear and horror. That was how they always took their victims.

Unscathed, the two still found themselves being forced down among the living gemstones by the crush of the foul specters. Jumping up on a pile of blazing sapphires, the Morrigan sheathed her knives and beckoned for the dog to leap. He only hesitated for a moment, for he saw the Morrigan grow in stature. She easily caught his huge bulk and then threw him like a guided missile into the advancing horde. Troubles had discovered that not only his teeth, but his body could disrupt the corporeal presence of the *sluagh*. When he landed among them, he sent a dozen of them into whatever passed for their eternity. The Morrigan leapt after him in a flurry of ferocious movement. She sliced, scythed and stabbed through their midst and, suddenly, none were left. At least for the moment. She and Troubles managed to heave the door up, close and seal it once again by placing the locking bar they found in the clamps on either side of the door.

Turning as one, they marched down the hallway, focused only on the screams they heard.

A NIGHTMARE BROKEN

Friday Evening, 11/13, Skellig Michael

FOR CONOR AND Jace, the nightmare seemed never ending. "They're dying, Conor, our friends are dying!" Jace managed to choke out between screams. Blackness was all around them and when they saw anything, it was glimpses of the battle over at *Staigue* Fort. Balor was not about to let them see the mettle of the defenders. He only showed them visions of soldiers dying, lines failing and friends faltering.

As the fighting grew worse and Travelers started to die, Conor was bereft. A sinking despair filled his heart. He was not in pain, but Jace was. The screams of his friend were terrifying. It was as if he was being flayed apart, piece by piece. What was even more heartbreaking, Conor realized that Balor left him physically pain free so he could mentally experience what Jace and his friends were going through, all the while knowing there was nothing he could do about it. He howled his rage into the darkness, knowing that no one else would hear.

But Troubles and the Morrigan heard. They rounded a curve on the walkway and saw a sight that horrified them. Before them stood two *sluagh*. One of them had his wing-like black robes surrounding a figure and the other had one robed wing-like arm around the throat of Jace. They couldn't see his face because he was turned toward the monstrosity sitting on the chair that only Michael had ever before occupied. Balor was flicking a barbed tentacle into the body of the Champion and splatters of blood and flesh were flying in the air.

The Morrigan and Troubles both shrieked in rage and charged. Troubles leapt at the *sluagh* that obviously held the hidden Conor. Hoping he didn't damage his master too much, he collided with both of them breaking the hold the wraith had on Conor. Conor slid out of the *sluagh's* grasp like a banana from a rotten peel. He lay stunned on the floor. After sending the specter into Death's own embrace, the panting Labrador stood guard over the fallen King.

The Morrigan for her part, took her knives and beheaded the *sluagh* holding Jace captive. The loathsome apparition promptly vanished from sight. Jace fell back into her arms and she gently laid his bloody body on the floor.

That's when Balor began to laugh, and it was that hideous sound that brought Conor back to consciousness. He chanced a look at the bloated being on that huge stone chair and had the most curious thought. The modern visitors to *Skellig* Michael constantly questioned the boat captains about the filming of Star Wars and here was a real live Jabba the Hut impersonator sitting on a throne. How freakish. Crazy ideas go through the head at times like this, he supposed. What's really happening is that I'm dying, at least he thought so. That was as far as his contemplation took him, for his eye caught movement among the beautiful pillars and mounds of colored gems that were beginning to shine a brighter light.

It was a figure, a woman, and she was smiling at him. "Mom?" he said. "Is it you?" The figure nodded and then held an index finger to her lips. Conor marveled in silence. He had seen her before when he was delirious. "I will always be with you," she had said to him, "even when you cannot see me." He looked at her again and she was nodding.

He mouthed the words, "What should I do?" as he chanced a fearful glance at the monster on the throne. He saw her look at Balor, and then she stepped out into the walkway leading to the throne. The laughing stopped suddenly.

"You!" raged Balor. He snapped out a tentacle to grab her but the slimy arm went right through her. She had made herself only partially perceptible in this reality. She had enough time though to reach her son. She looked into his haunted eyes and bent his head down to her lips where she kissed the exact spot where his invisible circlet Crown with its inert jewel lay unsettled on his head. He felt a click in his brain as he saw her recede and fade from his sight. Immediately he knew what happened. Whatever control Balor had over that symbol of kingship was gone and Conor felt new energy pouring into him. He also felt a furry muzzle nudging something into his hand. He knew it had to be the Lance. He used the dog as a brace to bend down and smash the stick he was given on the floor. Immediately, it became the Spear of Destiny and he swiveled his head to face Balor.

The thing was truly a blight on existence. Already it was lifting the lid of his one Eye, ready to blast Conor into eternity. But Conor struck first. The crown and the ruby had already become visible, and Conor looked at the ceiling of the cavern and sent a thought through the jewel, racing high to the beam above the chair. Shapeshifting was about transmuting matter, so he simply separated a five-meter section from the roof and sent it plunging down upon Balor before his evil glance could take him out. There was a satisfying squish and howl from Balor as the beam struck him off the chair. However, as Conor had discovered before, it was difficult to kill an immortal. He may have been injured, but Balor was nowhere near dead. He rose up on his bloated feet. Tentacles writhing, he flashed his Eye, missing Conor, but blowing a deep hole into the aisle. Both Conor and Troubles leapt the crater and plunged toward Balor. The Eye was moving side to side, causing great swathes of destruction in the hall. Both of them managed to evade the beam arcing from his swollen, putrescent body.

Troubles was faster than Conor and went for Balor's mouth, ignoring the ripping, writhing worms that protected it. He sank his teeth into the soft flesh and began tearing and shredding.

Conor, on the run, cocked back his arm and for the second time threw the Spear of Destiny at Balor. This time his aim was far more precise for it flew just above Troubles' head, plunging into the center of that orb. The beam of destruction winked out. A horrific screech echoed through the hall and Balor backed into the thronelike chair, his tentacles grasping it and breaking it out of the wall from which it was carved. Balor's obscene limbs smashed and tore wherever they fell. In his agony, he simply lashed out. Conor rushed forward to drag Troubles away, leaving a gaping wound where the mouth of the giant once was.

Conor would say later that he only saw a blur go by him, but looking towards Balor, he could see Jace rushing the titanic monstrous thing. With the Sword of Light in one hand, he plunged the weapon into Balor's Eye as well. The Champion took his other hand and pressed the Spear of Destiny even farther in. A fresh round of screaming and writhing took place as another tentacle smashed into Jace. The Morrigan jumped forward to pull his unconscious body away from the fray.

Balor was gushing green black fluid, and his cries became faint and movements weak. Soon he was still. Conor and Troubles rushed over to Jace. Conor gasped in horror. He had never seen someone so ripped apart before. Muscle and veins had been laid bare on Jace's arms and legs. His torso was pumping blood and he was lucky his abdomen hadn't been ripped completely open. There was no doubt he was dying.

Jace's head rested on the Morrigan's lap, but Conor took his hand. "Jace, Jace, buddy! Can you hear me?"

Jace's eyes lifted slightly, and he whispered, "Did we win? Is he dead?"

Conor looked over at the body of Balor, "I think so. We hurt the thing badly and it's not moving."

"Good," he gasped. "Our friends, though. We were getting beat. I saw Fr. Greavy die."

A sob burst out of Conor, "I saw it too, Jace. I saw it too. He was saving Scatha. I promise I'll check on them as soon as I can."

A huge noise came from outside of the hall. Conor and Troubles faced the doorway which took a huge thump and then the crossbar split and the door was flung down the hall. In the entrance stood a being of light, with six wings and flashing eyes and a trident lifted high.

"Michael!" said Conor.

"Awesome!" whispered Jace and then closed his eyes as his head dropped back.

Troubles leapt forward, joyfully barking, and the figure at the door shrunk into a more familiar sight, just an ordinarily splendid appearance of an angel with two wings—still impressive, but easier on the eyes.

Michael lifted up the dog and carried him to his friends. There was no smile on his face. "What a terrible yet momentous time," he intoned.

"You are late, *aingeal*," said the Morrigan.

"No, I'm right on time. The King and his Champion have done what they needed to do."

"The Champion is dying," snarled the Morrigan. "Is that what you foresaw? Is this what you ordained, what you wanted?"

"No," said Michael sadly. "But it is what the Dark wished, what Balor, his servant, tried to accomplish." Michael pointed over to Balor. As they looked, the tentacled beast began to change again.

"Can't that thing ever stay dead?" cried Conor. The Spear and the Sword fell out of Balor's Eye as the change accelerated. Conor made to go for the weapons, but Michael held him back.

"Watch for a moment."

When it was done, the body of Sir Hugh Rappaport lay before them. But he was not dead. Bleeding, blind, and sorely wounded, he was breathing.

"You," said Michael. "Hear me, now. You sold your soul for power and might. That might have been forgiven, but you used what you gained to hurt and destroy. Time and again you were given a chance to turn from your path, but you did not. You know what I am. You chanced to do your deeds knowing I could not directly interfere with humanity's choices. Blatant hatred still leaks from you. What cannot be forgiven is your choice to give despair to the human race. You chose to give them nothingness. And you are not repentant. Among my many duties here on this earth, I bear the dead, those saved and damned to their judgement. You know where I shall take you."

A moaning slobber was all that came from Sir Hugh's ruined mouth.

Michael turned to the Morrigan. "Can you heal the Champion?"

"Yes, I believe so," she said.

"Wisp!" cried Michael. A tiny blue ball appeared in the hall, and in a moment, Lettie was standing there. "Help the Morrigan tend Jace. She need not do this alone."

"Yes, I must," said the Morrigan. "He is my charge, and no one else touches him now." She turned to Conor. "Rest assured, my King, he will be returned to you whole and well."

A tear streaked down Conor's face. "Are you truly sure?"

She allowed herself a little smile. "I am many things, but a liar I am not. Farewell, for now." As if he weighed no more than a feather, she picked up Jason Michaels, the Champion and the Sword of Light, and strode out from the hall.

"Conor," said Michael, "those at *Staigue* Fort await their King. Take Brian; he is on the plain between the peaks of this island. The storm has dissipated."

"The Travelers and *Roan* won?" asked Conor. "But what I saw—they seemed to be losing."

"They lost much, and only you can determine how the outcome will eventually be viewed. The *Caorthannach* is contained, but Shiro Ishii is missing. Go now, and be who you were called to be."

A whimpering caught their attention. Sir Hugh Rappaport was trying to sit up. Michael walked over to him, took him in his hand, and vanished.

"That was amazing," said Conor.

"For us, yes," said Lettie, "but for Sir Hugh, I am afraid it is a one-way trip to nowhere."

ALL'S WELL THAT ENDS LIKE HELL

Saturday Dawn, 11/14, Staigue Fort

TROUBLES WAS TOO big to fit on Brian, the flying steed of Michael, so Conor asked Lettie to place him in wisp form and the two could follow Conor on the horse to *Staigue* Fort.

It was a trip of just a few minutes. Brian and the wisps circled the battleground, and Conor was sorrow struck to see bodies everywhere. He had no time for grieving for it was clear the battle was not yet over. The *Caorthannach* was not moving but was still upright. Four groups surrounded it on all sides, two groups of Travelers and two of *Roan*, Kevin was among them and seemed to be leading them. Conor could hear them chanting and realized it was that chant that was imprisoning the demon mother.

Abandoning the plan to re-unite with his friends, he had the stallion set him down close to the *Caorthannach*. Lettie and Troubles followed suit, transforming back into their human and canine forms. Calador from the groups of *Roan* came forward to meet Conor.

"Just in time," said the *Roan* leader. "We have been holding this thing in place but do not know what to do with it. Any faltering in our words, and it stirs."

"You think I know what to do?" said Conor honestly.

"Perhaps not, but you are the King, and we believe your advice will be most helpful." Conor turned and saw the speaker was Scatha, a smile on her face and arms ready to embrace. It was just a quick hug, but for Conor, it was exactly what he needed.

"I've missed you. So much has happened," he said.

"Indeed," nodded Scatha. "There is much sorrow and grief here but we cannot allow it to cloud our minds. The *Caorthannach* is the most awful manifestation of what has plagued our island. I doubt it can be killed, but we must do something with it."

Conor looked up at the thing and saw it observing him with cruel, calculating eyes.

"I thought this beast couldn't think," he said. "It's waiting for whatever we decide to hatch its next plan."

Colly loped up and butted Troubles in the shoulder and then morphed into his human form. "It's no Einstein, Conor, if that's what you mean, but it thinks and plans to survive. I say we try and kill it anyway."

Conor walked back to Brian and lifted up the Spear of Destiny. Showing it to the *Caorthannach*, he brought it close and could see the fear on the face of the demon mother. "I know this monster really exists. I can see it, no doubt even touch it if I try, but I know we can't kill it. Whatever it was under the waters of Lough *Derg*, it took new form from the hate, rage, despair and hopelessness that possess the souls of the people of this land. Until those things are diminished or vanquished, the *Caorthannach* will not even come close to dying."

"May I make a suggestion?" said Calador. "Perhaps we can imprison it again."

"Where?" asked Conor. "It's got to be someplace no one will look for it, and even if they find its resting place, no one will touch."

Scatha looked over at Calador and nodded to him. He said to Conor, "Bull Rock. It is the passageway to the House of the Damned. If it is sunk to the depths in the midst of that portal, that cave that pierces both sides of the rock, nothing will be able to surface it without us knowing that boundaries have been tampered with."

"Then we do it," said Conor, amazed at the force and authority his voice carried.

Phil came stumbling up, her shoulder bandaged but still bleeding. "How are we ever going to bury that thing in the ocean?"

Conor smiled mirthlessly, "I know someone who knows something about casting down demons and shutting them outside of both this reality and the Otherworld."

Conor turned toward the sea and shouted,

Michael, Michael of the morning,
Rider of the seas aborning,
Come to us in our need we cry.

Everyone looked out to where the morning mist wafted across the rolling waters, and just as the sun with its rose red beams ascended behind them, lighting the droplets flung heavenward from the ocean's waves, there came striding on the foam-flecked sea the figure of a seraph angel, clothed in white, a massive trident in one hand and a golden shield in the other.

"Who calls my name?" shouted the angel.

Conor answered shouting back,

"I, the King Over land, Under sea,
Pierced thrice for those I serve to see,
He who was destined and yet shall be,
Bringer of worlds together, am he."

Oh, my God, thought Conor, after he spoke, there I go being all Arthurian again.

"Both of you are show-offs if you ask me," harrumphed Lettie.

Ignoring her, Conor explained to Michael what they were asking him to do. The angel came forward saying, "I have no difficulty in agreeing to this. I just finished binding one worse than this to another hellish rock. The *Caorthannach* deserves its new home. I bid you now, stop the chanting."

The song ceased and Kevin collapsed exhausted to the ground. Conor ran to him and lifted him up, "So well done," he said.

Kevin couldn't even speak, but he smiled a tired smile.

Holding up his friend, Conor spoke to the seraph, "Always in your debt, we ask you to take the *Caorthannach* away. We cannot heal while it stays here."

Already, the monster sensed its chains loosening with the song ceasing, and it stretched and roared. Michael simply raised his trident and brought it down to the *machair*. Instantly, the demon mother crashed to the ground. Michael smashed his trident over its back and a golden lasso encompassed the beast rendering it powerless.

Michael lifted himself on wings of alabaster white, morphing himself into full seraph mode with six wings, flashing eyes and the trident held in one of its uplifted arms. The *Caorthannach* rose with the angel, imprisoned, unable to move or speak. Michael paused in mid-air and a sound came out of him that first sounded like distant trumpets but then resolved into a spoken voice,

"Look well upon that which has possessed this island. I take it away and imprison it under the waters. It goes back to where it once was birthed, but it will come again if people cannot change. You brave Travelers and People of the Sea, the only ones who could effectively challenge it, have won a great battle, but not the war. People's hearts are still too weak. You have much to do, to make the prison of the *Caorthannach* eternal. For it will wait beneath the seas, biding its time, when the hearts of men once again are poisoned by the Dark."

With that he disappeared with his prisoner through the mist and over the ocean towards the Bull Rock.

"Where's Jace?" said Colly. "I don't see him anywhere."

Conor turned a bleak face to his friend.

Phil saw and said, "Oh no!"

Conor looked at them all and said, "Jace has fallen in battle with Balor. He is not dead but is terribly wounded. The Morrigan has taken him."

Murmurs erupted through the crowd. "Enough!" said Conor, "She fought with me and with Jace against Balor. Whatever you think of her, at least in this she was on our side. Now what of Fr. Greavy, where is he?"

"Where he fell," said Scatha. "Up by the fort. We have composed his body as peacefully as possible."

"A terrible day," said Conor. "So many of us have lost so much. So many have lost their lives. Is this what victory costs? Is this what's going to happen whenever we go up against the Dark?"

Some saw a shimmering in the air; some only heard the voice. At first, the words sounded soothing and healing, "Yes, O King, anyone who goes against the Dark risks death, that journey into which we truly cannot see."

"But I have seen," said Conor, looking around for the source of the voice. "It is but a step into the Summer Country. I have seen those who walk in it."

"Bah!" said the voice, "visions given by things like that specter who took my friend away." The shimmering in the atmosphere began to twirl up dust and broken heather and it began moving. Swiftly, very swiftly. Touching Calador, it left him with his neck sliced open. It went through the two groups of *Roan*, leaving many gasping out their lifeblood on the *machair*.

"Ishii!" cried Conor, "It's Shiro Ishii!" He plunged forward to intercept the sorcerer before any more damage could be done, but he was too late.

Lettie, however, could see exactly where he was. Why she did it, no one know, but she managed to get between Conor and the invisible doctor and threw herself upon him, knocking him to the ground.

Conor got to her not a second later and pulled her off, but evil struck too swiftly. A gaping hole in Lettie's torso spilled her blood upon the earth. "No!" cried Conor again. He looked for Ishii, but all he saw was a faint shimmering going up the *machair*, avoiding the crowds. A faded burst of laughing was heard and then he was gone. Some chased after, but they never caught him.

Conor cradled Lettie. Both were covered in blood. He wept upon her face and she opened her eyes.

"Conor, my King, don't be sad. I'm a wisp, after all, hard to kill. This body, however, as you young ones are fond of saying, is toast. It may be I shall be given another and yet see you again. But if not, I die content, knowing that you live. I foresee much darkness ahead for you, but much light as well. As bad as all this evil has been, it has set you free Conor Archer. Now you know it. Now, you can fight it. Now, you can prevail."

"Don't talk," said Conor, "please don't talk. Let us help you. Scatha!" he shouted.

"I am here by your side," she said, bending down to touch Lettie's face. But the wisp had already closed her eyes.

"She's gone, Conor," said Scatha, gently pulling Conor away.

"We won, but we lost," said Conor.

"As is ever when we fight the Dark. This world is not the Summer Country my King, nor is the Otherworld you seek to join with this one."

"Don't I know it," said Conor. He lifted his head up to the people and allowed them to see the Crown on his head, the flashing ruby glowing brightly in the dawn's early light. He slowly stood before them, looking over the crowd.

Conor raised his hands and head to the sky, and the ruby in his crown burst out with light, mingling with the rising sun. Throughout the land of Ireland, people marveled at the sunrise with its multifaceted rays of beautiful glory shining upon the land. For a full minute, Conor stood there, everyone staring at him. When the ruby dimmed, he opened his eyes, lowered his head and spoke, "I have cleansed the land of the contagion spread by that mother of demons. Plague is gone from this island. But the victory we have won is at great cost and it is but a pause in our fight. Yet we did win, with your hearts, your strength and your courage. Go now, mourn our dead and at Ballinskelligs Bay this evening, I will light the fire of grief, the flame of victory, as a sign of the Light that never dies, that burns so our grief can pass away."

EPILOGUE

Saturday Evening to Sunday morning, 11/14–15, Ballinskelligs

BURNING BRIGHTLY IN the night, the bonfire illuminated Ballinskelligs Bay. Most of the Traveler mourners had retired to their own caravans. Even the *Roan* had returned to the sea. But Conor, Scatha, Colly, Phil, Moira, Kevin and family, and of course, Troubles still stood before the flames.

Moira clutched at her sweater, "I miss her already."

"All of us do," said Scatha. "Lettie was a force of nature around these parts for so long. And in the end, her heart was capable of a sacrifice that enabled us to continue the battle. This was the end she would have wanted."

"Would that many had that kind of generosity." A figure came into the firelight—St. Ita in her Otherworldly form. With silver circlet upon her nun's vesture and grey robes flowing, she was ethereal in presence. "The wisp was a perfect example of how we must live in peace as the worlds merge. For I have seen it. The worlds have touched and have not retreated. What has happened will continue, and what we have won here is this: the worlds shall come together blessed by the Light and filled with hope. There is darkness still; indeed, the Dark is not yet finished. It has yet the power to turn everything we have accomplished to Death itself. But it has suffered a terrible blow. For the moment, we can rest, at peace with our labors."

"Mommy!" cried Laura, clutching at Mary's hand. "There's a woman on the other side of the fire!"

The others looked, but all assured her no one was there. Only Conor and Ita remained silent. Conor could see the woman clearly, and she was looking directly at him, her raven hair lifting lightly from the heat of the flames.

"Mom," he whispered. She smiled warmly at him, raising her hands in blessing, and then she was gone.

"To the Summer Country, Conor. That's where she goes now," said Ita. "She could not really leave until she was sure you would become who you were meant to be."

"So, I'm perfect now?" he said, his sorrow taking out the sting of sarcasm in his voice. "I'd rather just be a kid again."

"I know," said Ita, placing her arms around his shoulders. "We all wish to be children again. Did you see her face? She is so proud of what you have become. Let her go now, for she deserves her rest. I will see her soon and give her your love, for I have overstayed my time here as well. The land is somewhat safe, and what is left to do, I leave in good hands."

"What about Jace?" said Conor. "I don't know how to get him back."

Ita laughed and said, "No worries there. The Morrigan will take good care of him and will see him back when he is needed."

"What happens to us now?"

"You are the King," said Ita. "You have unfinished duties at home. This nexus between the worlds is at peace, but I cannot say the same of the merging of the worlds at Tinker's Grove. There is still a darkness there to be exploited. Balor was hardly the only one capable of causing mischief. Others will sense their chance. But you have friends now and will never have to act alone again."

***

They rested that night at *Skellig* Pub. In the early morning, Moira was already up with a breakfast on the table. She said to Conor, "I tried to tell Phil she couldn't go, but she insists on traveling with Colly and you back to Tinker's Grove. I already know Scatha, Kevin and family are staying here to watch over things, but I'm still not happy about letting my only daughter leave."

"We'll keep her safe and sound," said Colly.

"Besides," laughed Conor, "I can't wait to see what her latest hair color will do to the folks of the Grove."

After breakfast, they walked to the portal behind the pub, and one by one disappeared into it. Conor was the last to go after pushing a reluctant Troubles through the portal. Hugging Moira goodbye, he looked past her to see if anyone else had come. And there she was, just around the corner of the shed. Scatha had come to say farewell. She walked up to him, and he stumbled for words.

Placing her finger on his lips she said, "Shh, my King. Soon we will meet again. The merging of the worlds will demand it. Remember what I have taught you and keep me here in your heart." She placed her palm on his chest, fading away into the morning mist.

As the rising sun arced over the world, the Hand of God nebula dimmed in the heavens, giving up its rule of the night. But before it faded from sight, Conor looked and saw from the Hand white wings shining, there in the light of the morn.

From the sky back down to the bay, Conor surveyed the rolling hills and flashing sea. "A beautiful land, Moira, with really beautiful people who have been given a second chance. I'll be back. Still, I'm glad to be going home." Conor smiled, stepping into the portal, and was gone.

Moira looked wistfully around Ballinskelligs Bay, sighing, "There's a King again for these green shores, and maybe, just maybe, all will be right with the world."

GLOSSARY

A

A dhearthairin: A ghrih-hawr-in. Celtic for 'little brother'.

Abbot Malachy: Leader of the *Stella Maris (Star of the Sea)* Monastery in Tinker's Grove. Not quite what he seems, Abbot Malachy is also a 'Walker of Worlds' who has watched over the town since its founding.

Amergin: *Ah-mer-gin.* The Bard of the West. Appearing in the novel *SKELLIG* as the head of the Tinker Clans, Amergin is the original druid of the same name who helped settle Ireland millennia ago, warring against the *Tuatha de Danaan.*

Aunt Emily: Sister of Conor's mother, Finola. She lives in Tinker's Grove on a family plot called 'Madoc's Glen'. She assumes guardianship of Conor after the death of his mother.

B

Baleros: Bay-lah-ross. The Celtic name for Sir Hugh Rappaport's huge cargo and research vessel. It means 'Deadly One' and is named after the ancient Celtic god, Balor.

Ballinskelligs: A village in County Kerry, Ireland, on the Bay of Ballinskelligs. It is the site of a now abandoned monastery where the monks of *Skellig* Michael retreated when the climate became too harsh for them to maintain the ancient monastery on that island.

Balor: *Bay-lore.* The ancient Celtic god of blight and pestilence. He is a Fomorian. He has a third eye in his forehead. Called the 'Evil Eye', if it ever opened it would destroy anything its gaze landed on. In *SKELLIG*, he is the personification of evil.

Bard: A druid singer and storyteller. The last name of Kevin, Mary and Laura. They are Tinkers. Kevin's father is Amergin and he takes his last name from his father's profession. In ancient Ireland, bards were very powerful. They acted as a check and balance on kings. Their songs and stories were often politically potent and could bring down or build up an unworthy or heroic king.

Beth Michaels: Twin sister to Jace, Beth is smart, attractive and full of personality. A leader in school, she is much like her brother, offering the newly arrived Conor much needed friendship. She senses his pain on losing his mother and seeks to make him feel at home in Tinker's Grove. As time goes on, she is deeply attracted to him and believes he feels the same. Her brother reluctantly watches the developing relationship, worried that the darkness that seems to pursue Conor will ensnare his beloved sister.

biodh se amhlaidh: bee-uck-say-owla. Celtic for the incantation or blessing "May it be so."

bodhran: bow-run. A Celtic instrument much like a small hand-held drum.

Brian: Bree-ahn. The Celtic name for the white horse St. Michael rides. He is a sentient being and immortal.

Bull Rock, (Rock of Donn): A barren rock off the coast of County Kerry, Bull Rock was seen by the pagan Celts as a portal to the netherworld. Donn, the god of the dead, would receive souls there and ease their passage into the afterlife.

C

Cahersiveen: A town in County Kerry, Ireland where the Tinkers park their caravans by the sea.

Caorthannach: Queer-haw-knock. A Celtic demon, its name is often translated as 'The Devil's Mother'. It is a fell beast, mother of demons, and is the most terrible evil St. Patrick ever had to encounter. He defeated this monster on the holy mountain *Croagh Patrick* and imprisoned it at the bottom of *Lough Derg,* a solitary lake often thought of as the entrance to the underworld. When loose, the *Caorthannach* ravages the countryside, killing people and poisoning the fresh water supplies.

Calador: A *Roan* prince.

Cauldron/Grail: In Celtic mythology, the Cauldron is one of the four great treasures possessed by the *Tuatha de Danaan*. Anyone mortally wounded, but put in the Cauldron, would be given back his/her life. As time passed and Christianity took over the Celtic lands, the Cauldron morphed into the Grail, the Chalice used by Jesus Christ at the Last Supper. It had the same meaning. It not only restored life but was the source of everlasting life.

celidh: *Cay-lee*. The Celtic name for a music/dance event usually held at the town hall. It showcases local talent and is always a major celebration for the community.

changeling: A *faerie* creature capable of taking many forms but usually appears in this world as a child exchanged for a human baby by the *fae*. It is not known to be particularly partial to humans as was shown clearly in the novel *ROAN*, but in *SKELLIG*, the one changeling encountered is Colly Roddy who seems to be on the side of humanity.

Colly Roddy: (Hercules Columba Roddy). Son of Joe Roddy, who runs the boat tours out to the *Skellig* Islands. He is eighteen years old. Colly's mother is Indian and his father is Irish.

Conor Archer: Conor is seventeen years old and helps his dying mother out by playing the tin whistle in a pick-up band in one of the Irish pubs in downtown Chicago. He's home-schooled, street-wise, and immensely talented musically. Conor has syndactyly, webbing between his fingers, which, while strange, does not affect his musical dexterity. But he knows he's different, and his encounter with a strange biker at the bar one night changes his life forever.

craic: *crack*. The Celtic word for an excellent time and good conversation.

Croagh Patrick:Crow Patrick. This is the holy mountain of St. Patrick on the west coast in County Mayo, Ireland. Always a holy mountain, it was Christianized when St. Patrick spent a Lent on its summit, casting the snakes from Ireland on this spot, and defeating the *Caorthannach*, the 'Devil's Mother', and chasing it all the way to *Lough Derg* where he imprisoned it underneath the waters.

cu sidhe: *coo she*. The original hell-hound. Usually this very large, dark green dog (or white with red ears, depending on which Celtic land you are visiting), travels in threes. They protect things and if they see you as a threat they will pursue you. One howl, they know of your presence.

Two howls, they are coming to get you. Three howls, they are upon you and your time on earth is over.

D

'dark ones': The 'dark ones' are the descendants of those Tinkers who coupled with *Roan* women, shortly before the voyage to America was made to escape the Irish famine of the 1840's. Recognizable by their webbed hands, they are shapeshifters in their pre-adolescent years who lose their powers as they reach puberty.

Dearg Due: *Dah-rag du-ah*. (The Red Thirst). The Irish vampire which may have inspired Bram Stoker to create character of Dracula. This female vampire has tortured the people of the Irish countryside for many centuries.

Deisil: deshil. A Celtic word meaning to turn sunwise or clockwise.

Dr. Nicholas Drake: First introduced in the novel *ROAN*, Drake comes to Tinker's Grove as a bio-geneticist invited by Caithness McNabb to build and develop DIOGENE, a research facility. His sole purpose, however, is to discover the secret of the 'dark ones' by whatever means necessary.

Droc ula: A small, vampiric creature, called a *droc*, for short, which travels in packs seeking out prey. Star Trek fans would be reminded of Tribbles on steroids with reptilian skins and clawed arms and legs.

Dullahan: The Irish version of the headless horseman, a powerful *fae* who seeks out its victims, holding its severed head high and letting the corpse head speak the victim's name who promptly dies. The *Dullahan* rides a kelpie and carries a whip made of severed human vertebrae.

Dun Scaitha: Doon Sky-tha. The Fortress of Shadows on the Isle of Skye. It is Scatha's home.

F

fae: Fay. The Celtic word for those creatures who dwell in the Otherworld. Also written as *faerie*.

Failte: Fail-cha. The Celtic word for 'welcome.'

Fr. Nathan Greavy: Father Nathan Greavy is the Catholic priest of Portmagee and Ballinskelligs. He is also a 'Walker of Worlds' like Abbot Malachy in Tinker's Grove.

Fomorians: Ancient Celtic beings seen by humans as gods of chaos. Defeated by the *Tuatha de Danaan*. Balor is a Formorian.

G

Gardai: Gar-die. The name for the police in Ireland.

Geas: gesh. An obligation or prohibition magically imposed on a person.

H

Hand of God Nebula: A gaseous, brilliant cloud 17,000 light years away that resembles a hand. It is surprising it appears in the sky over Ireland since it was first observed in the southern hemisphere.

Emperor Hirohito: The Japanese ruler before, during and after World War II who dealt with Shiro Ishii.

I

Ita: Celtic saint who began a famous abbey in Country Kerry that educated many well-known Irish saints. In *SKELLIG,* she comes from the Summer Country and befriends Conor and his companions acting as an advisor and healer.

Isle of Skye: A large island off the western coast of Scotland, named after the warrior, Scatha, who trained many heroes there. Majestic in this world, the Otherworldly version of Skye is even more stunning and beautiful and has its boundary with the Summer Country.

J

Jason Michaels: Captain of the football team in Tinker's Grove, Jace is big, friendly, and a natural leader. Seventeen years old, he has a twin sister, Beth, and is very protective of her. Blessed with a good intellect, he immediately befriends Conor Archer when he comes to town and senses that his friendship with the newcomer is going to lead to adventure and change. Always up for a challenge, Jace embraces that possibility with enthusiasm.

K

kelpie: In Celtic mythology, it is a water horse with the body of a horse, scorpion tail, and a coat somewhat reptilian and scaly. It has red eyes, breathes fire from nostrils and is dangerous to humans. Should a human try to ride a *kelpie*, that person will stick to the *kelpie's* hide and the monster will drag the human underneath the water to drown the person.

L

Lia Fail: Lee-ah fail. The Stone of Destiny upon which the Irish kings were crowned. Also called the Stone of Truth since it would shout out the truth of an Irish noble's right to claim the kingship once he sat upon the stone. It is one of the four great treasures of the *Tuatha de Danaan.*

Lettie Sporn: An old woman who is often found in the *Skellig* Pub. She is a friend of Moira's.

Lugh: *Lew.* An ancient Irish god who was a warrior, a king, a master craftsman and a savior who once possessed the Spear of Destiny that Conor now carries. Most similar to the Roman god, Mercury. Also, the name of Conor's son by Beth Michaels.

M

Machair: mah-care. Low lying plain near the sea.

Madoc: *May-dock.* Welsh Celtic prince, father of Conor, who traveled to America nearly eight hundred years ago and took up residence in the

Indian burial mound by the Wisconsin River near Tinker's Grove. He is of the *Roan*.

Malby: The old brown horse that draws Kevin's caravan.

The McNabb Family: Caithness McNabb and her three evil sons—Gordon, Rafe, and Fergal—are wealthy landowners in Tinker's Grove and formed an alliance with Piasa and Dr. Drake to bring down Conor and the 'Dark Ones'.

Meritaten: Daughter of Queen Nefertiti and Pharaoh Akhenaten. Legend has it that she briefly became Pharaoh and married a Greek prince, name Miles (*Mee-less*) but for some reason had to flee with her followers from Egypt. They traveled to the western coast of Spain and then onto northern Britain. Her other name was 'Scota' which she bequeathed to the northern British lands, and thus Scotland was born. She and her followers then went to Ireland and warred with the *Tuatha de Danaan*. Killed in battle, she was buried in Meritaten's (Scota's) Glen just west of Tralee in County Kerry. All the Scots take their name from her.

Michael the Archangel: First among all angels, the Celtic version of St. Michael is associated with high places and the sea. *Skellig* Michael is named after him and is one of the seven special sites in Europe dedicated to him. He drove Satan and the rebel angels from heaven. He is of the seraphim, the highest of all angels.

Milesians: *Mill-lee-zhens*. Descendants of Miles, the husband of Meritaten, are the same as the Scotians or Scots. When they invaded Ireland, they did battle with the *Tuatha de Danaan*. Amergin was one of the original sons of Miles and Meritaten.

Moira Sheehy: The proprietress of the *Skellig* Pub, mother of Philomena and godmother to Conor.

Morrigan: A *Tuatha de Danaan* often seen as the ancient Celtic goddess of death and the battlefield. Believed to be a tri-part goddess with forms of a young girl, battle maiden, and crone. She washes the clothes of the slain in flowing water. In the series, she is an ambiguous character often helping, sometimes hindering Conor and his friends.

N

neart: nearit. Celtic pagans saw this as the life force present in all things. Celtic Christians came close to equating this with God's grace, i.e. his love, power, energy present in all created things. Druids tried to harness it to do magic. Christians tapped into it to perform miracles and be one with God.

Niamh Finn: *Neeve* Finn. Proprietress of the *Foam and Finn,* one of the pub/hotels in Portmagee.

O

ogham: ahg-em. A primitive Celtic written language made up of lines usually carved into wood or stone.

Otherworld: A deeper, more real world upon which our world is based. Home of magical creatures and much that is beautiful and magnificent. Once the worlds were together, but long ago they were sundered. Our world, oftentimes seen as more concrete and physical, is a pale shadow of the Otherworld. Both need to be merged together for both to survive.

Oz: One of the 'dark ones' in Tinker's Grove who seems to be developmentally disabled but often is possessed by an intelligence that knows secrets and coming events. He is a large young man who wears earbuds in his ears that are not hooked up to any music, yet he hears something and often whistles tunelessly.

P

Phil Sheehy: Philomena, daughter of Moira and known for her rebellious nature.

pooka: A Celtic shapeshifting being known for taking the shape of a horse, goat, or hare. It can be beneficent or malicious but is always mischievous.

Portmagee: A coastal town in County Kerry known primarily for its tourism and boat trips to the *Skellig* Isles.

R

RAGE/RAGER: The designer drug developed by Sir Hugh and Dr. Shiro Ishii. RAGE is an acronym for Random Anger Graphic Encounter and is shorthand for the manifestation of the effects of the drug. The drug gives a concentrated high for fifty minutes which quickly devolves into a raging anger that seeks to do violence to any living thing. The violence lasts only ten minutes, so users and observers bet on when the rage portion will take effect and scatter before they are hurt. A RAGER is one who uses the drug.

Roan: These are the People of the Sea, the selkies, who are seals in the ocean and appear as human on land. They are shapeshifters and are kin to the *Tuatha de Danaan.* They are said to have fallen with the rebel angels from heaven but they are not evil.

Rory Nalan: The brother of Madoc, disguised as a biker. A *Roan,* he is an angry trickster and much like the Morrigan is an ambiguous character, sometimes helpful, sometimes not.

S

Scatha: *Skah-thah.* A warrior woman who gives her name to the Isle of Skye. In *SKELLIG,* she is also *Roan.* In Celtic lore, she trained all the great Celtic warriors in the ways of war.

Seanachie: *shan-ah-hee.* Celtic storyteller.

Shiro Ishii: Japanese doctor who headed the Japanese World War II effort in biochemical weapons. He experimented on people in the infamous Unit 731, developing plague cultures which he released into the Chinese population. One of the worst of all war criminals, he was never brought to justice because the Allies wished to use his knowledge to further their own development of biochemical weapons.

Sidhe: *shee.* These are the *faerie* folk that inhabit the Celtic landscape. Elves, leprechauns, other species of *fae* are included in this designation.

Sir Hugh Rappaport: Wealthy businessman, oil baron and part of the landed gentry who invents RAGE, he has high contacts among government and royalty, and many Middle-eastern connections. He is not who he seems since, in his pursuit of power and wealth, he has invited a much older and stronger personality into himself.

sluagh: sloo-ah. The restless dead who travel at night in flocks seeking out the sick and dying. They are the damned and try to snatch away souls to join them. Often looking like crows or ravens in the sky, they are robed with skeletal faces and grasping claws. Irish folklore says they come from the west, so west facing windows are always closed and locked at night when sick people are in the house.

Spear of Destiny: One of the four great treasures of the *Tuatha de Danaan,* it belonged to Lugh for a while and then entered the realm of myth till it surfaces again as the spear Longinus the centurion used to pierce the heart of Christ on the Cross. A nail from the Cross was fused to its blade. It has magical powers and many, including Hitler, have sought to possess it. Conor Archer is its caretaker now.

Summer Country: The Celtic name for heaven. It is a place of beauty and rest.

Sword of Light: Another of the great treasures of the *Tuatha de Danaan,* possessed first by Nuada of the Silver Hand, the first *de Danaan* king of Ireland. It has magical powers. Jason Michaels is its caretaker now.

T

Taoiseach: tee-shah. The Irish prime minister.

Tinkers/Travelers: Tinkers is a more pejorative word. The Travelers are the Irish gypsies. They are not loved by the Irish who often see them as thieves. They are called Tinkers because of their work with tin and other metals.

The Shandyman: Tom Shandy. Resident of Ballinskelligs who helps Conor and friends.

Tree of the World: The World Tree which, in mythology, holds up the world and is often the source of good and evil in it. Some say an ancient worm or dragon dwells at its roots, others say it represents the Tree of Life in Eden. In "The Tales of Conor Archer", it is a combination of all these things.

Troubles: The mysterious chocolate Labrador retriever who has connections with the Otherworld and is the companion of Conor Archer.

Tuatha de Danaan: Two-ah-ha day Day-nan. A supernatural race of beings who come from the Otherworld, invaded Ireland, and were later defeated by the Milesians. They are the *fae* who were often mistaken for gods and who have great power. Sometimes described as beings who fell with the rebel angels, they can be good or bad, but mostly good. Their enemies are the Fomorians who they defeated on their arrival in Ireland. The Fomorians represent the chaotic powers in creation.

W

Walker of Worlds: A human, given an extraordinary life-span, who is tasked to walk the various worlds, trying to preserve the presence of good in creation. The Walker belongs to a very secretive group whose origins are as yet unknown and whose ultimate purpose can only be guessed at.

wisp: A Celtic creature also known as a *will o' the wisp.* It is often observed as a simple blue light but is a shapeshifting creature as well.

My friends,

Thank you for becoming part of the Conor Archer family. We are a tight knit group of people looking for adventures that ennoble and celebrate humanity.

<u>THE TALES OF CONOR ARCHER</u>
by E. R. Barr

ROAN

SKELLIG
(both available from Internet bookstores)

DRIFTLESS
(coming soon)

Series, like <u>THE TALES OF CONOR ARCHER</u>, depend on the support of readers like you. One of the ways to guarantee more stories like these is to leave a book review on the Amazon or Barnes and Noble websites. If you enjoyed this book, please take a moment and write a review. It's the best way you can thank an author.

E. R. Barr

ABOUT THE AUTHOR

E. R. Barr spent his youth wandering around "Conor Country" known better as the "Driftless Area" of the southwest corner of the state of Wisconsin. The Mississippi and Wisconsin Rivers and the lands around them, dotted with Indian mounds and filled with stories and legends, fueled his imagination. Not till he started traveling world-wide did he truly begin to see connections between Ireland, Scotland, Wales and the lands where he was born. His forebears came from those ancient nations and settled there in Wisconsin. Always wondering why, he kept searching for answers. A Catholic Priest, a university professor, high school teacher and administrator, a popular speaker on all things Celtic and Tolkienesque, E. R. Barr makes his home in northwest Illinois. This is his second novel. Find out more about him and Conor's world by checking out the following website:

www.talesofconorarcher.com

ABOUT THE ILLUSTRATOR

Howard David Johnson, illustrator, is a classically trained artist with a background in the natural sciences and cultural history who works in many mediums. His realistic paintings of history, religion and mythology have been published all over the world by distinguished learning institutions and publishers including the Universities of Oxford and Cambridge.

www.howarddavidjohnson.com

Made in the USA
Monee, IL
24 October 2020